Anne Douglas, after a varied life spent elsewhere, has made her home in Edinburgh, a city she has known for many years. She very much enjoys life in the modern capital, and finds its ever-present history fascinating.

She has written a number of novels, including *Catherine's Land*, *As The Years Go By*, *Bridge of Hope*, *The Butterfly Girls*, *Ginger Street*, *A Highland Engagement* and *The Road to the Sands*, all published by Piatkus.

Also by Anne Douglas

The Butterfly Girls

Anne Douglas

PIATKUS

PIATKUS

First published in Great Britain in 2001 by Judy Piatkus (Publishers) Ltd
This paperback edition published 2009 by Piatkus

A CIP catalogue record for this book
is available from the British Library

ISBN 978-0-7499-3308-1

Typeset in Times by Phoenix Photosetting, Chatham, Kent
Printed and bound in Great Britain by
CPI Mackays, Chatham, ME5 8TD

Papers used by Piatkus are natural, renewable and recyclable
products sourced from well-managed forests and certified
in accordance with the rules of the Forest Stewardship Council.

Mixed Sources

Product group from well-managed
forests and other controlled sources
www.fsc.org Cert no. SGS-COC-004081
© 1996 Forest Stewardship Council

Piatkus
An imprint of
Little, Brown Book Group
100 Victoria Embankment
London EC4Y 0DY

An Hachette UK Company
www.hachette.co.uk

www.piatkus.co.uk

*This book is dedicated to all those doctors and nurses
who fought so valiantly against tuberculosis in the past,
and to those still carrying on the fight today.*

Author's Note

This story of young nurses, set partly in Edinburgh some fifty years ago, is entirely imaginary. It is true that the hospital where they work is based on a real hospital, and that certain locations of the city, even with invented names, will be easily recognised, but the story, the characters – nurses, doctors, patients – and the Fidra Bay nursing home are all completely fictitious. Only the fight against tuberculosis, which forms the background of the novel, really happened.

Of the works consulted for reference, I am particularly indebted to the following:

Crofton, Sir John, *Science and Society: Tuberculosis, Tobacco, Poverty and Crime*, Weidenfeld & Nicolson, 1995.

Dormandy, Thomas, *The White Death: A History of Tuberculosis*, Hambledon, 1999.

Eastwood, Martin & Jenkinson, Anne, *A History of the Western General*, John Donald, 1995.

Gullen, F. Doreen, *Traditional Number Rhymes and Games*, University of London Press, 1950.

MacDonald, Betty, *The Plague and I*, Mann, 1948 New ed., 1974.

Pipes, Rosemary J, *The Colonies of Stockbridge*, Lomond Books, 2nd ed., 1998.

Ryan, Frank, *Tuberculosis: The Greatest Story Never Told*, Swift, 1992.

Part One

Chapter One

'Two to the Jubilee, please,' said the nurses.

They were young, fresh-faced, shaking raindrops from their capes. A morning lecture at the Infirmary had kept them late, they'd had to run through a shower for the tram. Had only just caught it, which was a bit of luck.

'Might have missed our dinner,' said Martie Cass, settling into a wooden seat beside Alex Kelsie, as the conductor pressed the bell and the tram moved off. 'Such as it is. When are we going to get something decent to eat again? You'd think the war was still on.'

The Second World War had in fact been over for four years, but austerity was still with Scotland. There were still shortages of everything. Except, as Martie said with grim humour, TB cases. Always plenty of those.

The girls were in their second year at Edinburgh's Jubilee Chest Hospital, both good friends, not just as colleagues. They had been brought up together in the Stockbridge Colonies, a little community of terraces by the Water of Leith, a mile or so from Princes Street, where their parents shared a house. It was perhaps not too surprising that both should have chosen nursing, but Alex had had a particular reason for wanting to nurse tubercular patients, and Martie liked to joke and say she was only in it for the extra money.

In fact, if it had been true, Alex wouldn't have blamed her. Everyone knew that Martie's folks, Sid and Tilda Cass, were a pair of skinflints, and that Martie, cheerful and outgoing, liked to

3

spend, not necessarily on herself. Tall and strong, with honey-coloured hair and vivid blue eyes, she radiated vitality; she had been born to be generous. Looking at her in the tram that day, Alex thought again how life at home must have been for her an exquisite form of straitjacket.

Alex herself had loved her home. She had one brother, Jamie, who like her, had toffee-brown hair and eyes to match, and the pair of them had thrived in the atmosphere of home like loved and cherished house-plants. When everything changed and the cold wind of tragedy touched them, they had for a time withered, found it hard to recover. Jamie had gone into the army to do his national service and was now working with an insurance firm in Glasgow. Alex, as soon as she was eighteen, had followed Rose Burnett, a friend of hers and Martie's, into nursing. And Martie, whether or not it was for the money, had followed her. Both were doing well and looking forward to next year and Finals, when with luck they should qualify as State Registered Nurses.

'Then, who knows?' Martie once said. 'The world'll be our oyster!'

'The Jubilee's my oyster,' Alex had replied. 'I'm staying put.'

The showers had become heavy rain by the time they reached the stop for the Jubilee.

'Here we go!' cried Martie, and they raced up the drive to the nurses' home, a shabby old house, once part of a large estate that had been acquired for the original hospital many years before. In those days, the Jubilee had been almost in the country; now, it was surrounded by the city, its grounds a little oasis amongst stone and brick. Most patients were housed in large pavilions known as the butterfly wards because of their Y-shaped construction, though some slept in wooden chalets open to the weather. As fresh air was considered part of their cure, no one objected. Even on that cold wet November day, the two nurses could see a few brave souls walking round the lawns or digging in the allotments. Such activity after their long periods of rest in the wards gave them hope. And until the wonder drugs that everyone was talking about actually arrived, hope was mostly what the patients had.

4

'Bet it'll be mince again,' groaned Martie, when she and Alex had changed from their wet things and made it to the nurses' dining room. 'And that rice pudding they make from grit. Or tastes like it, anyway.'

There was no mince, only rissoles, equally disliked.

'What's in 'em?' asked Martie, 'we should be told.'

For pudding, there were small squares of pastry filled with strange jam. 'No' so bad with custard,' remarked a probationer, which turned out to be true, so they had second helpings and cups of tea. By which time they had to be on their way again, hurrying to Butterfly Two.

'Nurse Kelsie, Nurse Cass, may I have a word?'

Staff Burnett was coming down the corridor towards them, looking the very picture of crisp efficiency.

Alex's heart lurched. She still thought of the staff nurse as Rose, as her friend who had skipped and played games with the children of the Colonies, even though she was not from the Colonies herself but Cheviot Square, which was so much more grand. It had taken a huge effort to accept her as someone quite different at the Jubilee, someone always ahead, a second-year nurse, a third-year nurse, and now a staff nurse. Someone who must be called Staff and not Rose, who, in spite of always being there to help and advise, held Martie and herself at arm's length, because that was the way it had to be.

'Oh, Lord, what have we done now?' whispered Martie.

Alex, racking her brains to think, tried to find a clue in Rose's expression. But she was only looking her usual striking self: oval-shaped face pale, dark eyes steady under distinctive brows, black hair shining beneath her cap. Rose had always been more than pretty, even as a child, perhaps because the seriousness of her nature added the dimension of beauty. This was not something Alex could ever have put into words; she just felt it and knew others felt it too. Dr Chris MacInnes, for instance, though it was said Rose never gave him the time of day.

'You're on your way to Two?' Rose glanced at the watch pinned to her uniform. 'I won't keep you a moment.'

'We're no' late,' Martie said quickly. 'But we were held up at the lecture.'

'Oh, yes, the lecture – physiology and hygiene, wasn't it? Find it useful?'

'Very. We enjoyed it.'

'Good.' Rose hesitated. 'There's just something I wanted to tell you. My brother is to be admitted to the Jubilee next week. He has a small shadow on his left lung.'

Martie's jaw dropped. Alex's hands at her sides tightened. Neither spoke.

'I know it's years since you've seen him,' Rose went on. 'He had to go into the RAF when he left school. But you remember him, don't you?'

'Oh, yes,' said Alex.

'When he came back from the war, he went to university to read law, felt a bit unwell lately, had tests.' Rose paused again. 'Now he's coming here.'

'I'm very sorry,' Alex said softly.

Rose gave her a long dark look. 'The prognosis is good, he should make an excellent recovery.'

'So, what's wrong for you?' asked Martie with her usual bluntness.

'It's my opinion he shouldn't be coming to the Jubilee at all.' Rose shrugged. 'But you can see how it is. I'm here and my mother thinks I can give him special care.'

'Only natural, Staff.'

'Maybe, but it's not possible and the truth is he should be going somewhere privately. It's difficult to get to Switzerland at the moment, but he could have gone to the Highlands. I could have given him a list of places . . .'

Rose's voice trailed to a halt and she looked away, her eyes sombre. It seemed to them that they had never seen her so dispirited. This was not the Rose they knew of old, or the efficient Staff Nurse Burnett.

Suddenly she moved, snapping smartly back into her professional role. 'Time you two were on duty. It's my fault, I shouldn't have kept you.' With trembling fingers, she adjusted her cap that was perfectly straight.

Alex cleared her throat. 'Thanks for telling us about your brother, Staff. We'll look out for him.'

Rose gave an uncertain smile. 'Yes, well, remember, no special treatment required!'

They watched her walk swiftly away down the corridor, her nurse's shoes tapping, her back straight, her head, as always, held high. The nurses' eyes met. Martie gave a long low whistle.

'What do you make of that, then? Poor old Tim.'

'Come on, you heard what Staff said, we're due on the ward.'

'How about Staff, though? I mean, talking to us like that! She's never said a word before that wasn't to do with work. Shows how she's feeling.'

'Shows she's human. Needs someone to talk to, just like everybody else.'

'And we knew her brother.'

'We never knew him well.'

'Might have liked to, eh?'

Alex made no reply, but hurried on down the corridor, her cheeks rather red.

Butterfly Two, a men's ward, was quiet. It was the rest period, which every patient must strictly observe, and all in the different parts of the pavilion were lying motionless on their beds, eyes closed, systems shut down, in order that their lungs might have as little work to do as possible. While Martie conferred with Jill Berry, waiting to go off duty, Alex trailed in a wheelchair for Kenny Skene, who was to go to X-Ray.

He was from a slum tenement in the Old Town, only seventeen, cheeky and bright. It had taken several baths to cleanse him when he had first been admitted and his head had been almost completely shaved, but now he was scrubbed and rosy in hospital pyjamas, his ginger hair growing again and his eyes full of mischief. No one had told him how ill he was; all he knew was that he must lie in bed and do nothing, and he never complained.

'Come on, Kenny,' said Alex, holding his dressing-gown. 'Time to go for a ride.'

7

'Hallo, butterfly girl,' he whispered. 'Are you no' gorgeous?'

She was smiling as she pushed him along to X-Ray. It was silly, to be pleased with a name, eh? But Kenny called all the nurses butterfly girls, because they were beautiful, he said. Because they could fly away from the butterfly wards, and he could not. Because they were free.

Ah, Kenny, thought Alex, you can never tell who's free.

Chapter Two

Lying sleepless in her little room that night, Alex didn't feel that she was free. Not locked as she was in her thoughts. In her memories. As the autumn wind howled round the old house and she shivered under her thin blankets, Tim Burnett's fourteen-year-old face kept surfacing in her mind. The more she tried to block it out, the clearer it became, though she hadn't thought of him in years. It was hearing his name that had brought him back, had brought everything back. Not just that silly time she'd fallen in love with him and endured such terror in case Martie found out and laughed, but all her childhood when she'd been happy. For in spite of sometimes crying into her pillow because Rose's brother didn't know she existed, in spite of worrying about Martie, she had been happy. Ma had been alive.

Looking back, she knew that they'd all been happy because of Ma. She was the one, plump and serene, who'd held them all together, listening, soothing, quietly doing her chores or sitting crocheting while Arthur Kelsie did his recitations. Alex could see her father now, short and strong, prematurely silver-haired, snatching up the poker, ready to declaim—

'"Is this a dagger which I see before me, The handle toward ma hand? Come, let me clutch thee."' He lowered the poker to look at his audience. '"I have thee not and yet I see thee still . . ."' Are they no' grand mysterious words, Letty? Do they no' send a shiver down your spine, thinking o' that fellow seeing a dagger that's no' there?'

9

'Aye, they do,' her mother answered, her crochet needle spinning along with thread and the lace appearing like magic on the cloth she was edging. 'Is that Macbeth, then?'

'Letty, Letty, it's the Scottish play! Never, never say – you ken what. If ma dad had heard anybody say that—!' Arthur rolled his hazel eyes. 'Well, he was an actor, you ken, at the Royal Lyceum—'

'Sceneshifter,' whispered Jamie, laughing, and Alex remembered laughing too, because they'd heard it all before. All about Dad's father at the Royal Lyceum Theatre, who might or might not have been a great actor, or might just have made the tea. Anyway, it was true that the poor man had dropped dead of a heart attack in the wings and that Dad had had to leave school and help his mother. He always said he'd been wasted as a factory toolmaker, he should have been on the boards, should have been a household name by now.

As it was, he hadn't even been able to buy his home in the Colonies but had to rent, unlike Sid Cass on the lower floor, who only worked behind the counter in Dowie's Grocery, though it was true nobody could slice bacon thinner than Sid, or weigh out carrots closer to the nearest ounce. Never a fraction over for the customer, if you got Sid to serve you, and it was no' even his shop! Somehow he'd saved up the deposit to buy, though, and it had always been the aim of the Edinburgh Cooperative Building Company, who had built the original Colonies, that ordinary folk should be able to buy their own houses and have a bit of garden.

From a grand idea, they had produced a well worked-out scheme back in the 1860s, even arranging affordable loans for working men, but they hadn't been able to keep the ownership principle going. Over the years sub-letting and renting had come in, which suited Arthur Kelsie. He and Letty had been able to take the pleasant little house in Mason Street and if they had to have Tilda and Sid Cass below, at least those two scrimps were quiet because they wouldn't buy a wireless and always went to bed early to save the light. Poor old Martie, though!

'Och, you'd think her folks would give her something better than socks and vests for her Christmas!' Letty would exclaim indignantly, and always invited the Casses in for Hogmanay, to make sure that Martie had a good time.

Alex could still remember the first time she and the other Colonies girls had met Rose. They'd been skipping, with Martie as usual always stumbling on Rich Man when they played 'who shall I marry?' Rich Man, Poor Man, Beggarman, Thief. It was always Rich Man for Martie.

'Martie, you did that on purpose!' the girls had all screamed.

'I didnae! I didnae!' Martie screamed back, and what could you do? She went to church in a carriage, of course, not a wheelbarrow, and her wedding dress was silk, not cotton, but when they complained she only tossed her head and laughed.

'It spoils the game if you dinna play fair!' Jackie MacAllan had said earnestly, and they'd all been arguing when a tall dark-haired girl wearing St Clare's school uniform came down the Archangel Steps towards them.

'May I play?' she asked.

They'd been struck dumb. They didn't know her, she wasn't from the Colonies, who was she? Her name was Rose Burnett, she told them, and she lived in Cheviot Square at the top of the steps. Oh, yes, they all knew Cheviot Square. Big tall houses, maids to clean the brass, a garden in the middle with trees and lawns where you could sit.

'Why'd you want to play with us?' asked Martie, studying Rose's good shoes and wrist watch, her middle finger stained with ink.

'I was doing my homework and heard your voices,' Rose answered. 'I thought I'd come down, see if I could join in.'

'Are there no folk from your school up there?'

'No, there's no one.'

'You know how to skip?'

'Of course!'

'How about playing Giant Steps and Baby Steps?'

'I don't know that one.'

'That's Martie's favourite because she likes giving us orders,' Jackie explained. 'You all stand at the kerb, you ken, and try to get across the street, and the girl who's it tells you to take big steps or little steps, or do a banana slide, or something like that, and if you start crossing when her eyes are shut, you go back to the beginning!'

'I'll play that!' cried Rose.

She did and she won. That was the start of her coming down regularly, playing all their games, joining in as if she was a Colonies girl, born and bred. It didn't seem to make any difference that her father was a lawyer, or that her mother played bridge every afternoon and never did a hand's turn, Rose was just one of them. Unlike her brother. They saw Tim Burnett sometimes, when he came to call Rose home, but he never stayed. Rose said he had his own friends to meet from the Academy; it was understood he wouldn't stay. Whether he did or not, was of no interest anyway to Alex, she hadn't been in love with him then. That had come later, one summer afternoon in 1939, she could never understand why. What after all was different about him? But it was as though he had stepped that day from shadow into light. As though she was seeing him for the first time.

They hadn't been at school, it was the holidays. The grown-ups had been talking about the war but the children never listened. It meant nothing to them, all they knew was that they were finished with school for four lovely weeks. No more standing on the form if you got your sums wrong! No more strap if you were caught talking! Off streamed the boys to play Kick the Can or Tig, or Ginger Man, which involved knocking on doors and running away, and Alex just hoped that Jamie wouldn't get caught by the polis, or some cross house-owner. The girls, too, were out, ready to play – those who hadn't had to go for the messages for their mothers, or look after younger children at home. Alex might have had to do that, for she had once had two little sisters, but they had both died in infancy.

'Aye, they were only lent, the poor wee things,' her mother would sometimes sigh, and her brown eyes would fill with tears. 'But I've got you and Jamie, Alex, I'm lucky, eh?'

And Alex would put her arm round her mother's plump shoulder and kiss her soft cheek.

That day they had really exhausted themselves, Rose as well, playing one game after another, with only a break for their dinners. Finally they were too tired to do anything but sit on the Archangel Steps, where they got in the way of passers-by, who were all talking about the war. Rose seemed to know a lot about it. She said her dad had said Hitler was spoiling for a fight, and that if there was a war it might go on for years. Then her brother would have to go.

'And Jamie?' asked Alex, in alarm.

'Och, no' Jamie?' whispered Martie, whose blue eyes often followed Jamie tearing round the streets.

'They say they'll need women this time,' Rose answered calmly. 'If they do, I'd like to be a nurse. I think I'd like to be a nurse, anyway.'

'No' a bad idea,' said Martie. 'I might be a nurse, too.'

At which they laughed, because Martie was always saying she wanted to marry a rich man. How could she be a nurse as well?

'Maybe I'll meet a rich doctor,' retorted Martie, laughing herself, then turning to look up the steps, because Tim Burnett was there and calling to Rose.

He came slowly down towards them, smiling agreeably, a lanky, fair-haired boy in cricket shirt and flannels, telling Rose in a voice like hers, more English than Scottish, that she was wanted at home. Their mother had come back from bridge early and needed Rose to help with their packing. Had she forgotten they were going to Aberlady tomorrow?

Alex never heard what Rose's answer was, or what else Tim Burnett said, but that was the mysterious start of it. The light around Tim, the arrow in her ten-year-old heart, the fear that she would never see him again, the sorrow that he didn't even know who she was and wouldn't care if he did. Worst of all, maybe, was keeping it all hidden, from Martie, from Jamie, from her mother. There were the sleepless nights with the tears and sniffs, and strange looks from Ma, who never actually said anything, the walks round the square after the Burnetts had come back from holiday, always hoping he might appear.

13

When she did see him again, it was worse, really, than not seeing him, because those times when he came looking for Rose, or stood watching the boys play their games, never offering to join in, only made it more clear to her that he didn't know she existed. He was very well-mannered, always smiled and answered politely if anyone spoke to him, but those grey eyes of his never rested on anyone in the Colonies for long. Never rested on her at all. Or, at least, she didn't think so, but never actually had the courage to look. Sometimes she would order herself to be one of those who spoke to him. 'Go on, you daft thing, say something – ask him what it's like at his school – ask him what he'll do if there's a war – anything!' But she was only just beginning to believe she might find the courage to do that, when he disappeared, and for good. Had gone to boarding school, Rose said, somewhere safe, up north, her mother's idea. Rose might be going away to school, too.

'And we'll never see you again?' asked Alex fearfully.

'Of course you will! There are holidays, aren't there?' But though they did see Rose in the holidays, they never saw Tim. The strange thing was, it no longer mattered. Alex's love had suddenly died. Just went out, like someone switching off a light, switching off that light round Tim. She could pinpoint when it happened. Having breakfast, scraping out the marmalade jar. Feeling happy, as though released. From Tim Burnett? She was already on her way to forgetting him.

But she was remembering now.

Chapter Three

Rose was off duty, spending the afternoon at her parents' house with Tim, who was due to enter the Jubilee next day. They were in the upstairs drawing room, Rose by the elegant chimneypiece where a fire was burning, Tim stretched out on the sofa, his hands folded on his chest, his feet crossed. He was now twenty-four years old and handsome, with pale straight hair and regular features. Though he had lost weight recently and his eyes were sometimes anxious, he was remaining resolutely cheerful.

'Do I look like a Crusader?' he called to Rose. 'You know, on a tomb? Don't they have their feet crossed, like mine?'

Rose laughed, but he sensed the strain she was trying to conceal.

'Maybe I shouldn't mention tombs? In the circumstances?'

'Oh, Tim!' She shook her head and sighed, and he thought how young and vulnerable she seemed out of uniform, with her dark hair loose on her shoulders. Perhaps she was always vulnerable. Perhaps that was something else she had to conceal. They were both good at concealment, he and Rose.

'I wish you didn't mind so much,' he said, getting up to stand by the fire and look down at her. 'I mean, about my coming to the Jubilee. It doesn't help, you know.'

'I'm sorry. It's just that you can afford to go elsewhere, and there are so many people in Edinburgh who can't.'

'You're really annoyed with Mother, aren't you?'

Rose shrugged. 'She's just being Mother, as usual.'

'It's only natural she'd want me somewhere close at hand, where she could visit, isn't it?'

'Yes, but can't you see that apart from anything else it's very awkward for me? Everyone will know you're my brother and they'll be watching me, waiting to see what I'll do.'

'Expecting you to slip me cigarettes and whisky or something?' Tim smiled and flung himself back on the sofa. 'They know you, Roz. There's not a snowball's chance in hell of you doing anything you shouldn't.'

'Just don't play up, Tim, that's all. Just do as you're told.'

'You don't have to worry. I'm not going to embarrass you. I only want to get well.'

Rose lowered her eyes. She had heard those words so many, many times before, sometimes from those who never would be well. Hearing them now from Tim made her catch her breath with fear.

'That's all I want, too,' she said quietly. 'But, please, try not to worry. I know you're going to be all right. You'll be out of the Jubilee in six months, I promise you.'

'Six months,' he repeated stonily. 'Oh, God.'

They had been sitting for some time in silence, watching the afternoon darken and the lights coming on in the square, when the door opened and a large grey cat strolled in, followed by Mrs Burnett, struggling with the weight of a loaded tea tray.

'Isn't it ridiculous?' she gasped. 'No maids now. Only girls in to clean, so I've everything else to do. Rose, dear, help me to set this down, please. No, no, Tim, you stay where you are, I forbid you to move. You're supposed to rest all the time, isn't that so?'

'According to Rose I'll be flat on my back for months.'

'Maybe only a few weeks to begin with,' said Rose, taking the tray from her mother and setting it on a small table. She stooped to pick up the cat and hugged him close. 'Hallo, Smoky Joe, you darling! Have you missed me? He does miss me, you know, he's like a dog, he counts us all.'

'He'll miss me tomorrow, then,' Tim said lightly and Sylvia Burnett, pale and dark-haired like her daughter, gave a little cry.

'I can't bear to think of tomorrow, Tim, I really can't! It's like a bad dream. I keep thinking I'll wake up and feel so glad it's not true!'

'Tim's going to get better, Mother,' Rose said patiently. 'His case is not serious, he'll be well in no time. And he'll have the best of care at the Jubilee.'

'Exactly!' Her mother's dark eyes flashed. 'And you didn't want him to go there, Rose!'

'Let's not go into all that again,' said Tim, biting into a buttered teacake. 'Listen, what are the doctors like? And the nurses? Any pretty ones?'

'The doctors are excellent.'

'Especially Chris,' put in Mrs Burnett. 'Chris MacInnes, Tim. You know I play bridge with his mother?' She gave a meaningful glance at Rose. 'Joan says he's very fond of you, dear.'

'As for the nurses,' Rose went on, coolly disregarding her mother's remark, 'they're the best. Completely dedicated. Actually, you might remember two of them. Girls I used to play with in the Colonies.'

'And why you ever wanted to go down there, I don't know,' said Mrs Burnett. 'I was always very worried about your playing in the street.'

'All children like playing in the street, Mother.'

'Why would I remember these girls?' asked Tim. 'I never went skipping with anybody.'

'They remember you, they did meet you. One's called Alex Kelsie, the other is Martie Cass. You'll call them both Nurse.'

'Did you say they were pretty?'

'It doesn't matter what they look like, they're both good at their jobs. Alex Kelsie is particularly keen to help TB patients. Her mother died in the Jubilee.'

'Poor woman,' whispered Mrs Burnett, giving Tim a frightened glance.

'Oh, look, her case was quite different from Tim's,' Rose said hastily. 'She had miliary TB – that's when the TB gets into the bloodstream. Tim has only a small shadow on one lung; he'll be gardening in no time.'

'Gardening?' cried Mrs Burnett. 'Is that considered part of the cure?'

'Rest is the cure, rest and fresh air.'

'And what about these new drugs? Joan MacInnes said Chris had been talking about them.'

'They're not available here at the moment, and it will be years before they are. It's not sure if they work long term, anyway.'

'But Joan said they'd tried them in America. If it's a question of money, Rose—'

'Even if you managed to buy them, there's no guarantee they'd be right for Tim. Let's just leave it to the doctors to decide what's best.' Rose stood up. 'Look, I've got to go. I don't think I can wait to see Daddy.'

'He's here,' said Tim. 'I can hear him on the stairs.'

A moment later, Mr Burnett came into the drawing room, an older version of Tim, with fair hair receding and horn-rimmed spectacles. As he set down his briefcase and Smoky Joe weaved around his ankles, purring like an engine, Rose went to kiss him and he folded her in his arms.

'How's my favourite daughter?'

'Very well, Daddy. Just looked in to brief Tim about tomorrow.'

Mr Burnett looked over Rose's shoulder at his son. 'All set then, Tim?'

'All set, Dad.'

'Sit down, dear, I'll make fresh tea,' said Mrs Burnett.

'I'll put the kettle on for you before I go out,' Rose told her. 'Daddy, I'm sorry, I have to dash, I want to be back for six.'

'There's no need for you to walk!' exclaimed her mother. 'I'll ring for a taxi.'

'It's no distance.'

'No arguments!'

As Mrs Burnett hurried out, Rose hugged her father again, then kissed Tim's cheek.

'See you tomorrow, Tim. Remember what I said.'

'I'll be as good as gold, Roz. You'll be proud of me.'

'I know I will.'

Dark thoughts held her mind in the taxi taking her back to the nurses' home. It was true that Tim's case was mild and she had probably been right to tell him and her parents not to worry, but as a nurse she knew that mild cases didn't always stay mild. It all depended how well he responded to treatment, how well he co-operated. At least, he had given up smoking!

By the time she was back in uniform and busying herself with the medicine trolley, she was feeling better and even beginning to wonder if after all it was best to have Tim under her eye. She would see that he followed the regime to the letter and that should do it. He would be out of the Jubilee in six months, as she had promised.

'Rose, you're back!'

She looked up to find Dr Chris MacInnes beside her trolley, looking down at her with eager eyes. He was a broad-shouldered, ex-Rugby player, who had lost several years of his career to the war and gained a Military Cross he never talked about. With his open face and curly hair, he seemed younger than his age, but Rose knew he considered himself old at thirty-five because she was only twenty-two. To Rose the age gap didn't matter at all, but that was of no cheer to Chris, who knew he didn't matter, either.

'You didn't take the whole day off, then?' he was saying. 'I'd been thinking I wouldn't see you at all.'

'I had some time owing, just wanted to tell Tim about tomorrow.'

'How is he?' Chris asked gravely.

'Oh, in quite good spirits. He'll do his best to obey orders.'

'I'm really sorry, Rose. You know we'll do all we can.'

'You do that anyway,' she said calmly. 'Look, I must get on.'

'Couldn't we go out for a meal some time soon? To cheer you up?'

'Oh, I don't think restaurant meals are very cheering these days, do you? Let's leave it for the time being.'

'How about the cinema, then? Something highbrow, I suppose?' Chris grinned. 'French? Italian?'

'I'd rather see Danny Kaye,' she retorted, suddenly giving one of the smiles that could so transform her. 'I think I saw there was one of his old films on somewhere. We could go next week, maybe?'

Feeling guilty at the delight she read in his eyes, she quickly pushed her trolley away before Sister or someone should see her gossiping with one of the doctors. What would she have said to one of the junior nurses caught doing that?

'Rose, Rose, when can we go?' Chris was calling after her, but she only waved her hand and went through the swing doors into Butterfly Two. Tomorrow afternoon, this would be home to Tim, and at the thought of that, her face had no more smiles.

Chapter Four

At three o'clock the following afternoon, Tim arrived alone at Reception in the Admin. Department of the Jubilee. By a quarter past three, his personal details had been taken by Staff Nurse Maxwell, he had signed several forms, been given a copy of the rules of the hospital and told to go with 'Nurse', who would 'look after him'. The nurse was Alex Kelsie.

He hasn't changed, she thought, battening down the memories, I'd have known him anywhere. He was a man now, not a boy, but as handsome as ever. Rather thin, as most new patients were, even a little gaunt, but holding himself well. No round-shouldered look, no febrile flush. He would get better. In spite of her determination to feel the usual required detachment, Alex's heart lifted. For him, for Rose. Not for herself, of course. He meant nothing to her. No light shone for him now.

'I'm Nurse Kelsie,' she told him. 'I'm going to help you get ready for the ward. Would you like to give me your case?'

'My case? Oh, come on, I can't let you take that!'

Conscious of Anita Maxwell's bright eyes and flapping ears, Alex smiled politely.

'Mr Burnett, you're the patient, I'm the nurse, I carry your case. Would you please follow me?'

The rituals for incoming patients sometimes embarrassed them. Blood tests, injections, thermometers in their mouths – these were tolerable – but stripping for a bath, getting into pyjamas,

21

then stripping again for X-rays made some feel vulnerable. Not so Tim Burnett. It was Alex who was self-conscious as she ran his bath and took his clothes.

'I have actually had my bath today,' he told her, 'But I suppose it's a rule, is it? All new patients take a bath?'

'That's right.' She laid his pyjamas on a chair and hung up his dressing-gown, carefully not looking at him. 'I'll leave you to it, shall I? When you're ready, I'll take you to X-Ray.'

She felt ashamed of herself. Where was all her training? It was true, when you knew someone personally, the intimate aspects of nursing were difficult. But she couldn't be said to know Tim Burnett. He certainly didn't know her.

When he reappeared from the bathroom, wrapped in his dressing-gown, his fair hair plastered to his head, he surprised her, however, by asking if she hadn't once played in the Colonies with his sister.

'How did you know that?'

'Rose told me. She said you were nursing here.'

'You don't remember meeting me?'

'I'm afraid not. Did we meet?'

'Sometimes. If you'll wait here, Mr Burnett, I'll get your wheelchair.'

That shook him. 'Wheelchair? For God's sake, who says I need a wheelchair? I can walk, you know!'

'I'm afraid you'll no' be doing much walking for the next few weeks. When you're in your bed, Sister'll come and have a talk with you. She'll tell you why you have to rest.'

Without another word, he sat in the wheelchair and allowed himself to be pushed away.

Some time later, when his X-rays were completed and he'd had a brief interview with Dr MacInnes, Alex took him along to Butterfly Two. The rest period was over and in the wing where he had been allocated a bed, patients were awaiting his arrival with interest. Meeting new patients so lately in touch with the real world was always interesting, but this fellow was special, he was Staff Burnett's brother.

Tim himself was pleasantly surprised by the spaciousness of the wing, the number of windows, the general feeling of airiness. There were six beds, all at generous intervals from one another and all near open windows. Tim's was furthest from the door and as Alex pushed him across the expanse of polished linoleum, she introduced him to his fellow patients.

'This is Mr Burnett, everyone. Make him feel at home, eh? Mr Burnett, meet Mr Napier, Mr MacNicol, Mr Hardie, Mr Gibson and Mr Skene.'

'I'm no' a Mister!' cried Kenny Skene, whose bed was nearest to Tim's. 'I'm Kenny!'

The others, clearing their throats, called out their first names, too, but Tim knew it would take him time to pin the right label on everyone. George, Barrie, Jack, Andrew. Two were about his own age, two slightly older, and Kenny, of course, only a boy.

'I'm Tim,' he told them, sliding into icy sheets.

'Nice to meet you, Tim!'

'Dinna worry, the first six months is the worst!'

'That's enough talking,' said Alex. 'I have to unpack Mr Burnett's case.'

'Is she no' a sweetheart?' asked Kenny. 'Ma butterfly girl!'

Tim raised his eyebrows. 'Butterfly girl?'

Alex blushed. 'Take no notice, that's just Kenny's teasing. He calls us all butterfly girls, because we work in butterfly wards.'

'Och, it's no' just that!' cried Kenny, but Alex shook her head at him and put her finger to her lips.

'Mr Burnett, I've put your wash things and razor in your locker and your spare pyjamas in the little drawer. Try to keep your locker top clear. These cardboard containers here are for sputum; be very careful always to use them and keep them for collection. We take them for analysis, you see, the sputum count is very important. These are your paper tissues, use those instead of handkerchiefs, you'll get a fresh supply when needed. I'm no sure what you want to do with the books you've brought – we'll no' want you to be reading much to begin with.'

'I can't read? You're joking, aren't you?'

'It's just to begin with, like I say. Complete rest, you see, is what you need.'

'I'll go mad!'

'No, you won't.' She gave him a smile, so sweet, so compassionate, it made him lower his eyes. 'It'll no' be for long. Now – about your case and your clothes – is there anyone who could take them home for you? Most patients bring someone with them to do that.'

'I wanted to come in alone,' he said shortly. 'Maybe Rose'll take them. I thought she'd have been to see me by now.'

'I'm sure she'll come soon.'

'After Sister's pep talk?' he asked sourly, then cleared his brow. 'Sorry, I shouldn't take my feelings out on you, you've been very kind.'

'That's all right, Mr Burnett, it's what I'm here for, to look after you.'

'I did say my name was Tim.'

'For your friends in here.'

'Aren't you a friend?'

She looked round and whispered quickly,

'Don't say any more – Sister's here!'

As a tall woman in dark blue made her way down the ward, the patients lay quite still, arms by their sides, and Alex standing by Tim's bed seemed like a soldier waiting for the commanding officer's inspection. 'This is Sister Clerk,' she managed to say, and the ward sister nodded.

'Thank you, Nurse. You may get on with your duties. I will just have a quick word with Mr Burnett.'

She was a handsome woman, her features clear-cut, her eyes shining grey, her hair, her skin, everything about her, immaculate. She had clearly been born to be a senior nurse, a sister or a matron, one who would always have the welfare of her patients at heart, provided they did what they were told, who would be totally fulfilled by her career. It occurred to Tim that Rose could end up like her if she didn't watch her step, but young Nurse Kelsie – no, she'd be different.

'I hope you are settling in well, Mr Burnett?' the ward sister asked.

'Very well indeed, thank you, Sister. Everyone's been very good.'

'I'm glad to hear it. Now, I won't talk too long, I don't want to tire you, but I always try to explain to new patients why it's essential that they follow the hospital's regime without question.' She fixed him with her clear gaze. 'It is the only way to get well, do you understand, Mr Burnett?'

'Perfectly.'

'I know that some patients find it very difficult to accept that in the beginning complete rest means exactly that, and I agree that it is not pleasant to have to be blanket-bathed, to have to use bed-pans—'

'Bed-pans?' Tim looked stunned.

'It will only be necessary for a short time, Mr Burnett. As soon as you make progress and your temperature stays down, you will be permitted more independence. But, think about it – if you had broken your arm, you wouldn't expect to use it till it healed, would you? Your lungs are the same. They must be rested till they are well. Sometimes, surgery is required to collapse a lung and allow it to recover, but we need not go into that now.'

'Shall I need surgery?' he asked quickly, but Sister Clerk refused to be drawn. That would be for the doctors to decide. All Mr Burnett should concentrate on was following the rest-cure. In no time at all, he would find himself recovering and going home.

'My sister said six months,' said Tim.

'As I say, no time at all,' Sister Clerk agreed, smiling glacially. 'But again, that will be for the doctors to decide, not Staff Burnett, much as we appreciate her.'

'Speaking of angels—', Tim, seeing Rose approaching, was grinning, but Sister Clerk was not amused.

'I beg your pardon?'

Rose moved smoothly in. 'I'm sorry, Sister, I didn't realise you were here, I came to collect my brother's things.'

'That's quite all right, Staff, I am just leaving.'

When Tim had declared his humble thanks, and Sister Clerk had left them, her brow rather dark, Alex melted away, and Rose packed Tim's case.

25

'You didn't let Mother come, then? She's just rung me, feeling very aggrieved.'

'Couldn't face it.'

She laughed. 'Well, now you're here, how are you feeling?'

'Damned cold. Don't they believe in heating here? Apart from that, as well as can be expected, I think is the phrase.'

'Too much heating is not considered helpful. But, cheer up, you're not too bad.' Rose lowered her voice. 'When you get to know about other people here, you'll soon realise that.'

'Why can't they hurry up and let us have those new drugs? God, if I could just take a pill, instead of lying here for weeks! Why didn't you tell me I'd have to use bed-pans, Roz?'

'Thought I'd leave that to Sister,' Rose smiled. 'I knew you'd take it better from her.'

'Doesn't like you much, does she?'

'Sister Clerk? Why, what did she say?'

'I just got the impression. Maybe you're a rival.'

'A rival for what, for heaven's sake? Look, I'm going to leave you now. You mustn't talk any more. Just rest.'

He closed his eyes and Rose with his case walked quietly away.

' 'Bye, 'bye, Butterfly Staff!' cried Kenny, with an impudent grin.

Rose's look was indulgent. 'Now, now, Kenny, you know nurses keep their feet on the ground, they don't fly anywhere.'

'Speak for yourself, lassie,' said Jack MacNicol. 'I'll bet there's some that do!'

'Is he in?' Martie asked Alex, when they met up in the sluice.

'Who?' asked Alex.

'You know who – Tim Burnett. I've been in theatre, I've no' seen him.'

'He's settled in very well.'

Martie studied Alex's averted face.

'You're blushing, just like you used to.'

'What do you mean?'

'In the old days, when you talked about him, you used to blush.'

'I never did!'

'Och, you did, Alex. You were sweet on him, everybody knew.'

'They did not know!'

'Well, I did,' said Martie.

Chapter Five

As the days of Tim's initial bed-rest slowly passed, Alex concentrated on not showing any particular interest in him. As he meant nothing to her, it should have been easy. Yet every time she entered the swing doors of Butterfly Two, her eyes went instinctively to the bed at the end of the ward, and every time she found its occupant's cool grey gaze brightening as it met hers. She tried not to feel that that welcoming spark was especially for her. Probably Tim Burnett was glad to see anyone coming who'd break the monotony of his long dull days. Certainly, he never tried to flirt with her as some male patients did, never tried to whisper to her, or touch her hand. Yet she had the feeling that he did think of her differently from the other nurses. He gave her no messages; it was strange she received them, all the same.

His parents visited him twice a week at the appointed times, bringing glimpses of another world to his fascinated fellow patients. His father would sit by his bed, loosening his overcoat, polishing his glasses, looking so much like someone in authority, everyone in the ward would fall silent in case he noticed them and told them what to do. His mother, in her furs and expensive shoes, her face made up, her scent wafting from bed to bed, made every man try to see her better and any other visitors who were present at the time would murmur among themselves and say things like, 'Wha's the duchess?' and 'Whativer is she doing here, then, should she no' be visiting Holyrood?'

On one occasion, Alex was passing and Tim called to her to come and be introduced. In fact, Alex had already met Rose's mother back in the old days, but didn't expect to be remembered and wasn't. Not that Mrs Burnett wasn't very sweet and gracious, thanking Alex for all her kindness to her son, but Alex, moving on, had the impression that she was being thanked as a housemaid for making a specially good job of cleaning the silver or something.

'Och, I shouldn't be so touchy,' she told herself. Mrs Burnett had been brought up in a certain way, you couldn't expect her to change, even if times were changing around her.

Three weeks went by, then four, and on one wonderful morning, Dr MacInnes brought Tim the news that he could join the dressing-gown parade the following day. Alex had just taken his temperature and was writing it on his chart; her eyes met his and at their radiance, she smiled.

'Dressing-gown parade?' he cried, laughing weakly. 'Chris, I don't believe it! I go to the lavatory tomorrow on my own two feet? I take a bath and wash myself? Who'd have thought happiness would come to mean this?'

Chris grinned. Though others on the staff would not have approved, he and Tim had become friends, more because they both had wartime experiences to share, when Tim was allowed to talk about his, rather than because their mothers played bridge together. Now Chris clapped Tim on his shoulder.

'Your temperature's been down for some time, you've been a good boy, done your bit, and now you're due for your reward. But don't expect too much too soon. Your shadow's not gone, you still have sputum, you're not ready for dancing yet.'

'Dancing?' Tim glanced at Alex. 'Will you save me a waltz, Nurse? When I am ready for dancing?'

'I bet Nurse Kelsie'd be good at that old jitterbugging,' said Chris. 'Now you really have to be fit for that, Tim.'

Alex, still smiling, said she must get on with her temperature round, but at the next bed to Tim's her smile died. It was Kenny's bed, but he was not in it. In spite of a recent operation to collapse his right lung, his condition had deteriorated and he was being nursed in a side ward. After a moment's dark gaze at the pristine pillow and expertly cornered blankets, Alex walked on, while Tim and Chris exchanged glances.

'How is Kenny?' asked Tim.

'We're doing all we can.'

'What are his chances?'

'You know I can't discuss that with you, Tim.'

'You mean he's not going to make it?' Tim's delight was fading fast. 'Why the hell can't you get him some of that strepto-whatever it is?'

'Streptomycin? It's not necessarily the answer.'

'I understood there'd been a lot of success with it.'

'Yes, but there've been setbacks, too. Some people in fact can't take it, the side-effects are too bad.'

'One step forward, half a dozen back, I suppose.'

'No more talking,' Chris said hastily. 'In fact, if Sister catches me, I'll get shot for talking to you myself.' He leaned forward. 'I will tell you this, though. You're not going to need streptomycin, you're going to get well on your own.'

'I'm happy to hear it,' Tim said wearily. 'If I didn't know about Kenny, I'd be even happier.'

Chapter Six

When Alex had rare time off at the weekend, Jamie came over from Glasgow on Sunday to collect her from the Jubilee. It had been arranged that they would spend the day with their father and his second wife, Cousin Edie, at Mason Street. Alex would rather have been just nursing as usual, particularly nursing Tim Burnett and young Kenny, who was still very low, but she put on her New Look tobacco-brown coat, her woollen hat, mitts and boots and prepared for the December day.

Jamie didn't particularly want to go to their old home either. Neither he nor Alex had been happy when Cousin Edie had replaced their mother. In fact, it had been some time after the marriage before Alex could bring herself even to speak to her father.

'How could he do it?' she had cried to Jamie. 'How could he try to replace Ma? Specially with HER?'

'He's no' trying to replace Ma,' Jamie told her. 'Cousin Edie's just worn him down, that's all. Saw him as her last chance.'

Edie's parents, Arthur's Aunt Jean and Uncle Cameron, were long dead, but it was true that Edie had always claimed that looking after them had prevented her from marrying. With Letty gone and Arthur left, it must have seemed her chance had come. In no time she had become a regular visitor at Mason Street, always bearing jars of jam or apple pies, darned socks or ironed shirts, until Alex was at screaming point.

'I can do Dad's washing!' she had told Edie. 'I can darn his socks!'

'No, no, pet, you've your school work and your exams.' Cousin Edie's soft, florid face had not lost its sweet and indulgent expression, even though Alex was scarlet and ready to cry. 'You just leave your dad to me, and dinna worry your head.'

Just as Jamie had said, Edie had worn Arthur down, and he had been too dazed with grief to fight. With indecent haste, so his children thought, there was a wedding in the register office, a cake baked by Edie, a honeymoon in the Borders, and then Edie was sorting through all Letty's things and throwing most of them out.

'Now, what's all this crochet?' she asked pleasantly, pulling out yards of Letty's handiwork. 'This is no good, eh? I mean, what's it for?'

'It was for me!' Alex cried. 'A tablecloth for me! For my bottom drawer!'

'But, pet, where is the tablecloth? And you'd no' want old-fashioned stuff like that, would you? I'll put it on the pile to go, eh?'

'You won't!' Alex snatched up the crochet work and ran crying to her bed, where she lay thinking what she might do, how she would get away. It was then that the thought had come to her that she should follow Rose into nursing and TB nursing at that. She'd been so grateful to the people who'd looked after her poor bright-eyed mother, so painfully thin when she had been so plump, so gallantly hurrying away from life, anxious to be no trouble. The thought became a decision and one that gave her strength. If she went into nursing as soon as she was old enough, she could live in a nurses' home, she could be away, as Jamie too would be away, in the army. They need never see their father or Cousin Edie again. Of course, it hadn't worked out like that. Time had done a little healing, and there they were, she and Jamie, on their way for Sunday dinner back at home. It had become a regular event, whenever Alex was free.

'I'm thinking of getting a car,' Jamie said, walking with his head down against the winter wind.

'A car?' Alex was disbelieving. 'What sort of car?'

'Morris Eight. Been up on blocks through the war, no' much driven since. I'm getting it checked.'

'But can you afford it, Jamie? And what about the petrol? It's still on the ration.'

'I'm no' worried about the petrol, it'll be enough for what I want. And I can run the car.' Jamie pulled his cap further down over his brow. 'I've a bit put by.'

'You could take us for drives,' Alex said, beginning to accept the idea. 'We could go into the country.'

'Who'd you mean by us?'

'Martie and me.'

'Martie Cass? Why'd you make such a friend of her, Alex?'

'She's all right, Jamie.'

'She bosses you.'

'I know.' Alex suddenly raised her chin. 'But not when things really matter.'

'Then you take a stand?' Jamie laughed shortly.

'Yes, I do. At least, I will.'

'Talk's cheap.'

Alex deflected the attack. 'She likes you, you know, Jamie. Always did.'

'Martie? She wants to marry a millionaire.'

'Oh, and she's likely to do that, eh?'

'All I'm doing is thinking of buying a car,' Jamie said flatly. 'No' marrying Martie.'

They had come to Mason Street, one of the rows of parallel terraces that made up the Colonies close to the Water of Leith where it moved sluggishly through Stockbridge. In the early days, this district had been an independent village with its own flourishing markets, just as Canonmills, up the road, had had its industries. The site had been considered very desirable by the Cooperative Building Company, providing easy access to shops and employment for the residents, but times had changed. The villages were part of the city, the markets had closed, most of the old industries had faded, people now found work elsewhere. The shops remained, however, and the Water of Leith, which at least was a good deal cleaner than it had been in the old days, though still subject to flooding. And up the old Archangel Steps, there were still the grander houses of Cheviot Square and that different world known to Rose and Tim. How strange, thought Alex, that it should be so close and yet so far. But that was Edinburgh for you!

Her own old home, following the Colonies pattern, was built of stone and housed two families in two separate storeys connected by an external staircase. The Kelsies had the upper floor, with two rooms, the Cass family had the smaller apartment below, but both families had the use of the little garden at the front. It was here that Alex and Jamie met Mr and Mrs Cass coming out of their front door, dressed for church.

Tilda Cass, a thin-faced woman in her forties, with sharp wandering eyes, stopped to speak.

'Come for your dinner?' She made it sound as though that was the only reason they might have for visiting their father. 'Och, it's nice you've got your stepmother to cook for you, eh?'

Alex and Jamie looked away.

'What Arthur'd have done without Edie, I canna think.'

'He'd have managed!' snapped Alex. 'He'd have had Ma to remember!'

'Aye, but you canna live with the dead, you ken. Life goes on.'

'We'd better go,' said Jamie, holding Alex's arm tightly, as though warning her to say no more. 'Goodbye, then.'

'Wait a bit,' said Sid, who was tall and gaunt in a secondhand black overcoat that was too small for him. 'If you see our Martie, tell her it's time she came to see her folks. Dinna ken when she was last over.'

'Out of sight, out of mind,' sniffed Tilda. 'That's what you get for doing your best for a girl, eh? But we'll away to kirk. You sure you damped down the fire, Sidney?'

'Sure,' he replied, and the Kelsies hid smiles. There was no need for Sid to damp down the fire; in his house, fires and lights were always low.

'Life goes on,' Alex murmured, as she followed Jamie up the

staircase to their father's door. 'All folk mean by that is that you have to forget.'

'No, to be fair, it just means you have to get on with your own life, not live in the past.'

'You're saying I live in the past because I want to remember Ma?'

'Och, no!' Jamie swung back and pressed Alex's hand. 'I'm like you, I'll never want to forget Ma.'

They were round the table in the living room, scene of so many happy times in the old days. Edie had replaced their mother's curtains and pictures, changed the wallpaper and thrown out the rug in front of the stove, but she had not brought in new furniture. No doubt she had her plans, but for now the sideboard, the table and chairs, the tall press, where Letty had once kept everything that wouldn't go elsewhere, from string and writing-paper, to dishcloths and Arthur's tools, were still in their familiar places. Alex could never decide whether she was happy to see them, or whether it was too painful that they should be there and her mother not. But here were she and Jamie and her father still around and her mother not. Life goes on, the awful Tilda Cass had said. Yes, it was true, it was right that it should, as long as memories went on too.

Edie, her cheeks flushed from the oven and her auburn hair straggling from its combs, was dishing up the joint, while Arthur, his shoulders bowed, was sharpening the carvers. He never said much these days, never recited any Shakespeare. If asked, he would only shake his head and say he'd forgotten all that sort of thing. Jamie said it was Edie's fault – she liked to hear her own voice, not other people's. Alex knew her dad had just lost heart, but she wouldn't give him credit for grieving still. Not when he'd married Cousin Edie.

'No' a big joint,' Edie said comfortably, 'but the best I could do on the ration. There's plenty of roast tatties, anyway, and cabbage.'

'Looks very nice,' Jamie said politely.

'Better than you get at the nurses' home, eh, Alex?' asked

Edie, as Arthur passed the plates around. 'How you stick that life at the Jubilee is a mystery. All thae poorly folk coughing their heads off!' She stopped, remembering Letty, flushed a little, then carried on. 'But somebody's got to do that kind of work, right enough, and all credit to you, Alex, is what I say. Will you be coming for Christmas, you two? I've been promised a nice bit of pork.'

'I'll be working over Christmas,' Alex replied. It was true; she volunteered every year.

'I've been invited by a friend,' said Jamie.

'Girlfriend?' asked Edie, her cold little eyes twinkling.

'Chap I knew in the army.'

'There'll just be you and me, then, Art, but we won't mind, will we?'

As Edie jumped up to get more gravy, Arthur raised his eyes to Alex. Help me, they signalled, Please, help me!

Oh, Dad, thought Alex, Oh, God, poor Dad . . .

Her heart melting, she stretched her hand across the table, but before she could touch his, Edie was back.

'There now, who's for more nice hot gravy?'

'I was thinking, I might be able to get the day off at Christmas,' Alex said, not looking at her father. 'Can't promise, but I have worked the last two holidays, it should be my turn.'

'Why, Alex, that'd be grand!' cried Edie. 'Hear that, Art? Alex might come for Christmas, after all!'

'I hear,' Arthur said huskily.

It was evening before Alex could return to the Jubilee. There'd been the washing-up to do, then a walk to take in Inverleith Park with Arthur still scarcely speaking; finally tea, with potted meat sandwiches and currant tea-loaf. When they'd managed to get to the goodbyes, Edie had given them her usual soft hugs and kisses, and Arthur had shaken their hands and said he was looking forward to seeing Alex at Christmas. She'd had the courage then to look into his eyes again and seen gratitude, which made her feel bad. As soon as she'd kissed his cheek, she'd hurried out into the cold with Jamie, and had begun scolding him because he wasn't coming for Christmas too.

'All that stuff about an army friend inviting you! I'm sure Dad knows you've made it up, and I think you should say you'll come and help me out.'

'Hey, hey, hey, I didn't make anything up! It's true Terry Jeffrey has invited me for Christmas Day. He's just got married, wants to show off his wife's cooking.' Jamie strode down the damp pavement, with Alex almost running at his side. 'Anyway, you've changed your tune a bit, haven't you? I thought Dad was supposed to be the villain of the piece; now you're all for trying to please.'

'I suddenly felt sorry for him, that's all. Look, will you slow down, Jamie? Where's the fire?'

'Sorry, I was just thinking about the train.' He studied his watch under a street light. 'It's OK, I've plenty of time. Shall we have a drink before I take you to the Jubilee?'

'A drink? Are you crazy?' Alex laughed. 'I can't go back to the Jubilee smelling of drink, Sister'd have ma guts for garters!'

Jamie laughed too and took his sister's arm.

'It's good to hear you laugh, Alex. It's good you're feeling better about Dad, and all. He's had a bad time, too, remember.'

'I know. Cousin Edie's the problem.'

'Aye, well, let's no' think about her. She can live her life, we'll live ours.' Jamie scowled. 'Just wish she'd keep her nose out of our affairs, eh? Did you hear her hinting about me having a girl-friend?'

'No harm in that, Jamie. I sometimes wonder about your girl-friends myself. You'll want to get married one of these days.'

'Aye, when I'm ready.' He glanced at her face in the shadows. 'How about you, anyway? You used to go out with some of the lads I knew. No' found Mr Right?'

'I'm no' even looking for Mr Right.'

'How about a handsome young doctor?'

'We've only got one handsome one and he's booked himself for Rose. You remember Rose Burnett?'

'Yes, she's a looker. And rich with it, eh?'

'Her brother's in the Jubilee,' Alex said casually. 'Very mild case, though.'

37

'Well, there you are, Alex!' As they reached the gates of the hospital, Jamie stooped to kiss her cheek. 'He's the one for you. You were sweet on him in the old days, eh?'

'Oh, for heaven's sake!' cried Alex, speeding away up the drive. 'Does everybody know everything about me?'

'Now what've I said?' called Jamie.

Chapter Seven

Alex had intended to go straight to the nurses' home, where she would make herself some cocoa, go to bed, and forget her troubles. At the sight of the dimmed lights of Butterfly Two, however, she hesitated, standing beneath the trees lining the drive, listening to the night wind sighing through the bare branches. Something made her want to go to the ward. It wasn't the hope of seeing Tim Burnett, who should already be asleep, or at least settled for the night, as all the patients should be at this hour. She didn't in fact know what it was that drew her, but a strange, sick feeling of apprehension gripped her, making her turn her steps away from the home and towards the ward.

Everything seemed as usual as she opened the entrance door to one of the wings and slipped inside; not quiet, of course, for there were always sounds in a hospital – coughs, voices, taps, knocks, the humming of machines – but subdued, for this was evening. Alex listened for a moment, taking off her hat and unbuttoning her coat, then moved along the corridor that led to side wards and bathrooms. There didn't seem to be anyone about.

Suddenly a side ward door opened and Martie appeared. She was without her apron and carrying a bundle of linen; in the poor light of the corridor, her face seemed colourless.

'Alex – what are you doing here?' she asked without real interest, as though she was too tired to feel interest.

'I don't know.' Alex looked at the linen in Martie's arms. It was bloodstained. 'I think – maybe I came to see Kenny.'

'Kenny?' Martie gave a long deep sigh. 'You're too late. We've lost him.'

'Oh, no!' Alex put her hand to her lips. 'Oh, no, Martie! No, not Kenny!'

'Aye, he had a massive haemorrhage, nothing we could do. I'm just taking this lot to the laundry.' Martie glanced back at the side ward. 'You can go and see him if you like. Jill and me've got him ready. Jill's gone for tea, she feels pretty bad.'

'Is he – by himself?'

'Rose is with him. She's waiting to see his mother. They've sent transport for her.'

'Poor soul . . .'

'Aye. She might have to bring the bairns.'

Kenny had been the eldest of five. His mother, bravely cheeky, as he had been, was on her own. Nobody had seen his father since 1946.

'I hope she doesn't bring the bairns here,' Alex said. 'No' to a place like this.'

'They've all had their injections, they'll be OK.'

'Yes, but it's what they'll remember, isn't it?' Alex blew her nose. 'I'll – I'll go and see him then.'

'To say goodbye,' Martie said gently.

The little room was very quiet, filled with shadows cast by the one lamp by Kenny's bed. When Alex tiptoed in, Rose, who had been sitting by the bed, stood up and came to her.

'Aren't you off duty?' she whispered.

'I felt I wanted to come, I don't know why.'

'Nurses have that feeling sometimes.' Rose turned towards Kenny's bed. 'You heard what happened?'

'Martie's just told me.'

'There was nothing anyone could do.'

'No.'

They stood looking down at Kenny. Dressed in a hospital shroud, with his ginger hair smoothed back from his brow, he didn't look like Kenny. Too peaceful, thought Alex, perhaps because his eyes, that had always given such character to his face, were closed. The finality of death came over her. Never again would they see Kenny's eyes open, hear him laugh and tease, as they brought him his pills and injections, prepared him for his tests, his X-rays, his operation that had done no good. Her eyes misting with tears, she turned to Rose.

'Remember, we were his butterfly girls?'

'We still are,' said Rose.

After a few moments, Alex put her hand to Kenny's cold brow, and turned away.

'Mrs Skene should be here soon,' said Rose. 'Why don't you go back to the home and make yourself a hot drink?'

'I think I will, Staff.'

As Rose took up her melancholy watch again, Alex felt grateful that it was Rose and not she who would have to see Kenny's mother. But Rose would carry out the duty perfectly, as she did everything. Wiping away her tears, Alex let herself out into the corridor, anxious now to get away from Butterfly Two, back to the haven of her own room, to Martie's company and a cup of cocoa. But someone was there in the shadows. She could see a tall figure, a man's figure, in a dark dressing-gown. As he came towards her, she saw his face.

'Mr Burnett! What are you doing out of bed?'

'You forget, I'm allowed to go to the bathroom.' He was close beside her, his eyes taking in her off-duty clothes, her face marked by tears. 'But what's the matter? You've been crying, haven't you?'

'It's Kenny.'

'Kenny?'

'He's dead. He had a haemorrhage. They couldn't save him.'

Tim couldn't speak. He took Alex's hands in his, he stooped and pressed his face to hers. Only for a moment, then he released her hands and turned his head away.

'I have to go,' Alex whispered, acutely aware of Rose's presence beyond the door to the side ward; of Kenny, lying there; of this man before her who had taken her hands, put his face against hers, for comfort. Or more than that? She felt guilty even wondering. Felt guilty to be alive, thinking of herself, so close to the presence of death.

41

'Shall I see you tomorrow?' asked Tim, his eyes still fixed on her in the gloom of the corridor. 'I missed you today.'

'Better go back to bed, Mr Burnett,' she said evenly. 'You know you mustn't tire yourself.'

As he left her, walking slowly, head bent, she sagged with the effort she had scarcely realised she was making.

'Are you all right?' asked Martie, as they boiled the kettle on the landing gas ring in the nurses' home.

Alex, touched by a variety of emotions, shook her head. 'Feel terrible,' she answered.

'Aye, we all do,' sighed Martie, and Alex, stirring the cocoa, nursed guilt again. Yet if she was sheltering behind her grief for Kenny, the grief was genuine all the same.

'Shall we try to go to the funeral?' she asked.

'Aye, Rose says two of us could go. I thought, you and me.'

'Two butterfly girls,' said Alex. 'He'd have liked that.'

Chapter Eight

Kenny's loss was devastating to the men in his ward. It seemed to underline their own vulnerability, their own mortality. A young lad like that, so full of desire to live, to be put out like a candle, in the place where he should have been made well. It didn't bear thinking of, eh? Patients from other wards, women, too, who only knew Kenny slightly, felt his passing like a cold wind blowing over their own graves.

'Aye, shows you, the doctors canna do miracles,' they muttered among themselves. 'And miracles are what we're asking for, eh?'

'Praying for,' said some.

Alex and Martie, bracing themselves for the ordeal, attended Kenny's funeral. A charitable fund had helped to pay for the burial, which took place in dark, raw weather, and afterwards the mourners were invited back to Mrs Skene's tenement rooms.

'Och, you're no' away?' she cried, when the two nurses tried to excuse themselves. 'I've no' had the time to thank you for everything you did for ma Kenny, and thae lovely flowers frae the hospital and a'—' As they wavered, she added eagerly, 'I've tea laid on, and ham and everything, I've done ma Kenny proud!'

'We really can't stay long,' Alex said, yielding at last, 'we're due back on the ward, you see.'

'Aye, aye.' Mrs Skene knew they'd their wonderful work to do. Oh, but she wanted to be with them just a wee while longer, her last link with Kenny, eh? 'He was ma prop, you ken,' she told them, her eyes full of tears. 'He was going to take care of me and the bairns, he'd sich plans!'

Somehow, they got through the little wake, trying not to notice the smell of poverty that hung round the tenement like something you could touch, drinking strong tea, talking to Mrs Skene's neighbours and few relatives, finally managing to get away.

'Now, remember, you must bring the children into the clinic for regular checks,' Martie told Mrs Skene firmly, as they left. 'It's all free, you've nothing to worry about. Just make sure they don't go like Kenny, eh?'

With her promises ringing in their ears, they waited, shivering, for their tram.

'He never had a chance, did he?' Alex muttered, searching in her purse for change. 'Kenny never had a chance, of any sort.'

'Well, we have to make sure the others do. Get them checked, X-rayed, all that stuff. This mass radiography's going to make a difference, as well.'

'I suppose so,' Alex answered dispiritedly. So many things had been put forward as the magic way to defeat TB. Sometimes it seemed to her they were as far away as ever from success.

'Cheer up, here's the tram!' cried Martie, and leaped aboard with her usual energy. 'Two to the Jubilee, please!'

It was not long, of course, before Kenny's bed, if not his place, was filled in Butterfly Two. Neal Drover, who was admitted the day after the funeral, was a black-haired schoolmaster of thirty-two, tall and painfully thin, but so good-looking, he set the hospital jungle telegraph buzzing before he'd had his first X-ray. An amazing number of female patients found an excuse just to peep in the door of the ward, and arguments raged as to whether he looked more like James Mason than Stewart Granger, or could it be he was even more like that new fellow, Gregory Peck? He had just the same cheekbones, Jill declared, but Anita Maxwell said, Och, no, he was Cary Grant to the life! Someone terrific, anyway, and it was a shame, so it was, that he had a cavity on his right lung that was going to keep him out of action for quite some time. Tim Burnett, who was his neighbour as he had been Kenny's, took an immediate dislike to him.

'Thinks a lot of himself, that fellow' he told Alex, when she stopped to speak to him in the morning 'dressing-gown parade'. 'You should have seen him when Sister came round to give him her little talk. Puts his hand up, operates the dimples, and says, "No need to tell me, Sister, I'm an old hand at this, rest, rest and more rest, eh? But I'm waiting for my pneumothorax surgery, so don't expect me to spare too much time for the rest cure!"'

'He never said that to Sister?' cried Alex, giggling. 'Why, she must have had a fit!'

'She did. Blew him up on the spot for even mentioning surgery. That would be for the DOCTORS to decide, et cetera. So then he tells her that Dr Senior has already told him he can have it, knows him from another sanatorium, apparently. Seems Drover's been in at least two other places before this one. Listen, what exactly is this pneumothorax treatment?'

'It's just a way of collapsing a diseased lung. They put gas or clean air into the pleural cavity, so that the lung is compressed and forced to rest. Then you get topped up with the gas at regular intervals.'

'You don't think I'll have to have that?'

'No, Neal's case is more severe than yours. Look, I'm away. I mustn't be seen talking to you for too long.'

'You worry too much,' he said softly. 'What harm can it do?'

She lowered her eyes. There had been a change in their relationship since the night Kenny had died, something they both recognised. Nothing was said, but she called him Tim and he called her Alex, and in her heart was love again. What was in his heart, she couldn't be sure – how could you ever be sure? But she hoped she knew.

'I wish you'd try to understand what it's like for me, Tim,' she said quietly.

'Alex, you have no idea at all what it's like for ME!' He put his hand on her arm. 'You know how I feel about you, don't you?'

Her head shot up, her eyes fastened on his. She should be looking round, trying to see if anyone was watching, overhearing, but just at that moment she didn't care. This was the closest either of them had come to declaring love. She felt herself trembling with joy and surprise.

'It drives me crazy, the way we have to go on,' he went on, keeping his voice low. 'You understand me?'

'I'm away,' she said faintly. 'Don't keep me, Tim.'

'OK. But just don't go talking to that fellow Drover, that's all I ask. I suppose you think he's handsome?'

'Of course, the handsomest man in the hospital.' At Tim's look, Alex laughed. 'Oh, Tim, how can I even see him, when he's next to you?'

As she left him, Tim smiled.

It was some days later that Alex did talk to Neal Drover. Or, at least he talked to her. Though not the rest period, it was very quiet in the ward at the time. Tim, Jack and Andrew had gone for routine checks with the doctors; George and Barrie were dozing. Neal Drover, who had recently had a bad fit of coughing, was watching Alex move round the ward. He did not look so much like a film-star at that moment, she thought, glancing at him as she felt his eyes on her, far too pale and worn, poor man.

'You all right?' she whispered, approaching and bending over him.

'Fine.' There were deep shadows under his blue eyes, but their gaze on her was bright. 'How are you?'

'Me?' She laughed and smoothed his sheet. 'You shouldn't be asking about me, Mr Drover. Shouldn't be talking at all, in fact.'

'Oh, forget that peace and quiet stuff, doesn't do any damn good.' He began to struggle into a sitting position and suddenly jerked his head towards Tim's empty bed.

'Mind if I ask – are you getting fond of him?'

Alex's eyes widened. Scarlet colour flooded her face.

'What did you say?' she whispered.

'You mustn't be offended,' he said calmly. 'I'm a lot older than you and I've been around a lot more. This is my third time in a place like this, you know. I was in a sanatorium down south and another in the Highlands. I've seen it all before.'

'Seen what?' she asked angrily. 'What are you talking about?'

'These little love affairs. Relationships. Patients falling for nurses, nurses falling for patients, everybody falling for the doctors. None of it means a thing.' Neal smiled sadly. 'They're like shipboard romances. Fine when you're away from real life, but when you come ashore—' He waved his hands. 'Then it's bursting bubbles everywhere, and you're lucky if you don't get hurt.'

'I can't believe you're talking to me like this,' Alex cried, trembling. 'How dare you, Mr Drover? What gives you the right?'

'Oh, I've no right.' He crumpled a tissue in his fingers. 'It's just that – I see things. I see the way Tim looks at you, I see the way you look at him. And I'm afraid.'

'Please lie down and don't talk any more, you're doing yourself harm—'

'I'm afraid for you, Alex. You're a lovely girl, you're also a very good nurse. I don't want to see you risk your happiness for Tim Burnett.'

'It's no' the way you think, I'm no' risking anything!'

'He's going to get well, isn't he? He's going to go back to university, take up his life again. Where will you fit in?' Neal lay back, breathing heavily. 'Or, haven't you thought that far ahead?'

Alex stood looking down at him, her heart thudding with anger and fear. She wanted to shout denials, to make him take back all his cheek, to apologise, say he was wrong. What she and Tim had was real. Neal Drover didn't know anything about it. He didn't understand, he had just taken it upon himself to interfere; simply because he was so handsome he thought he could do whatever he liked.

'If you're so afraid of me being hurt, maybe you should try not hurting me yourself,' she said through clenched teeth and left him. At the door, she looked back, and saw that his face was flushed and that his eyes were closed. Damn him, she thought, damn him! But went back anyway.

'Let me take your pulse,' she said coldly. 'You've worked yourself up into a fine state, haven't you? I think I'll get the doctor to have a look at you.'

'See what I mean?' he asked faintly. 'You're a wonderful nurse.'

'No more talking,' ordered Alex.

*

When Tim came back from his check-up, he was exultant. If he carried on as he had been doing, he'd soon be allowed up for limited periods every day. 'Not just for the dressing-gown parade for the bathroom,' he told Alex as soon as he saw her, 'but for the library and the workshop. By February, I might even qualify for "own clothes" and short walks! Can you believe it?'

'I'm so happy for you,' she said, with truth. All she wanted was for Tim to get well, and Neal Drover's warnings meant so little they floated from her mind as though they had never been made. When Tim asked what was wrong with Dreamboat Drover, he seemed to be sleeping, which was not like him, Alex said casually that the doctor had given him something, he'd been overdoing things.

'The guy's his own worst enemy,' said Tim. 'Can't help talking, showing off, telling everybody what to do.'

'I expect he means well,' Alex murmured.

When Neal woke up and seemed recovered, she was relieved, all the same, that he never attempted to give her any more advice.

Chapter Nine

If they could afford it, most patients at the Jubilee handed out little presents at Christmas time. The nurses were usually given soap or talcum powder, the doctors handkerchiefs or, if lucky, bottles of wine. The staff, too, exchanged gifts and that year, after a lot of thought, Chris MacInnes gave Rose Burnett a fine silk scarf that had cost him far too much, and she gave him claret from her father's cellar, having left it too late to buy him a proper present. He didn't mind; the fact that she had bothered to give him anything at all was progress in his view.

'Shall I see you over the holiday?' he asked hopefully.

'Well, as we're both on duty, I'm sure you will,' Rose answered.

'You know what I mean. Can we go out somewhere, when we're free?'

'I suppose you've already got something in mind?'

'There's a staff dance at the Western, I think it's on the twenty-eighth.'

She sighed. 'I'm not keen on dancing.'

'There'll be reels. You like reels, don't you?'

'Yes, I like something with action, not drifting round in foxtrots.'

'OK, then?'

'OK. Got to dash. Happy Christmas!'

'Rose, listen, I just want to say, it's good that Tim's doing so well, isn't it? You must be very relieved.'

49

Her dark eyes shone. 'Oh, I am. I was pretty confident about him, but you can never be sure, can you? He should be out of here by the spring.'

'Know what he asked me the other day? Could he have one of the chalets?'

Rose stared. 'One of the chalets? I'm amazed. Tim likes his comfort. Not that Butterfly Two is particularly comfortable, but it has got four walls!'

'Probably wants to get away from Neal Drover.' Chris laughed. 'Those two don't get on!'

'Neal Drover is just too good-looking to be true,' Rose commented. 'I never like handsome men, they're always so conceited.'

'Now you tell me!' cried Chris, striking his brow. 'No wonder I've never got to first base with you!'

He was rewarded by one of Rose's rare laughs and went on his way, still filled with hope for his private festive season.

Tim gave Alex chocolates for Christmas. In fact, he gave all the nurses chocolates, luxury boxes bought from one of the best shops in Edinburgh by his mother, who seemed to have sweet points to burn.

'Oh, they're gorgeous!' cried Jill Berry. 'How'd your mum get so many, then, on the ration?'

'Never uses her ration, never eats sweets,' Tim told her. 'Nobody does in our family. We're sweet enough.'

'Cheeky!' retorted Jill, shaking her head at him. 'But these'll be a real treat. We don't get many sweeties from Logie's!'

All the nurses were delighted, except Alex, though she knew she was being unreasonable. For even if she was special to Tim, how could he be expected to give her a present that was special? He couldn't draw attention to their relationship by singling her out in any way. She was already worried enough by Neal Drover's noticing something between herself and Tim. If anyone else noticed, it might be the end of her career, all involvements between staff and patients being strictly forbidden. So why did she mind that she'd had chocolates from Tim just like everyone else? Och, because she wanted to shout it from the housetops that she was different from everyone else, Tim was in love with her and she with him. Wasn't it only natural?

On Christmas Eve, there was a carol concert, which Tim and Neal were unable to attend, both being confined to bed-rest, though Tim, of course, would soon be up and about, an ambulatory patient.

'I can do without the carols,' he told Alex. 'It's just being stuck with Drover that gets me.'

'You should try to get on with him, Tim. Don't want to send your temperature up, do you?'

'No, as soon as I possibly can, I'm moving out to one of the chalets.' Tim grinned. 'And getting away from Drover isn't my only reason for wanting that.'

'What do you mean?'

'Come on, I'll be on my own in a chalet, won't I? And you'll be able to see me, won't you?'

'Tim, the chalets aren't part of this ward. Some other nurses will be taking care of you there.'

'You're saying you won't be able to come to me?'

'I'll come to you,' she said fervently. 'Whatever happens.'

She thought of Tim throughout the concert, which seemed interminable. For God's sake, did they have to sing every verse of 'O Little Town of Bethlehem?' or 'O Come, all ye faithful'? But Martie was enjoying herself, bawling out all the words, 'Oh, come let us adore Him, oh come let us ADORE Him!' in Alex's ear, until she felt quite deafened and just longed to get away to Butterfly Two. The lined gloves she had bought for Tim's Christmas present were all wrapped and ready in the pocket of her apron, she was dying to give them to him and tell him they were for the walks he'd soon be taking round the grounds. Just as long as Martie didn't spot the package and ask who it was for . . .

As soon as the concert was over, she hurried away to Tim's wing and could have screamed when Rose stopped her to wish her a happy Christmas.

'Now, you're not in tomorrow, are you? Do have a lovely day, it'll be so nice for you to be with your father, won't it?'

'Yes, yes, it will. I'm sorry you've got to work, Staff.'

'Oh, I don't mind at all. My parents are visiting Tim in the afternoon and I'll try to spend a bit of time with them.' Rose smiled. 'It's our best Christmas present that Tim is doing so well.'

'I'm just going to pop in to see him before I go off,' Alex said with wonderful matter-of-factness. 'And all the other patients, too, of course.'

She skidded away, stifling her conscience that was stabbing a little over her deception of Rose. It wasn't her fault things had to be this way. As soon as Tim was better and out of the Jubilee, everything could be in the open. No more secrets! How she would be happy, then.

I'm not made for secrets, thought Alex, pushing through the swing doors to the ward. Then stopped. Tim had visitors. A young man with glasses, a young woman with short blond hair, both dressed casually and expensively, both talking in loud clear voices across Tim's bed. A large bowl of fruit had been placed on Tim's locker, where of course it would not be allowed to stay, and a large teddy bear with a bow had been set on his pillow.

'Why are those people still here?' Alex asked Martie, who was behind her. 'Surely, visiting time's over?'

'Have a heart, it's Christmas. Neal Drover's got a visitor, too. Another of his colleagues from the high school. Have you noticed how many of his colleagues are women? I'll bet they're missing him, eh?'

Alex wasn't interested in the sandy-haired girl talking earnestly to Neal Drover, whose eyes were wandering off round the ward. She tightened her lips.

'I'm going to tell them all to go, we'll be in trouble with Sister, if she comes in and sees them. Who are they, anyway? I mean, those two visiting Tim?'

'How should I know?' Martie's eyes were resting on Alex with lively interest. 'University friends, from the look of them.'

'You think that blonde would be at the university?'

'Why not? What's up with you, Alex? Is Tim no' allowed visitors, or what?'

Alex, feeling ridiculously annoyed, took a deep breath, straightened her shoulders and advanced towards Tim's bed.

'So sorry, I'll have to ask you to go now,' she said politely to the two young people at the bedside. 'Visiting time's over.'

'Oh, no!' cried the blonde. 'Oh, Tim, what a shame!'

'Should've thought we could have had a little longer, as it's Christmas,' the young man drawled. He favoured Alex with a smile. 'Why are you nurses such tyrants?'

'Visitors are tiring for patients,' she replied coolly. 'I'm sure you'll understand.'

'Mr Drover still has a visitor,' Tim observed.

As Alex's eyes swung towards Neal's bed, the sandy-haired girl leaped up, blushing.

'I'm just going,' she said breathlessly. 'I'm so sorry, Nurse. Neal, shall I see you tomorrow?'

'Thanks, Dad's coming in.' Neal's gaze had moved to Alex, and she was uneasily aware that he knew exactly why she was acting like Sister Clerk. She turned back to Tim's visitors, who were making their goodbyes. In fact, the blonde was leaning over Tim, trying to plant a kiss on his cheek, but with an apologetic grin he averted it.

'No kissing, Susannah, sorry. Strictly forbidden until I'm well.'

As the two young people sighed and waved and slowly left the ward, followed by the sandy-haired girl, Alex with a pang knew that Tim's words applied as much to herself as to his visitor. In all these weeks of touching hands, exchanging glances, they had never kissed, never caressed, never been close as lovers were close. As she had just been telling herself, everything would be fine, once Tim was well. But when would that be? At the thought of the long, long weeks stretching ahead, her heart grew heavy in her breast and even the thought of giving Tim his present seemed to have lost its savour.

'A bit hard on them, weren't you?' Tim asked her, as she straightened his bed. 'And now, I suppose you'll make me take my fruit off the locker, because nothing's allowed on the locker. Might as well be in gaol!'

'Better put the teddy away as well, before they fumigate it!' Neal called across with a laugh.

53

'I will take the teddy,' Alex said quickly. 'You can collect it when you leave, Mr Burnett.'

'It was just a fun present from my friend,' Tim told her. 'You can let the children's ward have it, if the poor kids are allowed toys, of course.'

'The rules are made for good reasons,' Alex murmured, glancing round to see if Martie was watching. Luckily, she was thanking Jack for the soap he had given her, her voice booming across the ward – 'lavender, ma favourite!' – and Alex quickly put Tim's present into his hands. 'Tim, this is for you.'

'Why, Alex!' Tim's expression softened as he unwrapped the paper, drawing out the leather gloves. 'Oh, for heaven's sake, you shouldn't have gone spending your money on me! These are perfect – how did you know my size?'

'I guessed.' Alex, still anxious, could see from the corner of her eye Neal Drover, watching. 'Tim, could you no' let anyone see them? Just for now? I'll take the paper, shall I?'

'Oh, hell, what a performance! OK, OK, put them in my locker.' Tim was smiling, looking very handsome, very well, as Alex slipped the gloves into his locker. 'What a darling you are, then, to buy those for me!'

'They're for when you're well enough to go out, you'll need them, then.'

'And when I'm in my chalet! But shall I not see you tomorrow?'

'No, I'm going to ma dad's, I told you.'

'You'll take my chocolates?'

'Yes, of course. I'm looking forward to them.'

'I think you'll like them.' His grey eyes seemed to be sending a message she couldn't read. Was it, I love you? She knew her own eyes were saying that to him.

'Merry Christmas, Tim. I'll see you soon.'

'Merry Christmas, Alex.'

She was moving down the ward, smiling at the other patients, her heart lighter now, as hope triumphed once again, when another voice called:

'Merry Christmas, Nurse Kelsie! Remember, too many chocolates aren't good for you!'

'Merry Christmas, Mr Drover,' Alex said frostily.

'Cheeky devil,' whispered Martie, grinning. 'I'm going to eat the lot when I come off duty tomorrow!'

Chapter Ten

Christmas dinner was over at One, Mason Street, the roast pork and trimmings cleared away, the remains of the plum pudding back in its basin, ready for re-steaming on Boxing Day. Edie was pouring out coffee – a rare treat.

'Would anyone like a chocolate?' asked Alex.

Edie looked at the box. 'Logie's Talisman Selection! Alex, how'd you ever get hold of these?'

'Present from a patient. We all got them.'

'My word, he must have some money, eh? And sweet points!'

Alex shrugged, but as she began to open the splendid box with its scarlet ribbon and picture of the Scott monument, Edie leaned forward, full of excitement.

'Wait a minute, pet. If I'm no' mistaken, that box has been opened already! What do you think, Art?'

Arthur put on his glasses and studied the box.

'Aye, you can see where it's been stuck down again.' He looked at Alex over the frames of his glasses. 'Hope the sweeties are all right.'

'Hope they've no' been tampered with!' Edie was in seventh heaven with excitement. 'Was there no' a story once, about somebody putting poison into chocolates and sending them off as a present?'

'Oh, for heaven's sake!' cried Alex, flushing, and tearing open the box. 'As though Tim – as though a patient would do a thing like that! Look – they're fine – they're lovely!'

Edie peered at the delicious-looking assortment and shook her head. 'There's something there that's no' a chocolate. Art, have a look, eh?'

'I'll have a look!' Alex scrabbled on the top layer, then raised her eyes to her stepmother's. 'I – I think you're right, Edie – there is something here.'

'Well, take it out, take it out! Let's see it!'

It was small and wrapped in tissue. As she unwrapped it, just for a fleeting moment, Alex thought it might have been – no, that was silly, it couldn't be. And it wasn't. But it was beautiful, anyway. She held it up, the fine gold chain with its tiny locket, and the three of them watched it dangle, glittering in the light, from Alex's fingers. They might have been hypnotised.

'A locket?' asked Edie wonderingly.

'Aye, a wee gold locket,' said Arthur.

'Gold? Real gold? Are you sure?'

'I know gold when I see it. No' that I see it very often, mind.' He smiled. 'But that's gold, all right. See if it has a picture inside, Alex.'

'A picture?' She was having difficulty in speaking.

'Folks used to put photos in lockets, or locks of hair.'

'No' these days, Art,' said Edie.

Alex opened the locket. 'There's no picture.' She laughed nervously. 'Or lock of hair.'

'Told you.' Edie was staring hard at Alex. 'I mean, who'd give you a lock of hair? Who'd give you a locket, anyway?'

Alex was silent, holding the locket as though it were a charm to keep her safe.

'Did you say it was a patient who gave chocolates to all the nurses? Did he give everybody a locket and all?'

'How would I know?'

'He didnae, did he? He gave that locket just to you.' Edie glanced at Arthur, who was sitting spinning his glasses by their frame, round and round. 'Art, what are you going to say?'

'Why should I say anything?'

'Well, it's no' ma place to tell your daughter what to do, but if she's taking up with one of the sick fellows at the Jubilee, surely you've got something to say about it?'

'Seems to me you're saying plenty, Edie.' Alex stood up. 'But I'm saying nothing.'

'It's only for your own good, pet, that I'm talking about it,' Edie said eagerly. 'I mean, we all know, what that consumption can do to a family!'

Arthur flung his glasses on to the table and leaped to his feet. 'Come on, Alex, time to do the pots. You stay there, Edie, have a rest.'

Her face flushing, her eyes glistening, Edie sat alone at the kitchen table. Then she pulled the box of chocolates towards her.

'Might as well have one,' she murmured. 'Let's see what there is.'

Alex and her father hung up their tea towels. Everything was tidy in the little kitchen, dishes away, the table scrubbed, Edie's trail of flour and crumbs swept from the floor. Alex turned to look at Arthur.

'Are you feeling any better, Dad?' she asked softly.

'No' so bad.'

'I thought you looked a wee bit happier.'

'Aye, a bit.' He put his hand on her shoulder. 'How about you? There is some fellow, isn't there? This patient at the Jubilee?'

'I don't really want to talk about him, Dad.'

His hazel eyes were filled with pain. 'If he's the one, Alex, you take him. Nae bother if he's sick, or no'. Life's short, you ken.'

She kissed his cheek. 'I know you're right, but it may no' be up to me.'

'He sent you that locket. Must mean something.'

'Yes.' Her eyes were alight. 'It must.'

Arthur turned aside. 'Better put the kettle on, eh? Edie'll be wanting to put out the Christmas cake.'

'Dad, we've just finished our dinner!'

'Och, it's Christmas, eh? Have to keep on eating.'

There was a feeling of exhaustion about Butterfly Two when Alex, on wings, returned that evening. All visitors had gone, all festive meals were over, patients were flat on their beds, exhilarated by the change in their routine, yet relieved in a way to be able to return to their rest. In Tim's part of the ward, only his eyes were alert on the swing door as Alex, in her uniform, came silently through. She wavered, smiling, then crossed to speak to Jill, who looked at her in some surprise.

'You're back early. You needn't have come in yet.'

'Just wanted to see how things were. Where's Martie?'

'Gone off with Staff. They've taken Neal Drover down for tests. He had another paroxysm today, might have to have his lung collapsed pretty soon.'

'Oh, no! At Christmas, too!'

'When did Christmas make any difference?' asked Jill.

Alex tiptoed away to Tim's bedside.

'Hello,' she whispered.

'Hello.'

'Had a good day?'

'Sort of.'

'Only sort of?'

He mouthed the words, 'I missed you.'

'I missed you. But I had a lovely present. Would you like to see it?'

She pulled out the locket that had been hidden by her collar. 'A kind friend gave me this. I'm sure I don't know where he got it from.'

'I expect he asked someone to buy it for him. That can be done.'

'It's very beautiful, anyway. Do you no' think so?'

'I do. The friend must think a lot of you.'

'Perhaps. I can't be sure.'

'You can be sure.'

Their eyes met, and it seemed to Alex that these long intense exchanges when their whole beings met through sight, were now almost like making love. They were all they had, these meetings of eyes, they had to make them mean as much as meetings of lips, of bodies. But, oh God, they longed for that meeting of lips, of bodies, even Alex who had so little experience. She knew it must be hard for Tim, who suddenly put a dry warm hand on hers and made her revert for a moment to being a nurse.

'Are you all right, Tim? You seem upset.'

'I'm OK. It's Neal – he had another bad do, they've taken him off for tests.'

59

'I know, I'm sorry.' Alex was feeling guilty that all thought of Neal had left her mind as soon as her eyes had met Tim's. 'I'll find out how he is.'

'I don't like him, but I don't want anything to happen to him,' Tim said morosely. 'Don't want anything to happen to anyone.'

'Well, try not to worry. Remember, you need a quiet life.'

His expression brightened. 'Not for much longer!'

'Had a good day?' asked Martie, putting her head round Alex's door late that night.

'No' bad. Edie'd gone to a lot of trouble.'

'Jamie there?'

'No, he'd been invited to go to a friend's in Glasgow.'

Martie came in and lay heavily on Alex's bed, putting her arms behind her head and groaning. 'I'm out for the count!' she announced. 'This is the first time I've been off ma feet all day. You heard about Neal Drover?'

'I looked in on him, but he was sleeping – how is he now?'

'Back on the ward, but they're scheduling him for the pneumothorax day after tomorrow. Hope it does some good.' Martie sat up. 'Listen, did you enjoy your chocs? You'll never believe this, but I'm too tired now to have any. I've just got to get to bed.'

'They were lovely,' Alex said evenly. 'The best I've ever had.'

'Aye, I'll say this for Tim Burnett, he's generous.' As Alex made no comment, Martie moved to the door. 'Well, I'll away. Thank the Lord I've got Boxing Day off!'

'You going to see your folks?' Alex asked.

'I might.'

'I think they'd like you to go round.'

Martie smiled darkly. 'I suppose I could see what they've got me for Christmas, eh? I'm giving them a bottle of port. 'night, Alex. Merry Christmas.'

When she was sure Martie had gone to her room, Alex undid the chain she had managed to keep hidden and sat with it in her hands, gently running her fingers over its links, over the surface of the little locket. Maybe she wouldn't ask Tim for a lock of his hair, but she wouldn't mind his photograph. She could put one of herself in the locket, too. For some time she stayed where she was, thinking of the future and what it might hold. In a week's time it would be 1950. A new decade. Maybe a new life? With Tim? 'You can be sure,' he had told her, meaning sure of him. And she was sure. He had given her a beautiful present made of gold. It had been foolish to think that the chocolate box might have contained a ring, as she had thought, just for a moment. He could scarcely have asked a friend to choose a ring for him! She laughed at herself and rose to put her locket safely away under her black uniform stockings in her drawer.

It was only when she was in bed that she remembered what 1950 would bring to her whatever else happened. Finals! Oh, God, she hadn't done any work for weeks! Tim meant everything, but so did being State Registered; she had worked for it for so long, she couldn't let it go. Tired as she was, she leaped up, found one of her textbooks and read until the small hours. Only then did her conscience release her and she was able to go back to bed. For some time, Tim Burnett's words travelled round and round in her mind. 'You can be sure . . . You can be sure . . . You can be sure . . . ' Finally, she slept.

Chapter Eleven

Changes came in the New Year, but then there were always changes at the Jubilee. Patients moving on, moving out, dying. Some changes were not connected with the patients, as for instance the departure of Chris MacInnes. He had asked Rose Burnett to marry him at the Western's Christmas dance; when she refused, he had taken a post at the Infirmary. Everyone felt like going into mourning. How could their favourite doctor desert them?

'How can you?' Rose herself asked him desolately. 'You know you're needed here.'

He gave her a long sad look. 'You think of me as just a doctor. I'm a man, I have feelings. Staying here, seeing you every day, knowing it's all hopeless – I just can't do it. Don't ask me.'

'I don't understand you, Chris. You've always put the patients first before.'

'Yes, and now I'm putting myself first. OK?'

She turned away, defeated, and he caught her arm.

'Rose, won't you reconsider? I mean, you're a wonderful nurse, you do a great job here, but the point is, you needn't give it up. Nurses can be married now. You don't have to end up like the old-fashioned dragons.'

'Dragons?'

'You know, the Florence Nightingales. Living for nursing, ruling everybody's lives like generals on campaigns. Things have changed, Rose, can't you see that?'

'Those dragons as you call them are just dedicated nurses,' she said coldly. 'I'd be proud to be one of them.'

'And what about your life apart from nursing? Don't you want love, Rose? Don't you want children?'

'Chris, women don't have to have husbands and children to be happy. They can be happy and fulfilled with a career, just like men.'

'It doesn't have to be either or,' he said desperately. 'You could keep your job and have me. But you don't want me, do you? The thing is, you're not in love. You've never been in love. That's why you don't understand why I have to leave the Jubilee.'

'People think far too much about love,' said Rose, and Chris, despairing, left her.

'Chris, I'm going to miss you,' Tim told him when he made his rounds to say goodbye at the end of January. 'You've made one hell of a difference to my life in here.'

'You'll soon be on your way, Tim. Own clothes next month, occupational therapy, gardening—'

'Don't forget the chalet. I can't wait to get out of this ward. They're all good chaps, but I just want to be on my own.'

'And away from Neal?' Chris asked in a low voice, but Tim shook his head. Since Neal's pneumothorax treatment, he and Tim were no longer in conflict. Maybe Tim had just been relieved that Neal hadn't died; maybe Neal was so happy to be recovering, he hadn't wanted to needle Tim any more. Whatever the reason, they rubbed along pretty well, somewhat amazed to find themselves already the oldest inhabitants of their wing. Jack MacNicol had been allowed to go home, George Napier, Barrie Hardie and Andrew Gibson, had all progressed to convalescent wards. Now three young strangers occupied their beds and it was Tim's task and Neal's to cheer them up, as they began the long dreariness of bed-rest. 'The first six months are the worst!' Tim almost called, remembering someone shouting that to him, but then remembered he hadn't found it so very funny at the time.

'You'll keep in touch?' he asked Chris, as they shook hands. 'You're not going very far, after all.'

'Oh, I'll keep in touch,' Chris answered. 'With you.'

'But not with Rose? Look, I'm really sorry that didn't work out, you know. I'd have liked you for my brother-in-law.'

'Goodbye, Tim, take care.'

When Alex first saw Tim in his own clothes again, she felt a strange dismay. She should have been pleased – she was pleased he was almost well – but back in his clothes he looked so ready to return to his own world, she wondered if he might forget hers. How handsome he was, though, in his tweed jacket and flannels, how much at ease! She was proud of him, and proud of his love.

'You look wonderful,' she told him. 'How do you feel?'

'As though I'm myself again.' Tim took a deep breath and squared his shoulders 'I think they've got it all wrong here, you know. The idea is for people to want to get well, but they feel so damned demoralised, slopping round in dressing-gowns, they lose heart.'

'It's only till they improve, Tim. And rest is so important, you see, and you can't rest fully dressed.'

Tim shrugged. 'Well, all that's over now, for me, at any rate.' His eyes held hers. 'And next week, I move into my chalet. You haven't forgotten what you said, about coming to me?'

'I don't think it'll be as easy as you think, Tim. People can see into those chalets.'

'There's nothing in front of them though, and a sort of door you can pull across. I've had a look at them on my walks. You will come, anyway?'

'I want to. More than anything in the world.'

'That's all right, then.'

The chalets in the grounds of the Jubilee were made of wood and could be rotated so that they followed the sun. Their fourth wall was open to the air but, as Tim had said, there was a door that could be pulled across when temperatures dropped very low. Each chalet had a bed, a couple of chairs, a locker and a small cupboard for clothes, but because patients sleeping out were on their way to recovery, rules were relaxed and they were allowed pictures, photographs and books. It was no surprise to Tim that his mother, as soon as she heard what he might have, lost no time in bringing things from home to brighten up his quarters.

'Photographs of all the family,' he told Neal with a grin, as he emptied his locker at Butterfly Two. 'A terrible watercolour painted by my aunt, two rugs, two hot-water bottles and a great plant I'm sure they won't let me have.'

'As long as she's happy,' said Neal. Though much improved, he was still some way from achieving 'own clothes' status and trying not to show his envy of Tim. 'Have to keep parents happy. So, when do you start gardening?'

'Any time now. Unfortunately.'

'You'll have to change out of that snazzy sports jacket.'

'Don't worry, I've got my casuals.' Tim grinned again and held out his hand. 'I'll see you about, Neal. Look after yourself, right?'

'I'm already booking my holiday chalet next to yours,' Neal answered cheerfully. 'Keep a place for me on the potato patch!'

As Tim stood for a moment, taking a last look round at Butterfly Two, Martie appeared and swung up his bag.

'Ready, Tim?'

'Oh, look, why do you butterfly girls insist on carrying a chap's luggage?'

'You're still a patient, even if you've got yourself a chalet, and patients get their luggage carried.' She gave her wide smile. 'But soon as you're better, you can carry my cases any time you like. 'bye, Neal. Get some shut-eye now, it'll do you good.'

But Neal kept his blue eyes on them until they had progressed down the ward and Tim had been escorted out of Butterfly Two for the last time.

65

Chapter Twelve

Finding the right time to sneak across to Tim's chalet was proving almost impossible for Alex. It had never before occurred to her, but every minute of her working day seemed to be accounted for, with fixed duties she could not escape, or places she had to be, patients she had to see. Snatching a few moments to talk to Tim when he was close at hand was one thing; absenting herself to go into the grounds perhaps for some time was quite another. She decided at last that the only way to see him would be directly she came off duty. Before supper, maybe, in the early evening, when it was dusk. But she would not dare to stay long.

There were beads of sweat on her brow when she ran through the trees towards the lights of the chalets; she was gasping when she reached them, not through exertion. Suddenly what she was doing seemed crazy. She longed to be with Tim, longed, after all these weeks of deprivation, for physical contact with him, but the risk was too great. The thought of being seen and reported, maybe sent to Matron, asked to leave the Jubilee, was terrifying. She couldn't face it. She would tell Tim so as soon as she saw him; this was the first and last time she would visit him. Surely he would understand?

When she looked in at him, he didn't at first see her. He was wearing a grey sweater and corduroy trousers and sitting by his bed, reading.

'Tim,' she called softly, and he leaped up instantly.

'Alex!' He threw away his book and held out his hands. 'Oh, Alex, you came! I never thought you would!'

She put her hands in his, he pulled her towards him into the chalet, their eyes met, then their mouths, and after that there was no question of saying anything to him. Only the sweet meaningless things lovers say in between kisses and caresses, in the pauses for the breath they had to take.

'I've waited so long for this,' Tim murmured, when they at last sank on to his bed. 'But oh God, it was worth waiting for! How have I done without you all these terrible weeks?' Her cap had long since fallen off, and he smoothed back her bright hair and looked into her face that was masked now in love and delight. 'Oh, Alex, darling, it's so good of you to come. I can't tell you what it means to me!'

'I wanted to come, Tim, I had to come.'

Already, she was forgetting that she had thought the risk too great.

'As long as you think it's all right, to be with me?'

She hesitated. 'Are you worried, Tim?'

'Only about you. I mean, I've read the rule book. No kissing, no physical contact. Even married couples are supposed to sleep with the bolster between them!' He gave a cracked laugh. 'Am I a selfish bastard, Alex?'

'Maybe I'm the selfish one,' she said slowly. 'But you don't need to worry about me. I've worked with TB for ages, I've had all the injections, I'm sure I'm immune.'

'I'd give anything to sleep with you, with or without a bolster.' Tim laughed again. 'But preferably without, of course. Would you do that, Alex? Would you ever sleep with me?'

'I might.' She ran her fingers gently down his face. 'But it's no possible.'

'Because we're not married, I suppose?' He gave an exasperated smile. 'I know what girls are like, don't want to "give themselves", as they call it.'

'Do you blame us?'

'You shouldn't talk about giving. Sex should be a partnership.'

'Men don't have the babies. But the rule book is right, Tim, sex isn't possible for us.'

67

'You are afraid, aren't you?' he asked quietly. 'I don't blame you.'

'Please try to understand, I'm thinking only of you. It's no' because of morality the doctors ban sex for folk with TB, it's because it's dangerous. You can have a flare-up, you can set yourself back months.' Alex stood up. 'In fact, I shouldn't even have let you kiss me just then. I must have been crazy. If your temperature's up tomorrow, I'll be to blame.'

'To hell with my temperature!' Tim cried. 'Oh, God, what's a few kisses? All right, I won't ask you to sleep with me, I've no right anyway, but you can't refuse to see me again, can you? You can't say you won't come back? Alex, please, don't say that!'

'It would be better to wait, Tim.'

'Wait? I've done nothing else but wait! I'm nearly well, everybody says so—'

'And I want to keep you like that.'

Alex was being so firm, so resolute, but Tim could see her lip trembling, could feel her body shaking as he put his arms around her.

'I love you, Alex,' he said gently. 'I need you. I need you to help me get well. What good will it do me to be in hell without you? If you could just see me sometimes, so that I could think of that, have that to look forward to, I know I'd be better. That's all I'm asking.'

'Oh, Tim, you wear me down!' Alex leaned against him, still shaking, and he stroked her hair, saying no more, knowing he'd won. A small victory, but something. She would come back.

They kissed quietly and tenderly, then Tim released her.

'You'd better go. But don't let anyone see you.'

'Of course I won't.'

'I mean, keep your face down, my darling, it's such a giveaway.'

She knew it was, knew she must be looking like a woman in love, a woman who was so caught up in passion, she could scarcely see the world for the face of her beloved. As she ran back to the nurses' home, she tried to think what she could do. She needn't have supper, she didn't feel in the least hungry, she could say she had a headache. But then if she went to Tim again, she couldn't pretend to have a headache every time. And she was going to Tim again, there was no question of it. All thoughts of Matron receded from her mind, for in her mind was only Tim. I'll wash my face and hope for the best, she thought. At least then I don't have to make excuses for not going in to supper.

In the event, no one took the slightest notice of her. Martie wasn't even there, it was her time off and she'd gone to the pictures with one of the boys who used to play Kick the Can with Jamie, only of course he wasn't a boy now, he worked in the Tax Office. As soon as she could, Alex got away to her room, where she sat in her chair without the light, until it came to her that someone might look in and she switched on her lamp, took up a study book and pretended to read until midnight. No one looked in, Martie must have got back too late, and finally Alex went to bed where she lay gazing into the darkness.

What have I done? she asked herself. The worst thing a nurse can do, jeopardise the health of her patient. Oh, but it would be too hard, not to see Tim again! Maybe he was right, maybe his frustration would make him even worse. And then it was true, he had waited so long. They had both waited so long. He was almost well. What were a few kisses? Remembering his kisses, Alex fell into bitter-sweet sleep.

Chapter Thirteen

Twice more, Alex went to see Tim without trouble. No one saw her, no one questioned her. She didn't stay long, just enough to enter into a world of bliss with Tim, for in spite of all her good intentions, she could not deny that to him, or to herself. They kissed frantically, they closed the two halves of the chalet door and lay on the bed, wrapped in each other's arms, they talked about how it would be when they could really make love. Then Alex would rise, straighten her clothes, put on her cloak, her crushed linen cap, and tear herself away.

After those two visits, she made a third, running through the grounds to the chalet as usual, but this time safely anonymous under an umbrella, for there was a steady, steely downpour. The doors of the other chalets were closed, the patients within shivering under rugs, but Tim's door was open. In the dusky interior of his chalet, his eyes seemed to glitter as she stood, shaking the drops from her umbrella. When she touched his cheek it was hot.

'Oh, Tim, your temperature's up!' Alex flung off her cloak and looked round for his chart. 'Let me see your chart – has your curve been rising?'

'No, it's fine, never mind it.' He tried to take her in his arms. 'Don't let's waste precious time looking at my damned chart!'

'I want to see it.' Kissing him briefly, Alex took his chart from the end of his bed and studied it. 'Oh, God, I knew it, you are up! Has the doctor seen you? What did he say?'

Tim shrugged. 'Said he'd be monitoring me. I told him it was all the gardening they make me do. He seemed to think that might be it.'

'You know it's no' the gardening, Tim. It's me, it's being with me. I'm the reason for your fever.'

'Alex, the fever's nothing, everybody has these ups and downs, you know that. Just come to me, let me hold you—'

She shook her head. 'I can't stay, Tim. This is my fault and I'm no' going to make things worse. What I want you to do is to lie down, lie down now, rest the way you used to do, keep very calm, that's the only way to correct this. Please, do as I say.'

'When you've gone, Alex. I promise, when you've gone, I'll put myself to bed and lie like a monk, but only when you've gone.'

He put out his arms to her but she backed away.

'Tim, I mean it, I'm going. I'll see you another time, I will, but now you must rest.'

At his look of utter desolation, her heart smote her and she went to him, holding his face in her hands, sinking her lips on his. 'Let me kiss you just this once,' she whispered against his cheek, and felt his arms tighten around her. 'But now I have to go.'

'You will come again? You promise? I have your word?'

'I promise I'll come again. But then we'll have to wait a while, till you're well. Don't look like that, it won't be long.'

'Won't it?'

'Come on, let's get you to bed. I'll help you to change into your pyjamas and fill a hot-water bottle.'

'Now you're my nurse again, instead of my lover,' he said quietly, as he allowed her to help him undress. Alex shook her head.

'I'm still your lover, Tim. I always will be.'

Returning to the nurses' home, she felt sick at heart. What were a few kisses? they had asked, she and Tim. Well, now they knew. When there had been no kisses, no passionate embraces, no hope of snatched meetings, Tim had progressed, had even had recovery in sight. Now, he had fever. He might even have to return to bed.

71

What was she to do? She couldn't give him up. In any case, she had faithfully promised to see him again. As she wearily climbed the stairs to her room, she knew, though, that the next time must be the last time. Until he was better.

Supper was an ordeal. She couldn't wait to be finished with it and on her own again, studying, maybe, if she could bring her mind to it. Sometimes she wondered if she had a mind at all, or was only a body, blown every way by feelings too powerful for her control. But she was going to have to stay away from Tim's chalet. One last time and then they must both agree to wait. They could do it, be strong; if necessary she would be strong enough for both of them. It was her job, after all, to be strong.

'Shall we have a cup of tea in your room?' Martie asked, leaning across the table, and it occurred to Alex that she had been unusually preoccupied throughout the meal.

'Oh, I don't know, Martie. I wanted to do some work.'

'Won't take long. I'd like to have a word.'

'All right, then, as long as it's just a word.'

They brewed their pot of tea in the corridor and carried it back to Alex's room. Martie took the one chair, Alex lay on the bed. She felt as lifeless as a doll propped against her pillow, watching Martie pour the tea.

'What did you want to talk to me about?' she asked, taking her cup.

'Got any sugar?'

'You should be giving that up.'

'Aye. Where is it?'

'In that little jar there.'

Martie stirred in the sugar, took a sip of tea.

'It's a bit awkward,' she said, at last. 'You'll think I'm interfering.'

Alex immediately sat up. 'Why?'

'Because I'm going to ask you about Tim Burnett.'

'You're right. I do think you're interfering.'

'Have you been seeing him? Since he moved into a chalet?'

Alex looked down into her cup. 'What if I have?'

'The devil,' said Martie 'I knew that was why he wanted a chalet, so he could get to see you. Soon as I saw you haring over there the other evening, I thought, oh no, she's going to Tim Burnett, and you see, I was right.'

'You saw me?' Alex asked dully.

'Sure, I did. Somebody'll always see you in the Jubilee, Alex, you know that. That's why I decided to speak to you. I can't bear to see you taking such risks.'

'All right, you've spoken to me. Will you go now, Martie? I want to get on with my work.'

'I've no' said what's in my mind yet. And you should listen to me, Alex. We've been friends since we were bairns.'

'And you've bossed me around since we were bairns. I get tired of listening to you. I don't care if you saw me going to Tim's. I've a right to go there. He loves me, and I love him, that's all there is to it.'

'Oh, Alex, Alex!' Martie gave a groan. 'I can't believe what you're saying, I can't believe you could be so taken in. I always knew you were sweet on Tim in the old days, but you're no' a kid any more. Have you no' learned anything?'

'Taken in? I haven't been taken in! I tell you, we're both in love, genuinely in love. Look, I'll show you—' Alex leaped up and took Tim's gold chain and locket from her drawer. 'See, this is what he gave me at Christmas. He gave you chocolates, he gave everybody chocolates, but he gave me this!'

Martie's eyes went over the chain. 'So? It's a very nice present. No' a ring, though, is it?'

'How could he give me a ring? He had to get a friend to buy the locket. He couldn't get him to buy a ring!'

'No, but he could ask you if you'd wear one, eh? He could ask you to marry him. Has he asked you?'

'It's none of your damn' business!'

'He hasn't, then. Oh, Alex, can you no' see what's happening? He's another of our frustrated patients, he's spotted that you're keen on him, and he wants what he can get. That's what love means to him.'

'You don't understand,' Alex replied. She was trembling, trying to hold on to her control. 'It's no' like that at all. He's no' asking me to sleep with him, he knows he's ill and he has to get well, all he wants is for me to be with him when I can. Is that a crime?'

Martie sighed. 'It is, in a way. You know the rules and what they're for. You've probably made him worse already, haven't you?'

A dark red colour spread slowly up to Alex's brow. She could not speak.

'These folk, you know what happens when they get the emotions going,' Martie went on, watching her. 'Their temperatures go sky high, their lesions flare up. Before you know it, they've ruined every single thing that's been done for them. That's why you can't play about with a patient, Alex. It's dynamite.'

'I'm no playing about,' Alex said huskily. 'I tell you I love Tim, he means everything to me.'

'What are you going to do, then? You can't keep on the way you are. Sister or somebody's sure to find out and that'll be the end of your career. I'm thinking maybe I should tell Rose, anyway.'

'Rose!' Alex turned so pale, Martie thought she might faint and put out her hand to her. Alex brushed it aside. 'Oh, Martie, you wouldn't tell Rose, would you? I don't think I could bear it, if Rose knew!'

'All right, I won't tell her. But what can I do to make you see sense?' Martie put her hand to her brow. 'I mean, it's crazy, isn't it? Getting involved with a patient, and Rose's brother, at that. What did you expect to happen? You know Tim'll never marry you. He's a lawyer's son, he's going to be a lawyer himself, he'll probably marry that blonde from the university—'

'Martie, that's enough!'

'All I want is for you to face facts.' Martie's face was solidly earnest. 'You've got Finals coming up, you've a good career ahead of you, doing what you want to do, helping people like your mum. Are you going to risk all that, for a temporary affair with Tim Burnett?'

Alex stood up. She moved across her tiny room to the window, where she pulled aside the curtain to look out at the wet grounds, the branches of the trees, writhing in the wind. From here she couldn't see the lights of the chalets, but she knew where they were, knew where Tim would be lying in his bed, thinking of her, as she was thinking of him.

'I'm no giving up my career,' she said over her shoulder. 'And I'm no' giving up Tim, either.' She turned back into the room to face Martie. 'But I won't go to see him again in the chalet, except for one last time. I promised I'd go once more and I will, but after that we'll wait for each other. Until he's well.'

'One last time?'

'I did promise.'

'So what happens after the one last time?'

'I told you, we'll wait.'

'You think he'll agree?'

'I think so.' Alex's voice trembled. 'He wants to get better.'

Martie moved slowly to Alex's door. She looked back, her gaze very direct. 'Did you mean what you said? About me bossing you?'

'Well, you did, Martie. You still do.'

'I never knew,' said Martie, and went out.

For some time, Alex tried to work. Didn't folk say work solved all ills? But the words of her textbooks blurred before her eyes and soon she gave up the struggle. Lay on her bed and thought of Tim. One last time to meet, and then the parting. But not for ever. That thought shone in her mind like the evening star.

Chapter Fourteen

The talk in the sluice next day was of the new young doctor who had replaced Chris MacInnes. Really nice guy, but married, eh, what a shame! And Sister Clerk was on the warpath because somebody unknown had left the steriliser on and it had been caught just in time. Two new women patients were being admitted that afternoon, and three men. Somebody had heard that more American patients treated with strepto-mycin had had bad relapses, so how was that for a wonder drug? But then there was another thing called PAS and if you put that with strepto, you got better results. Meantime, Tim Burnett was back on bed-rest and Staff B was looking furious. Keep out of her way today, was the advice, as the nurses scattered, but Alex didn't need it. The last person she wanted to see at that time was Rose. Seemed Rose, however, wanted to see her.

'Nurse Kelsie!'

Alex, taking temperatures some time later, froze. She turned her head very slowly.

'Yes, Staff?'

'Could I see you in the office, please, when you've finished the charts?'

'Yes, Staff.'

'In trouble?' Neal Drover asked pleasantly. He was in his dressing-gown and reading a newspaper, as he was now permitted to do. In the next bed, Tim's bed, a young man with a look of Kenny Skene lay waiting for Alex to remove the thermometer from his mouth. When she did, he smiled.

'Bet you never get in trouble, eh, Nurse Alex? Is it true they call you a butterfly girl?'

'Somebody did once,' she answered, filling in his chart. 'And no, I never get into trouble.'

'There's always a shoulder here if you do!' called Neal, and she gave a distracted smile.

The office was a small room where the senior nurses did their paperwork when they could snatch a moment. There was a desk and a couple of chairs, but Rose did not ask Alex to sit down and did not sit down herself. She stood with her back to the window, letting the light of the spring day fall full on Alex's small, anxious face. How hard Rose looked, Alex was thinking, how white. She was like a block of marble. Did she know? She couldn't know. Martie had said she wouldn't tell, and nobody else knew. Or, did they? Sweat was breaking on Alex's brow.

'Nurse Kelsie, have you seen my brother today?' Rose asked without preamble. Her St Clare's voice was cool and clear, sounding a knell in Alex's heart. Rose knew, all right. In spite of her promise, Martie must have told her.

'No, Staff,' Alex answered.

'Then I think you should know that he will be leaving the Jubilee very shortly.'

'Leaving!' For a moment the little room seemed to sway before Alex's eyes. 'Why?' she whispered. 'He's no' better yet, he can't leave the Jubilee!'

'I asked him to go. A bed has been found for him at Corrie House. That's a sanatorium up near Fort William. Dr Senior thinks very highly of it, Tim should do well.'

'But why did you ask him to go?'

'I think you know the answer to that well enough, Nurse Kelsie.'

'Tell me what you want to say to me,' Alex said desperately.

'A complaint was made earlier today, to me personally, not Sister Clerk, because my brother was involved. It was said that you'd been secretly visiting him in his chalet and that you must have been having some sort of affair. I didn't believe it. I went to see Tim. He admitted that there was a relationship and that you had been seeing him. So then I had to believe it.' Rose suddenly sat down at the desk, her composure cracking for the first time. 'For God's sake, Alex, what did you think you were playing at? You knew the risks, you knew the rules. Why did you let yourself get involved?'

'I fell in love,' Alex said simply. 'Do you mind if I sit down, Staff?'

Rose shook her head and Alex sank into a chair, facing her across the desk. Between them lay their old acquaintance, all those years of memories; but in their eyes was new conflict.

'You're a nurse,' Rose said, after a pause. 'That means you accept discipline to put your patient first. You didn't do that, Alex, and you see the result? Tim's worse.'

Alex's eyes filled with stinging tears and she pulled out a hand-kerchief and wiped them away.

'I know it's no use saying I'm sorry,' she said quietly. 'I've no excuse. But you don't know what it's like, to care so much—'

'No, perhaps I don't.' Rose straightened some papers on the desk. 'I do know about duty, though.'

Alex flinched, taking the blow. 'Are you going to report me?' she asked after a long silence.

'I don't know. You're a good nurse, you have the right instincts, the will to care. And you've got Finals coming up.' Two spots of colour splashed Rose's pale cheeks. 'Oh, I'm so angry with Tim! When I found out what had happened, I could have personally thrown him out of the Jubilee on the spot. He promised me he'd do everything he could to get well, but at the first temptation—'

'He loves me,' Alex said quickly. 'We love each other, that's how all this came about.'

Rose looked at her. 'So you believe. Well, the quicker he gets away to Fort William the better. He's been a bad influence on you.

Once he's gone, you can get down to work again, put him right out of your mind.'

'I can't do that, Staff,' Alex said bravely. 'I don't see why I should. I'll admit I was in the wrong, seeing him like I did, and maybe you won't believe me but I had already told him I wasn't going to risk his health any more. He knew we couldn't meet until he got better. That doesn't mean we have to forget each other.'

Rose gave a sigh. 'You're not making this easy, Alex.' She straightened her papers again. 'I really should send you to Sister Clerk, I'm not senior enough to deal with you myself. On the other hand, I feel you're too good at your job to be lost to nursing.'

'And I would be? If you reported me?'

'Well, you might be.' Rose got to her feet. 'Look, I'm going to take a chance. You said you knew you'd made mistakes, I believe you won't make any more.' She put her hand lightly on Alex's arm. 'I won't report you, Alex – I should say, Nurse Kelsie.'

'Thank you,' Alex said quietly. Her eyes on Rose's face were saying what she wanted to say. At the door, she looked back. 'Do you mind if I ask – who made the complaint?'

'It was Miss Alder.'

'Miss Alder?' Batty Miss Alder, their only elderly patient, who had had mild TB for years, who came in and out of the Jubilee, telling staff and patients what to do, taking the greatest pleasure in complaining about everything, never mind disgraceful doings in the next chalet. And I was blaming Martie, thought Alex, with a wild impulse to laugh. 'Oh, dear Lord,' she said aloud, 'I never even thought to check who was next door!'

'And those chalets may be detached, but the walls are very thin,' commented Rose. 'Better get back to Butterfly Two, Nurse.'

But Alex still hesitated. 'May I see him?' she asked. 'Tim, I mean, before he goes?'

'Of course,' Rose answered shortly. 'You can say goodbye.'

So it was back to eye contact and secret messages. 'Help me, help me,' Tim's grey eyes signalled, just as Alex's father had signalled before Christmas. There was nothing Alex could do to

79

help Tim, who was ready to get into the long black vehicle that looked like a hearse but was in fact an ambulance sent by the sanatorium. His mother, who had insisted on accompanying him on the long drive which they were to do in two stages, held his thin arm and looked daggers at Rose, whom she blamed for sending Tim so far from home, while Alex and Tim looked only at each other.

At least he was in his own clothes for the trip, thought Alex, and did not seem too unwell. Strained and angry, but trying to keep calm. Write to me, she willed silently. Keep in touch. Don't forget me!

As though I would! his eyes said, and she knew that there would be no forgetting.

'Ready?' asked the ambulance man.

'They're ready,' Rose answered. 'Mother, will you get in? Then they'll help Tim.'

'I don't need help,' said Tim.

'I'm closing the doors,' said one of the ambulance men as the other took the driving seat. 'Stand back, please.'

'Goodbye!' called Tim desperately. 'Goodbye!'

'Goodbye!' Alex shouted.

Rose, her face impassive, waved.

The long black vehicle moved off down the Jubilee's drive, rounded a bend and vanished from view. Rose turned to Alex.

'He'll be all right,' she murmured. 'And so will you.'

I would be, thought Alex, only I'm no' really here. This isn't me you're seeing, Rose. I'm away. To Fort William.

'Better get on,' she said, before Rose could say it, and walked slowly, stiffly, back to Butterfly Two.

'You poor soul,' said Martie later. 'Och, if you could see your face! Listen, what say we go out together on our next time off, eh? Have a bite to eat and go to the Empire or somewhere? Shall I see what's on?'

'Oh, I don't think so,' Alex replied. 'I don't feel like it.'

'You could bring Jamie, I could bring Denny, make a foursome maybe?'

'Martie, we've got exams coming. I'd rather study.'

'You're never going to spend all your spare time studying!' cried Martie.

'That's just what I'm going to do,' said Alex.

Chapter Fifteen

Summer days passed. The Labour government, elected in February with a much reduced majority, staggered on. There was trouble in the Far East. Princess Elizabeth was expecting her second child. None of these matters concerned Alex and Martie, who kept their heads down, working and studying, while Rose kept her professional distance. Only when Miss Alder, temporarily cured again, went home, did she relax a little.

'There's a piece of luck,' she told Alex, and Alex, with heartfelt relief, agreed.

From time to time, Jamie would come over in his little car and take Alex for a drive. Arthur and Edie would come too, marvelling at the luxury of being driven to see the Forth Bridge, or over to North Berwick to have a fish supper and sit by the sea. Once Alex asked Jamie to take Martie instead of Arthur and Edie, but the trip was not a success, with Martie showing off and trying to be funny and generally presenting herself in the worst possible light. Why does she do it, wondered Alex, but wasn't really involved enough to say anything. All she cared about was Tim's letter in her bag, because there always was a letter, a recent one to be added to her collection in the chocolate box that also held her locket and chain. Her great regret was that she still had no photograph of Tim for the locket, but that would come, and in the meantime she had his letters. Wonderful, passionate letters, sometimes written in reply to her own, sometimes just because he missed her and wanted to tell her so.

'I think about you all the time,' he wrote. 'You've no idea what it's like here, with this bunch of rich nitwits. Oh, they're all ill, but it hasn't improved their brain power and it drives me crazy to think I have to spend time with them, when I might have been with you. I miss you so much, my darling, my butterfly girl, miss those brown eyes looking straight to mine the way they used to do when you came in the ward, miss that dear, lovely body I never got to know, miss everything about you, as I hope to God you miss me!'

As though he needed to hope that, thought Alex, riding high on the crest of love, yet feeling Tim's absence every day like a sharp point in her heart.

The SRN exams came at last. Alex and Martie had passed the earlier papers, theoretical and practical, without trouble, but these were the Finals, the last hurdle. They were so nervous they wished they'd been smokers.

'Seems to help other folk eh?' groaned Martie. 'All I can do is chew my nails!'

'What'll we do if we don't get through?' asked Alex, who had even for the moment put Tim out of her mind.

'Take to drink!' Martie tried to laugh. 'Don't worry, we'll get through.'

They did. They couldn't believe it. State Registered Nurses? 'Us?' asked Martie.

'You,' said Rose, smiling, looking like their old friend again, when the results came out. 'Congratulations, both of you – but don't leave us straight away, will you? There'll be vacancies here for promotion, if you wait.'

'Oh, I'll wait,' said Alex, but Martie didn't actually say yes or no. Alex knew that she had been looking at job advertisements for some time.

'Well, well, SRN, eh?' Neal Drover murmured to Alex, when he heard the news. 'Does this mean you'll be flying away from us, butterfly girl?'

'No, I want to stay here.'

'Really? You're not, say, applying for a job up in the Fort William area?'

She made no reply to that, only urged him to step on the scales for his routine weighing. He was looking better these days, promoted to wearing 'own clothes' and gardening, and perhaps due to be going home quite soon.

'Haven't you even been up to see Tim?' he asked in a low voice, as Alex dealt competently with the weights on the machine. She shook her head, making a note of his weight, and he stepped away.

'I bet you are going to see him, though, aren't you? You'll want to tell him about your success.'

'I've already told him. We write, you know.'

'Ah, love letters.' Neal shook his handsome head. 'Wish there was someone to write love letters to me.'

'Half the hospital would do it tomorrow.' Alex gave a faint smile. 'The women, I mean.'

'I'd have to go away first. Think there's any chance of that?'

'Every chance. You're much, much better.'

'Till the next time,' he said quietly.

Love letters. When she was alone in her room that evening, Alex took Tim's letters from the chocolate box and read them through. Love letters. Oh yes, they were. Passionate, genuine, love letters. They made her heart bound, her body tremble, they brought Tim so close she felt him there, in her arms, and for a while gave herself up to the pleasure of imagining they were together again. Gradually, though, the bliss faded and she put the letters away, all except one. This was Tim's reply to the news of her exam success. It was the last letter she had received.

'How wonderful, I'm so proud of you,' he had written. 'What a clever girl you are, then. Not just a butterfly after all! You know, I can really see you in a staff nurse's belt now, not to mention sister's blue. Well done!'

Sister's blue. Was that what he wanted for her? Well, why not? She had her ambitions. But her ambitions included him. However her life developed in the future, he would be a part. But in this, his last letter, he had not mentioned himself. He had not said anything about being with her, or wanting her. He had not, in fact, said anything about love. So this letter could not be – she put it back in the chocolate box with a hand that slightly shook – this letter could not be described as a love letter. Friendly, cheerful, pleasant, but not a love letter.

Oh God, why should that be? What had happened?

For days now she had been asking herself that question, never trying to answer it, never wanting to answer it, in case the answer should be something she could not bear. How long could she go on, torturing herself with the unknown? She was a nurse, she had been trained to face things. Why could she not remember her training now? Suddenly she stood up, combed her hair, put on a dash of lipstick, and made her way to the Admin. building.

'Do you have any railway timetables?' she asked the secretary. 'I want to go to Fort William.'

'I hope you know what you're doing,' said Martie.

'Don't worry about that,' Alex replied. She was making a list of all that she needed to do. Take money out of post office. Book leave. Book train. Book guest-house. Buy new dress. 'I know exactly what I'm doing.'

'You've no' even told him you're going, have you? Is that no' risky?'

'Risky?'

'Well, supposing he can't see you for some reason. You'll have gone all that way for nothing.'

'He'll see me some time. I'll wait.'

Martie heaved a sigh. 'Makes no sense at all, rushing off like this, Alex. Could you no' phone him, at least?'

'Martie, will you for once let me do things my way?' Alex's face was flushed, her generous mouth set. 'Now, excuse me, I'm away to see Rose.'

'Best of luck,' said Martie.

At first it seemed that Rose was going to be reasonable about Alex's plan.

'I know you want to see Tim and I can't stop you doing that,' she said evenly. 'You're not Tim's nurse now, there's no reason why you shouldn't visit him.'

'Thank you, Staff. I just thought I should let you know what I was planning to do.'

'But I have to tell you I think it's unwise.'

Alex caught her breath, she tried to keep calm. 'Why d'you say that, Staff? You've just said there's no reason why I shouldn't go.'

Rose hesitated. 'Has he asked you to visit him?'

'No,' Alex answered reluctantly. 'But that doesn't mean he'd no' like to see me. He might just think I couldn't get away, or something.'

'You have told him you're coming?'

'I – I thought I'd make it a surprise.'

Rose's dark eyes flickered. 'I'd really advise you to give some notice. Every sanatorium has its own rules, procedures, as you well know.'

'I've checked on the visiting hours. You can go any afternoon.'

'Seems there's not much more for me to say, then. I hope all goes well for you.'

'You've still no' said why you think I shouldn't go, Staff.' A frightening thought suddenly came into Alex's mind. Her eyes sharpened. 'Tim is all right? You're no' keeping anything from me?'

'I haven't seen him myself, but my parents visit regularly. They say he's very well.'

Alex sighed gently. She put a piece of paper into Rose's hand.

'These are the dates I'd like to be away. Hope they're OK.'

Rose looked down. 'I'll check with Sister, but I don't think there'll be any problem. Look, just at the moment it seems I'm not Tim's favourite person, but if you see him, give him my love.'

'When I see him,' Alex said light-heartedly, 'I will.'

It was only when she was back on Butterfly Two that she remembered – Rose never had said why it would be unwise to visit Tim.

Chapter Sixteen

The train to Fort William passed through some of the grandest and most beautiful scenery in the British Isles. Lochs, forests, distant mountains, the fearful emptiness of Rannoch Moor – none of it meant anything to Alex. She had never been so far north before, in fact had scarcely been out of Edinburgh and normally would have been thrilled by the novelty of travelling and of what she was seeing. But all she could think of was meeting Tim. Her whole being was geared up to what lay ahead, for he was like the winning post in the races she'd run at high school; he was the prize she'd never won. She could almost feel her lungs getting sore, her heart straining, and though she'd scarcely moved from her seat, when she finally arrived at Fort William, she felt as though she had been competing in the mile.

Everything seemed hazy. The station, that was the site, someone said, of the original fort. The town, filled with climbers and walkers and dominated by Ben Nevis, Britain's highest mountain, even though you could only see a part of it. The guest-house, where a chatty little landlady tried to pump her about the object of her visit and other guests covertly stared. Somehow, she got through, ate a meal, went to bed, and next morning, wearing her new apricot dress and jacket and a small summer hat, walked the streets and looked in shops until it was time to go to the sanatorium. She knew where it was – she'd looked it up – and knew that she'd have to take a taxi because it was too far out of town to walk and buses were infrequent. No matter. She didn't mind paying for a taxi. She had the money she'd taken out of savings, and in her strange dreamlike state, didn't really care how much anything cost. After a cup of coffee at lunchtime and a bun she couldn't eat, she found a taxi and gave the address she could scarcely form into words.

'Corrie House Sanatorium, please. Do you know it?'

'Aye, I do,' the driver answered. He was a young man with bright brown eyes and a band of freckles over his nose. He reminded her of Jamie.

'Is it far?'

'No' far. A few miles down the Mallaig road. What some folk call the Road to the Isles.'

The Road to the Isles? Alex, fanning herself with her handkerchief, for the day was hot, repeated the words to herself. She wondered what it would be like to be able to follow that road with Tim, to cross to Skye, or Rhum or Eigg, or any of those places she'd only heard of and never seen. It would be wonderful, of course. A dream come true. But it would be enough for her just to be with Tim. Anywhere.

The sanatorium was not visible from the road. Its extensive grounds were bounded by high stone walls and a variety of trees; its drive was barred from entry by stone-pillared gates and a lodge.

'Have to say who you are,' the driver told Alex laconically, as he pulled up. 'You coming for a job, or what?'

'A job?' Alex was already panicking. Was she to be turned back now, having come so far? Oh, God, Martie was right. Rose was right. She should have given warning.

'Well, you could be a nurse,' said the driver, as an overweight, middle-aged man emerged from the lodge, opened the gates and raised ginger eyebrows of enquiry. 'Thought mebbe you'd come for interview.'

'I am a nurse, but I'm no' coming for a job.' Alex was winding down her window with slippery fingers. 'I'm visiting someone.'

'Name?' asked the lodge-keeper.

'Tim – I mean, Mr Burnett.'

'Your name,' he groaned.

'Oh—' Alex cleared her throat. 'Nurse Kelsie, from the Jubilee Hospital in Edinburgh.'

'Wait there.' The lodge-keeper rolled away but soon returned. 'You're no' on the list, Nurse Kelsie.'

'I'm – I'm afraid I forgot to phone ahead.'

'Should be on the list.'

'Och, come on!' cried the taxi-driver. 'You can see the lassie's no' going to burgle the place or something, eh? Let her in!'

'I'll have to ring the office.'

'Well, bloody well ring the office! My fare wants in!'

'Go on, then,' said Ginger Eyebrows, sighing. 'I'll phone up to say you're coming.'

'Thanks,' Alex murmured to the driver, as he took the taxi up the well-kept drive. 'I might no' have got in without you.'

'Anything to oblige a pretty lassie like you!' he sang. 'There now, there's the house. Big enough for you?'

She managed a smile as she got out of the taxi and took out her purse. Surely the house was big enough for anyone? A great, grey, turreted building that looked as though it had been intended for a castle, but at the last moment had been made into a private house. Rows of windows shining in the sun. Tubs of flowers on a long verandah. Climbing plants softening its stone. All very different from the Jubilee.

'It's lovely,' Alex said, trying to see the meter. 'How much do I owe you?'

'Wish I could let you off,' the driver answered with a grin, 'But I've a wife and four bairns to keep, eh? No, only joking, but that'll be four and six, please.'

She gave him an extra shilling and he touched his cap. 'Coming back? Give me a ring. There's my number.'

Going back? The idea hadn't even crossed her mind. Everything for her stopped here, where Tim was, where she would be with him. She couldn't think of anything else.

When the taxi had disappeared down the drive, she stood in the hot sun, her heart thumping. There seemed to be no one about, yet the rest period should be over. She supposed she should find the office the lodge-keeper had mentioned and ask for Tim, but still she stood where she was, her new cotton dress sticking to her in the heat, the brim of her hat biting into her brow. There had been admiration in that taxi-driver's eyes as they rested on her, and for a moment or two she had felt pleased and confident, but now the insecurity of her position rushed over her. She had no idea what she was going to find, how Tim would react, whether she would even be allowed to see him. Oh, God, she had been a fool, hadn't she?

She took off her hat and began to walk slowly over the gravel sweep in front of the house where several cars were parked. Suddenly, from the open front doors, a group of people appeared, all young, all dressed in casual clothes, all laughing together. They looked like any other young people, fit, bronzed, carefree, but Alex's professional eye was not deceived. These people were all patients, suffering in various degrees from TB. Only one looked really well. And that one was Tim.

Chapter Seventeen

They were in his room. Alex couldn't remember how she'd got there. Must have walked with him, after he'd done his double-take of staring, recognising, finally introducing her. His dear, kind nurse from Edinburgh, he'd said, and there'd been laughter from some of the young men and polite smiles from the young women. How wonderfully good of her to come all this way to see a patient! Oh, just passing, you know, Alex had felt like saying, and then mysteriously was with Tim in his big white room and he was ringing the bell and ordering tea from a uniformed maid. As though she wanted tea!

'I can't believe you're here,' he was murmuring, and laying her jacket and hat on his immaculate bed. 'It's just incredible! I mean – how? Why?'

Why? He was asking why? She stood in his room, staring at him. Oh, but he looked so well, didn't he? So tanned and strong, his grey eyes so bright. In his white shirt and light trousers, he looked like the boy she had first seen on the Archangel Steps, which made her want to cry. But she wouldn't cry. Not yet.

'I wanted to see you again,' she said stiffly. 'That's no' so strange, is it?'

'Of course not! And it's wonderful to see you, it really is.' As Alex watched, Tim moved nervously about his room. 'So, what do you think of it, then? I mean, the house? Bit of an improvement on the old Jubilee, eh?'

'It's very grand. Like a hotel.'

'Yes, could be. Used to belong to one of the local families, but it's been a sanatorium since the twenties, apart from the war years.'

'You seem to like it.'

'I do. Very much.'

Alex lowered her eyes. 'You didn't say that in your letters.'

'Didn't I? Well, I suppose, to begin with, I was just furious with Rose, sending me up here as though I was some sort of parcel.' He grinned. 'Then I realised I was a damn' sight better off.'

No tears, Alex told herself. Still no tears. She cleared her throat.

'Rose sent her love. She's upset that you haven't forgiven her.'

'Oh, I have. It's all worked out well. I'm better and I'm going home. I'll be back at the university in October.'

'Better?' she stammered. 'I'd no idea.'

'Yes, they've done a good job. Well, you did, too. But, look, why don't we sit down? The tea'll be here any moment.' As she made no move to take the chair he gave her, Tim smiled uncertainly. 'How pretty you're looking, Alex. No wonder those fellows didn't believe you were my nurse!'

'The taxi-driver thought I looked like a nurse.'

'Did he? Well, if you do, you're a beautiful one.' Tim was now looking anxiously towards the door, presumably waiting for the tea. She herself was standing very still, as though she would not move again.

'And of course you're fully qualified now, aren't you?' Tim ran on. 'I told you, I could see you as a staff nurse, didn't I? My word, it'll be up the ladder for you now, won't it? Staff nurse. Sister – before you know it, you'll be running your own hospital!'

'Tim!' Her voice was high, desperate, a cry over an abyss, and his face went white.

'Oh, Alex!' He took her in his arms, kissing her on the lips, and for a while they stood together like lovers. They were not lovers, though, and in that moment Alex felt they never would be. It was all over. Their little affair that had never been a real affair had died before it was born. A still-birth. One of the saddest things that could happen to a woman. She drew away, her shoulders shaking, and he made no move to hold her.

'I'm sorry,' he said in a low voice. 'I never wanted things to be like this.'

'What happened?' she asked tonelessly.

'I don't know. Just time, I suppose. Changed things.'

'Changed you.'

'Alex, I've said I'm sorry. I can't tell you how bad I feel. I never wanted to change, I swear I didn't! It was just – coming here – meeting new people—'

'We were on board ship,' she said, battling pain that she remembered from long ago. 'We were a shipboard romance, that's all.'

'Shipboard romance? What do you mean?'

'It doesn't matter. Tim, I think I'd better go.'

'No, wait – they're bringing tea.'

There was a knock at the door and the uniformed maid brought in a tray which she set down on a table at the wide window.

'Will that be all, sir?'

'Yes, thanks. We'll pour.'

When the girl had gone, Alex suddenly sank into the chair Tim had placed, as though her legs would no longer support her. He came to her at once.

'Alex, won't you have some tea? You look so pale. And what about something to eat? A cake? A scone?'

'Just the tea. Then I'll be going.' Alex sat up, pushing back her hair from her damp brow. 'Maybe you could ring for the taxi? I've got the number.'

'Are you staying in Fort William? I'll take you back. There's a car here I can use.'

'They let you drive?'

'I told you, I'm better. No fevers, no sputum, no shadow. They're giving me the OK to leave next week.'

'All right.' She lay back, sipping the tea. 'Drive me, then.' What did it matter if she accepted that last favour from him? She felt too exhausted to argue, felt drained, a ghost, sitting there in the lovely room, Tim watching over her, as though their roles were reversed, she the patient, he the nurse.

'I'll never forget you,' Tim said slowly. 'You know that, don't you?'

He made as though he would kiss her again but she moved her face and stood up.

'Could we go now? I'd like to get back.'

It was difficult for her to direct him to the guest-house, everything being so dreamlike still. There were times on the drive back to Fort William when she seemed to be floating in the heavens, looking down at her crazy self driving with Tim Burnett away from happiness.

'That road is the Road to the Isles,' she had said, pointing to the right, as they left the gates of the sanatorium, 'did you know that?'

'Yes, I believe it's very beautiful.'

'I thought I'd like to go to Skye one day.'

'You will, Alex. You'll have a wonderful life.' Tim glanced at her briefly. 'With somebody better than me.'

'You don't do any good, talking like that.'

'I mean it. You're a very special person. There'll always be people ready to love you.'

She smiled bitterly. 'No need for you to feel bad, then.'

For some time, he drove in silence. 'Tell me how to find this guest-house,' he said at last.

In the end, Tim found it himself, stopped the car and sat looking at the tall terraced house with its flowering tubs and little paved garden, its 'No Vacancies' sign hanging in its lace-curtained window.

'I can't just leave you,' he murmured. 'I mean, what will you do?'

'That's no' your worry.'

'Let me take you to dinner. I'll ring Corrie House and say I'm delayed. They won't mind, I'm practically off their hands. Alex, will you let me do that?'

'No.' She undid the car door, then stopped and put something into his hand. 'I almost forgot – you might as well have this.'

'What is it?' He opened his fingers. 'Oh, God – the locket.' He raised his eyes to hers. 'Won't you keep it?'

'I don't want it.' Alex stepped out of the car. 'Goodbye, Tim Good luck.'

He made no reply, remaining hunched over his open hand where the locket and chain caught the evening sun and glittered. From her bedroom window she saw him eventually drive away, and then at last she was free to cry. But the tears never came. Perhaps she would have felt better if they had. After all, she was mourning a death, the death of Tim's love, and everyone said you ought to cry so that you could grieve. But she was grieving, anyway.

Chapter Eighteen

'The rotter!' cried Martie. 'The cad! Och, did I no' tell you what he was like? I knew all along he'd let you down! Why you ever went up there to see him, I can't think!'

'Martie, please.' Alex, unpacking in her room, felt she was bending like a bough in the wind before her friend's onslaught. 'You were right, I was wrong, can we just leave it?'

'Yes, but why should he get away with it? He leads you up the garden path and then just dumps you, and you don't say a word? Have some spirit, Alex, do something!'

'Like what? He fell out of love with me, it happens all the time.' Had happened to her, all those years ago. It was hard to believe that she had once stopped loving Tim. 'Just tell me what I'm supposed to do?'

'You can stop taking it like some kind of martyr. You can stop making excuses for him!'

'I am not taking it like a martyr, I am not making excuses!' Alex, jumping to her feet, snatched up her hairbrush and hurled it across the room. 'You don't know what I'm feeling, Martie! You don't know what's inside my head and you never have! I wish you'd just get out of my room and leave me alone!'

There was a long silence. Both girls stared at Alex's hairbrush lying on the floor, its handle cracked apart.

'Lucky it was no' a mirror,' Martie said at last. 'That'd be seven years bad luck.' Alex gave a burst of laughter.

'Oh, Martie!'

'I'm sorry, Alex. There go my big feet again, eh?'

'It's all right. I shouldn't have got mad like that.'

'You'd every right to get mad, it's just what you should have done. I only wish you'd chucked that brush at Tim Burnett. Or something bigger. Say a brick. A boulder.'

'Wouldn't have done any good, would it?'

'Might have made you feel better.'

'I don't know when I'm going to feel better.'

'Well, listen, I've got something that'll help. Saw it yesterday in the nursing mag. No, don't sigh, Alex, it's just the thing.' Martie had produced a cutting and was waving it like a flag. 'A new job! Well, jobs. Jobs for both of us!'

Alex stooped to pick up her hairbrush and after studying it for a moment, threw it in the bin.

'New jobs? Where?'

'The Fidra Bay! It's a nursing home out North Berwick way. They want two SRNs to start as soon as possible. No' staff nurse posts, but with good prospects. I've already written out my application.'

'I don't know that I'm interested, Martie.' Alex took down her uniform dress from its hanger. 'I haven't the energy to apply for anything new.'

'Come on, you want to get away from here, don't you? What's it going to be like, remembering that bastard every time you go into Butterfly Two? I bet you see him now, eh? See him in Fred Cluny's bed, where he used to be? Think of him in that damned chalet where you used to run to see him every day?'

'Martie, will you just shut up?' cried Alex.

'Well, you see what I mean. You get your pen out and start writing. This is too good to be missed. I'll leave you the advert, shall I?'

'I'll think about it.' Alex was struggling into her uniform, doing up buttons, looking for her belt. 'But Martie, wait a minute, I want to ask you something.'

'What?'

'Do you think I need tell Rose – what's happened?'

Martie hesitated. 'Oh no, I don't think so.'

Alex gave a grim little smile. 'You mean, when she sees my face, it won't be necessary?'

'I didn't say that.'

'It's funny, I can't put my finger on it, but I look as though I've been ill, don't I?'

'Alex, you have been ill. No doubt about it.'

'And I'm no' better yet,' said Alex.

'I'm so sorry,' Rose said. 'I wouldn't have had you hurt like this for the world.'

She and Alex were in the office where they were taking a few moments of privacy, Rose looking sympathetic, Alex drooping before that strange, soft gaze.

'You know?' murmured. 'I thought you would.'

'He rang me last evening.'

'You didn't know before I went, then? When you said it would no' be wise to see him?'

'Of course I didn't! I was just going on what my mother had told me. That Tim was so well and happy up there at Corrie House, making so many friends.'

'No' pining?' Alex smiled coldly. 'Well, I don't regret seeing him. At least, I found the truth out for myself.'

'Yes, and you're being very brave about it. I admire you, Alex, I think you're a fine nurse, and if you put this behind you and concentrate on your work, you'll do very well.'

'Maybe I should tell you, Staff – Martie and I are thinking of moving on.'

Rose's dark eyes lost their softness. 'Moving on? Leaving the Jubilee? Why, where would you go?'

'There's a nursing home called the Fidra Bay wants SRNs. We're both going to apply.'

'The Fidra Bay? Near North Berwick? I've heard of it. Caters only for the rich, not your sort of place at all, you'd be miserable there. Alex, please listen to me, you can't do this, you really can't!'

'We're both applying, Staff.'

'You're different from Martie, you're more dedicated, you know what nursing really means.' Rose swept her hand across her fine brow. 'Oh, Alex, please reconsider. Don't give up what matters just because Tim's let you down!'

'I want to get away,' Alex said firmly. 'Martie's right. It's what I need. I'm writing out my application tonight. I'm sorry, Staff.'

Rose bit her lip. 'Look, I haven't told anyone this yet, but it'll have to come out soon. I'm leaving the Jubilee myself. I'm joining the QAs.'

Alex, shocked out of her own concerns, stared wide-eyed. 'You mean, the military nursing service?'

'Yes, the Queen Alexandra's. I've been accepted for a commission and start training in October.'

'But, why? Why do you want to do that? You're perfect here, you'll end up sister and it'll be just what you want!'

'No. Look, we're old friends, that's why I'm talking to you like a friend now. Things haven't been so good for me lately. I haven't exactly been under a cloud, but let's say a certain person has had her suspicions about Tim.'

'Sister Clerk?' Alex whispered. 'Oh, no!'

'She's never liked me and the way Tim was bundled away, she's sure there's been trouble that I've concealed from her. No, it's all right, Alex, she doesn't know about you. I made sure of that.'

'Oh, why didn't you tell me?' Alex moaned. 'Oh, God, I've landed you in it, I know I have – oh, I feel so bad!'

'It's all right, I tell you, she really knows nothing, but I've just decided to get away, do something else. What I want to say to you is that it's worthwhile work, it's proper nursing. Maybe you'd consider joining the service yourself?'

Alex was silent. 'I'd like to say yes, but – I don't know – I feel that life's no' for me. At the moment, anyway. You say I'm dedicated, but I just feel I'd like to stay in Scotland, do something nice and ordinary. Does that sound weak?'

'No.' Rose sighed. 'You've taken a battering, you deserve a break. But later, you might perhaps think about it?'

'Oh, yes, later!' Alex shook her head. 'But, Rose, I'm so sorry, I really am. I've caused you so much trouble, and you've been so good, never saying a word—'

'Don't think about it. I'm happy now to be going. I see it as a challenge, something I really want.' Rose shrugged. 'It's worked out for the best. Things usually do.'

Standing at the door to Butterfly Two and looking down the ward to Tim's old bed, Alex's mind was in conflict. Would she have done things differently, if she had been given the chance? Would she still have met Tim at the chalet as she had, when it had been like a stone thrown in a pool, sending ripple after ripple of trouble, not only for her? She didn't know. Love was selfish, love would drive you on, no matter what, until things went smash and you were left with broken pieces of your life to put together again. All she did know was that Martie was right, she had to get away from the Jubilee, and the sooner the better.

'Ah, you're back,' a voice murmured. 'How did it go?'

She turned her head to find Neal Drover at her side. He was in his dressing-gown, ready for bed, still the image of the famous star no one could quite place.

'How did it go? It didn't.'

'I'm sorry.'

'Oh, you're another one who was right. Everybody was right, except me.'

'Tim's a bloody fool, Alex. If he were here, I'd tell him so. If I didn't knock him down first.'

'I must get on, Neal.' Alex, conscious of the other patients waiting, was agitated. 'Excuse me.'

Later, she found a moment to ask when he was due home. Had they given him a date while she'd been away?

'Next week, if you can believe it.' He grinned from his pillows. 'Of course, I'll still need my regular fix of gas.' He tapped his chest. 'Keep the old windbag going.'

'It's wonderful, to see you so well.'

'How about you? What are you going to do?'

'I might be leaving, too. Martie and I are going to apply to a nursing home on the coast.'

'You'll be missed.'

'There'll be other nurses.' She smiled. 'Other butterfly girls.'

'They won't be the same.'

'I don't feel the same myself. Feel somebody's clipped my wings.'

'Don't say that. Don't let a fellow like Tim Burnett spoil things for you. I told you, he's a fool!'

She put her finger to her lips and shook her head at him. 'No getting excited. I'll see you in the morning.'

'Yes.' He smiled wryly. 'Mustn't get a fever at this late stage. Goodnight, Alex.'

'Goodnight, Neal.'

He left the Jubilee a week later, accompanied by his father, tall and handsome, a grey-haired version of himself. Everyone gave him a grand send-off, he being one of their successes, and Alex, like them, felt a special warmth as she waved goodbye. To see someone recover, that was the bonus they worked for, and though a success could not wipe out the failures, it helped to know they could succeed sometimes.

As the euphoria of Neal's departure faded, Alex tried very hard to put her mind on her future. Both she and Martie had been given interviews for the following day at the Fidra Bay and though it was the last thing she cared about just then, she had to work out what she should wear. It was important for her to look her best, she really wanted the job. Really couldn't wait now to get away from the Jubilee.

The Fidra Bay, she had discovered, was not on Fidra, a tiny island in the Forth, but facing it on a little headland some miles from North Berwick. It had been a hotel, Martie said, but that was back in the twenties when it had been run by the parents of the present owner, Mrs Raynor, a qualified nurse, and had the reputation of being a very exclusive and luxurious place to go, if you weren't too ill.

'We'll probably spend all our time arranging flowers and putting on bedjackets,' Martie said cheerfully, then laughed at the expression on Alex's face. 'Oh, come on, that was a joke! They asked for nurses, didn't they? And they're paying over the top, so of course we'll be doing proper nursing. Don't take any notice of Rose. She just wants you to join the army.'

Everyone knew now about Rose's decision to join the QAs and the shock had been profound. The Jubilee without Rose Burnett's calm presence was scarcely to be imagined, even though Sister Clerk was frequently heard to say with satisfaction that everybody could be done without.

'Isn't it strange?' Martie commented to Alex. 'Three of us leaving together? Three butterfly girls flying?'

'IF we leave together,' Alex retorted. 'We haven't got the jobs yet.'

'We'll get them, don't worry. Be positive, Alex!'

'You can be positive.' Alex tossed Martie a timetable. 'Find us the right bus.'

'No' want to take a taxi? Turn up in style?'

'A taxi? It's miles away, and the bus goes past the gates.' Alex tried to laugh. 'Remember, you haven't met your rich man yet, Martie!'

'Well, I'm still hoping.' Martie thumbed through the bus timetable. 'And you will wear some lipstick tomorrow, eh, Alex? You still look as though you've been ill.'

'Oh, well, I'll do my best to look convalescent!' snapped Alex, who did in fact make such an effort the following day, Martie, at the bus stop, said she looked terrific.

'And so do I!' she added. 'I tell you, we're going to be fine, Alex, you'll see. Did I no' tell you, the world was our oyster?'

'Just get the tickets,' Alex murmured, as the bus arrived and they took their seats.

'Where to?' asked the conductor, and Martie, sorting her change, said grandly,

'Two to the Fidra Bay, please.'

Part Two

Part Two

Chapter Nineteen

It was February, but you'd never know it. Not indoors at the Fidra Bay.

Martie, on her way to give old Mr Wray his injection, paused at an upstairs corridor window. Out of doors, yes, there was every sign of winter, and a hard one, too. See those heavy grey skies over the Forth? Could be more snow, but it would only come hissing down into the water, wouldn't lie on the shore. Wouldn't make you miserable, the way it did in the city, when you had to go ploughing through it, waiting for it to thaw, and when it did thaw, nursing chilblains and calling out the plumber for another burst pipe. Och, folk in this place were so cocooned from all that, eh? Me, too! thought Martie, revelling in the novelty.

There'd been a 'flu epidemic in January and patients were still booking themselves in, wanting to be cosseted, because that was what the Fidra was for, cosseting, and with its warmth and light and flowers, you could fool yourself that there it was already summer. No wonder the fees were off the scale! Who wouldn't pay out to be here, if they could afford it? Even the food was wonderful. How did Mrs Raynor manage it? Had to be black market – all those eggs, all that butter and good Scotch beef! So it was black market, so what? Rationing ought to have finished long ago, no one could blame a woman with her responsibilities for doing the best she could. Even if I do have to let my belt out another hole, Martie laughed to herself, knowing she should move on, but knowing, too, that old Mr Wray would be asleep when she got to him and she'd have to spend ten minutes bringing him back to the world again. In the meantime, her eye was caught by the sight of Alex down on the shore, wrapped in her cloak, but otherwise not in her uniform. It was her day off, she'd been in to North Berwick, hadn't come into the house yet. That was Alex, still wanting to be on her own whenever she could. Surely she wasn't still mooning over Tim Burnett six months on? Honestly!

Irritated by what she considered Alex's perversity, Martie marched away towards her patient's room. She'd been so sure that once they were appointed to the Fidra Bay, the new surroundings and the new life would have made Alex as happy as she was herself. And she, Martie, was happy, oh, yes! As happy as a lark in the sky! Every morning when she woke up in her delightful little room, she thanked God, or Fate, or whatever, for giving her this job. Sent up grateful acknowledgements for central heating and baths every day, for food that wasn't rissoles or rice pudding made of grit, for the whole way of life she was now enjoying that she had never known before.

'Aye, you've fallen on your feet,' her mother had said, when she'd gone back at Christmas and told her parents about the Fidra Bay. More fool she! It had only horrified them, to think of all that money being wasted on heating and lighting, on flowers in winter, flowers at any time being a luxury everyone could do without! Their faces had gone quite pale when Martie had described the fitted carpets and eiderdowns, the private bathrooms, the heated towel-rails, the telephones! They couldn't take it in, didn't want to take it in. Folk weren't meant to live like that, it could only lead to trouble – softening of the brain and body, maybe, or a complete breakdown of stability.

'I'd say it was no' the place for you,' her father said slowly, 'except your mum's right, you've fallen on your feet, because it's what you like, eh? You were always one for wanting what we couldnae afford.'

'That's no' true,' Martie said earnestly. 'It was you no' wanting a bit o' comfort when you could afford it that upset me. Look at the Kelsies! When Alex's ma was alive, they used to enjoy themselves, eh? And they'd no more than we had!'

'And spent every penny!' cried Tilda. 'That's no way to live, Martie! You have to save, you're meant to save, so you've money put by!'

'Put by? What for?' Martie leaped to her feet, losing her temper as she had promised herself she wouldn't do. 'For a rainy day? It's always a rainy day here anyway. Whyn't you open your cash box and buy yourself a couple of bloody umbrellas? I'm going to bed.'

There she'd cried angry tears until she fell asleep, clutching the stone hot-water bottle that was all she had to keep away the Arctic night. Even that lost its comfort as the hours went by and it began to follow her round the bed, pressing its iciness against her legs until she threw it on the floor with a satisfying thump.

'I'm sorry, Mum,' she said next morning over the breakfast porridge. 'I lost my temper, never meant to upset you.'

'That's all right,' her mother answered through shut teeth. 'But just mark my words, Martie, if you go on the way you are, you'll come to want.'

'Aye,' her father agreed, laying aside last night's evening paper that Arthur Kelsie kindly pushed through the letterbox for him every morning. 'I'm afraid that's true. You listen to your mum, Martie. Take heed, now, before it's too late.'

'OK, OK,' Martie sighed, looking at the clock and thinking, not long now. Jamie Kelsie would be collecting her within the hour, to drive Alex and herself back to the Fidra Bay. What a treat! She could hardly wait.

'I'd better get ma case,' she told her parents, who were preparing to go to work, Sid to the grocery, Tilda to a little knitting shop, both pleased to be getting back, they weren't keen on holidays. 'Jamie'll be coming with the car.'

'Car? Now whatever is he wanting a car for?' cried her mother. 'Talk about money down the drain! Why can he no' go on the tram or the train like everybody else?'

'Have we no' been saying what the Kelsies are like?' asked her father. He bent his thin face towards Martie's and suddenly kissed her cheek. 'Now, you take care, Martie, eh? And come back to see us soon.'

'Aye, come soon.' Tilda Cass was standing with her hat in her hand, her face suddenly and unbelievably woebegone. 'You're all we've got, you ken.'

'Mum, I'm only a bus ride away!' cried Martie, feeling a rush of contrition, feeling she should for once throw her arms round her parents and pretend they were all Kelsies. But of course they weren't and she didn't. She did kiss her mother and father, though, and when she ran upstairs for her case, felt bad enough to shed a few more tears. It was still a relief to pile into Jamie's car with Alex and go spinning away to East Lothian. To relax. Breathe again. Be free.

'Found your rich man yet?' Jamie asked, as under lowering skies they drove past the race course at Musselburgh and on towards the coast road that would bring them eventually to the Fidra Bay. Alex, in the back seat, laughed, but Martie next to Jamie was embarrassed.

'Och, Jamie, that was just my joke in the old days.'

'Was it? Should've thought where you work now would be just the place for you to find what you want.'

'There are rich patients but they're all at least sixty-five,' Alex put in. 'You don't find rich YOUNG men in nursing homes.'

'Can't have everything,' Jamie said blithely, and Martie angrily set her jaw and would not respond.

When they came to Aberlady, the picturesque village that had once been a thriving port and was now popular for golfers and holiday-makers, she twisted in her seat to look at Alex and found her with her eyes shut. So she would not even look at where Tim Burnett had spent his holidays?

'Oh, Alex, come on, open your eyes!' Martie cried roughly. 'Can you no' forget that fella?'

'What fella?' asked Jamie, then groaned. 'Tim Burnett, you mean? If I meet him, I'll give him what for, I can tell you! I'll spoil his arrogant face for him, TB or no TB!'

'Will you just stop talking like that?' cried Alex. 'I don't care about him any more, I don't even think about him. If I want to close my eyes, I suppose I can if I like?'

'It's all right, we're through,' said Martie. 'Let's enjoy the scenery.'

They were running along the coast road, where they could see the grey Forth churning white and the narrow stretches of shore filled with weed and tossed pebbles. Here were lines of trees bent as low as African scrub in defence against the battering wind, one or two fine houses, and everywhere golf courses, for this was golfing country and would continue so as far as North Berwick. Past Gullane Point and close to the village of Dirleton, were splendid yellow sands, though these they couldn't see from the car. Perhaps when the summer came, they would visit them, though? Perhaps, wondered Martie, with Jamie? She gave his freckled face a covert glance, but his eyes were fixed on the road.

'Are you coming in?' she asked, when they reached the gates to the Fidra Bay. 'For tea, or something'

He had slowed for the gates, looked at her in surprise.

'No, I'm going on to North Berwick. Did Alex no' tell you?'

'I didn't tell her,' called Alex.

'Going to see a friend,' said Jamie. 'Somebody from the office. Her folks live in North Berwick.'

'I see,' said Martie, making sure to smile. 'A girlfriend.'

'A friend who's a girl, put it that way.' Jamie grinned. 'But I'll take you two up the drive, I'd like to see this wonderful place for maself.'

The house stood on a small point of land overlooking the great sweep of the Firth of Forth. In the distance were the little islands of Fidra, Craigleith and The Lamb, though on that late December day they were scarcely visible through the mist, and no one was venturing down the steps that led to a sandy strip of shore.

'Very nice,' Jamie commented, turning his eyes from the view to the nursing home. 'I can see why you're impressed.'

'Martie's impressed,' said Alex, swinging her case from the car.

They all three stood looking at the elegant house, with its circle of drive before a tall portico and banks of trees giving shelter from the winds. There had been additions made at the conversion from the hotel – a long glassed-in sun lounge, a block at the rear for the nursing staff, a small operating theatre – but all had been discreetly done and nothing marred the image of a fine country house where people just happened to stay to get well. That had been Mrs Raynor's aim, and what Mrs Raynor aimed for she usually hit, bang on target. Martie was a great admirer of Valerie Raynor's. Dr Raynor, now, he was shadowy. Nice enough. He just didn't come into things.

'Take no notice of Alex,' Martie said now to Jamie. 'She loves it here, just doesn't want to admit it.'

'I think you're both happy enough, anyway.' Jamie glanced at his watch. 'Got to go. Have a good New Year, eh? Keep in touch.' He pecked his sister's cheek, shook Martie's hand, though she'd thought he might have kissed her, too, and got back into his car. As they shouted their thanks, he expertly turned the Morris, waved, and disappeared down the drive, his red lights winking in the gloom. They were silent for a moment, watching him go, then picked up their cases and walked quietly round to the nurses' block.

'Alex, you are happy here, eh?' Martie asked at last. 'I mean, you must be!'

Alex shrugged. 'It's OK. Just a bit too comfortable.'

'Too comfortable! You're joking!'

'I can't explain. Maybe I just can't find anything right at the moment.'

As Alex took out her key, smiling apologetically, Martie thought how well she was looking, her cheeks pink with the cold, her rich brown hair falling over her brow. Well and pretty and as though she were not pining at all. Only her eyes retained the lost look Tim Burnett had bequeathed them, but that look was enough to make Martie sigh. Eyes were what counted, everyone knew that. It was like when you wanted to assess a patient, you always looked into their eyes. Alex wasn't better yet.

'Come on, let's get in and put the kettle on,' she said briskly. 'Back to work tomorrow, eh? At least it's no' today!' It was only when they'd made the tea in the nurses' kitchen and had finished greeting colleagues and exchanging descriptions of their Christmas holidays, that she whispered to Alex—

'Why didn't you tell me about Jamie's new girlfriend, then?'

'I don't want to think about her,' Alex replied. 'Jamie should have been for you, but now I'm sure they're going to get engaged. I mean, why else would he be going to meet her folks?'

'Why indeed?' Martie gave her loud laugh. 'Och, nae bother! Plenty good fish in the sea, eh? And rich ones, too!'

'Even if they are sixty-five,' said Alex, laughing, too.

Wish Alex'd laugh more often, thought Martie. Wished she really felt like laughing herself. Och, what was it to her if Jamie Kelsie wanted to get engaged? There'd never been anything between herself and him. In fact, he'd always given her the impression he rather looked down on her. Cheek, if that were true! By the end of the evening, in the warmth and comfort of her surroundings, her spirits came back with a bounce. This was where she wanted to be, this was where she was happy, and if Alex didn't feel the same, there was nothing she, Martie, could do about it.

Seven weeks later, as she knocked on Mr Wray's door and let herself in, she felt the same.

'Hello, there, Mr Wray!' she cried. 'And how are we this afternoon? Going to open your eyes and sit up for me, then? That's the ticket!'

Chapter Twenty

Alex, on the shore, was chilled to the bone. She was wearing her sheepskin mitts and woollen hat, her thickest sweater, slacks and hospital cape, but still the cold got to her and she knew she must go in. Once inside the house, however, she'd have to change because otherwise she'd be too hot and though Martie soaked up warmth like a cat in the sun, Alex felt tired and irritable in the over-heated atmosphere. And – all right – ungrateful. Most people would have given their eye-teeth to be so warm in post-war Scotland. Was she just an old misery-guts? No, there was more to her feelings about the Fidra Bay than that.

'Happy?' her dad had asked her at Christmas.

'I should think she is!' cried Edie. 'My word, talk about living in the lap o' luxury! If ever I come up on the pools and fall ill, that'll be the place for me, Art, don't forget!'

They'd laughed, of course, but Arthur Kelsie had not missed Alex's evasion of his question. Later, when they were alone, he asked her again.

'You're OK at that fancy place, Alex? Glad you made the move?'

'Oh, yes, I think so,' she answered, not meeting his eyes.

'No' still pining after that fella?'

'No, that's all over.'

'And no' missing the Jubilee?'

'I miss Rose, that's all.' Alex began deftly to switch attention from herself. 'She's doing well in her training. Writes to me, tells me all about it. Next thing, she'll probably be off abroad. Hong Kong, or the Middle East, or somewhere.'

'Thank God that's no' you,' her father said with feeling. 'East Lothian is far enough, eh?'

'How about you, Dad? Things OK for you?'

'Aye. Ticking over, you ken. Doing a lot o' reading these days. Plays and that. Get them from the library.'

'That's wonderful. You'll be back to your acting next!'

He shook his surprisingly silver head. 'No, I just like to read. Lose maself, you ken.'

She understood. It seemed to her that that was what a lot of people liked to do, lose themselves in someone else's world. Wasn't it what she'd been trying to do in her new job? That world, though, had failed to provide the cover. She was still far too much aware of who she was and what she wanted, and that what she wanted was not to be found within the Fidra Bay. That did its work well, provided treatment and comfort for large numbers of patients, with nurses who had time to listen, assistants to do the chores, doctors who could solve all minor problems and call in specialist help if required. Why kick because the place seemed more like a hotel than a hospital? Because she missed the drama of nursing really ill patients? Because being cold and enduring indifferent food made life seem more real? More worthwhile?

She found her mind sliding away from these questions, and anyway she was getting frozen. Pulling her cape more tightly around her, she faced the biting wind. The day had darkened further still, she could make out nothing now on the Forth except cloud growing darker by the minute. Even the islands – Craigleith and The Lamb, Fidra, with its ruined chapel and tiny lighthouse, seemed for the moment to have vanished from view. Some said that Robert Louis Stevenson, who used to land on Fidra as a boy, had made it the setting for *Treasure Island*. No one knew for sure, but it might be fun to see it. Alex promised herself a trip, as soon as the weather improved. You could go on a boat from North Berwick, see the Bass Rock as well. Oh, but she must go in now.

On a sudden crazy impulse, she pulled off her glove, picked up a pebble and ran to the water's edge to try her hand at ducks and drakes. Jamie had been good at that game on the rare occasions they'd found themselves by the sea. How satisfying it must be, to send a stone skimming and jumping over the surface of the waves! She'd never managed it, and didn't now. Down plummeted the stone without a single touch, but as she shook her head at herself, pulling on her glove, a man's voice said over the wind,

'Wrong stone, Nurse Kelsie!'

She spun round to find Dr Raynor holding out a smooth flat pebble.

'This is the shape,' he said kindly. 'Want to try?'

It came to her with some surprise that this was the first time she had seen him out of his professional surroundings. He seemed very different, perhaps because the change from the medical white coat to windcheater and scarf made him seem less anonymous. Younger, too, though she knew he was in his forties, and his wildly tossing dark hair was thickly mixed with grey.

'Why don't you?' she countered, smiling. 'Show me how it's done.'

'I'll probably make myself look a perfect fool, but – here goes—'

Away went the stone, hopping, skipping, jumping over the water.

'One, two, three, four, FIVE times!' Alex cried. 'Oh, well done! I could never do that, never!'

'I tell you, it's just a question of choosing the right shape of pebble.'

They had forgotten the cold as they searched the shore, until Dr Raynor's keen eyes found what they were looking for.

'Now – take this, Nurse Kelsie, hold it so – parallel with the water, if you understand me – that's right, that's right – let it go, then!'

One, two, three times the pebble bounced before sinking, and Alex laughed with ridiculous delight.

'My best ever,' she told the doctor. 'All thanks to you.'

'Glad to be of help,' he said formally, and they laughed again, because it seemed such an absurd thing to be pleased about, throwing stones into the water on that chill February day. 'But you're getting too cold,' he added. 'I think we'd better go in.'

She felt a little self-conscious, climbing the steps before him, and felt she must look a terrible mess, with her cape all blown sand and her awful woollen hat pressed over her hair. Not that Dr Raynor was known himself for band-box neatness. It was well known that he left that sort of thing to his wife, who was always well dressed in tailored suits and hand-stitched blouses, her pale brown hair carefully styled, her make-up constantly renewed. She was not pretty, but seemed so, whereas her husband was handsome, yet no one noticed. Perhaps because he didn't care about his looks, thought Alex, who had taken very little interest in her own for some time. Even so, she pulled off the woollen hat as she turned to face Dr Raynor at the top of the steps, and knew she looked better with her hair blowing free.

'Your day off?' he asked. 'Mine, too. Half-day, at least, I never take a whole. Come into my study, we'll have some coffee to warm us up.'

Mrs Raynor was in the reception hall as they went through and her husband called to her.

'Val, want some coffee? I've just rescued Nurse Kelsie from the Forth – well, almost. She needs to thaw out.'

Valerie Raynor, beautifully dressed in a short cranberry-red jacket and matching pencil-slim skirt, smiled cautiously. Her brow was always a little puckered, her mouth tense; there were those on the staff who wondered if she ever really relaxed. There was no matron at the Fidra Bay, her two nursing sisters answered only to her, and as everyone who worked for her quickly learned, Mrs Raynor did not like to delegate.

'Take care, Alex,' she said now, 'You mustn't let yourself get chilled, you might go down with 'flu.'

'Don't worry, Mrs Raynor, I'm immune.'

'So nurses always think, till they collapse. Well, off you go and have your coffee. I won't have one just now, Hugh, thanks all the same, I have the accountant coming, you remember.'

'Oh, yes.' Dr Raynor looked vague. 'This way, Nurse Kelsie. Or, may I call you Alex, too? Seems terrible, you've been here for months, and I've never met you out of work hours.' He led the way to his office at the back of the house, a beautiful square room with a view of the Forth, and directed Alex to an armchair. 'I'm not usually so unfriendly, I assure you, I like to get to know the staff, see that they're happy, that sort of thing, but this 'flu epidemic seems to have knocked everything haywire. Wait there a sec, and I'll give Elsie a shout.'

While he was out of the room, Alex took off her cape and gloves, and gave her hair a quick comb, unsurprised that she had to manage without a mirror, which would be the last thing Dr Raynor would have in his study. Also no surprise was that her sweater was already feeling too heavy. She was sighing under its weight when Elsie, from the dining-room staff, came in with a tray of coffee and biscuits, looking her own surprise at finding one of the nurses in the doctor's private study.

'Thawing out?' asked Dr Raynor cheerfully, as Elsie withdrew. 'Or too warm already?' He was in shirt sleeves himself, she noticed. 'Maybe you're like me, and find this place too hot? Comes from working in a TB hospital, of course. Once you've got used to perpetual winter, you can't get used to summer.'

As she gratefully sipped her coffee, Alex raised her eyebrows.

'You sound as though you know about TB hospitals, Dr Raynor.'

'Should do, I used to work in one.' At her immediate look of interest, he smiled. 'At East Fortune, just down the road from here. Great experience there, we had every type of case, not just pulmonary, as at the Jubilee.' Dr Raynor bit with relish on a ginger biscuit. 'Odd, how so many people think TB only affects the lungs. Too many operas and films, I suppose, where the stars expire with gentle little coughs. In fact, you're damn' lucky if it doesn't spread to your innards or your bones, or if you don't get lupus – that's TB of the skin, often affects the face. Ever see a case of lupus vulgaris, Alex?'

'Yes, in training sessions at the Royal. We were supervised from there for our studies.' Alex shook her head. 'No' pleasant. There's so little that can be done.'

'There's been some success with Conteben. Limited, maybe,

118

but the big breakthrough's coming, you know, for all TB. Oh, yes. Just wish to God I could have been in on it. Worked on streptomycin, or maybe PAS. You know about PAS, the aspirin one? Of course you do, you're a TB nurse. Or were.' He laughed. 'But why am I talking to you as though I'm giving a lecture?'

'You're not! Anyway, I'm interested.'

'Yes, you are, aren't you? I can tell, I can always tell when somebody cares.'

'My mother died of miliary TB,' Alex said, after a pause. 'That made me care.'

'I'm sorry,' he said gently. 'Must have been hard for you.'

'Made me decide to work at the Jubilee.'

His intelligent eyes rested on her. She saw that they were grey, not unlike Tim Burnett's, but brighter, and with little gold flecks. 'And what made you decide to leave?' he asked quietly.

Oh, God. She wished he hadn't asked her that. When his wife had put the same question at the interview, she'd told her she just wanted a change. Martie had said the same and Mrs Raynor had accepted their reasons without comment. Perhaps it had seemed quite unsurprising to her that nurses would prefer to work in her lovely nursing home, rather than a Spartan hospital such as the Jubilee. But Alex didn't feel she could give Dr Raynor the same answer as she had given his wife. He would know it wasn't true, for even though this was the first time they'd talked, she had the feeling he already knew her very well. Felt he could turn those bright eyes of his on her and see beyond her pretty face to whatever it was that drove her. Which was remarkable, when she didn't know herself.

'There was a relationship,' she heard her voice saying, as her face grew hot and the collar of the woollen jumper chafed her neck and made the sweat start on her brow. 'I wanted to get away.'

'You must forgive me,' he said at once. 'I didn't mean to pry.'

It seemed the right time to make a move, thank him for the coffee, say she mustn't take up any more of his time. But at the door, she couldn't resist asking – why had he left TB medicine for the Fidra Bay? Had it been because of the war?

'No, no. By the time the war came, I was already here. I'd met

119

my wife and agreed to help her convert her father's hotel to a nursing home. Her mother was long dead, her father was failing, he gave his blessing to the project.' Dr Raynor gave a rueful smile. 'We'd just got the thing off the ground when it all had to be closed – the army requisitioned it. I was joining up anyway, and Val was going back to nursing. The patients went where they could, and we opened up again in 1947. Just in time for the big freeze! How we got through, I don't know, only Val could have done it. She's a marvel.'

'I'm sure,' Alex murmured. 'But it seems a shame, you know – all your TB experience—'

'Yes, we did think of making the Fidra into a sanatorium, but it was going to be much more expensive and more difficult. Anyway, I can do a useful job here, with the set-up we have.' He fixed her again with his bright gaze. 'And so can you, Alex. We need people like you.'

She smiled and left him, wondering if he was watching as she walked down the corridor. Somehow, she thought he might be, but did not turn her head.

'You had coffee with Dr Raynor?' Martie exclaimed later. 'What a way to spend your time off!'

'I enjoyed it. He's very interesting to talk to.'

'But why did he want to talk to you? I mean, specially?'

'He said he likes to get to know all the staff. Find out if they're happy.'

'He's never talked to me! Never asked me if I'm happy!'

'Anybody can see that you are, Martie.'

'Yes.' Martie smiled. 'Well, I am, and so should you be. Did you tell him you were?'

'I'm no' sure what I told him,' Alex answered thoughtfully. 'He seemed to know, anyway, what I felt.'

'I see, a mind reader. Well, I suppose he is a very good doctor, even if he is a wee bit boring, eh?'

'Boring? Why, I don't think he's boring, Martie! He's a lot more interesting than Dr Parr or Dr Best!'

Drs Parr and Best made up the permanent medical staff with Dr

120

Raynor. Stuart Parr was young and recently married, with his eye on lucrative private practice, while Wendy Best, some years older, had just returned to medicine after bringing up a family. Alex didn't consider either of them to be of Dr Raynor's calibre, though she had to admit she'd only just come to this opinion. She lowered her eyes before Martie's curious stare.

'OK, OK, Dr Raynor's a ball of fire,' Martie said, grinning. 'I'll bet you never gave him a thought before today. See what a cup of coffee can do, eh? But don't let Mrs Raynor catch you!'

'And what do you mean by that?' Alex asked frostily. 'If it was supposed to be a joke, I think it's no' funny.'

'Of course it was a joke! Och, come on, you know me!'

'Yes, only too well! I've no interest in Dr Raynor, Martie. His wife's got nothing to fear from me!'

'I'm sorry, Alex,' said Martie, looking far from penitent. All that concerned her was that Alex should for once have enjoyed talking to a man again, and that meant her feeling for Tim Burnett was well and truly dead. Or, dying, anyhow.

Chapter Twenty-One

It was quite true that Alex was not interested in Dr Raynor in any kind of romantic or sexual way. But she had to admit she was interested in him as a person. Though she had never again had coffee in his study, they still met off duty, still liked to walk by the water, still talked, mainly about new advances in TB, or allied medical matters. She knew that he felt a certain affinity with her because of her experience in what had been his field, and guessed she satisfied his need to talk with someone who understood what that field had meant to him. He satisfied a need in her too, which was a desire to look beyond the limitations of her life at the Fidra Bay. He made her feel a purpose in what she was doing, and as the weeks went by and winter changed to spring, she began for the first time to settle, to feel content. Not quite happy, but almost. As for Tim Burnett, his image grew more faint as Hugh Raynor's became more distinct. Not that she ever called Dr Raynor by his first name, of course, she couldn't imagine ever doing that. He was a father-figure to her, that was all.

At the beginning of May, a patient with a heart murmur was admitted to the Fidra Bay from one of Edinburgh's best hotels. Her name was Lois Adamson and she was on vacation with her husband from New York, where he ran the family bank. They were, according to Sylvia MacKenna, administrative manager at the Fidra, very rich indeed.

'Old money,' she told Martie, her crimson lips drooping with awe. 'Very grand.'

'Old money?' Alex repeated, when Martie retailed the information. 'What's the difference between old money and any other kind?'

'Search me. I suppose the folk have just had it longer, eh?'

'I wouldn't mind new money myself, would you?' Alex said, laughing.

'Any money would do for me!' cried Martie.

The staff at the Fidra Bay thought Mrs Adamson most attractive. Almost as attractive as Mr Adamson. The couple weren't young, she being in her late forties, he over fifty, but they had immense style, even what might be called glamour, and were, of course, Americans, which set them apart, anyway. In austerity Britain, the United States was still seen as a land flowing with milk and honey. Everyone remembered war-time GIs, providers of nylons and candy. When the war was over, it was America, with its Marshall Plan, that had donated billions of dollars to help rehabilitate Europe. Now, American tourists, just beginning to travel again, appeared to have money to burn. It was no wonder that the Adamsons, as Americans, with all the wealth that was expected of them, should have taken the Fidra Bay by storm. Everyone wanted to nurse Mrs Adamson and be as helpful as possible to her husband, who had opted to stay in a room near her, rather than remain at their hotel. But the nurses favoured by the Adamsons themselves, as it soon became apparent, were Alex Kelsie and Martie Cass.

'You're such a darling girl,' Lois Adamson said to Alex one morning after Dr Raynor's visit. 'It makes me feel better just to look at you!'

Alex, embarrassed, straightened the sheets, and blushed.

'You're much better, anyway,' she murmured. 'The doctor said so, didn't he?'

Lois lay back against her pillows. She had an unusual face, Alex thought. Very modern, with a large, generous mouth which she

123

insisted on making up, wide eyes under pencilled brows, high cheekbones also touched with rouge, in spite of Dr Raynor's frown.

'I like to see what colour my patients are,' he told her gently. 'Not what colour they put on from a box.'

Lois only pushed back her long sweep of hair, cleverly coloured greyish blond, and smiled her lipsticked smile.

'Doctor, I'm not me without my make-up,' she told him, in her flat, nasal, New York voice. 'You wouldn't have me lose my identity just because I'm sick?'

'Believe me, Mrs Adamson, you will never lose your identity,' he retorted. 'But as you're making such good progress, I'll say no more.'

'Am I really? Making good progress?'

'Yes, the regime is working. Bed-rest, medication – that leaking valve has got the message. You're not going to need surgery.'

'And I'll soon be able to continue my trip?'

Dr Raynor pursed his lips. 'I'm not sure about soon. We'll have to see.'

'That's what doctors have been saying to me since I was fourteen years old.'

'When you got rheumatic fever.' He nodded. 'It's left its legacy.'

'One I could have done without.'

Now, Lois was giving her smile to Alex.

'Dr Raynor did say I was getting better, it's true, but he wouldn't be pinned down about our trip. I guess we'll get going again sometime.' Her smile died. 'I hope so, for poor Warren's sake. He's worked so hard for years on end, he's just desperate for a break. We were going to look up my Scottish ancestors in Skye, you know. I was a MacDonald – that's where they are, right?'

'There are a lot of MacDonalds in Skye,' Alex agreed with a faint smile. 'Now, if you're settled, Mrs Adamson, I'll leave you.'

'Do you have to? I really like to talk with you, my dear.' Lois sighed and picked up the photograph of her only child, her son, Brent, that she kept by her bed. It was Brent who was looking after the bank, together with a board of trustees, while his father was in

Europe; his mother missed him dreadfully. 'But I know I mustn't keep you from your duties.'

'Just rest, Mrs Adamson, then before you know it, Mr Adamson will be back from golf to have lunch with you.'

'Yes, I'm so grateful he's got something to do. Oh, before you go, would you be very kind and pass me a bedjacket from that chest over there? Any one would do – perhaps the pink?'

'Of course, Mrs Adamson.'

Alex had had occasion to find things for Mrs Adamson before, and always, as her eye went over the drifts of silk and lace in the chest of drawers, the exquisite little bras and French knickers, the frothy jackets, silk-ribboned and scented, she was reminded of the time she and Ma had gone to see the Hitchcock film *Rebecca* together. How long ago? Years and years. She'd been quite young, her mother too, come to that. They'd had toffees that they might have saved from their ration – or maybe it was before you had to have 'points' to buy sweeties? She couldn't remember. What she did remember was sitting, open-mouthed, watching the timid little heroine scuttling round Manderley, while the dark-browed Max De Winter barked orders at everyone, and the sinister housekeeper hovered in the background. Oh, my goodness, how they'd enjoyed it all, she and Ma! Particularly that scene where Mrs Danvers, the housekeeper, had shown the heroine all Rebecca's beautiful clothes. Her furs and dresses, shoes, her filmy underwear. 'Made for her by the nuns,' Mrs Danvers had breathed, and Alex could remember wondering what it would be like to wear things like that instead of a liberty bodice and school knickers, and promising herself that when she was grown up, she'd have just such a collection and be like Martie, so keen for silks and satins, she'd even cheated in their skipping games. But now that Alex was grown up, she'd quite forgotten all about expensive underwear and wore her plain white cotton without a care.

Bet Martie wouldn't agree with me, she thought now, lightly sorting through Mrs Adamson's lingerie until she found her pink wisp of a bedjacket. Oh, yes, Martie would want all this! And as the silks rippled through her fingers, Alex did understand. What woman wouldn't?

'There you are,' she murmured, slipping the jacket round Mrs Adamson's shoulders. 'Comfortable?'

'Oh, yes! You're so kind, my dear, really kind. I'm sure I ask you to do things I shouldn't – I mean, you're a trained nurse, aren't you?' Lois Adamson's thin hand patted Alex's. 'But you don't mind, do you? Now say if you do!'

'I don't mind at all,' Alex told her, smiling, only looking a little rueful when she was out in the corridor and remembering Martie's joke. 'We'll probably spend all our time arranging flowers and putting on bedjackets . . . 'Suppose I'll be arranging the flowers next, Alex muttered to herself – Mrs Adamson's room was always filled with flowers provided by Mr Adamson – what of it? She liked Mrs Adamson, liked doing things for her, whether she was rich or not, and it was scarcely worthwhile ringing for a nursing assistant just to put on a bedjacket.

Other nurses were discussing the Adamsons at supper that evening. Had anyone seen Mr Adamson's watch? Oh, my God, cost a year's wages, eh? Or, two year's wages, or three? As for Mrs Adamson's rings – ! Plump Staff Nurse Shona Ward said she'd give anything for one o' thae diamonds! Anything!

'Anything?' asked Martie, grinning.

'Nearly anything,' Shona answered, grinning back.

'I'm no' greedy,' someone else whispered. 'I'd settle for her undies!'

'Lingerie, please!' Martie stood up, scraping back her chair. 'I wouldn't give anything for Mrs Adamson's, I'd want ma own!'

'Too right,' they echoed, and as they all began to move away to pour the coffee or tea that had arrived, Alex asked Martie if she wasn't wanting a cup of something?

'Got to dash,' said Martie. 'I'm away to North Berwick.'

Alex's eyes widened. 'This evening?'

'Aye, I'm due a bit of time off.'

'Doing anything special?'

'When do I do anything special? Now, if your Jamie had no' gone and got himself engaged—'

Martie laughed and before Alex could speak again, had hurried away.

She's up to something, thought Alex. I can always tell.

But what could Martie be up to, that she didn't want to talk about? There was no time to wonder. Alex had no time off, she was due back on duty and Sister Grey had already poked her head round the door with a meaningful stare. Neither Sister Grey nor Sister MacAlister was as stiff as Sister Clerk, but they would not have been employed by Mrs Raynor if they had not been efficient. Alex, trained in a hard school, liked to be efficient too.

'Just coming, Sister!' she called, and thought no more of Martie.

Chapter Twenty-Two

Martie was not happy on the bus taking her into North Berwick. Just what did she think she was doing, going for a drink with Warren Adamson at one of the best hotels? She must be out of her mind! Why had she ever agreed? Because she'd wanted to, that was why. Especially after being with him last week in the same hotel. That was after she'd met him accidentally on her day off. Bumped into him on the pavement outside a shop, had thought him so distinguished-looking, even in casual clothes, the pale sunshine lighting his strong features, his steel-grey hair, his flashing smile.

'Nurse Cass! How nice to meet you!'

'Mr Adamson!'

It had been the obvious thing, to accept tea with him, not in one of the little cafés, but the lounge of the good hotel, where they had looked out to sea and the Bass Rock, and the waiters had delivered the silver teapots and pastries with such panache, they must have known they were serving an American.

What folk'll do for a big tip, thought Martie, but she'd basked all the same in the attention that was as comforting as the warmth of a summer's day. And that attention was not just from the waiters. She couldn't fail to be aware that Mr Adamson's dark hazel gaze was scarcely leaving her face.

'How d'you like North Berwick, then?' she'd asked, feeling strangely at ease. This man, so different from any man she'd met before, seemed to treat her as though she were something special, and the way Martie looked at that was, if he thought her special, well, she was, wasn't she?

'Oh, I'm charmed,' Mr Adamson answered. 'It's the sort of place I'd like to roll up and take home. Unspoiled, I guess, is the word for it.'

'Unspoiled? They'd no' thank you for calling it that. They like to think this is a pretty high-class resort.' Martie, who knew the town well, added in her definite way, 'Come to that, it is! Folk come here from England and all over, stay at the big hotels, go boating, and all that sort of thing. You can go round the Bass Rock from here, you know.'

'I'd like that.' Warren Adamson had turned his gaze on the massive dark rock that towered at the mouth of the Firth of Forth, some few miles off North Berwick. He'd read something about it, knew it had once been a fort and a prison for Covenanters and Jacobites, and now was home to thousands of sea-birds. He looked back at Martie. 'Guess my poor Lois would have liked it, too.'

'Don't worry.' Martie leaned forward, her blue eyes sympathetic. 'Mrs Adamson's no' seriously ill. She'll soon be going out with you again, I promise.'

'Maybe. But I'm not sure we should try to continue our trip. I'd like her to see her own doctor again at home.'

'Dr Raynor's very good, Mr Adamson.'

'Oh, I know, you're all wonderful, don't think I don't appreciate you!' He smiled his expensive smile again. 'We'll just have to see how things go. In the meantime, Lois rests, and I play golf.'

'And have tea in North Berwick!'

They'd laughed, then Martie'd said she must go, and Mr Adamson offered her a ride back in his hired car. She'd been tempted, but what would folk think, if they saw her driving in with the husband of a patient? Had things to do, she told him, and they left the hotel together. It was then that he'd asked her to have dinner with him – a little thank you for all she'd done for his wife.

'Dinner? Oh, I don't think – I mean—' She floundered, as he waited. 'It'd no' be easy—'

129

'A drink, then? A drink after dinner? We could meet here. When you're free.'

That was how it had happened. He'd made the offer, and though she'd been too uneasy to accept the meal, she'd been too dazzled to refuse the drink. So, here she was, on the bus, on her way, on a lovely evening that was far too light, wearing a blue suit that she thought matched her eyes, and her best shoes. What the hell was she doing, she groaned again. Until she walked into the cocktail bar of the Towers Court, and saw him waiting. A man like that, waiting for her? She couldn't believe it. As he leaped up to pull out a chair, it came to her with an inward laugh – he was her Rich Man. The nearest she would ever get to one, that was for sure. But he was someone else's.

'Tell me about yourself, Martie,' he said, when he had a whisky in front of him, and she had a gin and tonic. 'You won't mind if I call you Martie?'

'No, of course not.' She watched the ice cubes melting in her drink. 'But I'm no' very interesting. There's no' much to say about me.'

'I'm listening, all the same.'

She sighed. 'Well, I come from Edinburgh. I live in the Colonies – that's just a group of little houses no' far from the centre of town. I suppose they called it after an artists' colony, or else a hive of bees, I don't know. They'd be worker bees, anyway!'

'Do you have brothers and sisters?'

'No, there's just me. Ma folks are shop-workers. There's nothing special about them. They both like money.'

'No harm in that,' Mr Adamson said, with a smile. 'I like it, too.'

'Aye, but they don't like spending it.'

'Ah.' He drank his whisky. 'Kept you on a short rein, then?'

'Sometimes felt it was round ma neck!' She laughed. 'Anyway, I trained as a nurse, and here I am. Let's talk about you.'

'You know most of what there is to know about me. I have my dear wife, Lois, I have my son, Brent, the apple of our eyes. I have an apartment in New York and a house in Rhode Island. I run the

130

bank my family founded many years ago. I've no worries, except my wife's health.' He rested his eyes on Martie's face. 'I suppose you'd call me lucky.'

'I suppose I would.'

'There is that question of my wife's health, though. She's always been delicate, from being a child. Now you, Martie, you're strong, aren't you?'

'Bit too strong, I sometimes think. Too big, anyway.'

'Don't say that,' he said quickly. 'It's your attraction. To be so wonderfully full of health ... vitality ... You're very attractive, you know, Martie. Very attractive indeed.'

She bit her lip, looking round the bar. Thank God there was no one in this smart crowd who knew her. It came to her that she should leave. This had been a crazy idea, after all. Warren Adamson's wife was delicate, she, Martie, was strong. She didn't need it knocking in with a hammer to see the way his mind was going, and if she left now there was a bus back in twenty minutes.

'Thanks very much for the drink,' she said, rising. 'But I'd better get back.'

'Oh, God, I've upset you!' He rose with her, putting out his hand, then letting it fall. 'Listen, Martie, this is just what it seems – a friendly drink. I love my wife very dearly—'

And she's delicate, thought Martie again. 'It's all right,' she told him. 'I'm no' upset. Just need to get back to the Fidra Bay.'

'Let me drive you.'

'No, I'll take the bus, thanks all the same. I mean, it'd look better.'

'For God's sake, what's wrong with my giving you a ride?'

'You know what's wrong,' she said quietly.

He shook his head. 'Martie, we shouldn't let ourselves be ruled by other people. I make my own rules, I always have. I'm going to take you back to the nursing home, but if it'll make you feel any better, I'll let you out at the end of the drive. All right?'

'All right,' she agreed, suddenly and shamefully looking forward to being with him in his car. There'd be no harm in that, would there? And how lovely it would be, not to have to go for that rattling bus!

The hire car was just as she'd imagined it, black, luxurious, purring – more of a carriage than a car. How Jamie would have admired this, thought Martie, and felt a pang, remembering his little Morris. But why was she thinking of Jamie Kelsie? If he could see her now, bowling along with a married man, he'd be looking down his nose, eh? As he usually did look down his nose at her. Anyway, he was someone else's, too.

The great car ate up the miles to the Fidra Bay and before she had had time to compose herself and work out how to make a graceful goodbye, Warren Adamson was slowing down and stopping at the entrance to the drive.

'Well?' He switched off the engine and turned his head to try to see her in the dim light of the interior, for now, she thanked God, it was dark. 'This where you want to get out, Martie?'

'Yes, please.'

Yet she made no move to open her door.

'May I just say something – before you go?' Warren asked. 'It was true what I said to you in the bar. All I was offering was a drink.'

'Oh, yes, I know,' she said hurriedly.

'You might have thought otherwise?'

She said nothing.

'You did think otherwise. I'm sorry, I wouldn't have had you worried for the world.'

'I wasn't worried!'

'All right, I wouldn't have had you think ill of me for the world.' Suddenly, he took her hand in a firm warm grasp. 'You're a very fine person, Martie. I've already discovered that. I was wrong to ask you to meet me, you'll have to forgive me. It's just that – hell, I don't know – I succumbed to loneliness, I guess. My poor Lois is asleep all evening, I have no one to talk to, I wanted to talk with you. It's as simple as that. Can you understand, Martie?'

'Look, it's OK—'

'But you do understand? I wasn't out to seduce you.' He laughed uneasily. 'I'm old enough to be your father, remember.'

Older than ma father, in fact, thought Martie. Sid Cass was only forty-seven. With a feeling of desperation for an evening that had gone so wrong, she finally opened her door.

'I won't ask you to meet me again,' Warren said, watching her. 'We'll just pretend this evening never happened.'

She nodded. 'Shall we say goodnight now, Mr Adamson? I'll see you in the morning.'

'I wish you'd call me Warren.'

'I'd get stick from Mrs Raynor if she heard me doing that!'

'Why should we care about Mrs Raynor?'

'Because she pays ma wages.' Martie climbed out of the car, then looked back at Warren leaning towards her, all his body language telling her he didn't want her to go, that however much of a fiasco the evening had been, he didn't want it to end. 'Goodnight,' she said gently. 'And thanks.'

'Thanks? For God's sake, what have you got to thank me for?' He shook his head wearily and drew back behind the driving wheel. 'Look, you go on ahead. I'll follow. No one need know we've been together.'

It had been too much to expect that she would be able to slide into her room without being seen, therefore no surprise that Alex should appear as soon as Martie had unlocked her door, pulled off her high heels and thrown herself into a chair.

'You're back early,' Alex remarked cheerfully. 'Had a good time?'

'Oh, yes. Just had a drink.'

'With anyone I know?'

'No.' Martie stood up and took off her jacket, hung it on a hanger. 'Mind if I say goodnight, Alex? I feel whacked.'

'You don't look whacked.'

'Oh, what do I look, then?'

'Excited.' Alex, making no move to go, looked at Martie consideringly. 'I'd say you looked like I did, when I was meeting Tim Burnett.'

Martie's eyes flashed. 'If you've got something to say, Alex, say it!'

'Same as you did to me?'

'If you want to put it that way, yes.'

'All right. I saw you come up the drive just now. And then I saw Mr Adamson's car. Don't ask me why, I just had the feeling there was a connection.'

'Oh, we're into sixth-sense stuff now, are we? Guessing games?'

'Had you been with Mr Adamson, Martie?'

Martie's face was scarlet. She stood with her arms folded, staring away from Alex to some point over her head.

'All right, I had a drink with him. If you want to make something of it.'

'I don't want to make anything of it.'

'Why are you here, then?'

Alex's brown eyes were troubled. 'Maybe I just don't want you to get hurt, Martie. Or Mrs Adamson, either.'

'No one's going to hurt her. It was one drink, no' grand affair. Mr Adamson just – you know – wanted somebody to talk to.'

'Somebody to talk to?' Alex's mouth twitched. 'Why'd he no' ask one of the fellows he meets at the golf club, then?'

'We just happened to bump into each other in North Berwick last week. He asked me if I'd have dinner with him, as a thank you, you ken, for looking after his wife.' At Alex's look of outrage, Martie added hastily, 'he was no' meaning you don't look after her, Alex, it was just—'

'An excuse,' Alex said coldly. 'He wanted you to go out with him, that was all there was to it. Why did you no' have dinner, then?'

'Och, I don't know. A drink seemed easier. Anyway, he said he knew he shouldn't have asked me and I can promise you it won't happen again. End of story, Alex. Don't say any more.'

'You were playing with fire, Martie. If Mrs Raynor found out, she wouldn't be too pleased, eh?'

'There's nothing for her to find out, is there? I mean, I won't be going out with him again.'

For some moments Alex looked steadily into Martie's face. 'That's a weight off ma mind, Martie. I know you think I'm interfering – just the way I thought you were – but it's only because I – well, you know the reason. I've already said.'

'Yes, I can't blame you for doing what I did,' Martie answered grudgingly. 'But you've no need to worry. I know I'd be a fool to get involved with Warren Adamson. To be fair, I don't think he wants to be involved, either.'

'Doesn't he?' asked Alex.

In her beautiful room, with its windows open to the Forth, their white curtains blowing, Lois Adamson was sleeping peacefully. She didn't hear her husband's entrance, or his approach to her bed, didn't feel his gentle kiss on her cheek. But then he said her name and clasped her in his arms, and her eyes flew open.

'Warren? What – what are you doing? What's happening?'

'Lois, just get well,' he stammered, holding her close. 'For God's sake, get well, my darling. That's all I want, I promise!'

'Why wake me up to tell me that?' she asked fondly. 'I already know.'

Chapter Twenty-Three

As the summer progressed and patients began to sit out on the lawns and even walk on the shore, Warren was as good as his word and made no attempt to ask Martie to meet him again outside the Fidra Bay. He could not, however, conceal the special interest he took in her, and some of her colleagues were quick to spot how he so often just happened to be where she was, how he would hold her in conversation, follow her with his eyes when she had to move away.

'That guy's sweet on you, Martie,' Shona said one lunch break. 'And sweet's the word, eh? He'd make a grand sugar-daddy!'

'What a thing to say!' Martie retorted. 'You should be ashamed of yourself, Staff, talking about Mr Adamson like that!'

'Better watch out that Mrs Raynor doesn't see what we've seen,' said Shona, unconcerned. 'He's married to a patient, right?'

'You going to say something to her?' Martie asked fiercely.

'Och, have a heart! I'd no' do that! I'm just saying, be careful.'

'Aye, watch your step,' other voices warned. 'We all know what happens when a nurse gets involved where she shouldn't, eh?'

Alex, who had remained quiet during this exchange, coloured to her brow and hastily went back to work. As soon as she could find the right time, she asked Dr Raynor how soon Mrs Adamson might be well enough to leave.

'Mrs Adamson? She's doing well. I'm pretty close to giving her the all-clear to go home.'

'Back to America? I thought she wanted to go up to Skye?'

'I wouldn't be happy about that. Going back to be near her own doctor and good hospitals, that's one thing. Racketing round Skye as a tourist is another. Anyway, I don't think Mr Adamson's keen. He wants to book sailings back home now.'

'I see,' said Alex, feeling relieved. The sooner the Adamsons left, the easier her mind would be for Martie. What would Rose have made of all this, she wondered, as though she didn't know! Conduct was always clear-cut for Rose, who was now at the Louise Margaret Hospital in Aldershot, though likely to go abroad quite soon. Alex still missed her. Maybe they could organise a get-together before Rose left the country? Alex promised herself that on her next off-duty period she would get down to writing to Rose.

'You won't have been to New York, Alex?' Mrs Adamson asked one morning. She was well enough now to get up and dress, sit in a chair by the window and look out at the Forth as she loved to do. That day she was wearing a pale green suit with a silk scarf at her throat. Her hair had been set by the visiting hairdresser, her nails polished by the visiting manicurist, and as usual she was exquisitely made up. Alex thought she looked so charming, it was difficult to understand why Warren Adamson's eyes should have strayed to Martie. On the other hand, Mrs Adamson still seemed so fragile. As though if she ventured out, one of the strong winds from the Forth would lift her up and blow her away.

'Have I been to New York?' Alex smiled, as she gave Mrs Adamson her tablets and a glass of water. 'Well, no, I haven't. To tell you the truth, I've never even been out of Scotland.'

'How silly of me! There's been a war, and then you're so young.' Lois swallowed her tablets, making a face. 'Of course you won't have done any travelling. But I'd love for you to see New York, you know. It's a wonderful city.'

'Oh, it must be. All those skyscrapers – I've seen pictures.'

'Manhattan,' Lois said dreamily. 'Central Park. Fifth Avenue. Restaurants, department stores – there isn't a thing you can't get, believe me! And then the people – here in Scotland, you've no idea – so many people, every colour, race, religion – it's just a world of its own!'

'Maybe I will see it one day.'

'I was thinking—' Lois hesitated. 'Maybe, quite soon.'

Alex stared. 'What do you mean, Mrs Adamson?'

'Well, I don't want to spring it on you. It's just an idea, you see—'

'What is? What are we talking about?'

Lois smiled uncertainly. 'You know I'm pretty well better now? Dr Raynor doesn't want me to go to Skye, and neither does Warren, but I'm certainly well enough to go home. We're going to try to get an earlier sailing and I was wondering – if you'd agree to accompany us? As my nurse?'

There was a long silence in the lovely room. Outside on the water, ships passed, slowly. A tanker moved, dark against the horizon, small boats bobbed nearer the shore. Alex watched, quite unseeingly. New York. Manhattan. Skyscrapers. Central Park. Restaurants. Department stores. So many people. Just a world of its own.

'I don't know what to say,' she said at last. 'I mean, I don't know how I could do that. I'd like to. Oh, I'd love to. But there's ma work here – I wouldn't like to let Mrs Raynor down—'

'It wouldn't be for ever, only a visit,' Lois said eagerly. 'You'd come back, take up your job again, do anything you liked. It's just that I'd feel so much safer if I had you to look after me, you see. Because now I feel so vulnerable. I'm better, but I'm still – oh, I don't know how to put it. Sometimes, I'm afraid.'

'There's no need for you to feel that, Mrs Adamson. You are better, you really are. And you'll be in good hands on the ship, they always have excellent doctors.'

'I'd feel happier if you were there, my dear. And then I'd just so love to show you everything back home, we could have such a wonderful time!' Lois's eyes were full of appeal. 'Won't you say yes?'

Alex was opening her mouth to speak, still not sure of what to say, when the door opened and Lois, looking round, gave a radiant smile. 'Why, it's Warren! Come here, my darling, let me tell you my idea!'

He was in sports shirt and flannels, said he'd been running on the shore, felt wonderful.

'And you look wonderful too, doesn't he, Alex?'

'I must go,' Alex said quickly, but Lois held her back.

'No, wait, just see what Warren says. He'll be thrilled, anyway.'

He bent over her, kissing her brow. 'What's this great idea, then? What have you dreamed up for me?'

'It's not for you, it's for me! I've asked Alex to accompany us to New York, as my nurse.' Lois gave a triumphant smile. 'There, what do you think of that?'

He straightened up, sending a surprised gaze to Alex, but as she looked away, embarrassed, he smiled.

'Why, that's terrific,' he said slowly. 'A brainwave, no less. Why didn't I think of it?'

'She hasn't said yes yet,' Lois told him, almost purring with pleasure. 'But she will, I know she will.'

'I think so, too, because I've got an idea myself. Why don't we ask Nurse Cass to come as well?'

'Nurse Cass?' Lois repeated. 'Martie?'

'Why not? She and Alex are friends, isn't that right? They'd be perfect as a team, and I think we'd need a team. Alex couldn't be on duty all the time, you know.' He smiled again at Alex. 'And with Martie, Alex wouldn't feel lonesome, so far from home.'

'I guess not,' said Lois eagerly.

'Why don't I ask her, then? Or would you like to, darling?'

'No, no, you ask her, Warren. See if you can find her now.'

'New York!' Martie whispered. Her eyes had a glazed look, as she held Alex's arm fast. 'Oh, God, Alex, New York! Am I dreaming?'

'You can let go of my arm, Martie, I'm no' going to run away.'

They were in an upstairs corridor on their way to patients, Alex chafing because this was not the time or place to talk, Martie oblivious, starry-eyed, almost intoxicated with surprise and delight.

'Oh, but can you believe it?' she went on in the same, low bemused tone. 'Can you believe they've asked us to go to New

York? With passages on the Queen Mary! All our meals and dancing, deck quoits, or whatever they play, seats at the Captain's table—'

'We will not be at the Captain's table!' Alex cried, pulling away from Martie's hand. 'And we've been asked to look after Mrs Adamson, not play deck quoits! Oh, Martie, what are you thinking about? You know we shouldn't go!'

'Are you crazy? Of course, we should! As soon as Mr Adamson asked me, I said yes, didn't you?'

'I was going to say I'd think about it, but that was before I knew you were going.'

'But is it no' better that I'm going? I mean, there'll be the two of us, it'll be the chance of a lifetime for both of us. Alex, are you no' thrilled?'

'I'm worried.' Alex's brown eyes had lost their usual warmth. 'I'm worried about you, Martie. Going to New York for the wrong reasons. Be honest, you've no' given a thought to Mrs Adamson, have you?'

'Of course I have, I'm very fond of her, but you're her favourite, eh? I've just been asked to make up a team with you.'

'You can look me in the eye and tell me that?'

'Yes, it's true! But it's a wonderful opportunity for me and I'm no' turning it down.'

As Alex turned and began to walk swiftly away down the corridor, Martie followed, still talking.

'And that's why you've got to come too, Alex, because it'll be the same for you. The sort of opportunity that never comes twice, so you have to take it when you can, eh? Come on, put Mrs A.'s mind at rest. You know she needs you.'

'So does this place. We owe it something.'

'We'd no' be going to the States for ever, we could come back here, couldn't we?'

'If Mrs Raynor would have us, after messing her about.'

'Let's ask her. Put our cards on the table. I think she'd no' want to hold us back.' Martie again caught at Alex's arm. 'And you don't need to worry about me and Mr Adamson. There's nothing in that, honest.'

140

'No?'

'If you come, you'll be able to see for yourself.'

Alex stared hard into Martie's bright blue eyes.

'I'll see Mrs Raynor,' she said shortly.

But it was Dr Raynor she saw. They walked again on the shore, snatching a few minutes' break at lunchtime, though neither was thinking about lunch. Once or twice, Hugh Raynor skimmed a flat stone across the calm water, but mainly he kept his eyes on Alex as she talked. When she'd finished, he rubbed his sandy fingers together and sighed.

'Private nursing, Alex – is it what you want?'

'It wouldn't be for long. And I'd be working in America.'

'Oh, I can see the attraction.'

'But you think I shouldn't go?'

'Didn't say that.'

'No, but you don't have to spell it out. You think I should be looking for something different.'

'I'm just trying to guess which way you want your career to go. Taking care of Mrs Adamson – it's not going to stretch you, Alex.'

She lowered her eyes. 'I know, but it's such a wonderful opportunity to see something of the world. I mean, how else would I get the chance?'

'You're right. Of course you are.' He suddenly took her arm and tucked it into his. 'You know what it is, Alex? I'm just being damned selfish. I don't want you to go.'

'I'll come back, if Mrs Raynor will let me.'

'If she'll let you? She'll be crazy to have you back, I promise you. And I'll be crazy, too. Will you write to me? Tell me what's happening in America on the TB battleground?'

'As though I'd know!' she answered, laughing uneasily, conscious of her arm in his. 'I'd better go, Dr Raynor, my lunch break's up.'

'It's time you called me Hugh, you know,' he told her, following her up the steps from the shore. 'We're friends, as well as colleagues, aren't we?'

But Alex had stopped short at the top of the steps. Valerie Raynor, slim and elegant in a linen dress and jacket, was waiting for them.

'Been for another of your walks?' she asked, putting a hand to her immaculate hair. 'My goodness, I wish I had the time to go walking!'

'It is lunchtime,' Hugh said mildly. 'I don't normally go for walks in working hours, nor does Nurse Kelsie.'

'You mean Alex, don't you? You always call her Alex.'

Hugh glanced at Alex, whose face was pink, whose eyes were large with apprehension. 'Did you want to speak to me, Val?'

'Oh, no, I don't have anything to talk to you about, do I? I can't go in for heart to hearts about the latest cure for TB, I just run a nursing home!' Valerie Raynor's eyes were bleak. 'But there is a telephone call for you, as it happens. It's Hawkins Pharmaceuticals, about some antibiotics you ordered, they want you to ring back.'

'Thanks, I'll make the call now.'

As Hugh left them, walking rapidly, Mrs Raynor turned to Alex and said in tones that could have formed ice on the Forth, 'Nurse Kelsie, I'd like to see you in my office, please.'

'Certainly, Mrs Raynor.'

But as she followed her employer into the house, Alex's heart was hammering, her cheeks had turned from pink to scarlet. Nurse Kelsie? Not Alex? What did Mrs Raynor think she had done?

Chapter Twenty-Four

Mrs Raynor's office, smaller than her husband's and with no views of the Forth, was clearly the workplace of a woman dedicated to her job. Though flowers were a feature of the Fidra Bay and everywhere throughout the building there was evidence of comfort and luxury, the owner's office was Spartan. No flowers, no decoration. Only a large, uncluttered desk, filing cabinets and cupboards, two telephones and a few chairs, none that could be described as easy. All that was decorative was Valerie Raynor herself, though as she motioned Alex to a chair before her desk, she was obviously finding it difficult to retain her control. Perhaps because of that, she wasted no time in preamble but moved straight into attack.

'Nurse Kelsie, this can't go on.' She rolled a pen between trembling fingers. 'I'm sure you can see that for yourself.'

Alex's eyes widened. 'I don't understand,' she said hoarsely. 'What can't go on?'

'Please don't make things difficult. I mean, this relationship of -yours with my husband. All this walking and talking, all these little chats down on the shore. I don't know what you think you're playing at, but it's got to stop.'

'Mrs Raynor, there is no relationship! All we talk about is work. Medical matters!'

'Oh, of course.' Mrs Raynor's lip curled. 'Medical matters. I don't see him talking to Stuart Parr, I don't see him talking to Wendy Best, about medical matters. They are doctors, you're a

143

nurse, and you're the one my husband chooses to talk to about medical matters?'

'I suppose, it's just because we've both worked in TB hospitals,' Alex said desperately. 'We've something in common, you see, that's all it is, honestly. Dr Raynor's no' interested in me as a person.'

'Please don't patronise me!' Mrs Raynor flared. 'I know what my husband's interested in! Like all men, someone pretty, someone young!'

'No, Mrs Raynor, no! It's no' like that, I swear it!'

'You can cut out the dramatics, Nurse Kelsie. I wasn't born yesterday and I have eyes in my head. You're a very good nurse and I don't want to lose you, but unless you leave my husband alone, I'm going to have to ask you to leave.'

Alex rose slowly to her feet, struggling to rescue some kind of dignity from the nightmare that had enfolded her like a storm descending from an innocent blue sky. 'You needn't ask me to go, Mrs Raynor. I'm leaving, anyway. Mrs Adamson has asked me to accompany her to New York as her nurse.'

'Mrs Adamson has what?'

There was some satisfaction to Alex in seeing the incredulity in her employer's eyes.

'I hadn't made up my mind what to do, I was going to ask your advice, I felt some loyalty to you, you see—'

'Loyalty!' cried Mrs Raynor.

'But now I'll tell Mrs Adamson that I accept her offer and I'll put ma notice in to leave with her.'

'Just let me get this straight – Mrs Adamson has asked you to go with her to New York? She's going to pay your passage, put you up in her home—'

'And Martie's passage, too. We're both going.'

'Martie Cass?' Valerie Raynor's expression was a mixture of astonishment, relief and possibly envy. 'Well, I don't know what to say!' she cried. 'Except that I was planning to have a little talk with Martie Cass, too – you might tell her that. I did say, didn't I, that I have eyes in my head?' Mrs Raynor put her hand to her brow. 'Oh, why do things have to work out so badly? I try to find

144

good staff, and you two were so good, I was so pleased, then I find – you know what I found—'

'I'm sorry if you think we've let you down, Mrs Raynor, but we haven't, we really haven't. Please try to understand.'

'You're both leaving, that's all that need concern me now.' Mrs Raynor stood up. 'You'd better let me have your notice in writing as soon as possible.'

Outside the office, Alex stood very still. She felt quite sick. Humiliated. As though Mrs Raynor had taken from her all that made her respect herself as a person and left her naked to the world. What hurt the most was the injustice of it all! There had been no relationship with Dr Raynor. He hadn't talked to her because she was young and pretty, she hadn't talked to him to try to take him away from his wife. They'd had a friendship, that was all, and now that friendship was over. Only a word or two had done it, only a drop of two of accusation, of jealousy, and everything was poisoned. She found a chair and sank into it, not even checking her watch, though she knew she should have been somewhere, seeing someone. How could she face anyone with her eyes full of unshed tears? When she had lost her good name?

'Are you all right, Alex?' Dr Best, pausing with an armful of case notes, stood gazing down at her with some concern. 'You look as though you've just been taken ten rounds!'

'I'm all right, thanks.' Alex stood up, bravely meeting Wendy Best's considering eyes. She had never had much to do with Dr Best, who was tall and angular, with a long thin face and dark hair so casually cut, the nurses joked that she cut it herself. Perhaps she did, she wasn't one to care for appearances. All the same, Alex guessed she had been less than fair to her, when she had described her as uninteresting. A person of Dr Best's intelligence was never going to be that.

'I should make yourself a cup of tea and pull yourself together before you meet any patients,' she crisply advised Alex now. 'You've had a shock, haven't you?' As the tears overflowed and began to trickle down Alex's cheeks, Dr Best clicked her tongue with impatience. 'Oh, for heaven's sake – look, you'd better tell me about it.'

She hurried Alex down the corridor into a small side ward, rarely used.

'Now, what's happened? Quickly, tell me. You're not going to be able to cope unless you do.'

'I – don't want to talk about it.'

Dr Best's eyes shone with understanding. 'Has Mrs Raynor been getting at you?'

'I said – I didn't want to talk about it.'

'Come on, I can guess what she said. Hands off my husband, eh? Oh, Alex, couldn't you have seen it coming?'

Alex, dashing the tears from her eyes, was stung to reply.

'It wasn't true what she said, Dr Best! There's nothing between Dr Raynor and me, there never has been! All we've done is have a few talks, walked on the shore—'

'And if he'd been your husband, would you have been happy about that?'

'Yes, because I'd have trusted him! I'd have known it meant nothing!'

'Would you?' Wendy Best gave a cynical smile. 'You'd have trusted him to become friendly with a young and very pretty nurse? Enjoy being with her? Seek her out?'

'Just to talk, Dr Best! Just to talk about medical matters!'

'What the hell does it matter what you talked about? He wanted to be with you. He's a middle-aged guy whose wife is married to the Fidra Bay. He's a specialist who gave up his specialty and who now regrets it. Is it any wonder he's trying to find comfort?'

The tears were drying on Alex's cheeks. Her eyes were fixed on Dr Best's face with as much concentration as though she were trying to translate words from a new language.

'What are you saying?' she whispered. 'I tell you, there's nothing between us.'

'But Mrs Raynor doesn't know that. She thinks he's planning to trade her in for a younger model. I believe you, I'm sure he isn't. But can't you see it from her point of view?'

Alex drew back, colour flooding her face again.

'I thought – I thought she didn't mind. All this time, I thought – she understood. Oh, God, I've been a fool, haven't I?'

Wendy put her hand on Alex's shoulder. 'You're still very young. Have a lot to learn. My advice would be to move on. This set-up's not for you.'

'I am moving on.' Alex laughed bitterly. 'To New York, as it happens.'

Somehow she found the courage to get through the rest of her duties. Washed her face, put on shadow to conceal the redness of her eyelids, saw to her patients. Finally, she told Mrs Adamson she would go to New York with her. And Mrs Adamson's delight gave her the first comfort of the day. Someone wanted her. Someone needed and appreciated her. New and different tears started to her eyes and mixed with her eye make-up, but Lois was so engrossed in her happiness, she didn't notice.

'Oh, my dear, I'm so glad, so glad! Oh, I can't tell you what a relief it is, that I'm going to have your support! Now pass me my bag, would you, please? And my notebook and pencil? We have work to do!'

'Don't tire yourself, Mrs Adamson, take it easy. There's no need for you to make the arrangements.'

'Surely I can at least make lists?' Lois was already happily writing away. Warren could book the passages, Warren could send the cables home. Alex and Martie must have their photographs taken and apply for passports. Alex and Martie must also buy steamer trunks and new clothes, lots of new clothes . . . Lois looked up into Alex's face.

'Now, you won't mind if I help you girls out, will you? You really will need a nice wardrobe for the voyage, and I know you don't have a lot of money to spare. Why should you be out of pocket because of me?'

'Mrs Adamson—'

'No, I'm going to insist, Alex, and you're going to have to humour me. All my life, I've wanted daughters to dress and now I've got the chance to dress you two, I'm not letting it go. Warren will take you to your lovely Princes Street shops and you can choose what you need. Or, if I'm well enough, I'll come too!' Lois lay back in her chair, laughing. 'Oh, Alex, my dear, we're going to have such fun!'

Throughout that long afternoon, Alex had managed to evade Dr Raynor, but he caught her at last, as she was bracing herself to face supper. Would folk have heard of Mrs Raynor's accusations? There was no one who would have told them, yet somehow word could have got around. Brooding on this possibility, she was on her way to the nurses' dining room when Hugh Raynor appeared at her side.

'Alex,' he said softly. 'May I speak to you?'

'I don't think it would be a good idea.' She was already looking over her shoulder, fearing to see Valerie Raynor's icy eyes.

'I must speak, all the same. Won't you stop a moment, please?'

'Dr Raynor, I'm in enough trouble as it is, don't make things worse.'

'Alex, what can I say? My wife has made you suffer for something you haven't done. You know and I know the truth of the matter, but she won't believe it. I've tried to explain, but she sees what she wants to see.' He reached for Alex's hand. 'I'm sorry, my dear. It's my fault. I should have foreseen how things might have looked to her.' He gave a short laugh. 'When you're married, you can't just be innocent, you have to be seen to be innocent.'

'Seems when you're no' married, too.' Alex withdrew her hand from his. 'Look, it's all right, I was a fool maself no' to guess what she might think. Let's no' talk about it any more.'

'You'll be away soon,' he said quietly. 'You'll be free.'

For a moment, she was reminded of Kenny. Butterfly girls were beautiful he had said, butterfly girls could fly away when he could not, butterfly girls were free. She had not thought it true, yet here she was, leaving this clever middle-aged man caught in the trap of his own choice. He was as much a prisoner in his own way as Kenny had been in his, and her eyes meeting his were suddenly filled with compassion.

'I shan't forget you, Dr Raynor. I'll always feel glad I knew you.'

'Thank you for that,' he said simply. 'You've made things easier for me.'

She knew that if they'd been alone, he would have kissed her, a sweet sad kiss of farewell, but they weren't alone, they were never alone, except when they walked by the Forth. And even there, they had been watched.

'Coming to supper?' asked Martie, passing and looking back at her.

'No need to say goodbye just yet,' Hugh Raynor said quickly.

'Not yet,' Alex agreed, and slid away.

No one looked at her differently at supper, no one seemed to know about the row with Mrs Raynor. What they did know now was that Alex and Martie were to go to America with the Adamsons, and though some were admiring, others were resentful. Why Alex and Martie? Why not them?

'We're just lucky,' declared Martie, her truculent gaze going round the table daring anyone to say more.

No one did.

After supper, in her room, Alex told Martie what had happened between her and Valerie Raynor. Martie was suitably disgusted.

'Good God! She's crazy if she thought there was anything between you and Dr Raynor. Everybody knows you just talked work. I mean, most people would have died of boredom if he'd talked to them like that, eh?'

'You told me once to watch out for her, though, didn't you?'

'That was a joke!'

'I should have thought more about her feelings, all the same.'

'Oh, give me strength!' cried Martie. 'Why do you always have to see other people's point of view?'

'I didn't, did I? See her point of view?'

'So, you don't mind that she nearly gave you the sack?'

'She didn't give me the sack. Or, you, either.'

'Me? Where do I come into this?'

'She told me she'd eyes in her head and had been planning to have a little talk with you, too.'

'I'm in disgrace as well as you? She's got her nerve! I haven't done anything!'

'Seems you have to look innocent as well as be innocent.' Alex gave a weary smile. 'So Dr Raynor says.'

'Seems he's right. Oh, to hell with it all!' Martie suddenly laughed. 'We're off to New York with the Adamsons, why should we care?'

Trouble is, I always do care, thought Alex, getting ready for bed. Tomorrow she was beginning night duty. That meant long hours when thoughts could come to her, for there were rarely emergencies at the Fidra Bay. She would have to concentrate on the good times that were to come. Put everything else right out of her mind.

Chapter Twenty-Five

'New York?' cried Arthur Kelsie, 'Alex, when'll I see you again?'

'New York?' sniffed Edie. 'My word, Alex, you're a lucky girl, eh? Wish somebody'd take ME to New York!'

'What a good idea,' murmured Jamie. 'Alex, you'll be able to bring me back a wedding present from some jazzy store, eh? If Martie leaves anything. I expect she'll go crazy in New York.'

'New York?' wailed Sid and Tilda. 'Och, what a place to go! You'll just have to carry on until the wheels come off, Martie, and then it'll be too late, eh?'

'Too late for what?' asked Martie. 'To save for ma old age? I'm no' having one!'

'New York?' wrote Rose to Alex. 'That should be a wonderful opportunity for you and for Martie. But don't stay too long. By now you should both be staff nurses, you know, climbing the ladder in some good hospital.'

'Climbing the ladder in some good hospital?' Martie repeated. 'I tell you, if I meet a Wall Street banker, I'll no' be climbing any ladders except ma own!'

'You're still looking for Mr Rich?'

'You bet. And if I don't find him in America, where will I find him?' Martie gave Alex a sidelong glance. 'No date yet for Jamie's wedding, eh?'

'He says they need time to save. Wants to put down a deposit on a flat.'

'You might still get to go to the wedding, then? Might be back in time?'

Alex looked at her in surprise. 'Won't you? Be back in time?'

'Well, we don't know exactly how long we'll be staying in America, do we?'

'They're pretty strict over there, I mean about how long they let folk stay. We'll probably only be allowed to do temporary work.'

'What are you talking about? We don't need jobs, we're going as private visitors. Mr Adamson's visitors.' Martie smiled, a little smugly, Alex thought. 'He'll fix anything that needs to be fixed, he told me so.'

'I see.' Alex studied Martie for some moments. 'And then of course, if you find your rich man, you won't be coming back anyway, will you?'

'That's right!' Martie's smile had become quite sunny. 'Listen, have you made out your list of what clothes you need? We're due to go to Logie's next week, remember. Oh, Alex, are we no' lucky? To be given so much?'

'I've told Mrs Adamson I'm only taking the money for the clothes as a loan. I'd rather be independent.'

'Oh, why say that? What they spend on clothes for us will be peanuts to them!'

'Maybe, but they're going to be giving us such generous salaries, I reckon I'll be able to pay back a loan. It's what I'd rather do, Martie.'

'Well, I'm no' offering,' Martie snapped, her face clouding. 'Why'd you always have to make things so difficult, Alex?'

'When Shona called Mr Adamson your sugar-daddy, you didn't like it, did you?'

'It's Mrs Adamson who's paying for the clothes.'

'I just want to make ma position clear from the start.' Alex set her chin in the way she did when she was not to be moved. 'Mrs Adamson understands.'

'Well, I don't!' cried Martie.

However the clothes were to be paid for, buying them was a joy.

'It may be frivolous, but it's true, buying new clothes gives women a lift,' said Lois, in the hire car on the way to Logie's in

Princes Street. 'Whenever I've had a little tiff with Warren – does happen, you know – I've always managed to cheer myself up by buying a hat or a dress. Now, Warren would never try to make himself feel better by buying a suit, would you, dear?'

'I should say not,' Warren replied. 'Men like wearing old clothes, not buying new ones.'

In the back seat, Martie knocked Alex's arm. Both were thinking that if Warren Adamson didn't like buying new clothes, he must suffer a lot, for they had never yet seen him in anything old. Their eyes met and they wanted to giggle, for no real reason except that they felt happy. Everything was working out so well. It was a beautiful day, they had managed to switch shifts so that they both had time off, they were going shopping in one of the best stores in Edinburgh, and Mrs Adamson felt well enough to come with them.

'This is what they call a red-letter day,' Martie whispered. 'Sometimes I have to pinch maself to make sure I'm no' dreaming.'

'You can pinch me, too, then,' Alex replied, her toffee-brown eyes dancing. 'I'm dreaming with you.'

Out of nightmare, into dreams. That was how it seemed, for suddenly she felt able to put the bad times behind her. Surrounded by the affection and good will of the Adamsons and with a rosy future to look forward to, Mrs Raynor's suspicions seemed very far away. As for Tim Burnett's rejection, she had no room in her mind for that at all.

'Now you girls had better tell me where I can park,' Warren called, as they drove into the city. 'And when we get to the store, I guess you'll be wanting me to make myself scarce?'

'Just come back to pay the check dear,' said Lois, smiling. 'Shall we say we'll meet you here for lunch at one o'clock? That all right with you, girls?'

'Mrs Adamson, everything is all right with us,' said Martie fervently.

Letty Kelsie had never shopped at Logie's, though would have done if she could, for she always used to say she liked 'good'

153

things. It was, however, far too expensive for her, and Alex's experience of it as a child had been restricted to gazing at the commissionaire who stood outside the swing doors ushering in the customers as though they were royalty. And sometimes they were, for Queen Mary and the Princess Royal often came over to shop when they were staying at the Palace of Holyroodhouse. Tilda Cass, of course, would not have patronised Logie's, even if she could have afforded it. Why waste money on things you could get for far less at the Stores? she used to ask, and if you shopped at the Co-operative Stores you got your dividend, too!

'What Mum never understands is that shopping at a place like Logie's is something special in itself,' Martie murmured, as they were welcomed through the swing doors by the present commissionaire, not so grand as the old one, but grand enough. 'It's the atmosphere, eh?'

'Oh, yes, it's lovely!' cried Lois, eyeing the elegant furnishings and beautifully made-up assistants. 'You know, it's just as good as anything back home, but different. Scottish, you see! Oh, my God, will you look at those tartan drapes?'

'You mustn't stand too long, Mrs Adamson,' Alex reminded her gently. 'Let's find the lift.'

'Elevator, Alex,' corrected Martie, with a grin.

'We're no' in New York yet, Martie.'

'And, remember, I haven't even finished my vacation!' cried Lois. 'I'm not quite ready to say goodbye to Scotland!'

She was bearing up well for this, her first outing, thought Alex, as they were whisked up to Ladies' Gowns, though she was a little pale. They would have to watch that she didn't do too much.

Oh, but Lois didn't want to be watched, she was having far too much fun! Perched on an elegant sofa, she superintended proceedings like a general organising troops, and superior assistants jumped to do her bidding just as soldiers would have jumped to obey orders. Because she had the rank, thought Martie, she had the money, and Logie's assistants were expert, no doubt, at recognising money, old or new. Whatever would they think of Alex and Martie herself? Probably knew by what they were wearing, underwear especially, that they weren't used to shopping at Logie's. So what? Martie tossed her head. She didn't give a damn what they thought, she was replacing everything, anyway, and as long as the bills were paid, why should they care?

'Evening dresses first!' commanded Lois. 'You'll need at least three.'

'Three?' echoed Alex in dismay.

'Three, minimum,' declared Lois. 'And we'd better be working out something for the costume night, too. There's always a costume ball, you know, and some people go to such trouble to bring something really extraordinary! Warren wears a tuxedo and a black mask and makes that do, but you girls will want to do better than that. After the evening wear, we'll want to see cocktail frocks, day dresses, sports things—' She opened her eyes at the assistant. 'Oh, are they not in this department? You'll bring us a selection, won't you, my dear? And sweaters – it can get chilly on deck.'

'If we've nothing else, we've got sweaters,' said Martie. 'We're Scots! Let's see this evening wear, eh?'

Alex and Martie had never truly appreciated the power of clothes, until they saw themselves in the dresses so haughtily presented by Logie's grand assistants. Alex, in guipure lace and apricot chiffon, Martie in midnight blue; Alex in cream silk, Martie in dark red; Alex in emerald green, Martie in shining white! They were different people. They had no connection with themselves. Butterfly girls? Oh, they were flying now. If they'd ever had chrysalis cases, they'd certainly left them behind.

Lois seemed quite overcome by their transformation. 'Now, didn't I say you'd need three dresses, minimum?' she asked, touching her brow with a scented handkerchief. 'And wasn't I right? Because you'd never be able to choose between these dresses, would you? You look so lovely in them all!' She caught an assistant's black-sleeved arm. 'We'll take them, my dear.'

'All of them, Madam?'

'All of them. Please have them sent to the Fidra Bay Nursing Home. Could we see your cocktail wear now? Thank you so much.'

*

155

'I never realised it was so tiring, spending money,' gasped Martie, when they were giving themselves a break for coffee in the restaurant. 'But you know, Mrs Adamson, I've decided I should do what Alex is doing and pay you back out of salary. It's just too much, what you're giving us, we can't let you do it.'

Lois raised her hand. 'I'm not even going to discuss it at this point. I'm enjoying myself so much and I'm feeling so well, I won't let you spoil things with money talk. Alex, dear, would you pour me some more coffee?'

'Are you sure, Mrs Adamson? You know it's no' good for you.'

'A tiny cup won't hurt.'

Alex, frowning slightly, was concentrating on filling Lois's cup, when suddenly Martie gave a cry.

'Why, there's Rose! Now, what's she doing in Edinburgh? I thought she was in Aldershot?'

'Rose?' Alex gave Lois her coffee and swung round. 'Where? Where is Rose?'

'There – look, she's seen us, she's coming over!'

Chapter Twenty-Six

How well Rose was looking! She'd had her hair cut and it suited her, made her seem less severe, defined the lovely shape of her face and brought new brilliance to her dark eyes. In a light summer suit, with a blouse open at the neck, she was far removed from Staff Burnett of the Jubilee. But we've all changed, thought Alex. She'll see we're different, too.

There were smiles and greetings, introductions, questions.

'Mrs Adamson, this is our friend, Rose Burnett,' said Martie. 'She's a nurse, too, we were all at the same hospital. Rose, this is Mrs Adamson, from the Fidra Bay.'

'The lady from America?' Rose smiled and bent to shake Lois's hand. 'I'm so glad to be able to meet you. How are you?'

'Oh, so much better, Miss Burnett, thanks to the Fidra Bay. Please, won't you join us? Let me order more coffee.'

'Thank you, I'll bring my shopping over. But please don't worry about coffee, I've had too much already!'

'Snap,' murmured Lois, watching Rose threading her way through the tables to fetch her shopping. 'Goodness, what a beautiful girl!'

'Looks even better than she used to do,' commented Martie. 'Wonder why she's here?'

'Took some leave to do some shopping,' Rose explained on her return. 'I'm going to Cyprus in September.'

'Cyprus? How lovely!' Lois exclaimed. 'Don't they call that the jewel of the Levant?'

'I believe it is very beautiful.' Rose put her parcels to one side and sat down at their table. 'Though to be honest, I'd rather be going to Korea, or somewhere where there's a bit of action.'

'Trust you!' said Martie. 'Anyone else would give their eye-teeth to be getting some Mediterranean sunshine!'

'Action?' Lois repeated. 'But why should you want action, my dear, as a nurse?'

'I'm an army nursing sister. A member of the Queen Alexandra's Imperial Military Nursing Service.' Rose smiled. 'A QA for short.'

'Now I do know about Queen Alexandra!' Lois said proudly. 'She was the wife of your King Edward and you have an Alexandra Rose Day for charity, don't you? I remember buying a little pink rose flag when I was over in London before the war.'

'I was named for that Queen,' Alex put in. 'My mother once saw her when she came to Edinburgh, and thought she was so lovely.'

'And I always thought you were called after the flag day!' Martie teased. She turned to Lois. 'But do you know that at our last hospital, some folk called us the butterfly girls? That was because we worked in wards that had a butterfly shape. Seems funny to think we're all going so far away now, Rose to Cyprus, Alex and me to New York!'

'Butterflies on the wing,' said Lois. 'That's such a sweet idea.' To Rose, she added, 'I'm so grateful to Alex and Martie, you know, agreeing to go back with me to America. They've really put my mind at rest.'

'It's a wonderful opportunity for them,' Rose said smoothly. 'I shall have to wish you all *bon voyage*.'

'Yes, it won't be long before we're off. We've been buying new clothes today, we're all ready.'

'I've been buying clothes too. Thought I'd better come up for summer things before the autumn stocks arrive.'

'I guess it's hot in Cyprus?' asked Lois.

'Pretty hot, though it's a dry heat, usually quite comfortable.' Rose smiled. 'They say even the winter is like a Scottish summer.'

They laughed and gathered their things together, Lois shaking

Rose's hand and wishing her all the best before she and Martie retired to what Lois called the 'Powder Room'. Rose put her hand on Alex's arm.

'Don't rush off,' she murmured. 'Tell me how things are with you.'

'Fine. I'm OK. Quite over – you know who.' Alex hesitated. 'I will ask if he's still well, though.'

'He's still well. He's just graduated, joins my father's firm in October.'

'Good for him. Rose, it's lovely to see you. You will write from Cyprus? I can give you the New York address now.'

'Of course I'll write.' Rose took the scrap of paper Alex gave her. 'But I meant what I said before, Alex. Don't stay in America too long.'

'I'm no' planning to do that.'

'Mrs Adamson is charming, I can see you're going to have a wonderful time, but it might be like living on chocolate over there. You'll want a proper diet, eventually.'

'Oh, Rose!' Alex gave a rueful smile. 'Everybody's allowed chocolate once in a while!'

'Yes. All I'm saying is, don't eat too much.' Rose glanced at her watch. 'I'd better go, Mother's expecting me for lunch. Just one more thing – Mrs Adamson, she's the heart case, isn't she? Didn't you tell me she had valvular disease?'

'Yes, but it's no' too bad. They say she doesn't need surgery.'

'All the same, I think she could be trying to do too much, spending the whole day shopping. I suggest you take her back, to rest.'

'She's really quite recovered, Rose. I mean, she'd have been discharged from the Fidra, if she'd had a home here.'

'Maybe, but she's looking tired. Excitement isn't good for people like her.'

Alex nodded. 'All right, better be safe than sorry. I'll tell Mr Adamson we won't stay on for lunch.'

After Rose had left, Alex went to find Lois and Martie. They needn't buy anything more that day, then when Mr Adamson came, they could drive back to the nursing home.

*

159

'I'm so sorry we didn't get your costume outfits,' Lois said in the lift back at the Fidra Bay. 'And the lunch. I wanted to give you girls something special.'

'And you don't think you've given us something special?' asked Martie. 'Seems to me we're loaded with things you've given us, and what we're no' carrying is being sent!'

'I meant a nice meal, just to round off the morning.' Lois sighed as the lift doors opened and Alex took her arm. 'But you were very wise to tell me to come back. I really feel all in.'

Alex and Martie exchanged glances.

'Early bed!' Alex said briskly. 'And I think I'll get one of the doctors just to give you a wee look-over.'

'No, no, there's no need to trouble anyone, I'm not feeling ill, just weary.'

'It'll be no trouble. Martie will find who's on duty and I'll help you to get ready for bed. You'll feel much better after a nap.'

Lois obediently allowed Alex to prepare her for her rest, though she said it did seem hard to have go to bed when the afternoon sun was still shining. Whatever would Warren do with the rest of the day?

'What will I do?' asked Warren, coming in after parking the car. 'Play golf, I guess.'

'It's too late, surely?'

'OK, I'll take a nap myself.' He grinned. 'I find department stores very tiring.'

'Why, you were all morning in the Royal Mile, weren't you?' Lois, lying back against her pillows, was already sleepy. 'I bet you spent as much as we did, on books and stuff!'

'Honey, we'll argue about that later – here's the doctor to see you.' As young Dr Parr came in with his stethoscope, Warren said he would wait in his room. 'You'll let me know how she is, Doctor?'

'Of course.'

Alex, moving to the door with Warren, looked down at Lois's notes in her hand. 'I hope we didn't tire her out today, Mr Adamson.

'I'm sure you didn't. She was fine.'

I'm no' so sure she's fine now, thought Alex.

160

But Dr Parr, a soft-voiced young man with a pleasant bedside manner, assured everyone after his examination that there was no need to be alarmed. Mrs Adamson had done a little too much and with hindsight maybe shouldn't have been given permission for the day out in town, but after a good long rest, she'd be as right as rain in the morning.

'Why does everybody say as right as rain?' Lois asked drowsily, as Warren held her hand. 'I'm sure rain isn't particularly right!'

'Time to close your eyes, darling,' said Warren. 'I'll look in on you later, see if you need anything.'

'Do you think Mrs A.'s OK?' Martie asked Alex.

Alex hesitated. 'Stuart Parr said so. There are no murmurs, no chest pain. I think it's true, she's just exhausted. I feel bad, don't you? We shouldn't have let her come with us.'

'Och, she was happy, Alex! It was her first bit of fun for weeks!'

'As long as it was worth it.'

'You'll see, she'll come up like a flower after a rest. There's no' really a lot wrong with her, and she's no' that old.'

'What upsets me is that it was Rose who told us to take her home. She's still ahead of us, Martie.'

'Always will be,' said Martie without concern.

That night, Alex found it difficult to sleep. If she hadn't changed her shift, she'd have been on night duty and for the first time that she could remember, wished she was. Then she could have looked in on Mrs Adamson. Why was she still so anxious? Conscience, perhaps. In spite of what Martie had said, Alex felt in her heart that she shouldn't have allowed Mrs Adamson to come with them to Logie's. 'Excitement isn't good for people like her,' Rose had said, and Alex herself knew that well enough. Everyone could make a mistake, of course, but nurses shouldn't make mistakes and this wasn't her first. Folk said she was good at her job, but she had risked Tim Burnett's progress when she'd visited him in his chalet, and now she had risked Mrs Adamson's. Oh, God! But things seemed worse at night, didn't they? She'd be better if she could sleep.

But when sleep finally came, it was as tiring to her as though she'd stayed awake. She dreamed she was back in Logie's, trying on dresses again. But they were all grey and black and purple, funereal colours, and she kept desperately trying to persuade Mrs Adamson not to buy them. 'They're for death, they're for funerals,' she cried, 'don't buy them, don't buy them!' 'Oh, but I must, my dear,' Mrs Adamson answered, smiling, 'you'd never be able to choose between them, would you, and you look lovely in them all! Have them sent, please.' 'Where? Where? Have them sent where?' the assistants asked, but Mrs Adamson wasn't saying.

'Mrs Adamson, where are you?' Alex screamed. 'Mrs Adamson, come back, come back! Mrs Adamson!'

She was still dryly screaming when she woke up, her hands flailing, as though she were fighting off an attacker, her sheet twisted round her neck.

Oh, what a dream, what a nightmare . . .

She sat up in bed, staring into the darkness of her room, shivering now as the sweat cooled on her body. Her alarm clock, when she snapped on the light, showed the time as only two o'clock, the low point of the night. Hours to go before morning, when she could go and check on Mrs Adamson. Maybe she should get up and make herself some tea? No, she would pull her bed together, put the light out, and try to get back to sleep. But if she went to sleep, would she dream again?

'To sleep: perchance to dream: ay, there's the rub . . . ' Seemed she shared something with Hamlet. How her father had loved spouting those lines, 'To be, or not to be!' It soothed her a little to remember him in the happy days, her mother too, and as she felt easier, her eyes closed and she slept again. This time she did not dream, though in the morning, when her alarm shrilled at six, she couldn't say that she felt at all refreshed. It was a relief to get up, wash and dress, and sprint out of the nurses' wing, up to Mrs Adamson's room.

'Why, good morning, dear,' Lois said, sitting up in bed with one of her lacy jackets round her shoulders. 'You're an early bird, aren't you?'

'I felt such a fool,' Alex said to Martie at nurses' breakfast. 'Worrying about her all night and there she was, looking as fit as a fiddle!'

'Told you,' Martie replied. 'There's steel inside that thistle-down. She'll probably outlive us all.'

'All the same, her pulse was a wee bit fast, I think I'll just look in again, after this.'

It was another beautiful day, the morning sun streaming into the upper corridor, as Alex made her way back towards Mrs Adamson's room. She paused to look out of the window at the dancing waters of the Forth, saw where she had walked with Dr Raynor, felt a little pang because she would not walk with him again, and turned away.

'Alex! Alex' someone screamed, and it was Jeannie, one of the domestic helpers. She was standing at the door of Mrs Adamson's room, her face as white as chalk. 'Oh, Alex, come quick, come quick! I canna wake Mrs Adamson!'

'Wake her? She is awake!' cried Alex, already running, her heart thundering in her chest, 'I spoke to her maself!'

'Aye, and I took in her breakfast.' Jeannie stepped aside as Alex hurtled past her. 'There's the tray, see – toast and coffee-that's all she wanted – she hasnae touched it—'

And she never will, thought Alex, a shaking hand at her lip. Mrs Adamson would never eat breakfast again.

It was just like the time Kenny died, back in the Jubilee. Everything that could be done was done, but there was never any hope. Lois's heart had stopped and could not be made to beat again. There had been no attack as such, she would have known none of the pain, none of the terror. As Dr Raynor told Warren, summoned from his bath, his wife's face told its own story. She looked as tranquil as a child sleeping, and without her make-up, almost as young. Her hair fell across her brow, her eyes were closed, the lines of her mouth sweet in their repose.

'Sometimes death comes quietly like this, without pain, without

163

struggle.' Dr Raynor put his hand on Warren's shoulder. 'When it does, we must take consolation that the person knew nothing, it would simply have been like falling asleep, the gentlest, most peaceful way to go.'

Warren, wrapped in his damp towelling robe, nodded.

'You'd like to be alone for a little while, Mr Adamson?'

'Please.'

They left him with his dead.

Chapter Twenty-Seven

'At least, we won't need a post-mortem,' Valerie Raynor murmured, her face twisting with anxiety over this death that shouldn't have happened in her nursing home. 'You and Stuart were treating her, Hugh, the Fiscal will accept your death certificate.'

Hugh was leaning against the wall, spent with effort and emotional strain, wrapped in his own thoughts. 'If only we could have done more,' he muttered. 'If we'd had better techniques, we might have saved her.'

'Her heart was exhausted,' Stuart Parr declared. 'She had no symptoms of her complaint when I examined her last night, clearly the heart was just tired of pumping. We did all we could, it was nobody's fault.'

Alex, standing with Martie, gave a strangled sob, but Martie made no sound. She seemed bewildered. Shell-shocked, thought Hugh, glancing at her. An old-fashioned term for a state that was as old or as new as you liked, the inability to take in a reality that was too terrible to bear. He whispered something to his wife, who nodded.

'Martie – Alex – go and make yourselves some tea. You were close to Mrs Adamson, I'll get someone else to see to her.'

'I want to see to her,' Alex said clearly. 'I want to do whatever's necessary.'

'We can't do anything until we've discovered what Mr Adamson's wishes are,' Hugh said gently. 'And first we must inform the Fiscal.'

'I'll ring his office now,' said Valerie. 'And then I think I should get the funeral directors out. If Mr Adamson wants to take his wife home, they'll need to do the preparations.'

'Take her body home?' whispered Martie. 'On the ship? On the Queen Mary? Oh, no, no! No, it's too horrible, it's too awful!'

As tears began to pour down Martie's cheeks, Alex took her by the arm. 'Come on, let's go across and make some tea, eh? Look, it's all right, you'll feel better soon.'

'Usually such a strong girl, Nurse Cass,' Stuart Parr remarked, as the two nurses made their wavering way towards the lift. 'Who'd have thought she'd crack like that?'

'Have you forgotten?' asked Hugh. 'Those two were to have gone back with the Adamsons to New York, they were to have been Mrs Adamson's private nurses. Now her body is going back without them.'

'Oh, my God, of course!' Stuart shook his head. 'I wonder what they'll do now?'

'What indeed?' asked Valerie Raynor.

'Alex, I can't take it,' Martie said brokenly. 'I can't, I really can't. It's too much, you see. It's just too much.'

They were in the sun-filled nurses' kitchen, luckily just the two of them; at that time of the morning, no one was making elevenses. Alex stirred sugar into Martie's tea and pushed the cup across the table towards her.

'I know, I know. I feel the same. And so guilty. We should never have let Mrs Adamson come with us to Logie's, I'll never, never forgive maself for that.'

'You're talking about Mrs Adamson. I'm talking about us.'

'Us?'

'Us no' going to America. No' going on the ship. No' going anywhere.' Martie's drenched blue eyes were shifting away from Alex's wide brown gaze. 'You think I'm selfish, saying that? Think I don't care about Mrs Adamson? I do, I do! And I care about Warren. I'm thinking of them both, all the time. But it's just so hard, you ken, to be so close, and have to give it all up.' She drank some tea, nodding drearily. 'First time in ma life I was going to get the chance for the good life. Travel on one o' the Queens, mix with the rich, wear pretty clothes – och, Alex, think of thae dresses! Did you see me in that gorgeous blue? And the white? I'd never seen such material, had you? And now what happens? We never wear them, we go nowhere. I tell you, I can't take it, Alex, I can't!'

'Martie, these things happen, there's nothing anyone can do.' Alex refilled Martie's cup. 'Drink some more tea, try to be calm. You'll feel better in a little while. It's just the shock.' Alex's eyes were apprehensive on Martie's face. 'Anyone'd feel shock, after what happened. But think of poor Mr Adamson, Martie. All alone now.'

'I told you, I am thinking of him!' Martie suddenly jumped up and took a packet of cigarettes from behind a tin of tea in one of the cupboards. 'Shona's,' she muttered. 'Keeps them here to make it difficult for herself to have a smoke. She'll no' mind if I take one. Want one, Alex?'

'You know I don't smoke.'

'Neither do I. Usually.' Martie lit a cigarette and blew smoke. 'But I feel like one now. If I'd a whisky, I'd drink it.'

'Martie, let's go and see Mr Adamson! Let's tell him how much we care.' Alex rinsed the cups under the tap and turned to Martie, drying her hands. 'I think I might feel better, if I could talk to him. If he could say he doesn't blame us.'

'You said once you'd never feel better.' Martie blew her nose. 'That's how I feel now. Like I'm wrapped in black curtains that block out all the light. There's no light, Alex, no light anywhere. Never will be.'

No light. It did seem like that. A totally dark future. Alex dashed her own tears from her eyes.

'Let's go,' she said quietly. 'Let's get back on duty.'

Mr Adamson was very kind. He was in his room when they found him, immaculately dressed in grey, with a grey silk tie, gold cufflinks, white handkerchief in his pocket, all just as usual, except for his poor face that was as grey as his suit. When they tried to tell him how they felt, how devastated, how guilty, he said

167

there was nothing to feel guilty about. What had happened to his Lois could have happened any time, in fact he'd been expecting it for years, which didn't make it any easier, now that it had come. But they weren't to worry at all about the day in Logie's. Everyone had thought she was well enough to shop, and he personally was glad her last day had been so happy. He was glad, too, and very grateful, that she'd had two such wonderful nurses to take care of her in her last illness. They had been like daughters to her, and he would never forget their kindness.

'It was Alex, mainly, who looked after Mrs Adamson,' Martie said, clearing her throat. 'You should no' give me the credit.'

'No, no,' cried Alex. 'It wasn't just me. Everyone here was really fond of your wife, Mr Adamson, everyone wanted to help.'

'Well, I'm certainly grateful.' Warren's eye sharpened. 'Listen, did you hear anything out there? I'm waiting for the funeral directors. I have to make arrangements.' He faltered for a moment, then regained his composure. 'And I want to see Lois one last time.'

Tears sprang again to Alex's eyes. 'We'll leave you,' she said softly. 'But don't worry about the arrangements. Mrs Raynor will tell you when the funeral directors arrive, she'll fix everything for you.'

'Yes, I know she's very efficient.' Warren heaved a long painful sigh. 'Everyone's being so wonderful. And I won't forget you two. I'm really sorry about the trip, you know. Lois was so looking forward to taking you to our home. Talked about it all the time.'

'Oh, please, what does a trip matter, at a time like this?' Alex sent a desperate signal to Martie, but her swollen eyes were cast down. Warren's gaze rested on her.

'How do you feel, Martie? ' he asked quietly.

She looked up. 'I'm just so sorry for you, Mr Adamson. It's so terrible – going back alone—'

'I know. I was in touch by telephone with my son just now. He wanted to come right over, but I said, what's the point? I'm bringing your mother home. He said to take a plane, but I can't face that. Lois always hated flying. We'll go by sea, as we always planned.'

*

As the girls came out of Warren's room, they saw the undertakers approaching, carrying a coffin. They grew cold inside. Experienced as they were, they had never become used to the terrible divide between those who were living and those who were not. Mrs Adamson, so pretty in her silk bedjacket, smiling, talking, was now something very different, something to be placed in a box, set apart from all she had loved. How could you truly accept that? They were trained to accept it, but there were times, all the same, when feelings took over.

'I wanted to lay her out,' Alex whispered. 'That should have been my job.'

'We'd better get out of the way,' Martie said, sniffing. 'Here's Mrs Raynor, she'll be fetching Mr Adamson.'

They backed away to the lift, bracing themselves for work elsewhere. Probably there would be a lot of calming down to do with the patients. Death was always unsettling, and in the Fidra Bay not as common as in those nursing homes catering for the elderly and the seriously ill. No one had believed Mrs Adamson to be seriously ill. She shouldn't have died, that was the point.

Crossing the reception hall, they saw a delivery man bearing in a load of long elegant boxes. As he approached the desk and spoke to Sylvia MacKenna, Martie clutched Alex's arm.

'Deliveries for Miss Cass and Miss Kelsie?' asked the man.

The clothes from Logie's had arrived.

Chapter Twenty-Eight

Gradually, things returned to normal at the Fidra Bay. The Procurator Fiscal, whose responsibility it was to investigate sudden deaths, accepted Hugh Raynor's death certificate for Mrs Adamson and her body was allowed to 'rest' at the funeral parlour until it was time for the last voyage home. As soon as he could, Warren removed himself to the North British Hotel, after having made, it was rumoured, a very generous donation to the nursing home when he paid his bill. No one knew for certain, of course, but Mrs Raynor was looking distinctly sweeter, and it was the sort of thing Americans did, so everyone believed. Nor was there any doubt that Mr Adamson's tips to the domestic assistants were really quite extravagant, and when the doctors and nursing staff refused to accept money, he brought in chocolates and fine wine. When asked how he had managed to obtain them, he only answered, 'Ways and means, there are always ways and means.' By which, they knew, he meant the almighty dollar transformed into the Scottish pound.

To Alex and Martie he insisted on giving the clothes his wife had helped them to select at Logie's.

'It may not be possible for you to go on the trip, but you will at least take the dresses?' he urged. 'You know my wife would have wanted you to have them, without any question of paying back loans or anything of that sort.'

'Mr Adamson, you're very kind,' Alex replied, 'but when would I need three evening dresses and all those cocktail frocks? I don't have the sort of life for clothes like that.'

'You'd make me very happy, if you kept them. Please.'

Alex and Martie exchanged glances.

'I'd like them,' Martie said at last. 'Thank you.'

'Alex?'

She gave a sad smile. 'I'll keep them too, then, if you're sure.'

'I'm absolutely sure. And before I leave for New York, I want you two to have dinner with me in Edinburgh, as a last farewell. Will you do that?'

They agreed, of course, though it was Alex's view that such a dinner could only be an ordeal. Wouldn't they feel the presence of Mrs Adamson at the table with them? Wouldn't she be in all their hearts? If it made Mr Adamson happy, though, it would be worth going through with it. Time was hurrying by. Soon, he would be out of their lives for ever. They would have to give some thought to where they wanted to go, once they themselves had left the Fidra Bay.

All their colleagues were being very nice to Alex and Martie, now that their good fortune had failed to materialise. No trip to New York, eh? What a shame! But the sympathy was genuine, especially as most knew how attached they'd been, Alex in particular, to Mrs Adamson.

Mrs Raynor was being nice, too. There must certainly be some truth in that rumour about Mr Adamson's donation, for she was pleasanter than anyone could recall, even to Alex. Possibly, she had come to realise that Alex was indeed no threat to her marriage, and now that she wasn't going to America, should be persuaded to stay on at the Fidra Bay. It would certainly be a pity to lose her.

'Have you given any thought to what you might do now?' Valerie Raynor therefore asked Alex one afternoon in her office. 'I know it must have been a terrible disappointment to you, losing the trip to the States.'

'Yes, but I think more than anything I was upset about Mrs Adamson.'

'You'd become very close.' Mrs Raynor gave a sympathetic smile. 'But life goes on, doesn't it? Eventually, you have to think of yourself. I've been wondering whether you and Martie would consider staying on here?'

Alex hesitated, deciding how best to be tactful. 'I can't answer for Martie,' she said at last. 'I've been very happy here maself, but the truth is, I'd rather go back to TB nursing.'

'I was afraid you'd say that.' Mrs Raynor sighed. 'I'm sorry we had that little disagreement, you know. I'm afraid I did get hold of the wrong end of the stick, I see that now.'

Alex's heart lifted. She murmured a word of thanks.

'If you should change your mind, you'll let me know? Sister Grey and Sister MacAlister both speak very highly of you. I might be able to offer you promotion.'

Alex was polite, but knew she would not be changing her mind. Though it was a great relief to have Mrs Raynor's apology, her accusations had left their mark, and with the death of Mrs Adamson, there was sadness too. The time had come to go, at least for Alex. What Martie wanted was uncertain. She said she hadn't made up her mind.

One heavy August afternoon, when she was hurrying back to duty from the nurses' wing, Alex was surprised to see Martie with Warren Adamson. They were walking together across the front lawn, heads bent, completely absorbed, it seemed, in conversation. But Martie, glancing up, saw Alex and waved, calling her to come over.

'I haven't got time,' Alex answered.

For a reason she couldn't define, she was already alert to possible trouble. Martie was looking so happy, wasn't she? Almost radiant. What could have happened so suddenly to make her look like that? Only something Warren had said. Instinctively, Alex felt she didn't want to know what it was.

'Oh, come on, won't take a minute!' Martie grabbed her arm and drew her towards Warren, whose look was rueful, yet oddly defiant. He reminded Alex of a child found out being naughty and not sorry, though aware he should be.

'Alex,' Martie was saying in a low breathless voice, 'Warren's got something to ask us.'

172

'Is this the place to talk?' asked Alex. 'Everyone can see us from the windows. And it's so hot!'

'I'm sorry, I won't keep you long,' Warren said quickly. 'It's just that it came to me – quite suddenly – that you and Martie should still be going to New York.' He wiped his brow with his immaculate handkerchief and gave an uneasy smile. 'It was like a flash, really, I saw that it would have been Lois's wish. She'd never in this world have wanted for you two to miss out on your trip because of her. And the strange thing is that I never tried to cancel your tickets. It was as though I knew, subconsciously, that you'd still be needing them.'

There was a silence, as the afternoon sun beat down and the eyes from the windows of the nursing home beat down too; or so Alex imagined. She looked from Warren's face, now so anxious, to Martie's, filled with exposed delight. What was she supposed to say to them? If they had fooled themselves, did they think they could fool her?

'Alex, what do you think?' asked Martie, so excited she could scarcely keep still. 'It's lovely, eh? Of course, Warren is no' suggesting it'd be the same for us on the ship, I mean we'd no' be going to parties or dances, because that wouldn't be right.'

'No, it wouldn't,' Alex said tightly.

'He's just saying the passages have no' been cancelled, so we could still go, be a help to him, maybe, then attend Mrs Adamson's funeral and – you know – help out there. And then, do some sightseeing, that sort of thing—'

At the look on Alex's face, Martie swallowed and blinked her eyes hard in the sunlight. Some of her euphoria seemed to be evaporating, but she still had plenty to say and was determined to say it.

'Thing is, Alex, it would still be a terrific opportunity, because we might even get jobs for a bit, and we do need something. We've given in our notice here and you want to leave, anyway, so, this would be the answer and at the same time we'd get a trip abroad that we're never likely to get again.'

Martie paused and looked expectantly at Alex.

'Will you no' say something?' she cried. 'It's right what Warren says, for God's sake! Mrs Adamson would have wanted it for us, she would! You know that's true!'

173

'No, I don't know it!' Alex answered sharply. 'Mrs Adamson wanted us to go to America as nurses and companions for her, no' for her husband. It isn't the same thing at all, for us to go with just him!'

'Alex, please!' Warren murmured, and Alex turned on him.

'How can you even suggest it?' she demanded. 'How can you even think of going to the States with your wife's body and a couple of young women like us? What are people going to say? How are you going to explain it?'

'Quite simply,' he replied with dignity. 'I shall say, if anyone asks, that I am doing what my wife wished, taking her two devoted nurses back to the States for a holiday. Not with me. I am not suggesting you stay with me. That would of course be quite inappropriate.'

'No' with you?' Alex flashed a look at Martie. 'Where, then?'

'With his sister!' cried Martie. 'You didn't wait to let me tell you that. Warren is going to ask his sister to put us up in New York. She's very kind and has a daughter our age.'

'Just the people to show you round,' Warren added. 'You'll have a far better time with Ursula and Bonnie than you'd ever have with me. All I'm offering is a very quiet voyage as a thank you for all you did for Lois. I'm sorry if you don't like the idea.'

'I didn't say that.' Alex was aware that in some way the tables had very neatly been turned on her, and that it was now she who appeared in the wrong, not Mr Adamson. But of course, he was a banker, an experienced man of the world, used probably to squashing much cleverer people than she. 'It's very kind of you to think of us,' she murmured, trying to recover ground, 'and I am grateful, I really am—'

'So you'll agree to go?' pounced Martie.

Alex put her hand to her head, throbbing in the sun. 'I don't think so, thanks all the same. I told Mrs Raynor I wanted to work in a TB hospital again and that's what I'm going to try to do. You go, Martie, if you like. It isn't for me, to tell you what to do.'

'Alex, you know I can't go without you! Two of us going – that'd be all right, but if there was just me—' Martie halted, her face scarlet. 'Alex, you have to come with me, there's no other way!'

174

'But if you're staying with Mr Adamson's sister, I don't see the problem.'

'You do see the problem,' Martie moaned. 'You do, and you won't help!'

'Mr Adamson could still say you were his wife's nurse, that would be perfectly true.'

'Alex, can't you see that for Lois's sake I want both of you to come?' Warren asked in a low voice. 'Martie is right, it wouldn't be the same without you, but not for the reasons she thinks.'

'It's no good,' Martie cut in, as Alex stood in misery. 'Once she's set her chin like that, you can't shift Alex. Always says I dominate her, but when it comes to it, she calls the tune. Every time.'

'Oh, Martie!' Alex whispered. 'I don't want to spoil things for you. It's just that – well, if it isn't the same without me, it isn't going to be the same without Mrs Adamson, is it? That's the way I see it.'

'All right,' Warren said with decision. 'Let's leave it, shall we? I have to get back to Edinburgh, anyway.' He gave Alex a pleasant smile. 'Don't forget our dinner, will you? Martie has the date.'

'I'll look forward to it.' Alex glanced at the watch on her uniform and shook her head. 'Oh, God, I should have given Mrs Thornwell her pills half an hour ago! I'll get shot!'

With immense relief, she left them, not wanting to know what they might say to each other, and went skimming over the warm grass into the house. They watched her go.

'I'm sorry, Warren,' Martie murmured. 'That's Alex for you.'

He fixed her with his dark hazel eyes. 'You won't consider the trip without her?'

'You wouldn't want me to, would you? It's right enough, you see, folk would talk.'

'Not if I explained things. The voyage is just a way of getting you to the States so that you can have your vacation. You'd be with my sister, once we reached New York.'

'That's true.'

'And you'd be a great help to me, Martie. I can't tell you what a difference it would make to me, knowing you were around. Can you imagine what it's going to be like, taking my Lois back?' Warren's voice faltered. 'I don't honestly know how I'm going to get through.'

Martie, glancing back at the windows of the nursing home, put her hand on his arm.

'Warren, I'll come.'

'You will?' He covered her hand with his. 'And you do understand how things are? Alex doesn't, you see. Thinks because I want your company, I'm forgetting Lois. It's not like that at all.'

'I understand how things are.' Martie's blue eyes were very direct. 'Don't say any more.'

Chapter Twenty-Nine

It was goodbye time. Goodbye to Rose, soon going to Cyprus. Goodbye to Warren Adamson, going home. Goodbye to Martie, going with him, much to everyone's disapproval. Goodbye to Alex, going – where? She didn't yet know, but she was saying goodbye anyway.

'I can't believe you're really leaving,' Hugh Raynor told her on her last morning. They were standing outside his office, not attempting to slip inside for a few moments' privacy; Mrs Raynor was nowhere to be seen, but they still looked round for her, as though they were dissidents fearing the secret police. Hugh's face wore the defeated expression it had taken on in recent weeks, but if he was unhappy, he would be blaming only himself, thought Alex. That was his way.

'I can't believe it, either,' she told him. 'But I'm all packed and ma brother's coming over to drive me home this afternoon.'

'You're going to your father's?'

'Till I find something.'

'No luck so far? I did my best for you with my reference.'

'Oh, you did, and I'm very grateful. But there's no TB nursing advertised at the moment. I've written to several places, just on the off-chance, but they had nothing.'

'How about the Jubilee?'

Her face darkened a little. 'I haven't tried there.'

'Keep on, Alex. Something is sure to turn up in your field.' He smiled grimly. 'At least, one of us will be happy.'

177

'Don't talk like that,' she said quickly. 'You're doing wonderful work here, you're needed!'

'Am I? All the people here could be as well treated elsewhere, only they might not be so comfortable.'

'You shouldn't look at it that way.'

'Think I'm an ungrateful bastard? Think I have a very good life at the Fidra Bay? You're right, of course.'

'The truth is, I just wish you could be doing what you really want.'

'If I'm not, it's my own fault. Should have gone for it, shouldn't I? Be like Martie Cass. Do what you want and to hell with what people think.'

'You make her sound worse than she is, Dr Raynor.'

'Hugh,' he said gently. 'For this last day, call me Hugh. Sorry, I don't mean to run Martie down, I admire her very much, but she's a tough one, isn't she? So's Adamson, of course. He goes for what he wants, too.'

'I'm sure he loved his wife.'

'Oh, he did. But now he's lost her, he's not prepared to lose Martie, is he?' Hugh shrugged. 'Just hope it works out for them.' His eyes softened. 'And for you, Alex. I wish, you know, things could have been different.'

'Yes.' They exchanged long tender looks.

'I suppose we can't say keep in touch?' asked Hugh heavily.

'We'll get news of each other somehow.'

'Have to make that do. Oh, God, I hate this saying goodbye!' He took her hand and held it. 'But listen, when you're playing ducks and drakes, remember you need a FLAT stone and hold it the way I showed you. Don't forget!'

'I won't forget, Hugh.' Alex's smile was tremulous. 'I'll never forget!'

She and Martie had a last lunch with their colleagues, at which they were presented with travelling clocks as leaving presents and Mrs Raynor said a few diplomatic words, wishing them both good luck in the future, to which they made embarrassed replies. Afterwards, they went to say goodbye to the patients, a task that brought tears to Alex's eyes, for many of them expressed real fondness for her and sadness at her departure.

'Such a lovely, kind girl, my dear,' sighed arthritic Mrs Thornwell, taking her pills from Alex for the last time. 'The other nurses here are very good, but they don't all care like you, you see. I've been in so many nursing homes, I can always tell the people who care.'

'I shall miss you,' Alex told her. 'I'll think about you. I'll think about you all.'

'And I believe you will,' said Mrs Thornwell. 'I suppose you won't take my pearl ear-rings, will you? I never wear them and I'd like you to have them.'

'I couldn't do that, Mrs Thornwell, thanks all the same.'

'Some chocolates, then. I got my daughter to spend my sweet points at Logie's. The Talisman Selection, do you like them?'

'Oh, yes, I love them, how very kind!' Alex, ignoring the stab of pain memory could still sometimes deliver, took the chocolates and kissed Mrs Thornwell's wrinkled cheek. 'Goodbye, take care!'

'Are you coming?' cried Martie from the corridor. 'Somebody says Jamie's car's at the door!'

'I must just have one last look out.'

Alex ran to the landing window and looked out at the Forth and the distant islands. Fidra, Craigleith, the tiny Lamb. She realised she had never taken that boat trip to Fidra, never gone round the Bass Rock. Where had the time gone? The afternoon was fine, with a high blue sky and cotton wool clouds; just the day to walk on the shore and play ducks and drakes, but there was no one to do that. She turned away, conscious of Martie waiting by the lift, and walked slowly to join her. It was along this corridor she had flown to Mrs Adamson's room that terrible morning. The room was just there, she would have to pass it, but there was no point in stopping, someone else had it now.

'Wish you'd get a move on,' said Martie. 'We've still got our cases to collect.'

'What's the rush? Jamie'll wait.'

Jamie was now working in Edinburgh, sharing a rented flat with two friends while he struggled to save the deposit for a mortgage. The housing shortage was acute; even if he found the money, he didn't know if he'd find a property, but the provisional date for his wedding had been set for Christmas. Alex was secretly hoping it would never happen, for she found Heather Craik, her future sister-in-law, rather difficult, but what Jamie decided to do, he usually succeeded in doing. Martie, who had never met Heather, said she didn't sound at all right for Jamie, but then Martie was never likely to approve of anyone Jamie married.

'I just want to get going,' Martie muttered now. 'I'm tired of everybody here looking at me sideways.'

The farewells were over at last and they were waving from Jamie's car, as it moved from the portico of the Fidra Bay and those who had come to see them off. Alex, from the front seat, craned her neck, hoping to see Hugh, but it seemed he hadn't made it. Mrs Raynor was there, however, waving a manicured hand, which made Martie, in the back seat, smile.

'Glad to see the back of us,' she commented, 'Of me, anyhow. Doesn't approve of me. I told her what I did and where I went was none of her business.'

'How about your folks?' asked Jamie.

'My folks?'

'What do they think about you going to America with just an old guy?'

'Alex, you told Jamie!' Martie was colouring furiously. 'You needn't have done that.'

'Alex didn't tell me, I worked it out for maself.' Jamie drove out of the gates of the Fidra Bay and made the turn for Edinburgh. 'She just said the trip was off because this Mrs Adamson had died, so when I heard you were still going, I knew what to think.'

'Oh, God, Alex, did you tell your folks as well?' cried Martie. 'About Mrs Adamson?'

Alex twisted round. 'Yes, why not?

'Why not? Because they'll have told mine and I'll be out on the street if they think I'm going to New York with just Warren!'

'The old guy,' muttered Jamie with scorn.

'My folks mightn't have said anything to yours,' said Alex, troubled to think that Martie had not told her parents about Mrs Adamson's death, or that her original trip had been cancelled. Could that mean that all along she'd secretly been hoping she might still go? That Warren would still ask them? Or, at least, her?

'She's a tough one,' Hugh had said, 'so's Adamson, of course.'

Tough, because they knew what they wanted and took it. How little you can ever know of other people, thought Alex. After all these years, she could still be surprised by Martie.

'Hope you won't mind if I come round to your place, asking to be taken in,' Martie said darkly. 'Or maybe I could try yours, Jamie?'

'You could try,' he said shortly.

'I suppose Heather wouldn't approve of you sharing with another woman?'

'Let's no' talk about Heather. When do you leave, anyway?'

'On Wednesday. The day after our dinner with Warren, Alex, don't forget. I'm taking the train to Southampton.'

'Lucky you.'

'Yes!' Martie cried. 'Lucky me!'

It seemed she was indeed lucky, for her parents had not heard of Mrs Adamson's death and made her as welcome as they usually did, within their own limits. Two days later, following a quiet and uneasy dinner with Warren at the North British Hotel, Alex saw her off at Waverley Station, standing in for Sid and Tilda, who could not, they said, get away from work.

'Trust them!' commented Martie. 'It'd take World War Three to get them to give up work for five minutes!'

'Well, at least, you're leaving on good terms,' said Alex. 'It would have been awful, if they'd really thrown you out.'

'Aye, and if they find out about Mrs Adamson when I'm away, it'll no' matter.'

Alex's gaze sharpened. 'Martie, you arc coming back?'

'Who knows?' Martie's eyes were wandering over the people on the platform. The guard had his flag ready, the great steam train was hissing and throbbing, ready to start. Porters were closing doors. 'I told you I might get work over there. Private nursing, probably.'

'You'll write to me? Keep in touch?'

'Do you have to ask?' Martie suddenly gave a sob and flung her arms around Alex. 'You write to me, eh? Tell me where you end up?'

'Oh, Martie !' Alex pulled herself away, as the guard put his whistle to his lips. 'Take care, and good luck!'

'And to you! Give ma love to Rose, if you see her.' As the train began slowly to move, Martie leaned out of the window, frantically waving. 'And dance for me at Jamie's wedding, eh? Goodbye, Alex, goodbye!'

Away went the train, rattling out of sight, and Alex, feeling flat, as those who are left usually do, turned to leave the platform.

Goodbye, Martie, she said to herself. Shall we ever meet again? She had her doubts.

Chapter Thirty

Strangely, even though she was jobless, Alex found she was quite enjoying being back at home. Until it was over, she hadn't realised how strained life had been latterly at the Fidra Bay; now, when she no longer needed to worry about Hugh or Mrs Raynor or Martie, she luxuriated in peace of mind and never ventured up the Archangel Steps in case she should see someone who might change all that. As for work, something would turn up. If necessary, she could always try England. She'd seen advertisements for posts there, one at the famous Papworth hospital, which would be very good experience. Meanwhile, she was glad to spend time with her father again, even treating him and Edie from her savings to Festival nights out at the theatre. It was worth every penny of the ticket price to see Arthur's pleasure when the house lights went down and the play began.

'Opportunity lost, eh?' he muttered during one interval. 'Should ha' been me up there on the boards!'

'Och, you're better off out o' that,' Edie told him, licking her ice-cream spoon. 'Acting's a risky business, Art, you're better off knowing where you are.'

But it seemed to Alex that her father knew only too well where he was and wouldn't have minded being somewhere else.

Sometimes Jamie came round to the Colonies with his tall, slim fiancée from North Berwick, who spent her time studying her engagement ring and yawning behind her hand.

'Och, now what sort of wife she's going to make, I canna think,' grumbled Edie. 'Niver does a hand's turn when she's here, eh? Niver so much as dries a cup!'

'And doesn't seem to want to be part of the family,' commented Alex.

'Too stuck up, and for why? It's no' as if her folks are anything grand, and she's no' even pretty. No' like that lovely friend of yours, Alex. I mean Rose. Now she's something special, eh?'

Rose. Alex hadn't heard from her, wondered if she'd already left for Cyprus. Then she received a postcard. Rose was coming up to say goodbye to her family. Could they meet at Logie's for coffee?

Not Logie's, Alex wrote back. She didn't want to be reminded of that euphoric time when they'd gone on the spending spree with Mrs Adamson. She named instead a little café in the West End, and Rose wrote back: 'Fine'.

Rose, looking as lovely as ever, appeared to have resigned herself to her Cyprus posting. She would be based in Nicosia, the capital, but was going to buy herself a little car – she'd passed her test two years before – and tour the island. From all accounts, there was plenty to see, from beaches to mountains, not to mention all the antiquities, the relics of the island's chequered history. You could even go skiing up in the Troodos mountains, and Rose thought she might give that a go.

'Sounds a perfect place for a holiday,' Alex observed. 'So, why are there British forces there?'

'Well, Cyprus is a British Crown Colony and Middle East base. I suppose the army and the RAF have to keep an eye on things. Sometimes there's trouble between the Greeks and the Turks, and some of the Greeks would like to see the British leave.'

'Where've I heard that before?' asked Alex, smiling. Rose passed a plate of shortbread.

'Alex, I was so sorry to hear about Mrs Adamson, she seemed such a nice person.'

'Yes. I was very upset by her death.'

184

'And you didn't want to go to New York without her? Unlike Martie?'

'You know Martie,' Alex murmured uncomfortably.

'Yes.' It was impossible to read the expression in Rose's dark eyes. 'But you could have stayed on at the Fidra Bay, couldn't you?'

'It wasn't really for me, Rose, you were right about that. I'd put ma notice in, so I just decided to go, anyway.'

'And you're not fixed up, at the moment?'

'Not yet.'

Rose's look was thoughtful. 'You really wouldn't consider joining the QAs? It's a wonderful life, Alex. Everyone's very professional, very dedicated, just like you. And then there's the travel – you could go anywhere in the world!'

'It's perfect for you, Rose, but I'm no' so—'

'Not so what?'

'Brave, I suppose I mean.'

'What nonsense! You don't have to be brave. Just good at your job, which you are.'

'Well, I still don't think it's for me. To tell you the truth, I'm really keen to get back to TB nursing, but so far, I've had no luck.'

'No luck? You haven't tried very hard, then. There's a staff nurse vacancy at the Jubilee.'

'The Jubilee?' Alex caught her breath. 'I hadn't heard. Who's going?'

'Anita Maxwell. She's getting married. Moving to Aberdeen.'

'You keep in touch with Anita?'

'No, I just happened to meet Jill Berry in Princes Street. She told me. The post's due to be advertised next week.'

Alex looked down at her plate. 'I'm no' sure I want to go back to the Jubilee, Rose. I pretty well blotted ma copy-book there.'

'Come on, that's all water under the bridge! And Sister Clerk's gone, you know.'

Alex's head jerked up. 'What happened to her?'

'Got a matron's post at one of the London teaching hospitals, lucky devil. . . Alex, there's no reason on earth why you shouldn't go back to the Jubilee. You have the experience and the qualifications, and I bet you've got terrific references, haven't you?'

'Dr Senior gave me a good one,' Alex admitted. 'And so did Dr Raynor.' She smiled a little. 'He's in charge at the Fidra Bay.'

'And would have been sorry to lose you?'

'You could say that,' said Alex.

The September day was fine and warm, the city pleasantly quiet after the Festival that had recently ended. After coffee they walked slowly home through the New Town, and so down into Stockbridge, from where they could reach Cheviot Square and the steps that led to the Colonies.

'Don't look so worried,' Rose said softly. 'He's in France, on holiday.'

'I'm no' worried!' Alex retorted. 'It wouldn't upset me to meet Tim again. That's all over.'

'Yes, of course.' Rose paused at her own door. 'Talking of holidays, why don't you come out to see me in Cyprus, when I'm settled? We could do some of those trips I was telling you about.'

'Cyprus?' Alex laughed. 'Rose, I've no' even got a job! There's no way I could afford to go to Cyprus!'

'You will have a job and pretty soon, too. And I've heard it's sometimes possible to get cheap flights with the RAF. If they're going out with empty planes, they let people have seats.'

'No' people like me, I'm sure.'

'I don't know, but I could find out. I'll write to you, anyway.'

Alex looked up at the solid façade of Rose's home, remembering the time she'd skulked round here, trying to catch a glimpse of Tim Burnett when he was a schoolboy. She put that memory from her with the resolution she always brought to memories of Tim. Aware of Rose's eyes on her, she straightened her shoulders and smiled.

'Don't look at me like that, Rose. I tell you I'm OK.'

'I just feel guilty, that's all. He is my brother.'

'You're no' responsible for him.'

'That's true. I don't know why I should feel like his older sister when I'm not.' Rose shrugged. 'Something to do with Mother, maybe. She always expected so much of me.'

186

'And no' so much of him? Some mothers are like that with sons.'

'But not yours, Alex. I always envied you as a child, you know, being so close to your mother.'

'You envied me?' Alex stared. 'I never knew!'

'Why should you? We all had our secrets, didn't we?'

They embraced quickly – Rose was not one for prolonged touching and kissing – and made their promises to write.

'And you'll try to come out to see me?' asked Rose.

'I'll certainly try. If I can get a job and some money together.' Alex laughed. 'I've no faith in your cheap RAF flights!'

'You'll get your job, Alex. Don't wait for the advert, put your application in right away to the Jubilee – that's where you belong.'

'A butterfly girl returning to base?' asked Alex, and when Rose looked mystified, reminded her of Kenny's name for the nurses.

'Butterfly girls? I remember poor Kenny, but I'd almost forgotten that.'

'Well, Martie's gone and you're next to fly, Rose.'

'Courtesy of the RAF?' Rose asked, smiling, and raised her hand in farewell, as Alex left her to run down the Archangel Steps home.

That evening, Alex wrote to the Jubilee, asking for details of any staff-nurse vacancies, and when an application form was returned, filled it in.

'You're niver going back there?' cried Edie. 'When you could've gone to America like Martie Cass!'

'I didn't want to go to America.'

'Well, Cyprus, then, like your friend, Rose. Alex, you'd have looked lovely in that QA uniform, eh? Nice grey dress and little red cape? Och, I can just see you in it!'

'Must have good eyesight, then, because I'm no' wearing it,' Alex said shortly. 'Look, Edie, I'm doing what I want to do, do you mind?'

'Aye, and what I want you to do too,' said Arthur, lowering the evening paper to look at her fondly. 'The Jubilee's just up the road, and that suits me.'

Alex folded her application form into an envelope, wrote the address and stuck on a stamp.

'I'm away to put this in the post, but don't forget, you folks, I've no' got the job yet.'

'As though they'd no' want Alex!' cried Arthur, when they heard the street door bang.

'Aye, but who'd ha' thought she'd turn down New York for the Jubilee?' asked Edie.

Chapter Thirty-One

Some ten days later, Alex received two postcards and a letter. She read the postcards first. One, from Martie, showed a picture of the New York Statue of Liberty. The other, from Rose, was of Kyrenia Harbour.

> *'Am settling in well,'* wrote Rose in her neat, straight hand, *'reorganising the medical centre, getting to know the island. Have bought an old Ford and am learning to avoid the grape juice on the roads! Visited this place the other day with a friend – it's quite beautiful and I hope to show it to you when you come. Do let me know about the job, Love, Rose'*

So, Rose had already made a friend, thought Alex. Male or female? Men would always be attracted to Rose, but whether she would ever let herself be sidetracked from her work was doubtful. Alex turned to Martie's card, so filled up by her outsize writing, there was very little space for news.

> *'Terrific place and everyone very kind,'* she had written. *'Things pretty sad, though, with the funeral and everything. Hundreds came, wish you could have seen the flowers. Hope all is well with you, Love, Martie.'*

H'm. 'Things pretty sad . . . ' Well, they would be. Martie could hardly have expected otherwise. But what exactly had she expected? Alex thought she could read a certain feeling of disappointment between the bold dark lines, but she could be wrong, and hoped she was. Maybe a letter would tell her more, if Martie ever got round to writing. Now that Alex had the address – care of Mrs R.W. Mayfield, obviously Warren's sister – she could write herself, anyway. Tell Martie about the job. If there was anything to tell. With shaking fingers, Alex opened her letter which she already knew was from the Jubilee, seeing as it had the name of the hospital on the envelope.

'Good news?' asked Edie, shaking crumbs from the tablecloth at the back door. Arthur had already left for work.

Alex gave a radiant smile. 'I've been called for interview to the Jubilee.'

'I'm sure that's the least you could expect. They ought to give you the job without an interview, eh?'

'Doesn't work like that. Would have been nice though.' Alex carefully studied the letter again, as though it might have said something different. 'Wonder what I should wear?'

The day of the interview was autumnal. A chill sunlight showed the leaves already drifting from the trees lining the drive; there was the smell of a bonfire burning somewhere in the grounds. Alex, wearing the same brown suit she had worn for the interview at the Fidra Bay, paused for a moment, letting the memories return. Water under the bridge, flowing fast. From here she could see the nurses' home and Butterfly Two. Through the trees were the chalets. Why look? She would have to look, if she came back here to work. Anyway, she didn't mind looking. Water under the bridge. She walked on, watching patients in the distance working in the vegetable garden; children exercising with an instructor, coughing as they swung their arms and bent and stretched, poor little devils. This is the place for me, thought Alex, I want to come back, I must come back.

'Alex?'

A man was coming towards her. Tall, rangy, dark-haired, a face that was well-known.

'Mr Drover?'

At the look of delighted recognition in his eyes, she felt an answering pleasure. He took her hands and his were dry and strong, the hands of someone well.

'Oh, it's so good to see you,' he told her. 'How come you're back?'

'I've got an interview. Staff Nurse Maxwell's job.'

'Ah, yes. I saw the ring on her finger. Well, if they go on looks, you'll walk it, Alex, you're looking wonderful! The Fidra Bay has done you good.'

She brushed that aside. 'What about you? You're well?'

'Never been better. Just had my check-up – I'm doing very well.'

'I'm so glad. Look, it's been really nice seeing you again, but I have to go—'

'Ah, come on! What time's your interview?'

'Three o'clock.'

'You're early! You've plenty of time.' He took her arm and steered her towards the trees. 'Just spare a few minutes to tell me how you are. Are you happy? Did you like the Fidra Bay?'

'Mr Drover—'

'Neal. You can call me Neal now. I'm not a patient, and you're not my nurse, we can talk together like ordinary people.' He hesitated. 'That's if you want to talk to me?'

'Of course I do.' She looked distractedly at her watch. 'Some other time, though?'

'You mean that? Could we have a drink, or something?'

'Neal, I really must go.' She laughed. 'I'll need to comb my hair.'

'It's beautiful. Take that hat off, let them see it.'

'I'll be in touch, I promise.'

'No, let's fix it now. Could you meet me in town next week? Shall we say Wednesday, seven o'clock? We could have a meal.'

'Where?' She was already turning away.

191

'At the Caledonian. I'll book dinner.'

'The Caledonian? Heavens, are we celebrating?'

'Sure. Why not?'

'I've no' got the job yet.'

'There are other reasons for celebrating.'

She ran back and pressed his hand. 'I know, your health. All right, I'll see you on Wednesday. Goodbye, Neal.'

'Good luck!' he called after her, as she walked quickly up the drive. 'But I don't think you'll need it.'

There were three people on the interviewing board – Dr Senior, a man from the health authority and the matron of the Jubilee.

Please God, may she not have heard any rumours about me, thought Alex, taking her seat and preparing to put on her big act of calmness and composure. But Matron was smiling. Surely she wouldn't have been smiling, if she'd known about that episode with Tim? Or have agreed to Alex's being called for interview in the first place? Alex breathed a sigh of relief. She felt a boost of confidence that was instantly dispelled by Mr Frazer, the man from the health authority, asking,

'Why did you leave the Jubilee for the Fidra Bay, Nurse Kelsie?'

Her eyes went round the room. She could hear the clock ticking on the wall behind her. Noises off, from the hospital corridors. Someone calling, 'Nurse, nurse!' Why had she left the Fidra Bay? To get away from memories? Couldn't say that.

'I'd just made SRN,' she said at last. 'I thought I'd go for different experience.'

'Private nursing home experience is not usually as demanding as hospital experience.'

'No.' Alex cleared her throat. 'I suppose I found that out.'

'And wanted to come back to our sort of hospital?' Matron asked kindly.

'Yes. Particularly a TB hospital.'

'Now, at the Fidra Bay, you were working for Hugh Raynor,' Dr Senior commented. 'He was a TB man himself, as I remember.

I knew him years ago at East Fortune.' He shifted papers on the desk. 'I see he's given you a very good reference.'

'We sometimes used to discuss new developments in TB treatment.'

'So, for someone working away from the field, you haven't lost touch with what we're trying to do?'

'I've tried not to, Dr Senior,' Alex added sincerely. 'It's always been ma real interest.'

For some time, they looked at her consideringly, then after a number of routine questions on nursing practice, asked her to wait outside. There were no other candidates in the side ward, where a chair had been placed for her, but Anita Maxwell put her head round the door and asked if Alex would like a cup of tea.

'Anita, congratulations!' cried Alex, gratefully taking the tea. 'Let me see your ring. Oh, it's lovely! When do you go to Aberdeen?'

'Next month.' Staff Maxwell herself looked down admiringly at the sapphire on her left hand. 'Barney's going as Senior Registrar up there – you remember Barney Henderson from the Infirmary? Ear, Nose and Throat?'

'Oh yes,' Alex replied, not remembering at all and wondering when the butterflies in her stomach would stop fluttering. Talk about being a butterfly girl . . . 'I do wish you all the best.'

'Thanks, I'll wish you the same. And, if I'm no' mistaken, it'll be congratulations for you, too.'

'For me?'

'Well, they've let all the others go,' Anita said carelessly. 'Och, it was always in the bag for you, Alex. You're a natural for ma job.'

'Nurse Kelsie?' A girl from Admin. had appeared, someone new since Alex's time. 'Would you step this way, please?'

It was only afterwards that Alex took in all that was said to her in the interviewing room.

The most satisfactory candidate . . . official contract to be sent by post . . . attend for a medical, present all necessary documents, be ready to start work on November 1 in Butterfly Four, a women's ward ... All she really heard at the time were Dr Senior's words, as he shook her hand, and Matron and Mr Frazer looked approvingly on:

'Welcome back – Staff Kelsie.'

Part Three

Part Three

Chapter Thirty-Two

It was the fourth Thursday in November. America's Thanksgiving Day. Martie Cass had been invited to the Adamsons' family dinner.

It'd be something the same as Christmas, she decided, only with cranberries and pumpkin pie, as well as turkey. Not that she'd had much experience of turkey Christmas dinners; at home, they'd sometimes had a chicken, but her mother was of the opinion that chickens didn't go very far, not compared with a nice joint that'd do you right up to Hogmanay! At the thought of Edinburgh's Hogmanay, Martie was mortified to find her eyes full of tears. Och, you great soft thing, she told herself, you're no' feeling homesick still?

Not really. She'd settled away pretty well, she thought, considering. Considering what? Well, the funeral and everything. And her own position, as neither friend nor member of the family. It hadn't been easy. Hadn't been easy from the word go, when she'd boarded the Queen Mary and found that Warren was too absorbed in grief to do anything but stay in his cabin and think about Lois. Martie had understood, had appreciated his feelings, in fact, and thought herself a fool for not realising how it would be, when poor Mrs Adamson was as she was in the hold. The voyage never could have been anything but a nightmare, it was just that Martie'd thought she could have been more of a help to Warren. Wasn't that why he had invited her along? As it was, she hadn't been able to do a thing, just sit at meals with strangers, not daring to wear anything but her own dreary wardrobe, not in fact, wanting to.

And then there was the arrival in New York that should have been so exciting, but was only an ordeal, because there was Brent Adamson to face, and he, so tall and handsome, like his father, had made it plain he found her presence quite unacceptable.

'Mother's nurse?' he had said, raising his dark eyebrows. 'Oh, of course, the one who's come for a holiday.'

And the way he'd said 'holiday' – as though Martie was out to enjoy herself while the family sorrowed – had made her cringe. His girlfriend, Julia Conway, a slender blonde in well-cut black, had made Martie cringe, too, just by running her cool eyes over her. Pricing ma clothes, adding pounds to ma weight, thought Martie, who'd hoped she'd fare better with Warren's sister, Ursula Mayfield. But the immaculately presented Mrs Mayfield seemed only baffled by her brother's inflicting a visitor on her at this time, and oh, God, thought Martie, can I blame her? When George Mayfield, Ursula's husband, hardly seemed to recognise her existence, and Bonnie Mayfield turned out to be just such another distant blonde as Julia Conway, Martie had begun to feel that Alex had been right. She should never have come.

But she had come, and there wasn't much she could do about it. She'd held back her tears and melted into the background as far as she was able, avoiding Lois's friends and Warren's home, enduring the days until the funeral was over and things had become a little easier. That had been the time when she'd begun to appreciate the comfort and elegance of Mrs Mayfield's Upper East Side apartment; to feel at last what it was like to be surrounded by money, even if none of it was hers. And that was when Ursula and Bonnie began to unbend and took to showing her New York.

New York! What a city! It made remembered Edinburgh seem small, and even quiet. So many people of every colour and nationality, always on the move. Everything on the move. Martie had never seen so many automobiles in her life, so many traffic lights changing, people flooding across famous streets, impossibly high skyscrapers looking down. She came to recognise the Empire State Building, the Woolworth Building, the Chrysler Building, the Flat-Iron. She went window-shopping on Fifth Avenue, climbed up the Statue of Liberty, went walking in Central Park, looked at pictures in the Metropolitan Art Museum, and when she was encouraged to go out alone, clung on to tramcars, or found her way round the subway. The tears of homesickness died, only to return occasionally with sudden poignant reminders. I could really get to like it here, thought Martie, but at the end of four weeks in Ursula's house, she told Warren it was time for her to move on.

'Move on, my dear?' He looked at her with eyes that were beginning to look his own again and not some bewildered stranger's. 'Where on earth would you move to? You like New York, don't you?'

'I love it, but I'm thinking I'd like to find some sort of temporary job, if I'd be allowed.'

He smiled. 'There's no need for you to work, Martie. I didn't bring you here to do that.'

'I'm no' so sure now why you did bring me,' she said, after a pause. 'I'm no' really much help to you.'

'That's not true, Martie. I'm really glad you're here, you've no idea, I assure you.'

'The time's come for me to go, anyway. Mrs Mayfield's been very kind – wonderful – but I can't stay with her for ever. I want to get some sort of private nursing and maybe a place of ma own, before I go home.'

'Go home?' Warren appeared stunned. He grasped her hand. 'You're not thinking of that? Why, what would be the point? This is your chance to see America. We haven't even taken you to Rhode Island yet, and then there's all New England in the fall to see, you couldn't miss that. My God, you don't want to go home, do you?'

'Not now,' she answered patiently. 'But I'll have to go back sometime. I'm no' planning to emigrate.'

Warren released her hand and stood looking down at her. 'What sort of job did you have in mind?' he asked heavily.

'As I say, private nursing. I shouldn't think I'd get a job in a hospital, anyway.'

'Well, you're very experienced, and Scottish. The Scots are very highly thought of here. I'm sure we can fix up something.'

'I'd be very grateful.'

'But what's all this about a place of your own? What's wrong with Ursula's?'

Martie grinned faintly. 'Nothing at all, it's beautiful. But I've been there nearly a month and that's long enough.'

'For her, or you?'

'Both. I'm an independent sort of devil, Warren. You understand, don't you?'

'I do.' He touched her cheek briefly. 'Don't want to be grateful all the time, of course you don't, I should have seen that for myself. Look, leave this with me. I think I know the very job for you – if you'll take it.'

One week later, Martie was installed as private day nurse to Mrs Geraldine Adamson, Warren's invalid mother, with her own suite in the family house facing Central Park, and her own generous salary. It was all above board, Warren assured her. A temporary appointment that would upset no one, but would, he hoped, please his mother and Martie.

'What do you think?' he asked anxiously. 'I know Mother seems a bit of a dragon—'

You can say that again, thought Martie, remembering Warren's ill-concealed trepidation when he had first brought her into the old lady's presence.

'Mother, this is Martie Cass, Lois's nurse in the last weeks.'

'Lois's nurse?' Mrs Adamson, straight-backed in her wheelchair, had fixed Martie with a penetrating stare. She was a handsome woman still, in spite of the stroke that had twisted her mouth and robbed her of the use of her right leg. She had a high, scarcely lined forehead, her hair, dark silver like Warren's own, was thick and glossy, her nose aquiline and powerful. As for that stare, from dark-hazel eyes, it filled Martie with dread.

'And what's Lois's nurse doing here?' asked Mrs Adamson, her speech only a little slurred.

'Well, Lois had fixed up the trip for her and we thought – I thought – it would have been Lois's wish for Martie – Nurse Cass – not to lose out, you see—' Under his mother's gaze, Warren, once again her little boy rather than the family banker, had ground wretchedly to a halt, and Martie, before anyone could mention the word holiday, had put in:

'I really want to do some nursing here, it'd be a wonderful opportunity.'

'I'm sure.' With her 'good' left hand, Geraldine Adamson put a handkerchief to her mouth, which dribbled and infuriated her. 'Well, if you took good care of my dear Lois, I'm very grateful to you. Lois was like my own daughter, not a daughter-in-law. Her mother and I were at school together many, many years ago. We always said, when we had children, if one of us had a boy and the other a girl, they'd marry. And so they did!'

'So we did,' Warren agreed softly.

'And you were very happy, weren't you?'

'Very happy.'

Mrs Adamson lowered her sharp gaze and seemed to be struggling against tears. When she looked up again, she had mellowed a little. 'I hope you'll have a very pleasant stay here,' she said to Martie. 'And if you want work, I hope you find it.'

Well, I have found work, and with her, thought Martie, crossing her fingers as she told Warren she was very happy about her new job and he needn't worry about her and his mother, they'd get on like a house on fire.

'As long as you don't burn each other up,' Warren answered, laughing uneasily. 'I have the feeling you're two of a kind.'

Chapter Thirty-Three

On the evening of that Thanksgiving Day, Martie was helping Mrs Adamson to finish dressing for the dinner that was by tradition always held in her home, the old Adamson house where she had lived since her marriage. Both Warren and Ursula had been born there, following the long line of their forebears; their father had died there just before World War Two. Mrs Adamson's night nurse, Prissie Smithson, had told Martie in her fascinating, gossipy way, that old Mrs A. had wanted Warren and Lois to move in with her after she'd had her stroke, but young Mrs A. wasn't having any. ' And you can't blame her for that!' wheezed Prissie, who was overweight and often smoked three packs of cigarettes during the day before she came on duty. She and Martie both agreed, a little of Warren's mother went a very long way.

'Being British, I guess you won't know about Thanksgiving?' Mrs Adamson asked now, as Martie fastened her pearls for her and fixed in her matching ear-rings.

Martie's blue eyes met the hazel eyes reflected in the dressing-table mirror. 'As a matter of fact, I do know about Thanksgiving, I looked it up. It began in the seventeenth century, when the Pilgrim Fathers first gathered in their harvest. Now it's a national holiday, a bit like Christmas.'

'Very good.' Mrs Adamson gave her crooked smile. 'You're a bright girl, Martie. You'll go far. Whether in nursing, or something else, I couldn't say.'

'Nursing'll do me for the moment.'

'You don't have a young man, back in Scotland?'

'Nobody special.'

'I'm surprised. You're very attractive. Comb my hair again, will you, dear? That's right. And brush my collar.'

As Martie combed her hair for her and straightened her lace fichu, Mrs Adamson looked at herself approvingly. 'I'll do,' she pronounced. 'Now, you'd better put me in my chair and go get ready yourself. Don't be afraid to put on something colourful. We've all agreed that Lois would have wanted us to celebrate Thanksgiving just the same as if she were with us. In fact, we feel she is.' She gave a quick glance at Martie. 'Warren feels that, you know. Lois is with him all the time. You don't forget a person quickly when you've been married as long as Warren was married.'

'That's true.' Martie brought up her employer's wheelchair and helped her into it; she was feeling a little apprehensive about the way the conversation was going.

Mrs Adamson hesitated. 'You won't mind if I say this, my dear, but though Warren is obviously attracted to you, it can't mean anything. You do understand that, don't you?'

A bright, rose-red colour swept over Martie's face, her eyes flashed. 'Mr Adamson is no' particularly attracted to me,' she said shortly. 'I was his wife's nurse, that's all he's interested in.'

'Oh, come!' Mrs Adamson laughed. 'If you'd been a homely little bluestocking, do you think he'd still have been keen to bring you to New York?'

'There were two of us coming, ma friend, Alex Kelsie, and me, we were both due to come, we both nursed Mrs Adamson, you see.'

'But she didn't come? I wonder why?' Mrs Adamson studied the rings glittering on her now useless right hand. 'Well, never mind. Off you go and get changed. I don't want to be late for Thanksgiving in my own house.'

Martie, her colour still high, strode off to her own small suite, where she tore off her clothes and ran the wonderful American shower she loved so much. Damn the old devil, she thought, as the jets hit her skin, making her wince and gasp for breath, damn her for spoiling things between Warren and me! I want to stay, I do, but how can I, with her watching and guessing and thinking she knows something? What the hell could she know, anyhow? There's nothing to know. OK, he might be attracted, but he's never even kissed me! She lathered soap over her breasts and shoulders, luxuriating in the scent and warmth, letting her thoughts about Mrs Adamson run wild until she felt calmer, able to leave the shower, towel herself dry and very carefully dress.

She had been waiting a long time to wear one of the dresses Lois had bought her, and tonight was the night. Which should it be? 'Don't be afraid to put on something colourful,' old Mrs A. had said, but all the same, Martie didn't think the red would be appropriate. Nor the shining white, though it was so beautiful. The blue, the midnight blue, that was the one . . . 'Silk, Satin, Cotton, Rags . . .' The old skipping rhyme ran through her mind, as she took the dress from its hanger, running her fingers caressingly down the delicate silk, holding it against her body, closing her eyes, swaying and dancing round the room. She didn't need to trip on the chanted word 'Silk' any more. Here it was, the real thing. Silk. She'd got it. No' a wedding dress, of course, but who cared? That would come. The way she felt just then, she could have danced her way to the stars.

She laid the dress aside and put on her Logie's underwear, including a lightweight girdle that clinched her waist and made her groan. Oh, God, see how all those American doughnuts had taken their toll! She just wouldn't be able to eat anything at dinner, or else not breathe. If she looked good, it would be worth it.

When she was ready, she looked in her full-length mirror and gave a little sigh of satisfaction. She looked good, all right. Someone very different from uniformed Nurse Cass. A little bosomy, maybe, but her shoulders rising from the dark blue silk were smooth and rounded, not a salt-cellar to be seen. And the girdle had done a good job on her waist, for there it was, she had one, and from its slimness, the full skirts of the dress shimmered and rustled in a way that made her feel excited and special. Different. Oh, very different!

After a little while, however, the euphoria caused by her transformation faded. Maybe it wouldn't do for her to look too different? Too attractive? This was Lois's family she was joining for Thanksgiving, Lois's and Warren's, and Warren's mother had already put into words what the others might be feeling. It might be better to keep to her old place in the background, until she removed herself from this house as she had now planned to do. Och, yes, there was no reason why she should put up with old Mrs A.'s sniping!

Martie looked at herself again, in the stunning blue dress. Must she really take it off? Put on that old black skirt and cream blouse she'd been wheeling out for evenings until now? Lois had bought her the blue dress, would she not have wanted her to wear it? Martie put her hands on her waist and twirled herself round, sighing. Yes, Lois would have wanted her to wear it, but when she herself was alive. Things were different, now that she was dead, and Warren was alone.

'Goodbye, blue dress,' Martie whispered, returning it to its hanger. 'For now, anyway.'

'I'm ready,' she told Mrs Adamson, preparing to push the old lady to the elevator.

'Oh, my goodness, I thought I told you to put on something colourful!' Mrs A. cried, eyeing the black skirt and dreary blouse: 'Don't you have any pretty clothes, child?'

'I thought this'd be suitable.'

Mrs A. looked at her shrewdly, then gave a curiously knowing smile, made sinister by the droop of her lip.

'Ah, I see. I said you were bright, didn't I? And I wasn't wrong. But if that's the way you want to play it, that's fine by me. Come, push me along, then. The family's due any minute.'

This was the life! For the first time since Lois's funeral, Martie was able to see the way the Adamsons lived with all the stops pulled out. Ever since she had arrived in New York, the atmosphere in the family homes had been subdued, the style low-key; it was only to be expected. Now, with Thanksgiving, there was the

205

feeling that a celebration should be a celebration. It was what Lois would have wished and, after all, life must go on, right? Out must come the Adamson silver and crystal, the candles and dazzling table-linen, the finger-bowls, place-cards, great set-pieces of autumn flowers, peaches and grapes tumbling from ornamented epergnes that must take for ever to clean.

From her place at the foot of the table, a long way from Warren, of course, Martie's eyes went over the faces of the family and their guests. Warren and Brent, Ursula and George, Bonnie and her current escort, Hartley Parry, with his parents; Julia Conway with her parents, together with two senior partners from the bank and their wives. Mouths working, eyes sparkling, all so composed, so much at home, all belonging. Only Martie herself couldn't describe herself as that. Odd man out. Odd woman. The only one who didn't belong. Somehow, as she was served her turkey and cranberries and talked to one of the bankers (who said, as everyone did, 'Hey, I love the accent!'), she didn't care. It was enough to be breathing in this strange atmosphere, this oxygen of money, that went to her head more potently than the wine in her glass. I'd better watch out, she thought, better no' let maself get whoozy. But who would notice? Only old Mrs A. at the top of the table, who never missed a trick. Goodbye, Mrs A.! The time has come for you and I to part, to part! She almost sang the words of the old song.

At the end of the long meal, Mrs Adamson 'collected eyes' and with Martie smoothly pushing her in her wheelchair, led the women from the dining room.

'My, how pretty everyone looks'!' she exclaimed, in her upstairs boudoir, from where everyone was making for the bath-rooms. 'Now, don't they, Martie?'

'They do,' Martie agreed. She had of course already scrutinised Bonnie's strapless white taffeta, Julia's ice-blue satin, Ursula's heavy brocade, and knew that the clothes of even the elderly bankers' wives outdid her own outfit in style. What of it? The thought of the superb dresses hanging in her closet was something warm and comforting. Their time would come. She was happy to wait, and if Mrs A. thought she knew what she was waiting for, let her think it.

'Let's go down for coffee,' Mrs A. announced. 'If the men haven't finished their port by now, they've lost out, I say!'

'Quite right, Mother,' commented Ursula. 'All this splitting up of men and women after dinner is absurd, anyway.'

'Not at all, dear, it's a custom with a purpose. Gives everybody a chance to get to the WC without embarrassment. Martie, take me to the elevator!'

So used to eyes meeting hers and sliding away, it gave Martie a little thrill to find Warren's fixed on her and staying, as the women went into the drawing room.

'Martie,' he said quietly. 'Come and have coffee.'

'I'll just see to your mother—'

'Mother's fine, she doesn't need you, and I haven't seen you all evening, I want to talk to you. Who the hell put you so far away from me at dinner?'

Martie smiled, as she drank her coffee. 'You know whose house this is, don't you?'

'Mother'd have no reason to separate us,' he said quickly.

'Wouldn't she? Warren, I want to talk to you maself.' Martie glanced around. 'Though this is maybe no' the time or place.'

'That doesn't sound so good.'

Warren also looked around, as though he were some sort of conspirator, but no one was near them. The long room was alive with groups of people talking, as staff deftly served coffee; the flames of two log fires were leaping and dancing. Mrs A. from her wheelchair was discussing the President's mistakes, while the bankers agreed, and their wives' eyes roamed elsewhere. Brent and Hartley were talking cars, Bonnie and Julia, clothes; Ursula was asking if anyone else had bought a television set yet? George had insisted on installing a great monster in his den, but what could you see on it? Not a damn thing! Parlour games and news reports, and all in black and white!

'So what did you want to talk to me about?' Warren asked Martie in a whisper.

'I'm really sorry, but I think I'll have to leave.'

'Leave? What do you mean? You've just settled, you said you were happy!'

'It's your mother—' Martie lowered her voice. 'She thinks there's something between us.'

Warren turned pale. He set down his coffee cup. 'That's nonsense. She couldn't think that.'

'She said it was obvious you were attracted to me. I told her you weren't – well, no' the way she meant. But she laughed. Warren, it's no' easy for me, to put up with that. I'd rather work somewhere else.'

'Martie—' Warren was biting his lip, his expression hunted, when Brent came up, glancing briefly from Martie to his father.

'Dad, Grandma would like a word.'

'What in hell about?'

'I think she wants you to circulate.'

Warren took a deep breath. 'You go back and tell Grandma I'll circulate when I'm good and ready.'

'You really want me to say that?'

'Yes! Well, you could be polite, of course.'

As Brent shrugged and left them, Warren said quickly:

'Martie, we can't talk here. Tell me when you're free and I'll meet you. Anywhere you like.'

'I've got Saturday afternoon off. The agency nurse comes in then.'

'Right, I'll collect you, we'll walk in the park.'

Martie looked dubious. 'Collect me from here?'

'The next block, then. Or, by the mailbox. Mother won't see.'

'What time?'

'Two o'clock? We could have lunch—'

'Better not. Two o'clock'll be fine.' Martie gave an encouraging smile. 'Now, I'd better see if your mother wants anything.'

'I've a pretty good idea what Mother wants,' Warren muttered, before he turned to mingle, smiling, with his guests.

Chapter Thirty-Four

It was cold in Central Park. They had to keep walking, watching the children running and screaming through the last of the leaves, grown-ups hurrying briskly, birds wheeling, on the look-out for scraps. Martie was wearing her old Edinburgh navy-blue coat, with a round hat that made her feel like a nurse maid. Warren was elegant in black, with a wide-brimmed trilby, leather gloves and cashmere scarf. Martie thought he looked pretty good, for his age.

'Winter comes quickly to New York,' Warren remarked. 'Once Thanksgiving's over, the thermometer drops.'

'I'm used to cold winters,' Martie replied. 'Try walking up The Mound in January!'

'It may seem cold in Edinburgh, but I'll bet it's never as bitter as here. You'll see, when the first snow comes.'

Martie tightened her scarf against the wind. 'Why are we talking about the weather, Warren?'

He took her arm. 'Because it's easy.'

'You'll have to say what you want to say sometime.'

'I know. I'd better say it, then.' He stopped and taking her arms turned her towards him. 'When the time comes, Martie, when I can really ask you, will you marry me?'

It seemed they couldn't go on walking and somehow found themselves in a small café where Warren said no one would know him, and judging from the clientele, who seemed to be students in huge sweaters and baseball caps, Martie thought he was probably right.

All she wanted by then was to be warm and have something hot to drink and comforting to eat so that she might pull herself together, and when Warren brought coffee and great sugary doughnuts, she managed to smile and thank him. Beyond that, was a block. She didn't know what to think, or what to say, though he was looking at her, and waiting. She knew she must say something.

'I guess I'm in shock,' she said, at last.

'In shock, or shocked?' He pushed his own doughnut away – (well, she'd never expected him to eat it – Warren, with a doughnut?) – and took out his cigarette case. 'I suppose you think I'm a heel, don't you? Somebody who wants another woman before his wife is cold in her grave? It's not like that, Martie.'

'I never said I thought it was, Warren.'

'I did love Lois,' he went on, with quiet intensity. 'And I am grieving for her. She was my friend. My friend and companion, the dearest person in the world.' He offered his case to Martie. When she shook her head, he slowly selected a cigarette himself, and lit it. 'But we hadn't had sex for years, you see. We didn't really have a marriage at all.'

Martie wiped sugar from her lips with a paper napkin. She called for a refill and drank the coffee black and strong.

'Because of Lois's health?' she asked huskily.

'Yes. She'd never been fit from her schooldays, but when we were first married, we were happy. Ecstatically happy. We thought it would last for ever.' Warren drew on his cigarette, keeping his eyes down. 'Then we had Brent and he was fine, but after that, things were never the same again. Lois was told, no more children. What the hell were we supposed to do? We took all the precautions, but I was terrified. I felt I was handling glass. I thought she'd break.'

'Maybe I will have one of your cigarettes,' said Martie. He lit it for her.

'In the end, the lovemaking died out. Lois worried about it for me, but I knew it was a relief to her. We just learned to live a different kind of life.'

'And Brent is – what – twenty-eight?' Martie shook her head. 'All those years, Warren? You lived all those years like a monk?'

He hesitated. 'There was someone else in my life once, a long time ago. She was a divorcee, a very attractive woman. We – I suppose we comforted each other. She married, there's been no one since.'

'Did Lois know about her?'

'I can't be sure. If she did, she might not have minded.'

'She'd have minded.'

'No, it was my love she wanted, not the sex. Anyway, she never said anything.' Warren stubbed out his cigarette. 'It's sometimes better, not to put things into words.' He raised his eyes to Martie's. 'Perhaps you think I shouldn't have put into words what I want to do? Shouldn't have mentioned marriage?'

'It's a crazy idea, Warren, whether you say it or not.'

'Crazy? Because of my age?'

'No, because of your position. Och, come on! How could you ever fit me into your life? How'd I ever be accepted by your family? All those guys at the bank!' Martie blew smoke. 'And I've no' even mentioned your mother!'

'I'm not saying it would be easy. Everyone will be very loyal to Lois, and that's how it should be. But people do get married again, Martie, and I'm not suggesting it happens tomorrow.' Warren leaned forward, his gaze very bright on her face. 'The thing is, if we want to, we can make it work. If we cared enough for each other – loved enough—' He drew back and glanced around the café, but no one was listening to anything except the juke-box thudding in the background. 'I'm not hoping that you'd love me straight away, Martie, but I have to tell you – ' he dropped his voice to a whisper – 'I do love you.'

Martie put out her cigarette and rolled sugary crumbs to and fro on her plate. 'You say that,' she said in a low voice. 'I can't believe it's true.'

'It is true. I think I fell in love with you that first time we really talked, when we had a cup of tea together in North Berwick. Do you remember?'

'I remember.'

'You were so fresh and different, so much alive! I couldn't help myself, Martie!' He gave a faint smile. 'But you didn't trust me, did you?'

'I didn't know you, Warren.'

'You'd no need to worry. I never wanted an affair with you. I knew from the start that you were more special than that, but I loved Lois and Lois was ill. There was never going to be anything between us.'

'You asked me to come to New York. Why did you do that?'

Warren ran his hand through his hair. 'I don't know, I guess that was crazy, if you like. But Lois had asked Alex and I thought if you came too, I'd be able to see you. That was all I wanted.'

'And then Lois died.' Martie looked at him sombrely. 'And you still wanted me to come.'

'Yes. I was suffering over Lois, but I felt I couldn't let you go.' Warren was silent for some time, staring down at the table. Finally, he looked up. 'Martie, what do you think? Will you consider me? I mean, when it's possible?'

'I think I'll need some time, Warren.'

'Take as long as you like. As long as you like!'

'In the meantime, I can't go on working for your mother. I'm sorry, I just can't. Not after what you've told me.'

He nodded, picked up his gloves and scarf. 'All right, I understand. I'll try to pull a few strings for you. Would you still want private nursing?'

'I might prefer a nursing home, something on the lines of the Fidra Bay. Or even a sanatorium. I could be a butterfly girl again.' At Warren's raised eyebrows, she smiled. 'That's just what one of the patients at the Jubilee used to call us, because we worked in butterfly-shaped wards.'

'Butterfly girl.' He laughed. 'Kind of suits you. Look, I'll do what I can to find you something. Now, we'd better go.'

Wrapped in their coats and hats again, they faced the street. Martie found she was too embarrassed to look Warren in the face, but his eyes on her were bright with hope.

'You haven't turned me down out of hand,' he said quietly. 'I'm allowing myself to feel optimistic. Please, Martie, dear, think about the good things, not the snags.'

'There are so many snags,' she sighed, staring into the traffic.

'We'd wait, say, a year, then take a long trip. When we came

212

back, people would have gotten over the shock, they'd have accepted the situation.'

'Your mother? Brent?'

'If they see I'm happy, yes, why not?'

He's right, he is being optimistic, thought Martie.

Back at his mother's house, she made hurriedly for her own rooms, not wanting to be caught by Mrs Adamson, tossed as she was in a storm of feeling. Fortunately, Mrs A. was holding forth to the agency nurse in her downstairs sitting room and Martie was able to close her own door and collapse in a heap on her bed.

She still couldn't believe what had happened. Although she'd denied it to his mother, she'd known, of course, that Warren was attracted to her. But to offer her marriage – that was something out of the blue. As she had told him, it was crazy. Even to think about it, made her dizzy. She, Martie Cass, to be Mrs Warren Adamson! Running the apartment in New York and the house in Rhode Island, mixing with the bank dignitaries and all Warren's superior friends, going on trips, buying clothes, spending OLD money . . . Martie lay back, half-laughing, half-crying, then sat up, putting back her hair and holding her head. She must think what to do.

No, that was stupid. She didn't have to think what she was going to do. She knew. She was going to accept Warren, of course she was. There might be difficulties ahead, she would surmount them. It would be just as Warren had said, folk would come to accept the situation. What else could they do? If old Mrs A. and Brent looked down their noses, let them. A marriage was a marriage.

Of course, Warren was not young. Not really old, but certainly way out of her own age-group. What had Jamie said – 'What do your folks think about you going to America with just an old guy?' Martie began to pace her room, wondering what her folks would think if she upped and married that old guy and made her home in another country? Come to that, what would Jamie think? His cheerful, freckled face came into her mind. She saw him playing with the lads again, knocking on doors and running away. Ginger Man! Imagine Warren as a boy, playing like that!

213

Impossible, but so what? Warren was offering her more than Jamie could ever have offered in his whole life. Anyway, Jamie wasn't in fact offering anything. He was engaged to be married to the most boring girl in the world and happy about it, so let him get on! I'll be happy, too, thought Martie. I've found ma Rich Man!

If only she could tell someone! Someone who'd know how much it meant! Her eye fell on the bureau that was so well-stocked with pens and ink, paper and stamps. There was someone who'd know. Not here, just a few thousand miles away in another country. As soon as she'd thought of her, Martie sat down at the bureau and began to write, in her large round hand.

'All a secret at the moment, don't breathe a word,' she ended. 'I'll keep you posted. Be happy for me. All my love, Martie.' Then she addressed the envelope.

'Miss Alexandra Kelsie, c/o The Nurses' Home, The Jubilee Hospital for Chest Diseases, Edinburgh, United Kingdom.'

Chapter Thirty-Five

Coming home. That was how returning to the Jubilee seemed to Alex. It was true that her responsibilities were greater now and she was on Butterfly Four instead of Two, but these differences didn't matter. She was back in her niche, she was happy, and if, occasionally, Tim Burnett's face seemed to come to her amongst a crowd of dressing-gowned patients, she soon forgot it. She had a real face to think about, anyhow, and that was Neal Drover's. What a fine face it was, too! She'd taken a lot of pleasure just looking at him, that time he'd taken her to dinner, and knew she wanted to see him again. Not for any romantic reason, they'd neither of them any interest of that kind in the other, but because they'd talked so easily, had such real rapport. It was rare to find anyone like that. Thank God he was better. More important than anything else, though, was getting to grips with work again. Am I turning into another Rose? Alex asked herself. She didn't really think so. No one could be as dedicated as Rose.

There was no doubt that looking after the women patients of Butterfly Four was not the same as looking after the men patients of Butterfly Two. It was always said that men made worse patients than women, but it was Alex's experience that those women who had children worried more about themselves than men. Not because they cared about their own health, but because they were afraid for their families.

'Who'll take care o' ma bairns?' was the cry Alex dreaded to hear from the hollow-eyed young mothers on her ward. For what could be said? There was no question of the women being released from hospital until they'd been made fit, and that could take months, sometimes years, if it happened at all. Very often, their children would not be allowed to visit for fear of infection, and the sight of mothers waving and trying to talk through windows at little figures huddled outside was heartbreaking. Ill-at-ease husbands would sit by their wives' beds, trying to find words of cheer if they were the sympathetic kind, or reading the sports pages if they were not, but all of them, in any case, would rise with alacrity when the bell rang for the end of visiting and speed away, waving, while the women left behind stared bitterly into space.

It didn't take long for the patients of Butterfly Four to discover that Staff Kelsie was particularly sympathetic, and they would urge her to speak to the doctor, eh? Get them out of here? Och, hen, if it was just a' this resting and that, they could get well at home!

'You can rest at home?' asked Alex, knowing full well what their homes were like. 'I don't think so. Come on, you be good now, follow instructions, take your rest periods, and you'll be out before you know it!' God forgive me for that, she added to herself, but knew they didn't believe her, anyway.

Sister Clerk's replacement, a heavy, ginger-haired woman named Sister Piers, would sometimes declare that those girls would drive her to drink, so they would! Always getting out of bed, doing each other's hair, listening to the wireless, anything but rest!

'They're no' used to resting,' Alex once reminded her. 'Being women.'

'Yes, well, in here, you do as you're told,' was Sister Piers's retort, her blue eyes snapping behind her glasses. 'That's if you want to get well. If you don't want to get well, you can leave the bed for somebody who does!'

There were those who believed that Sister Piers was just as tough as Sister Clerk, but Alex knew she had a soft spot for her patients. Nothing was too much trouble for their welfare, and frightened new arrivals, especially, were given her own comforting introduction to the hospital and even the occasional hug. She quickly recognised that Alex was a nurse after her own heart, and together they tried to make Butterfly Four as bearable as possible.

Sometimes, of course, it didn't seem bearable at all. As when a young, emaciated girl named Ginnie Fleck was told she must have surgery and couldn't face it. Grasping Alex's hand, she burst into tears.

'I have to have ma ribs removed, Nurse, and it's no' fair! I mean, how can I manage without ma ribs? I'll no' be able to stand up!'

'Oh, Ginnie, it's only a small section of your ribs that they're going to remove, just so they can collapse your lung.' Alex squeezed Ginnie's bony fingers. 'There are several ways of giving a bad lung a rest, and this is just one of them. You'll have it done with anaesthetic, you won't know a thing about it. And afterwards, you'll feel better, I promise you.'

'Will you be there when I go for it?' Ginnie asked fearfully.

'Yes, I will, and I'll hold your hand just like I am now.'

'OK, then, but dinna tell ma mum what they're doing, else she'll have a fit. She thinks it's terrible, carving folk up!'

'Everything that's done here is to help you get well, Ginnie. Think of it – being well, like your friends!'

'Like you,' Ginnie murmured, coughing into a tissue, as she lay back. 'You look awfu' fit, Nurse Kelsie. And pretty. Have you got a young man?'

'No, I haven't, but that's enough about me.' Alex was smiling as she took out her thermometer. 'I have to take your temperature now, so no more talking.'

'Staff Kelsie, telephone!' a probationer called from the door. 'It's Neal Drover!'

'Hang on, hang on, do you have to tell the whole ward?' cried Alex. She looked down in embarrassment at Ginnie, who gave a rare smile.

'Knew you'd have somebody!' she whispered.

'I'll be back in a minute,' said Alex.

'Neal, what are you thinking of?' she asked in a sharp whisper. 'You know you shouldn't ring me up on the ward!'

217

'Well, how can I contact you, then? If I ring the nurses' home, I get a whole lot of giggling and questions before I get to you, and mostly you're not there.'

'I'm sorry, it's no' easy.' She softened her tone. 'Why were you calling, anyway?'

'Could we meet again? Have dinner?'

'There's no need to pay for those expensive dinners, Neal. You need all your money for your bookshop now.'

When they'd last met, Neal had told Alex that he'd thought it best to leave teaching and with his father's help had bought a small second-hand bookshop in Stockbridge. Though he didn't expect to make his fortune, he was enjoying his new life and could still afford to take Alex for a meal, as he said now.

'Yes, but why do we no' just go to the pictures? That'd suit me.'

'Would it? What do you fancy, then?'

'I don't mind, as long as it's no' sad.'

'My taste exactly!'

They arranged to meet on her next free evening and Alex, returning to the ward with a buoyant step and a smile on her face, put up with the teasing she received with a good grace.

'Where you goin', Staff Kelsie? Is he takin' you dancin'? Are you goin' out for your tea? Save us a bit, eh?'

Smiling still, Alex shook down her thermometer and approached Ginnie's bed, but Ginnie, her young face gaunt against her flat pillow, had drifted into sleep.

There was a letter waiting in her pigeon-hole when Alex returned to the nurses' home. Blue envelope. American stamps. Martie! Alex's eyes lit up. She'd heard nothing from Martie since that first postcard of the Statue of Liberty and had so often thought of her, hoping things were going well. As Carol Shannon, a young first-year nurse joined her, looking for her own post, Alex tore open Martie's letter.

'Oh, dear, not bad news?' asked Carol, seeing the expression on her face.

'No, no – it's from Martie Cass – you won't remember her. She went to America.'

'Lucky so and so! She doing OK?'

'Fine.' Alex smiled. 'I'd better go and wash.'

In her room, she read the letter again, her heart plummeting. She couldn't take it in. Martie to marry Warren Adamson? Lois's husband? For so Warren still seemed to be to Alex. Martie to marry Warren, a man older than her own father, and stay in America, never come home? Of course, he was her Rich Man. Was that all that mattered? Be happy for me, she had written. How can I be? asked Alex, rising and gazing unseeingly from her window at the leafless trees outside her window. She leaned her brow against the cold pane and said the words aloud.

'How can I be happy for you, Martie?'

The thought came into her mind – what would Rose say?

But the news was secret for the time being. Martie wouldn't want to tell Rose, and Alex, when she next wrote to Rose, mustn't say a word.

Chapter Thirty-Six

Rose, with Alex's latest letter in her bag, came out of the RAF Officers' Mess in Nicosia into bright December sunshine. By British standards, the day was warm; by Cypriot standards, winter cool. Come Christmas, everyone said you'd need a coat, but today Rose was still wearing a summer dress and light cardigan. Her tanned legs were bare, her dark hair uncovered, and the eyes of Pilot-Officer Simon Dawson, walking with her, told her she was beautiful.

They'd met at an RAF cocktail party shortly after Rose's arrival and almost immediately had arranged to meet again. Simon wasn't to know that that was unusual for Rose. He did tell her afterwards that he knew he'd been lucky in getting to her first, before all the other guys could ask her out and boy, would they have wanted to do that! There weren't many new arrivals at RAF Nicosia who looked like her. As for himself, he still found it hard to believe that she was willing to spend time with him. He was tall, with a long, English face, thinnish fair hair, blue eyes; a rather ordinary-looking fellow in his own opinion, what did Rose see in him? She'd laughed and said she wasn't sure, which was not the answer he wanted, maybe, but happened to be true. All the same, she did see something.

They were taking his car that day to a quiet beach he knew along the coast from Kyrenia, which would make a change, they thought, from all the famous places they'd visited so far. Famagusta, the Troodos mountains, Bellapais Abbey, the ruins at Salamis. They'd certainly been able to get around. Amongst the other good points about a posting to Cyprus was the fact that you got most afternoons off. As Simon put it, who wouldn't work like hell from first thing in the morning, if you could be free by lunchtime? But Rose would work like hell anyway, wouldn't she? Now you make me sound a bore, she had told him. But that Rose liked work was something else that happened to be true.

'You've got the drinks?' Rose asked, as she climbed into the front seat of his open sports car and put on a pair of dark glasses. 'Can't afford to get dehydrated.'

'Soft drinks galore,' he told her, driving away. 'But it's getting cooler these days.'

'You think so because you've been right through the summer. This is still hot for me!'

'Wait till you've been through a summer too. Nicosia's like an oven.'

'I have a friend in Edinburgh – she's also a nurse. When do you think would be the best time for her to come out to visit? April ?'

'Perfect. Wouldn't be too hot for her then.'

Rose, looking at the modern blocks of flats lining the streets in this part of the city, thought how harsh their white surfaces seemed, how strongly the sun must beat down on their flat, unprotected roofs. She much preferred the traditional Levantine architecture of the older Nicosia, where the houses were shuttered and mysterious, and inner courtyards lined with flowers, and orange trees gave fragrant shade. She had already been a guest at one or two of these houses, where she had either met Turks or Greeks, but never the two together. That was the Cypriot problem, she had learned. Greeks and Turks would never meet.

It was siesta time. The city was quiet. Soon they would be out on the twisting road to Kyrenia. Rose glanced at Simon's profile.

'I don't like to ask, but do you know how I could get my friend a cheap flight out?'

'An indulgence flight, you mean? They mostly go to relatives, but you might be able to swing it.'

'I want you to swing it.'

He laughed. 'It all depends on how many empty seats they've got in the planes, coming or going. You need to have the cash for a commercial flight in case you don't hit lucky.'

'I could easily give Alex the fare, if she'd take it.'

'A proud Scottish lassie, is she?'

'Something like that,' Rose answered with a smile. 'Will you see what you can do, nearer the time?'

'Rose, I'd do anything for you, you know that.'

Her smile did not fade. For some reason, she seemed willing to accept the way he talked in a way she had never before accepted men's *badinage*. Perhaps because she believed in his case it wasn't *badinage*. It seemed to her that he meant every word he said.

The sun was still high in the sky when they arrived at Simon's quiet cove, where the only signs of life were a few goats grazing above the beach, and a middle-aged Greek who was setting out a refreshment stall. Simon put up the umbrella he always carried in the car, and Rose, without shyness, stepped out of her dress and lay down on a towel, wearing a well-cut Logie's swimsuit. Simon, stripped to shorts, lay down too, unable to take his eyes from Rose's body, as she could not help but notice.

I wonder what I'm playing at? she asked herself, sitting up to rub herself with oil. It was not the first time they had lain on sands together, but they had never made love. He had kissed her once or twice and she had let him. What more did she want? What did Simon want? The way he looked at her, she was sure she knew.

'This is the life, eh?' he asked, finally dragging his eyes from Rose to look at the line of sea not stirring under the sun. 'Feel like something to eat?'

She sat up, shading her eyes, to see what was happening at the makeshift café. The seller had now laid out his wares – rolls and pasties made of minced meat and egg, bottles of Coke, glasses and cups for Turkish coffee. There were the usual little wooden chairs standing ready, but so far he had no customers.

'Want to risk it?' she asked, laughing.

'Sure, I've a tin stomach.'

'Me too.' Rose slipped her dress over her swimsuit. 'Come on, let's go.'

As they sat under the thatched roof of the shelter, trying out the pasties, an ancient goatherd arrived to check his flock. The refreshment seller, opening a bottle of Coke for him, wandered across for a conversation.

'His only customer, apart from us,' Simon whispered, 'and he's not paying.'

'Somebody must eat his food, or he wouldn't be here.'

'Maybe he needs new customers every day.'

'Because the others collapse?' Rose laughed and looked so young and carefree, Simon shook his head.

'You know, no one looking at you now would take you for a highly responsible nursing sister,' he told her. 'You're so different, out of uniform.'

'I think most people are.'

'But your uniform means a lot to you, doesn't it? Your job?'

'Yes, it does.' She dabbed at her mouth with a handkerchief. 'Shall we walk by the water? I'll just get my hat. You should wear one, too.'

'Yes, Sister, certainly, Sister.'

For some time, they walked hand in hand by the sea, sometimes letting the warm water lap over their ankles, while the goats' bells jangled and the goatherd eventually led them away. It was so peaceful, so idyllic, neither of them wanted to break the spell, but finally Rose pointed out that the sun was lowering and there were little clouds mounting the sky.

'Shall we go back to Kyrenia?' she asked. 'I want to buy some lace for Christmas presents. I suppose I'm late for posting already.'

'Not by air,' Simon answered, following her up the beach to their towels. As Rose began to dry her feet, he threw himself down and reached for her hand. 'Rose, just how keen are you on your work?'

'Very keen, you know that.' She loosed her hand from his and put on her flip-flops. 'Nursing means everything to me.'

223

'I suppose you see yourself as some hawk-eyed matron of a military hospital somewhere?'

'Why not?' She sprinkled sand over him. 'Wouldn't I make a good matron? I was just thinking, I've come to Cyprus too soon. They were saying at work yesterday, there are plans to build a huge military hospital in Dhekelia. I could have worked my way up the ladder there, couldn't I?'

'You're not joking, are you?'

'No, I'd really like to work somewhere like that, see how far I could go. If they bring troops over from Egypt, and they might do that, apparently, there'll be plenty to do.' Rose began to comb her hair. 'Why do you think they'll need more troops here, Simon? You think there'll really be trouble?'

'There's always trouble between the Turks and the Greeks, anyway. This is a shared island, bound to lead to problems.'

'I know that, but we haven't been too much involved so far.'

'The Greeks want us out, they want to be part of mainland Greece. The Turks want us to stay. It was the Turkish rulers who more or less asked us to take over Cyprus way back, anyhow.'

'Do you think we're in any danger?'

'Not at the moment.' Simon smiled. 'You're not the sort to mind, are you?'

'No. As a matter of fact, I wanted to go where there was some action. But I ended up here.'

'Thank God you did! I don't want you mixed up in action, I want you here, all right, with me.'

'You'll be posted yourself one day.'

'Not for a long time,' he said firmly. 'And then—'

'Then what?'

'Nothing.' Simon leaped to his feet. 'OK, let's go back to Kyrenia. When you've done your shopping, we can have dinner. Those pasties didn't go very far. I'm starving.'

'It's wonderful the way you never put on any weight!' Rose suddenly laid her hand over his flat stomach. 'See, no flab!'

'Oh, Rose!' he caught at the hand, which she left for a moment in his, then pulled away.

'Come on, I'm hungry too!'

224

'And you don't put on weight either.'

They stood looking into each other's faces, blue eyes searching dark eyes, until Simon kissed Rose lightly and turned away to find his shirt and shoes.

'Hell, I can't get my shoes on,' he said, laughing. 'Too much sand on my feet.'

'You can drive in flip-flops.'

'Oh, I know.'

As they left their special place, they looked back to give a last wave to the Greek, now sitting on one of his chairs, smoking a small black cigar, still waiting for customers. He bowed his head with a melancholy smile, and Rose said,

'Poor man, he hasn't made much today. I do hope someone comes for him.'

'Bit late now.' Simon glanced swiftly at Rose. 'But we'll come back, won't we?'

'Yes, I could bring Alex.'

Simon looked back at the road. She could feel his body tensing in his seat. 'You'd bring your friend?'

She touched his hand on the wheel. 'Maybe not.'

He smiled. 'We'll take her to Kyrenia, shall we? She'd probably like that. Shops, restaurants, little boats in the harbour.

'I like it too. Especially the restaurant bit.'

They laughed and drove on.

Would anyone from the Jubilee recognise me? Rose asked herself, in her room that night. A great moon was dipping down a velvet sky, as she stood at her window in a thin nightdress, her arms crossed over her breasts. Cyprus had changed her. Or, was it Simon? She could still feel the kisses they'd exchanged when they'd said goodnight, could still see the love in his eyes that he was unable to conceal. Poor chap, he was being so circumspect. He was afraid, wasn't he? Afraid of her rebuff. She was afraid of that herself.

It was true what she had told him, nursing meant everything to her. Some women managed to combine their career with marriage, with children. How did they do that? She couldn't see herself stepping off her ladder in that way. Yet for the first time, she felt herself drawn to a man, felt her body reacting to his, her heart responding. Chemistry, she'd heard it called. Or, maybe a trap. Nature's trap. Nature's little trap to carry on the race.

Seems I'm just like everyone else, after all, she thought, slipping under her one sheet and closing her eyes, as though she might even sleep. But she wasn't sure she was the same as everyone else. Things weren't so simple for her. Never would be.

Chapter Thirty-Seven

Alex had received Christmas presents from Rose and Martie, which, of course, she'd keep to open on the day. Martie's was large – might contain something to wear, probably from some grand New York store. Rose's was no more than a package and Alex guessed it held lace, she'd heard that the Cyprus lace was beautiful. There was also a card, on which Rose had written a few lines with her greeting:

> *'Am still doing a lot of sightseeing, with this nice young air-force fellow called Simon. He comes from Kent, very English! Everything very hectic here at the moment, with parties at RAF Nicosia and army do's etc. Sometimes think I never want to see a kebab again! I expect Auld Reekie is festive too. So glad you're enjoying life back at the Jubilee. Lots of love, Rose.'*

The words sprang out before Alex's startled eyes. 'This nice young air-force fellow called Simon' . . . Well, well, so that was the name of the 'friend', was it? Rose must have changed a lot, to be spending time with a young man, away from work! Oh, but that was good. Alex was pleased for her, as she could not be for Martie.

As she put Rose's charity Christmas card up in her room, Alex felt the usual nagging reminder that she had not yet replied to

Martie's news about her engagement, but what was there to say? 'All good wishes, hope it doesn't come off' Congratulations just weren't possible, in Alex's view. There was one piece of news she could give and that was that Jamie had postponed his wedding, because he hadn't saved enough money. Would it make Martie think twice about marrying Warren? Probably not, Jamie was so obviously no Rich Man. Alex sighed. She would have to get a move on, anyway, and write something to send with her present of a tartan scarf. Not a very original gift, but might help to keep Martie warm in the winter, New York winters being so cruel, according to Neal. The thought of Neal brought another worry. He was still in good health, but lately had been low in spirits. Alex didn't know what to do, didn't think there was much she could do. Perhaps her father would cheer him up. She was taking him to see Neal's bookshop on her next Saturday afternoon off.

The only bright spot in her life came from work. Ginnie's operation had gone well, she had made a quick recovery and was already feeling the benefit. Alex had held her hand when she was anaesthetised and had been there when she came round, which was something she had promised to do and felt good about. Especially as Ginnie was feeling so well, and her terrifying mother had been pacified. Just once in a while, it seemed, things worked out. That would be something to tell Neal, perhaps, when they were cooking supper in his basement flat below the bookshop. They'd taken to cooking, lately, to save money on meals out after the cinema or theatre. Alex didn't want to turn into another Mrs Cass, but she was saving hard now for her trip to Cyprus, and didn't want Neal wasting money, either, as he wasn't making much.

'Why don't you stock new books?' she'd asked him. 'Folks'd buy them for Christmas presents, wouldn't they?'

'I'm a bookman, I stock old books,' Neal replied. 'I'm not interested in new books. I may not make much money, but I'm happy.'

Oh, Neal, thought Alex, I wish you were.

*

Edie had been invited to come to the bookshop, but had said she'd give it a miss, she was no' interested in books. As for meeting Mr Drover, she thought not. A Jubilee patient? No, better be safe than sorry, eh?

'Edie, he's an ex-patient,' Alex told her, 'he's better.'

'Aye, maybe, but you canna be sure with folk like that. I'd be careful, if I was you, Alex.'

'I don't know what you mean by careful. Neal and I are just friends.'

As Edie gave a knowing smile, Alex turned away, tight-lipped.

'Come on, Dad!' she called. 'If you're ready, we can go.'

Neal's bookshop was in St Stephen's Street, an intriguing part of Stockbridge, where the gateway to the old butchers' meat market, long since closed, could still be seen. Small shops sold second-hand clothes, materials, antiques and battered furniture, while cafés and pubs, some in tiny basements, catered for workers who walked down from city offices. Neal had rented a ground floor for his shop and turned the storage basement below into a one-bedroom flat, but where he'd managed to find all his stock was a mystery to Alex. She'd never seen so many books, shelved, stacked, slipping from heaps, and would have given a great deal to create some order. But Neal had said under no circumstances was she to tidy the books. People liked turning over the stock and browsing, it was part of the interest. If you wanted nice neat shelves of books arranged in order, you went to the public library.

'All this dust, though, Neal, can't be good for you.'

'I love it. The smell of dust and old leather, beats your disinfectant every time!'

'Aye, it's grand,' said Arthur, looking round his eyes alight. 'This is the place for me, Mr Drover, I could spend ma life here!'

'I'm glad you like it, Mr Kelsie, but please call me Neal. Is there anything special you'd like to see?'

Arthur, who was wearing his good jacket and a tie he was supposed to be keeping for Christmas, told Neal to call him Arthur and said he'd like to see the plays. Shakespeare, eh?

'Did you know I was all set for the boards when I was young? Did Alex tell you that? Aye, ma dad was at the Lyceum, wanted me to follow in his footsteps, but circumstances were against it.' Arthur shook his head. 'Life's like that, eh? Man proposes, God disposes, as folk say.'

Neal's handsome face darkened. 'I don't know if it's God or not,' he muttered, 'but somebody seems to knock you down every time you stand up.'

'Why, Neal, what a depressing thing to say!' Alex exclaimed. 'Especially when you're so much better!'

He made no answer, but led her father to his Shakespeare collection, of which he was rather proud.

'As you see, Arthur, I have the New Cambridge, also the Arden, but that's being replaced by a completely new edition starting this year, which of course I haven't got, my stock being second-hand. But I've a few Oxfords and all the Penguin – first-rate, I'd say, for the general reader—'

'That's me,' said Arthur, looking bemused. 'Och, I never knew there was all these different editions! I thought I'd just be able to get one big book, like I've got now. It was ma Dad's, you ken, but it's falling to pieces, and I'm wanting to save it.'

'And I'm going to replace it for him for Christmas,' Alex explained. 'It'll no' be a surprise, but he wanted to choose it himself, you see.'

'Of course, I have the very thing.' Neal was smiling, his dark side no longer in evidence, as he handed down an inexpensive one-volume Shakespeare for Arthur to look at. 'Will this do, d'you think?'

'It's perfect, Neal, perfect.' Arthur had put on his glasses and was reading the price pencilled on the fly-leaf. 'Alex, if that's too dear, I can put a bit to it—'

'You won't put anything to it,' Neal said firmly. 'This is a present from me.' He rubbed out the price and wrote, "With all good wishes to Alex's father, from Neal". There you are, Arthur, there's your new Shakespeare, and I hope it brings you many more happy hours.'

'Neal, you can't do that!' cried Alex. 'That's a piece of nonsense!'

'Aye, I agree,' said Arthur, looking over the tops of his glasses, first at Alex and then at Neal. 'You're meant to be selling your books, Neal, no' giving them away!'

Neal briefly put his hand on Alex's shoulder. 'Your daughter did a lot for me when I was in the Jubilee, Arthur, and this is a small way of saying thank you. Apart from that, I want you to have the book personally. It would give me a lot of pleasure for you to take it.'

'Well, if you're sure?' Arthur said doubtfully.

'I'm absolutely sure. And I've written in it, haven't I?' Neal grinned. 'I see a customer. Will you excuse me a moment. Alex, maybe you could take your dad downstairs and give him a cup of tea?'

In Neal's low-ceilinged basement kitchen, Arthur drank his tea and took one of the biscuits Alex had brought. His newly wrapped Shakespeare was on his knee.

'Alex, that's a nice fellow up there, giving me this. And that good-looking, eh? He's Tyrone Power, to a T.'

'Sure you don't mean Gregory Peck?' Alex asked, with a smile. 'Or, maybe Stewart Granger? People at the Jubilee had him like every film-star you've ever heard of!'

'How come he's no' married, though? Somebody like him?'

'He's been ill, Dad. Not able to marry.'

'But he's better now?'

'Yes, he seems to have made a good recovery.'

Arthur ate another biscuit. 'He's fond of you, Alex.'

'We're good friends.'

Her father's smile was less knowing than Edie's but showed his mind was on the same track.

'I've lived a few years now, pet, but I've never yet met a man and a woman that was what you'd call friends.'

Alex, remembering Valerie Raynor's views on Hugh's friendship with herself, abruptly stood up and began to clear away the tea things.

231

'That's old-fashioned talk,' she said, over her shoulder. 'We're supposed to be more mature these days.'

Arthur tapped his new Shakespeare. 'Alex this here'll tell you all you need to know about men and women – mebbe I should get you one for Christmas.'

'As though I'd have time to read Shakespeare, Dad!'

Chapter Thirty-Eight

When her father had gone home, proudly carrying his present ready to show Edie, Alex set the table in the corner of Neal's living room and began to make preparations for supper. There were two gigot chops in the meat safe – courtesy of one of the Stockbridge butchers who was always generous with Neal's meat ration – and a few potatoes in a bag. No other vegetables, though, which would mean she'd have to run out and get some, unless there was a tin of peas or something. Typical man, she thought, to make sure of meat but not vegetables.

'Of course I have a tin of peas,' Neal said irritably when he came down from closing the shop. 'Why do women always think men can't housekeep?'

'I can't see it, that's all,' Alex said patiently. 'And you really should be having fresh vegetables, Neal. Maybe I'll go out for a cabbage.'

'Don't bother.' Neal, looking at the sparse contents of his cupboard, was drawing his well-shaped brows together. 'Hell, I must have used that tin. Look, I'll get the cabbage, you start the chops.'

Alex took him by the hand and led him to his chair. 'Sit down, Neal, you're looking tired. Just leave things to me.'

'I suppose I can at least make up the fire? It's freezing in here.' He flung a shovelful of coal on the fire and stood rubbing his hands. Aware of Alex's watchful gaze, he turned his head. 'You don't need to look at me like that! There's nothing wrong with me, I'm fine.'

'I know.' She put on her coat, still hanging on to her patience, though with some effort. 'I won't be five minutes, just take it easy.'

When she looked back from the door, he was in his chair, lying back with his eyes closed.

They did not talk much over supper, though Neal seemed to cheer up slightly after he'd opened a bottle of red wine and had drunk a good deal of it. His father had given him a case, he told Alex, and pressed more wine on her, but she said, no, she didn't want to be rolling back to the nurses' home. She would like some coffee, though, when she'd washed up.

'I've only got the powder stuff.'

'That'll be OK.'

'And we'll both wash up. Why should you do everything?'

'All right, if you insist.'

Alex, avoiding Neal's glittering gaze, cleared away and put on the kettle. She had never seen him in this sort of mood before, and it made her uneasy. Perhaps he sensed that, for when he came to dry the dishes, he said in a low voice, 'Sorry I've been a bit prickly, Alex. I don't usually let people see me in a mood.'

'I didn't even know you had moods,' she answered, smiling readily.

'My dark secret.'

They took their coffee to the fireside, where Neal sat in his worn armchair and Alex pulled up a stool near him.

'I want to thank you, Neal, for being so nice to ma dad. Giving him that Shakespeare – that was so kind! He'll never get over it.'

'I wanted him to have it, I admire him.'

'Because there aren't many toolmakers who read Shakespeare?'

'Because there aren't many people at all who read Shakespeare. He's gifted, Alex, yes, he is. You smile at him, but maybe he should have been an actor. As he said, things were against him.' Neal shrugged. 'As they are for most of us.'

234

Alex sighed. 'Why do you keep looking on the black side, Neal? I know I shouldn't talk about cases, but there's a young girl at the Jubilee who's been so miserable, she was told she had to have some ribs removed—'

'Thoracoplasty?' Neal nodded knowledgeably; he had made a point of learning as much as possible about his disease and its treatments. 'Poor kid. She had adhesions?'

'Yes, she couldn't have the pneumothorax, and she was so afraid – I mean, you can imagine – having ribs removed—'

'I can imagine.'

'And she's only nineteen, been ill for so long. Anyway, what I was going to say was, that she's had the op and she's fine. She's doing really well, her mother's happy, we're all happy. So why not think of the good things, as well as the bad? After all, you're better, too.'

As he said nothing, her look sharpened.

'You are better, aren't you?'

'Yes, I'm better.' He fixed her with eyes from which the glitter had gone, leaving a darkness that was no less disturbing. 'I'm better, but not cured.'

'I thought you said you were doing very well?'

'For the time being, yes. But you know with me, it could come back.'

'Neal, you can't live all your life with that fear hanging over your head. You have to put it out of your mind, just not think about it.'

'That would be easy. If it weren't for you.'

Alex sat back on her stool, locking her hands together, trying to smile. 'Me?'

'How do you think I feel, knowing we can never have a relationship? Knowing I can't even kiss you?'

Relationship.

The word was like something thrown that hit and stunned her. Relationship? He wanted a relationship? All along, that had been in his mind? Alex thought again of Mrs Raynor. Why don't I see things? she asked herself bitterly. Why do I keep on making mistakes?

235

'Of course you can kiss me,' she said, seizing on something safe to say. 'You're clear now, and in any case, I'm immune.'

He was not sidetracked. 'You're looking poleaxed. Is it such a shock I want a relationship? I thought women always knew what men were feeling.'

'I didn't know what you were feeling. It never crossed my mind that—'

'I might be in love with you? Because I'm ill, I suppose?'

'You're not ill, Neal, you're better!'

'Was ill, then. That would be enough to put me out of the running?'

'How can you say that?' Alex lowered her eyes. 'Tim was ill, wasn't he?'

'Tim was a slight case. You knew he'd get well.'

'Why are we talking like this? You were the hospital heart-throb. Everyone was crazy about you, you'd admirers all over the place. I never thought you'd be interested in me.'

'Heart-throb?' Neal gave a wintry smile. 'Is that what they called me? You're right, they were crazy. But why shouldn't I be interested in you?' He took her hand. 'Come on, you must have guessed.'

'No, I never did.'

'Even when I left the Jubilee and thought I'd never see you again, you didn't realise what that was like for me?'

She was a little ashamed. 'I never knew, I had no idea.'

'Well, how about lately?'

'I thought we were just friends.'

'Friends!' He let go her hand and lay back, laughing again, and Alex was suddenly afraid he would cough. Oh, God, don't let him cough, she prayed. He didn't cough, but sat up. 'Let's have some more coffee. Or else, a drink. How about a drink?'

'Neal, I have to go. I'm going on night duty, need a bit of time.'

'I'm sorry.' He leaped to his feet. 'I'll walk you over.'

'There's no need.'

He didn't argue, just fetched her coat and put on his own. At the door to the area, he stopped, and stood looking at her. She could almost feel his heart thudding.

'I can't believe you didn't know,' he murmured. 'I thought it was written all over me in letters three feet high.'

'Oh, Neal, I'm so sorry!'

'Don't be. The last thing I want is pity.'

'I'm no' giving you pity. I only meant I was sorry you'd been bottling everything up for so long.'

'What else could I do?' He put his hand to her face, smoothed back her hair. 'If I'd told you, would it have made any difference? Has it made any difference now?'

'Well, I suppose I know the situation.' She gave an uncertain smile. 'Didn't know it before.'

'I suppose I know it, too. You don't love me.'

'Neal, try to understand. I'd never thought about it.'

'I didn't need to think about it.' He gently put his arms around her. 'Thing is, will you go on seeing me?'

'Yes, I want to.'

'Even though I'm as I am?'

'I tell you, there's no risk.'

'There might be risk to me. I might feel even worse than I do now and I'm not talking about my health.'

'Neal, I'm no' promising anything.'

'No, I know. I understand.'

'We'll just see how things go.'

'Perhaps start with this.' He kissed her briefly, then passionately, shaking a little as he let her go. 'If you say that's safe. And I'll take any risks going.'

It was a relief to be back on duty. Even at night, in Butterfly Four, there was no time to think of anything but work. No doubt when she was trying to sleep next day, Alex would ask herself why she had ever said she wanted to go on seeing Neal. She would blame herself for not wanting to hurt him, when it would have been better to make a break that would heal as quickly as a clean surgical cut. On the other hand, she had said she wasn't promising anything, and love might come. It happened. She had certainly enjoyed his kiss. If he could stay well, they might be happy together. And if he did not stay well? Alex blanked out that thought. Thank God for night duty.

There was no real quiet on Butterfly Four, even in the small hours. Always someone coughing, or calling, needing a drink or a word, or sometimes more. Sal MacNicol had just been sick.

'Missed the dish, as usual,' groaned Jill Berry. 'Sal, could you no' think of us, eh? Now we'll have to change the whole bed.'

'Hen, it's no' easy hittin' one o' thae wee pots in the dark,' wheezed Sal, a forty-year-old spectre, who went in and out of the Jubilee at regular intervals. 'And I get nae warning, you ken!'

'We know, we know,' Alex said cheerfully. 'Just roll on to the chair while we get the sheets off. That's the idea!'

'And ma throat's as dry as sandpaper,' Sal went on, coughing and holding her side. 'How aboot a cup o' tea, eh? Och, I could do wi' that! Wouldnae take you a minute.'

'Sal, it's two in the morning!' Jill cried, but it was only a little ritual they all went through. Everyone knew Sal would get her tea, and probably those around her would be given it too, she having woken them all up. That was the way the night went.

'What a life, eh?' asked Jill, carrying away the soiled bed linen. 'Are we nuts, or what, to do this job?'

'Nuts is the word,' Alex agreed, pausing at Ginnie's bed because she'd seen the young girl was awake.

'All right, Ginnie?'

'Fine, thanks.' Ginnie's eyes went over Alex's face. 'Are you OK, though, Nurse? You look dead beat.'

'I've just got one or two things on ma mind. You know how it is.'

'Aye, I do!' Ginnie agreed with feeling. 'Nurse, are they having tea down there? Any chance of some for me?'

Sister Crosby, the night sister, was writing up her notes at her desk, the light from her table-lamp providing a little centre of comfort in the shadows. She looked up as Alex went by and gave a weary smile.

'Sal again? Does that woman never sleep?'

'Just getting her settled, Sister.'

'That'll be the day!'

A kind of peace descended, as the patients gradually fell into restless sleep, from which they would soon be wakened by the ward maids with their soap and water for washing. Then the coughing would start again in earnest.

'Are we nuts, doing this job?' Jill had asked.

Alex, scrubbing her hands yet again, smiled wryly to herself. She thought of Rose, strange new Rose, going to parties on a Mediterranean island. Of Martie, mixing with the rich in astonishing New York, spending money, Warren's money, like water, probably by now planning a gorgeous wedding. Silk, satin, cotton, rags . . . Och, everyone knew what Martie would wear.

Looking down at her raw, cold fingers, Alex wondered, who would think her crazy? Not Rose. However different she had become, Rose would never think it strange to nurse on in difficult conditions. She might go to parties, but only when her work was done, and if Alex knew her, that work would be tough and selfless and always in the forefront of Rose's mind.

Martie? Alex shrugged. She could no longer be certain of what Martie would think. All she knew was that Martie would never for the world swap places with her, and that she would never swap places with Martie. After all, she did have Neal Drover. If she wanted him.

'Alex! Alex! Are you there?'

'Coming, Jill!'

In the ward, waking up to another day, one of the patients on bed-rest had insisted on getting up and had collapsed on the floor. A young girl, quite new, had brought up blood and was crying at the sight of the scarlet drops on her white sheet. And Sal MacNicol had been sick again.

'Och, I couldnae help it, Nurse – I niver get any warning, eh? Do you think it was that cup o' tea? You should niver have let me drink it, hen. Still, I think I could eat ma breakfast. When it comes.'

Chapter Thirty-Nine

Alex had been right about Rose's being different yet the same, going to parties though still working hard, but she had been wrong about Martie. Even though Christmas was on the horizon, Martie was not leading a brilliant social life in astonishing New York. Quite the reverse. She was working in a TB sanatorium in Massachusetts, and surprising herself by enjoying it. Of course, Mount Forest, a costly establishment set in the Berkshires, was not exactly the Jubilee. On the other hand, nursing there was harder than at the Fidra Bay, because the patients, if rich, were truly ill. Martie had rather forgotten the satisfaction that came from being needed. Perhaps it was not surprising, then, that she was enjoying herself, now she'd found that satisfaction again. And was still surrounded by money.

There had been some sticky moments when she had announced her plans to Mrs Adamson, especially as she had not been able to give much notice. A flu epidemic had run riot through the staff at Mount Forest, the director was desperate for her to start as soon as possible. All of which suited Martie, but not Mrs A. As soon as Martie broke the news she would be leaving at the end of the week, the temperature, as she told Warren afterwards, dropped to zero in his mother's boudoir.

'So this is the thanks I get for taking you into my home?' Mrs Adamson had asked, her voice crackling with ice. 'I gave you a job as a favour to Warren. I could have had someone who'd want to stay, who'd get to know my ways, be a real companion, but I was a softie, as usual. I thought I'd please Warren and do his little Scottish girl a good turn. And look where it's got me! You're on your way before you've been here five minutes!'

'I'm really sorry, Mrs Adamson,' Martie had said humbly. 'It's just the way things have worked out.'

'The way you've worked them out, you mean.'

Mrs Adamson's eyes snapped, as they so often did. 'Well, there's no point discussing it. I'll have to get myself an agency nurse and do the best I can.'

'The agency nurses are very good, Mrs Adamson. I'm sure you'll get one to suit.'

'Maybe.' The old lady waved a dismissive hand and said she would take her nap. When she was settled on her bed, her head against her pillow, she gave Martie a dark penetrating look.

'I suppose Warren is driving you to this sanatorium?'

'That's right.'

'And he fixed up the job?'

'It's only temporary.'

'Done a lot for you, all the same, wouldn't you say?'

'Yes, I'm very grateful to him.'

'I'm sure you are. But just remember, any relationship with Warren will be as temporary as your job. Don't hope for anything more.'

'I'll leave you to your rest, Mrs Adamson.' Martie walked quietly to the door. She had felt rather proud of her own restraint.

But all the New York tensions were behind her now, as she revelled in doing a job she knew and in being made so welcome. No one seemed to think it at all strange that she, a Scottish nurse, should be working in New England. Scots, apparently, were famous for roaming the world, and who, wanting the best experience in a certain field, would not want to come to the US of A? The owner and director of the sanatorium, Dr Frank Viner, a gifted TB specialist, made it plain he was particularly grateful to have someone of Martie's background helping out in his crisis, and at her interview had offered her a senior nurse's position at what seemed to her an amazing salary.

241

'It's all of a piece with things here,' she had reported to Warren, driving with him on her first afternoon off. 'Everything's on a bigger scale than back home.'

'And better?' he asked, grinning.

'Well, I'm no' so sure about that. Our doctors and nurses are the best.'

'But do you have the best equipment?'

Martie thought of the superb operating theatre at Mount Forest, and shrugged.

'Maybe we don't. But it's no' fair to compare this place with the Jubilee. Folk are paying here, and paying well. It's no wonder Dr Viner can afford the best there is.'

'Well, that includes you, dear Martie. But don't let him work you too hard. I don't want you worn to a shadow before our wedding day.'

Their wedding day. In all the pressures of her job, Martie hadn't thought of it, except perhaps as something far away. But in a year or so, it would be with her. It was hard to comprehend.

'Haven't forgotten about it?' Warren asked, not exactly teasingly. He stopped the car under trees and took a small box from his pocket. 'Perhaps this will remind you.'

Inside the box was a ring cushioned on pale velvet. The central stone was a sapphire, the perfect choice for Martie, who so loved blue. Around it, winking and glittering, even in the poor light of the winter afternoon, was a delicate hoop of diamonds. As Warren gently lifted the ring from the box and fitted it on Martie's finger, she sat, speechless. Before the power of the ring, everything there had ever been between herself and Warren grew and held her. In a way, she realised now, she had only half believed in her destiny, just as she had put aside the thought of the wedding as being something far away and scarcely to do with herself. But now the ring made everything real. This was her ring on her finger, put there by Warren. With this ring, he had staked his claim to her. Wearing it, she accepted. She was his.

'It fits, doesn't it?' Warren whispered. 'I had to guess the size. If it's not right, it can easily be adjusted.'

242

She could not take her eyes from it. She felt hypnotised by its light, its beauty, by what it meant.

'It fits perfectly,' she said softly. 'Everything about it is perfect.'

'I'm glad. I wanted it to be.'

'But, Warren, I can't keep it. No' yet. How could I ever wear it?'

'I don't mean you to wear it yet. We'll have to wait until our engagement is announced and that'll be some time off.'

'What shall I do with it, then?'

'Just put it somewhere safe.' He drew the ring from her finger and returned it to its box. Then he closed the box and placed it in Martie's hand. 'There you are. The symbol of what we mean to each other.'

'Warren, I can't just leave it in ma room, it's too valuable.' Her lips trembled a little. 'Too precious.'

'There must be something you can lock. A drawer? A cupboard?'

Martie thought for a moment. 'Yes, there is. There's a chest of drawers that has a key. I could put it there.' She opened the box to take another look at her ring. 'Och, though, it seems such a shame to lock it away, eh?'

'It won't be for ever.' Warren cupped her face in his hands and slowly sank his mouth to hers. 'But, oh God, it feels like it!'

As he drove her back to the sanatorium, she sensed a change in him. Away from New York, he was at ease. Safe. No one knew him here and alone with her, he was himself, as he could never be, surrounded by his family. Also, and this was something that mattered to them both, Lois had never been in this place. Her shade that could bring guilt, however much they reasoned against it, could not trouble them here. Martie, firmly clutching her ring box, felt wonderfully warm and content. It had been a good idea to come to Massachusetts. Already, she was coming to love it. Coming to love everything.

'You're happy here?' Warren asked, as they entered the drive and drove up through trees to the long white building that was the sanatorium. The balconies were empty now, but there were lights everywhere, and coloured balls on a giant Christmas tree twinkled through the dusk. In the distance, hills rose in dark outline; when the better weather came, Martie had promised herself to get to know them. She and Warren could climb them together.

'Yes, I am happy,' she answered without hesitation. 'This is the sort of place for me.'

'It's a damn' sight colder than the Fidra Bay. Don't they allow you any heating?'

'Not much. Doctor's orders.' Martie laughed. 'You get used to it.' She studied Warren's handsome face, pale in the half light. 'I suppose I can't kiss you?'

'Under all those windows?' He grinned fondly. 'The time will come, Martie, when we won't have to worry about windows.'

'I can't wait!'

As there was no way they could kiss goodbye, they pressed each other's hands, and Warren said he would be up the day before Christmas Eve, if she could get an hour or so off. If only she hadn't had to work! If only she could have come to New York! They both knew she hadn't wanted to spend Christmas in New York, but she'd agreed to come for New Year's, which was what Americans called Hogmanay.

'Let me know if you can get that time off,' Warren said, as Martie opened her door. 'I want to give you your present.'

'Warren, you've given me the ring!'

'That's separate. Quite, quite separate.'

She got out of the car and stood in the air that was cold enough for snow to watch him reverse down the drive. He was staying the night at the hotel in Great Barrington, then would make for New York at first light the following day. Dear Warren. Her heart swelled with feeling, as her fingers curled round the box that contained her ring.

Chapter Forty

Massachusetts was an amazingly varied state, stretching from the woods and hills of the Berkshires, across a central valley to Boston and then to the ocean, to Martha's Vineyard and Cape Cod. There was industry, fishing and whaling, but also beautiful country, pretty little towns, large estates of the wealthy. One of the pretty little towns was called Stockbridge, so very charming, with its Main Street and colonial dwellings, it could not have been more different from Stockbridge back home. Though not better, Martie told herself loyally. Different, but not better! The coast of Cape Cod she had visited only briefly, but of course she wanted to go back. That was another date she'd made for herself for when the better weather came, but then there was Boston, and Boston didn't need summer temperatures. Warren could drive her down some weekend, if and when she could manage a whole weekend free.

Would he ask her to stay in a hotel with him, she wondered, if they did go to Boston together? Would he risk that? More to the point, would she? There hadn't been much lovemaking between them so far; in fact, she couldn't even picture it. Not with Warren. When they were married, it would be different. Better wait till then.

When she was not enjoying her time off in the countryside, Martie flung herself wholeheartedly into her work at the sanatorium. Och, Rose would be proud of me, she sometimes said to herself at the end of another long day, and would think of getting a letter off to

Cyprus, maybe tomorrow. Writing letters was not her strong point, and it was no lie to say that she really didn't have much time. Mostly, what she liked to do when she got to bed, was curl up under her eiderdown and not put her nose out until her alarm went in the morning, for her room was no warmer than the patients' apartments.

It was true, as Warren had said, that Mount Forest was cold, but the management was only following accepted practice for TB sanatoria in that respect. The rooms were pretty Spartan, too, though all patients had private bathrooms, and what furnishings there were, were of the highest quality. The food was the same. Even better, in fact, than at the Fidra Bay, and Martie, still remembering rationing, could only marvel at the quantity and excellence of the meals. All kinds of tubercular cases were treated at Mount Forest, and some were very seriously ill, but as long as they could they indulged their one last pleasure, which was eating. And who could blame them? asked Martie, who loved to eat heartily herself. Food was what they paid for, along with their treatments; it had to be the best, just as the treatments were the best, too. Not only the techniques of the wonderful operating theatre were available to them, but the new medications as well, including some that were experimental, for Dr Viner and his team of doctors were co-operating in various studies, testing out new drugs. It all came back to money, didn't it?

She said as much to Dr Viner himself, for he was easy to talk to, never stood on ceremony, was always interested in what his staff had to say. He was quick to agree with her.

'Yes, all comes back to money, Martie. That's America for you.'

He laughed, as though he were not American himself. In fact, he had been born in New York, his parents being Austrian immigrants, and with his blond crew-cut and serene blue eyes looked as American as apple pie. Martie knew that most of his female patients idolised him, but he had been divorced twice and had been heard to say that there would be no third time lucky marriage for him, he was now wedded to his work. That appeared to be true.

Did he ever rest? his young doctors wondered. Rest was not a word that appeared in his vocabulary, except, of course, for the patients.

Rest, however, was now considered only one option in patients' recovery, now that the 'miracle' drugs were coming more and more into use, though side-effects were still hampering progress. The trick, Dr Viner said, was to find out just how to use them. Everyone was working on that.

'Gives me a good feeling,' he finished, 'to think we're all working together to defeat that sonofabitch bug. And there's news lately of another drug said to be even more powerful than strepto- mycin or PAS. I'd hoped to be involved in trials, but I think they're keeping it under wraps for the time being.'

'I bet it'll turn out to be the same as all the others,' Martie commented. 'Two steps forward, one step back.'

'Maybe, but so far, it sounds dynamite. Just what we've been waiting for.' Dr Viner shook his head. 'If it is, if it's the real breakthrough, who knows – I might be out of a job!'

Martie's eyes widened. 'I don't think so, Dr Viner. Look at the number of cases here alone!'

'Oh, I know. There are thousands of new cases world-wide every year. Millions have died in the past. But I'm talking about the future. It could be very different, Martie.'

'Well, I hope you're right. Even if you are out of a job!'

'I can always change specialties!' he said with a grin.

Later, over coffee, some of the nurses were discussing the chances of achieving a real cure for TB. Martie had relayed Dr Viner's hopes, but most were sceptical. There had been so many claims for wonder drugs before, and every time the TB germ had won the battle. It was so strong, so varied, it could spread to bones, kidneys, intestines, every organ. Consider the patients at Mount Forest, for instance. Some had responded to the drugs and appeared healed, but who knew when the disease would return? Then there were all those who had not responded, or who had developed side-effects, or could not tolerate the treatment anyway.

'I don't see any end to it,' Alice Penn, an attractive blonde declared. 'They'll never be able to close places like this, they'll never be able to do without surgery.'

As others were murmuring agreement, a young nurse put her head round the door and said there was a visitor for Martie. A Mr Adamson.

Warren? Martie flushed. He'd already arranged a meeting. Why come to ask for her today? Aware of her colleagues' interest, she said she'd really no time to see him, but he was her old employer, probably was in the area, just wanted to say hello—

'Go ahead,' they drawled. 'See the guy, Martie.'

But the man waiting for her in a small room off Reception, wasn't Warren. It was Brent.

Chapter Forty-One

Her first thought was that something had happened to Warren; her second, that if anything had happened to Warren, the last place Brent would have come would be Massachusetts to see her. But Brent did not look well. As he stood, with his heavy damp coat on his arm and his winter scarf still round his neck, he seemed strained and weary, older than his years.

'Hello, Martie,' he said, in his usual cold tones. 'I hope you can spare me a few minutes? I really want to speak with you.'

'You've come all the way from New York? Must be important.' Hearing the tremor in her own voice, Martie pushed forward a chair to give herself time. 'Like to sit down?'

'I'll stand, thanks. This won't take long.'

'That's good, I have work to do.'

His wintry gaze met her defiant stare. He cleared his throat.

'A few days ago, Martie, my father's signature was needed for certain documents at the bank. They were to do with a deal I'd organised, I wanted it to go through, and I tried to find him. He was nowhere to be found.'

Martie looked out of the window. It was snowing, she noticed.

'I spoke to my father's secretary, Betty Heimer.' Brent laid his coat on the chair Martie had offered him, took off his scarf and placed it on top of the coat. 'I don't know if you've met Betty, Martie?'

She shook her head.

'Betty's devoted to Dad. If he burned down the White House, that'd be OK with her.' Brent gave a faint smile. 'She said she didn't know where Dad was. I said, supposing there's an emergency? She said signing the papers for my deal wasn't an emergency. So, I knew she knew where he was and she wasn't saying. There wasn't a damn' thing I could do, so I waited to call him till late that evening. He wasn't home. I didn't see him till he came to the bank next day. Then I made him tell me where he'd been. As I'd guessed, he'd been with you.'

'Not at night, he hadn't!' flared Martie. 'He came to see me in the afternoon and we drove for a while. Anything wrong with that?'

'Plenty!' Brent's eyes were starting from his head. 'He'd been with you and he'd asked you to marry him. He said I might as well know, though it was a secret for the time being. A secret! I'll say! When my mother's not cold in her grave!'

Martie bit her lip, as the colour flooded her face. 'I know how you feel, Brent. I know how it must seem.'

'You don't know how I feel. You don't know what my mother meant to me.' Brent suddenly sat down and put his hand to his eyes. 'To think of her place being taken by someone else – so soon – it makes me sick to my stomach! I can't accept it. I won't accept it.' He took his hand from his eyes and stared up at Martie, whose own eyes were cast down. 'Do you understand what I'm saying?'

'Yes. You won't accept it. I never thought you would.'

'None of the family will accept it. It's not as though you'd anything in common with us. You come from a different country, a different background, you could never fit into our lives – or Dad's, for that matter. If he hadn't taken leave of his senses, he'd see that for himself.'

Martie gave a grim little laugh. 'I thought this was God's own country? I thought everybody was equal here? Or is it just the folk in your world who are equal, and the rest of us don't measure up?'

'You know what I'm talking about, Martie. You know there are some things that matter, and fitting in is one of them.' Brent softened his tone. 'I mean, what's it going to be like for you, trying to fill Mother's shoes? Can't you see you're just going to make yourself very unhappy?'

Martie moved to the door. 'No, it's you who's going to make

me unhappy, Brent. You and your family, when what you should be thinking about is your Dad's happiness. He's older than me, but he's no' an old man. He's got his life to live and he's a right to live it how he likes. I know it seems wrong for him to be thinking about marriage so soon, but it won't really be soon. We're going to wait a long time. There'll be no scandal, unless you want to make it yourself.' She opened the door. 'I've got to get back to work now, Brent. Will you go?'

He picked up his coat and came to her. He put his hand on her arm.

'Martie, listen. I do have my father's happiness in mind. That's why I'm asking you to give him up. It wouldn't work out. You're too young, you'd grow tired of him, and I don't want to see him hurt. Look me in the eye and tell me that if he weren't a rich man, you'd still want to marry him.'

Her eyes that had been fixed on his wavered and fell. No words came from her dry lips.

'I understand,' Brent said gently. 'But I know you're no gold-digger. You're just very young and you were dazzled. No one could blame you. I don't blame Dad, either. You're very attractive, and I guess he was dazzled, too.' He took his hand from Martie's arm and drew his chequebook from the pocket of his jacket. 'Who can make decisions when they're dazzled? But there's no reason why you should miss out. I've already written something for you here. It's quite generous. Very generous, really, and I'm sure Dad won't mind if you keep the ring he said he'd given you. What do you say?'

She wanted to hit him, to hurt him as much as he'd hurt her. But she knew she could never do that. Stepping into the corridor, she looked back at him, her eyes glinting.

'I'll keep the ring, all right, because I'll be wearing it when your father announces our engagement. But you can keep the bloody cheque. Goodbye, Brent.'

'Doesn't your guest want coffee?' asked Theo Rushworth, the receptionist, as Martie swung past her desk.

'Thanks, he's no' staying.'

'It's snowing out there. Hope he's got chains for his car.'

251

'If he needs them, he'll have them. He's that sort of guy.'

Theo smiled uncertainly. 'Well – there's some mail for you. You want it now?'

Martie said she was late for duty already. She'd pick it up before dinner.

After some hours of hard physical work, changing beds, mopping up blood and worse, moving patients, banging around in the sluice, she felt a little better. Not quite so raw, not quite so furious. But still pretty raw, still pretty furious. Not to say humiliated. She longed to be with Warren, have him comfort her, but hadn't decided yet if she would tell him of Brent's visit. Brent might not tell his father what he'd tried to do, it might be better for her to keep it from him, too. Oh, but what an outlook, eh? Maybe she and Warren could move right away from his family? Start life afresh? Thing was, she couldn't imagine him permanently away from New York, away from the bank. As she had said herself, he wasn't old, he wasn't ready for handing everything over to Brent. But the thought of living in the same city, the same planet, as Brent Adamson, made her feel so angry, she thought maybe she should take her own blood pressure. The worst of it was she could almost – almost – see his point of view. But the way he'd put it to her – oh, God, she'd better not think about that . . .

Her mail would take her mind off things. She collected it on her way to her room to wash before a hurried meal. Two or three Christmas cards from home. A soft little package from Alex – she'd keep that for her Christmas morning. A large envelope from her parents, a calendar, she guessed, and when she opened it in her room, found she was right.

Ah, look at that, then! Mum and Dad had really excelled themselves! A calendar from the grocery where her father worked. 'With the compliments of John Denny and Sons, Purveyors of High-Class Foodstuffs, Provisions, and Cold Cuts, since 1907.' Then pictures of Edinburgh. One of the original shop, with the assistants, all male, wearing long aprons and drooping moustaches. The Castle, Princes Street, Calton Hill, Charlotte Square, John Knox's House, Holyrood, the Meadows, the Lawnmarket, the Grassmarket, Advocates' Close, and last of all, for December, and marked with a cross by her mother, 'Children playing in the Stockbridge Colonies, at the Turn of the Century.'

There was one of the familiar streets running down to the Water of Leith, with the dear old two-storeyed houses. Girls in pinafores and boys in knickerbockers, bowling hoops, women in long dresses standing at doors. A horse and cart in the distance, a man carrying a ladder. All long, long ago. Before Martie's time. Yet, timeless. Her home, frozen, for ever, with people she had never known yet felt for with strange, heart-wrenching affinity. The Colonies. Despised when she wanted to get away. And now? She blew her nose and wiped her misting eyes. Would she really go back? Her eyes went to the chest of drawers, where she had locked Warren's ring. Honestly, what a fool she was! Of course, she wouldn't go back. Talk about being sentimental!

She took the key and opened the top drawer, removed the box and looked at the ring. It was as beautiful as ever, the symbol of all that she had ever wanted, and just for a moment she slipped it on her finger.

'Martie, honey, you coming?' Alice called outside her door, and she jumped like a guilty thing.

'Coming!' she sang, and locked away her treasure. Alex's present and her cards she put with her other Christmas things, her parents' calendar she looked at again, then laid aside. Couldn't put that up till Hogmanay. New Year's. Whatever. She felt a long way from home.

Chapter Forty-Two

Alex was worrying about Martie. Why didn't she put pen to paper and say what was happening? All there'd been from her since Christmas was a thank-you letter for the tartan scarf and a postcard from Boston. 'Great city, having a lovely time.' What sort of news was that? At least Rose kept in touch, sending instructions for Alex's coming trip to Cyprus. 'Bring sun-oil, sunglasses, summer clothes, cardigans, a light raincoat.' But Alex wasn't worried about Rose.

'Do you think Martie's all right?' she asked Neal.

'I've no idea. But from what I remember of her, I'd say she could take care of herself.'

'I get the feeling things aren't going as well as she'd expected.'

'Why don't you phone her?'

Alex looked scandalised. 'In America? I couldn't do that!'

'It wouldn't cost much. You could call from my place.'

'Oh, no, thanks all the same. I'll stick to writing.'

'Need two people to write if you want communication.'

'Maybe if I write from Cyprus, she'll be so staggered she'll reply!'

Neal laughed. 'She has crossed the Atlantic herself, remember.'

'Yes, but Cyprus sounds so exotic, do you no' think?' Alex's eyes shone. 'Folk like me don't usually go to exotic places.'

'My guess is that everyone will go to exotic places in the future. And then they won't be exotic any more.'

'Ah, don't spoil things,' said Alex.

It was almost April. Reports from New York of yet another amazing TB treatment had caused interest at the Jubilee in February, but like everyone else, the staff had been stunned by the death of King George the Sixth in that same month. Public gloom swept the country; no one could even imagine spring. Then suddenly there it was, on the horizon. The new Queen looked more cheerful, the weather was better, everyone took breath and started again. Including Alex, who was now all set for her trip and so excited, she could hardly get through the last days before she was due to fly to Nicosia. She had booked a one-way flight from London on a commercial airline, though was hoping for an indulgence passage home if the dates worked out. She had her passport and traveller's cheques ready, her cases packed, her flight bag organised. All she had to do was say goodbye to people. As though she was going for a long long time, instead of a fortnight!

She laughed about it to Neal, but on her last night, he said seriously, 'I feel you ARE going for a long, long time.' He'd given her dinner in the West End, they were walking back to Stockbridge on a beautifully light evening, arms entwined as though they were lovers. In a way, they were, for there was certainly love between them, though it was not equally divided. They had never spoken of marriage, never slept together, or done more than exchange kisses, but Alex knew that Neal was living on hope and getting by, and that she was waiting and seeing. Not waiting to see if Neal could stay completely well, but for her own heart to tell her something. It must, soon. Neal couldn't live on hope for ever. Maybe this little time away would be the turning point.

'I'll be gone all of a fortnight,' she said, still laughing.

'But I'll miss you so much!'

'I'll send you lots of postcards.'

'One every day?'

'One every day, but they'll probably arrive after I get back.'

'I'll have them to keep, though. Something in your hand-writing. I haven't got much.'

'That's because you see me all the time.'

'Not all the time,' he said quietly.

In his flat they made coffee and Neal put a match to his fire, for though spring was in the air, the evening wasn't warm. Alex said she couldn't stay long, she must get home, get to bed. She had a very early start tomorrow.

'I wish you'd let me come to the station,' said Neal, drawing her to his knee. 'I could have closed the shop for a bit.'

'I hate goodbyes at stations, even if I'm only going on holiday.' Alex moved awkwardly in Neal's restraining arms. She always had the feeling she would damage him, lying against his chest, though she knew she was being foolish. Neal was very well.

'Aren't you?' she asked gently, twisting round to look into his eyes.

'Aren't I what?'

'Very well?'

'You don't miss much.' He hugged her tight. 'I was going to tell you – I had another check today. I haven't had any refills of gas for some time, they wanted to have a look at me.'

'And?'

'My lung has healed.' His hands holding her shook a little. 'I don't need any more treatment. They don't think this time I'll have any recurrence and don't want to see me again for twelve months. I'm cured.'

'Neal!' She flung her arms around him and kissed him. 'Why did you no' tell me before when we were having our meal? We could have celebrated!'

'I wanted to tell you now.' He quietly released her from his arms and as she left his knee, he stood up and stirred his newly burning fire. 'Wanted to tell you something else, too.' He glanced back at her, saw her standing quite still, waiting for his news. 'When they told me I was really better, I took the opportunity to ask Dr Senior something. I suppose you can guess what it was?'

'No,' she whispered, guessing all the same.

256

'I asked if it would be possible for me to marry. Know what he said?'

'I expect he said you could.'

'He did! In fact, he said he would give me his blessing. I was one of their successes and he didn't see why I shouldn't remain so.'

'That's wonderful, Neal.' Alex's smile was genuine, though her eyes were wary. 'I'm so pleased for you.'

'Pleased for me? What about yourself?' Neal gave a little laugh. 'You know I asked about marriage with you in mind. You're the one I love, I told you that.'

'Yes, you did.'

'So, you know what I'm asking.' Neal moved closer to Alex and took her hands. 'Let's do it the old-fashioned way, with me going down on one knee. Alex, will you marry me?'

As he began to kneel, smiling, yet with a deadly serious look in his eye, Alex pulled him up.

'Neal, don't be silly!'

'OK, let's skip the formalities. But what do you say? Will you have me?'

She turned her head away from his intense gaze. 'I don't know, Neal. It's all been a bit of a shock.'

'Why? You've known for some time what I felt about you.'

'Yes, but marriage – I hadn't thought about it.'

'You thought you were safe? I couldn't marry?'

'No! Don't talk like that! Oh, look, I know I haven't been fair. I was happy, seeing you, but it was never right, taking and no' giving, making you wait. But I thought—'

'I had to wait?' He pulled her gently towards him. 'I don't now.'

'Neal, I'm sorry, I don't know what to say. I care for you so much, I love being with you—'

'But you don't know whether you love me or not?' He touched her face with his thin hand. 'The trouble is, you still see me as a patient, that's what's wrong. But things are different now, aren't they? I'm a man as good as any other. I won't break if we make love!'

She winced a little as the shot went home, and he smiled wryly.

257

'Look, let's sit down again. I want to tell you about my prospects.'

'Prospects? Oh, Neal!'

'No, you need to know.' As he took his shabby chair again, and Alex sat on the stool near him, Neal looked earnestly into her face. 'It's true I'm not earning much with the shop, but now that I'm well, I can go back to teaching and have a proper salary again. Then, my father has some inherited money. If I married, he'd make some of that over to me, enough to buy a decent house. We wouldn't have to live in this basement.' Neal suddenly brought Alex's hands to his lips and kissed them. 'You see, my darling, I could provide for you. I'm not offering just my love.'

Alex lowered her eyes. She could think of nothing to say, nothing that would make Neal happy, and that was all she wanted.

'Will you think about it?' he asked quietly.

'Of course I will!'

They drew together in a long hard kiss that was almost a lovers' kiss, as when they held each other, the embrace was almost a lovers' embrace. Not quite, though. Alex drew back, trembling.

'Of course I'll think about what you've said, Neal. I'm honoured, I really am—'

'For God's sake, don't say that!'

'Well, I am. I think it's wonderful that you should love me, I want you to know I appreciate it.'

'OK.' He stood up, his expression dark. 'Shall we say that when you come back from your holiday, you'll give me your answer?'

'Yes, let's say that!' She felt a tremendous relief at the postponement. After all, two weeks in another country was a long time. Maybe, she would feel quite different then. Though to tell the truth, she didn't precisely know how she felt at that moment. There was so much love in her, welling up for someone, and it might be Neal. It should be Neal, who cared so much for her.

They left the flat and made their way slowly towards the Colonies, neither speaking, but holding hands. At the steps leading to her home, Neal paused and looked down at her.

'Have a wonderful time,' he whispered. 'And give my regards to Rose.'

'I will, Neal.'

'Come back safely, you're very precious.'

They kissed again, briefly, then Alex ran up the steps to her father's door and waved. Neal waved back, and as she let herself into the house, walked away.

'My word, you look as if you've no' had a wink of sleep!' Edie exclaimed next morning, as Alex drank a cup of tea standing up and watched the clock for the taxi. 'Have you been lying awake all night, you silly girl, thinking o' Cyprus?'

'Yes,' Alex answered, and it was true, she had been lying awake for what seemed most of the night, but she had not been thinking of Cyprus.

Chapter Forty-Three

The first thing that struck her when she arrived at Nicosia Airport was the quality of the light. The second was the change in Rose, who had come to meet her.

'Heavens, this sun!' Alex exclaimed, when she and Rose had made their restrained embrace and were on their way to Rose's car. 'It's so—'

'Strong? Yes, even in April, it's powerful.'

'I was going to say, so different from home.'

'That, too.'

As Rose shaded her eyes and looked around the lines of cars parked outside the airport buildings, Alex stared at her with such fascination she felt embarrassed and forced herself to look away. But what was different about Rose? It was not just the glow of her face that had once been so white, or her bare arms and legs, or her varnished red toenails, though these were enough to make Alex's mind reel. No, it was something else she could not place, until Rose gave a sigh of relief, and cried, 'There he is!' And took the arm of the young man who came running, and looked up into his face, smiling. Then Alex knew what was different about Rose. She was in love.

Rose? In love? Well, of course, Alex had had clues already. She should have been prepared, ever since Rose had written about 'this nice young air-force fellow', the 'friend' who'd been with her on her sightseeing trips; should have realised that Rose was only human, after all, and as capable of falling in love as anyone else. And Simon Dawson, shaking Alex's hand, looked a really nice chap who so obviously adored Rose he would probably have married her tomorrow. Were they already lovers? Alex felt guilty at the thought, feeling that the old Rose would not have approved. But who knew what the new Rose would do? Just the way she and Simon looked at each other and touched hands as they put Alex's luggage into the boot of Rose's car, convinced Alex that they were sleeping together. Such golden rapport – that came from sex, didn't it? Oh, God, I'm a gooseberry, thought Alex, but knew she didn't have to worry. With two such well-mannered people looking after her, she wouldn't be made to feel unwelcome. In fact, as soon as they left the airport, they were already vying with each other to point out all that she should see in the capital city.

'What you have to remember, Alex,' said Simon, who was driving Rose's little car, with Alex next to him and Rose leaning forward from the back seat, 'is that Nicosia's had a pretty chequered history, so you get reminders of that all over the place. The Venetians built great stone walls and gates, and the Turks built mosques and minarets, and in the middle of Ataturk Square there's a huge monolith that probably came from Salamis. That's where there are some amazing Roman remains. We'll take you there.'

'We'll take you everywhere,' put in Rose. 'But this is Ledra Street. It's the main shopping area, you'll be able to get your souvenirs here, but don't buy lace. I know a wonderful little shop in Kyrenia where I want to take you for that.'

'Rose knows wonderful little shops everywhere,' said Simon, grinning. Alex turned round brown eyes on her friend.

'And you never used to care about shopping, Rose!'

'Didn't I? I must have changed.'

The nurses' quarters, where Rose had managed to obtain a guest-room for Alex, were in a plain, modern building, which Rose said was very dull but comfortable. Anyway, whatever it was like, it didn't matter. She, Rose, was scarcely ever there; nor would Alex be. During the fortnight she was due to spend in Cyprus, her feet wouldn't touch the ground, Rose could guarantee it.

'We'll meet tonight, then,' said Simon as he lifted out Alex's case. 'Eight o'clock OK for dinner? And how about a night club afterwards – if Alex is not too tired?'

'A night-club? I'm not sure Alex will approve.' Rose laughed. 'She'll probably be shocked by the belly-dancers!'

'I will not!' cried Alex, stung. 'Nurses don't get shocked.'

'Ah, but when did you last see a belly-dancer performing in the Jubilee?' asked Rose. 'Now that would cheer up Butterfly Two, wouldn't it?'

Oh, Rose had changed, all right, thought Alex.

Later, when she had showered and changed into a sleeveless pale green shift, she looked at herself in the dressing-table mirror with some dissatisfaction. How pale she looked! Anyone could see she was straight out of a Scottish winter and beside vivid Rose would probably fade right away. Not that it mattered. No one would be looking at her, anyway.

'How pretty you look!' cried Rose, joining her. 'Watch out for the fellows, Alex, they'll be round you like bees to honey. New talent, you see.'

'Talent?' Alex shook her head. 'Rose, I can't get over you! You're so different!'

Rose smiled. 'Don't be deceived. I'm still the same old Rose underneath. All this is packaging.'

'I'm no' so sure. I think something about you has changed. Something pretty fundamental.'

'And what might that be?' Rose lay on Alex's bed, her dark eyes dancing. 'Or, shall I guess? You think I've found love?'

'Yes. Yes, I do. I saw it straight away.'

'Oh, dear. Are we so transparent?'

'To me, anyway.'

Rose leaped off the bed, straightening her white dress that showed off her splendid tan. 'Well, I suppose I might as well admit it. Simon and I are in love.'

'Are you – engaged?' Alex asked cautiously.

'No. That's my problem. How to be married and still have a career. If Simon weren't in the RAF, if I weren't a QA, I daresay we could work something out. As it is, we're compromising.'

'What exactly does that mean?'

'I'm sure the great Sherlock Holmes has guessed already,' Rose said lightly. 'Not shocked, are you?'

'Why do you think I'm going to be shocked at everything? Of course I'm not!' Alex put a compact and a lipstick in her evening bag. 'As long as you know what you're doing.'

'Oh, I know what I'm doing, don't worry about that.' Rose threw a bright pink stole around her shoulders. 'But what's all this talk about me? How are things with you?'

Alex hesitated. 'I suppose you mean, is there anybody to replace Tim?' she asked at last. 'Well, I have been seeing Neal Drover. And before you say anything, Rose, he is better. Dr Senior's given him a clean bill of health.'

'I'm glad to hear it,' Rose said coolly. 'A very handsome man, if I remember rightly. But why should I say anything?'

'I thought you might not approve. Because of his history.'

'There's no harm in going out with someone who's better, Alex. As long as you don't get too involved. I mean, obviously, you'd have to steer clear of marriage.'

'You think so?' Alex had turned away and was combing her hair at the mirror.

'Of course. Clean bill of health or not, people like Neal shouldn't marry. Come on, let's go, Simon will be waiting. We're eating Turkish tonight. You must try the shish kebab.'

The restaurant was small and crowded, rather noisy but colourful, the very place, Alex thought, to feel truly abroad. There was nothing like it in Edinburgh, anyway. Over the meal, which she found spicy but good, Simon and Rose talked knowledgeably away about life in Cyprus. How everything was either or. Either Turkish, or Greek, but never both. There were a couple of minority groups in the population – Armenians and Maronites – and of course there were the British, but when talking of Cypriots, you had to say which kind you meant. Turkish, or Greek.

'Nice thing is, a good many people speak some English,' said

Rose. 'But I've been trying to learn a little Greek. You know, just a few phrases, to show willing.'

'The Greeks'll never be happy with us in Cyprus, whether you learn a bit of their language or not,' Simon told her. He glanced at Alex. 'Want us out, you know. Want to be joined with mainland Greece. They call it *Enosis*.'

'Might that happen?' asked Alex.

'Not if the Turks have anything to do with it!'

'Will they fight over it, do you think?'

'Yes, I'm sure they will. There are already a few fellows around who want that.'

Alex looked at Rose with some apprehension.

'There's no' going to be violence where you are, Rose?'

'No, no. Don't worry about it. The young men often have a few skirmishes, but there's no real sign of anything more as yet.' Rose smiled. 'Let's change the subject. Tell me what you've heard from Martie lately. I think she's given up writing to me.'

'And me,' Alex said hastily. 'But she did tell me she was working in a TB sanatorium in New England.'

'Is that right?' Rose opened her dark eyes wide. 'Good old Martie! A true nurse after all!' She turned to Simon, explaining that Martie was a colleague of theirs who had gone to America. 'With the intention of marrying a rich man, I believe, but seems she's nursing instead. I must say, I'm pleased.'

So, it was true, Alex thought, in some ways Rose hadn't changed.

'Hey, what's wrong with marrying money?' asked Simon, laughing. 'How much have you got, Rose?'

She laughed, too, as Simon filled up her glass with sweet white wine, then rested her lovely eyes on Alex, who was quietly blushing with the effort of keeping Martie's secret.

'Strange, isn't it, how we've scattered? We butterfly girls?'

'I often think that,' Alex replied. 'I'm the only one back where we started.'

'Butterfly girls?' echoed Simon.

'Oh, don't ask!' cried Rose. 'It was just a name a patient gave us. Alex, can we tempt you to something else? A Turkish pastry?

They do a lovely one here, filled with honey and nuts.'

'Not for me.' Alex shook her head. 'I don't know how it is, but somehow I can't seem to keep ma eyes open—'

'Oh, Simon, look at her! The poor girl's falling asleep at the table! No belly-dancers for you tonight, Alex, I'm going to have to get you home to bed!'

The day had been so filled with experiences, Alex could not clear her mind as she lay in her narrow, army-issue bed. The Turkish meal lay heavily on her stomach, the pungent smell of the charcoal-cooked meat seemed still in her nostrils, and though the temperature had dropped, she felt too hot. Her guide-book had said April nights were cool, so perhaps she should be grateful she hadn't come in August, but just as at home in Edinburgh, she still couldn't sleep.

'People like Neal shouldn't marry,' she seemed to hear Rose's clear voice declaring again. Then: 'Obviously, you'd have to steer clear of marriage . . .' And: 'There's no harm in going out with someone who's better . . . as long as you don't get too involved.'

Too involved . . . too involved . . .

But I am involved, thought Alex, and stared into the strange heavy darkness of the Cyprus night, longing for it to enfold her. Which it must have done, eventually, for the next she knew her room was filled with yellow light and Rose was smiling down at her.

'Want some tea? The milk's tinned, but it's not too bad.'

'What – what time is it?'

'Time to get up, I'm afraid. Come on, we've things to do!'

Chapter Forty-Four

Cyprus was a kaleidoscope. Every day another shake and there it was, a new pattern. A new picture. People, places, flowers, views, clear seas, quiet beaches. Every night, a different restaurant. Dancing. Talking under the stars.

Rose had been right, Simon's air-force colleagues were interested in Alex. She was a new face, and a pretty one. New talent. There was always someone to make up a foursome for a meal or dancing at a Nicosia night-club, to laugh with Alex over the gyrations of the belly-dancers, which she found only astonishing. ('I mean, if you've done a bit of anatomy, it's hard to see how they can do what they do, eh?') There was always somebody urging her to 'talk more Scotch' and calling 'Hoots, mon, och aye!' until Simon would say, 'Come on, fellas, give it a rest!' and Rose would frown, though Alex didn't mind in the least. OK, the fellows were teasing her, but they were nice about it, and always said they loved to hear the way she talked and that it suited her. Though she would not have admitted it, she found it pleasant to be in a relaxed, carefree atmosphere after so much time spent with Neal. No, she would never admit that.

Every day, she sent him the promised postcard. Views of the castles of Buffavento and Kantara, snow on the Troodos mountains, the birthplace of Aphrodite, Roman ruins at Salamis. Sometimes, just a camel on the sands, or pretty girls working in the vineyards, and once for fun, her own drawing of an octopus. 'Guess what,' she wrote, 'I saw one of these in the market at Famagusta. Rose says they're good to eat, but I said not for me!'

'Hey, who is this lucky guy you write to every day?' asked Simon, whose job it was to post the cards as forces' mail. 'Should I tell the fellas you're spoken for?'

'No, of course she isn't,' said Rose before Alex could speak. 'Neal's just a friend, isn't he, Alex?'

'Well – I have got to know him well,' Alex said, feeling treacherous.

'There's no need to tell anybody anything,' Rose said firmly, and Alex said no more.

Even in the short time she'd been there, she was beginning to get the feel of Cyprus, island of contrasts. A place steeped in history, yet struggling to come into modern times. Tarmacked roads, and peasants tending sheep. Blocks of luxury flats, and crumbling squares, where old men sat under trees, and women dressed in black gossiped over lace-making and stitching. The young men were handsome and volatile, sometimes flashing smiles, sometimes not, but the girls, even in their bright colours, seemed subdued. There were things they couldn't do, and whether they were Turkish or Greek, their dark eyes on foreign women were filled with the same wonder.

'They're under here,' said Rose, indicating her thumb. 'Their menfolk give them their orders.'

'Quite right,' commented Simon, grinning. 'No, I don't mean it!'

'Things will change for them, I suppose,' said Alex. 'But it looks as if it will take a long time. We're lucky, eh?'

'Took us long enough,' Rose answered dryly. 'And we've still got some way to go.'

But Cyprus was beautiful, and on the surface, romantic. Daytime skies were a hard, cloudless blue, but at night the heavens were black velvet, often with a great moon. Perfect for lovers, thought Alex, with a great knot of sadness in her chest. No wonder Rose and Simon had 'compromised' as they had, in a place like this.

Under the obvious beauty, however, were occasional marks of unease. Little straws in the wind. Averted eyes from villagers, waiters who pretended not to see them. Nothing much. Only signs.

'They want us out,' Simon had said, and though neither he nor Rose ever expressed anxiety, Alex sometimes shivered a little in the sunshine.

It was towards the end of her second week that Rose and Simon drove Alex to Kyrenia, together with Don Evans, an easy-going flight-lieutenant who had accompanied them a couple of times before. Though only sixteen miles from Nicosia, the distance seemed longer for the road was full of twists and startling hairpin bends, compensated for by exquisite views glimpsed from time to time. No doubt it would all be straightened out one day, Simon remarked. Which, of course, would spoil it, said Rose.

'Kyrenia is my favourite place,' she told Alex, as they made the descent into the little town. 'I've been saving it till last.'

'It's heavenly,' said Alex, surveying the harbour, filled with fishing boats and small yachts. There was a medieval look to it, with ancient walls built to hold the sea at bay, and a great castle, begun by the Byzantines, finished by the Venetians, that was so much like everyone's idea of a castle, it was almost theatrical. You felt you could roll it up and put it away like a play's scenery. Just as you could imagine making a jigsaw of the harbour, all sparkling sea and sunlight, and filling in the people sitting at the cafés, sipping cold drinks and Turkish coffee as they looked out to sea. Yes, Kyrenia was just heavenly, but a little unreal. A little too perfect. Are we really here? thought Alex, and wondered at herself for her strange mood. Perhaps she was sad, thinking of going home so soon, her holiday over. Talking of going home, she'd better buy that lace she wanted for Edie.

'Where's this good shop you told me about?' she asked Rose.

'Just on the waterfront, but first, we must have something to drink. Mustn't get dehydrated.'

'Rose takes good care of us,' Don said, with a laugh. 'She'll be telling us to put our hats on soon.'

'Not under the vines,' Rose said seriously. 'Look, this café is perfect, completely in the shade.'

The afternoon was hotter than usual, almost like full summer, and the town was filled with strolling visitors, some families, some

268

young women, but quite a number of young men, Turks and Greeks. There were one or two scuffles. Nothing serious. Just young men playing about, shouting, calling each other names.

'Kyrenia' s mainly Turkish,' Simon told Alex, 'but as you can see, there are all sorts here.'

'Some look British,' Alex observed.

'They are. Service folk like us, or else ex-pats, retired people, members of the Yacht Club, living the life of Riley on their pensions.'

'That's for me,' said Rose, and they laughed, because retirement was so far away for all of them.

Don ordered more cold drinks. Alex had another Turkish coffee, which she'd quite taken to, and they all had more pastries.

'Now, we really must do our shopping,' said Rose. 'You fellows can stay here, if you like.'

'No, I think we'll stick together,' said Simon, rising. 'Don't want you girls getting caught up in anything.'

'Caught up in what?' asked Alex.

'Simon, don't frighten Alex.' Rose shook her head at him.

'Sorry.' He smiled. 'But some of those young guys are a bit aggressive. Out for a fight.'

'Not with us. Come on, Alex.'

The shop on the waterfront sold pottery as well as lace, and a variety of curios. After the brilliant sunshine outside, it was filled with shadows, but when her eyes adjusted, Alex saw that there were other women looking round, and that the Greek proprietor was at everyone's elbow, showing his wares. As soon as he saw Rose, he recognised her, and came up, all smiles, to be introduced to Alex.

'A young lady from England?' He bowed deeply.

'Scotland,' said Rose. 'Looking for a present to take home. Something nice.'

'Everything nice, madame!'

'We'll be outside,' Simon said, groaning, as the traycloths, tea-cosy covers, dressing-table sets, were brought out and Rose began to turn them over. 'Just having a smoke, OK?'

'OK,' Rose said absently. 'What do you think, Alex? The tea-cosy is beautiful – so intricate – but might be too expensive?'

'I think Edie might prefer these mats.'

'Is a duchess set,' said the proprietor proudly. 'So the ladies tell me!'

'Just right for Edie,' Alex said with a laugh. 'I'll take it, please.'

She was opening her purse and Rose was studying a rather handsome jug, when a young man burst through the open door. He was silhouetted against the light, they couldn't see his face, but they could smell his sweat, smell his fear. He shouted something to the proprietor, who turned white, then ran past Rose, pushing her out of his way. As he did so, another male figure appeared in the doorway. Something went flying from his hand, and one of the women customers screamed. The proprietor, holding his heart, sank to a chair. The first young man leaped through a door at the back of the shop, the second had already gone. Melted away. Alex, who had been standing rooted to the spot, turned to Rose. But Rose, too, had gone.

She was lying on the floor, a red stain spreading on her pale yellow dress. There was a knife in her chest.

'Rose!' cried Alex. 'Oh, God, Rose!'

Down she went, on her knees, but Simon was there before her, holding Rose fast.

'Simon, Simon, let me see to her, let me see to her!'

The knife had dropped to the floor, he had kicked it to one side, and was cradling Rose in his arms, his face ashen, his eyes sightless. Only when Alex shrieked his name again, did he let Rose go, and then Alex flung herself down beside her friend.

'There is a pulse!' she cried frantically, 'But we must get her to hospital, she's losing blood fast. Find a phone, quickly!'

'Is too late,' groaned the proprietor, rocking himself to and fro. 'Is too late!'

'Get me some cloths, help me stop the bleeding!'

A crowd was gathering in the shop and Don appeared, pushing his way through, gasping for breath, covered in sweat.

'I lost him – I lost him – but the police are coming. Oh, God, what's happened to Rose?'

'There's a pulse,' said Alex, trying to staunch the blood with cloths someone had pushed into her hands. 'I tell you, there's a pulse, she might be all right, we just have to get her to hospital!'

But long before the ambulance arrived, there was no longer any pulse. Rose was dead.

Chapter Forty-Five

Nightmare. How did you escape from nightmare? You woke up. But Alex was already awake, that was the problem. There was no escape.

Everyone was so kind. All Rose's colleagues tried to comfort her, all the young men who had made up their foursomes brought flowers and wrote notes. An army doctor prescribed a sedative, but she refused to take it, for how would she feel when it wore off? The only person she wanted to see was Simon, for she felt only she could understand his pain, but Simon had been given compassionate leave and was nowhere to be found.

'He's gone away for a little while,' Don told her. 'Can't face seeing anyone, but he'll be back. He's strong, he'll cope.'

'I must see him before I go,' Alex said earnestly. 'I have to go home, you know, I'm on duty.'

'It's all right, you needn't go yet. The Station Commander's been in touch with your hospital, they've given you extra leave.' The thing is –' Don hesitated. 'There'll be an enquiry, you might be called as a witness.'

'Oh, no, no, I couldn't be a witness, I couldn't!'

'If they catch the chap, surely you'd want to be?'

Alex put her hand to her eyes. 'Will they catch him?'

'Probably not. He'll be away to some little village where they'll hide him till the heat's off.' Don stubbed out his cigarette and lit another. 'He didn't even mean to kill her.'

'What happened?' Alex asked, after a pause. 'No one's told me. No one wants to talk about it.'

'Apparently, some young men, Greeks and Turks, were having a scrap over *Enosis*, some drew knives, some scattered. One guy ran into the lace shop, another followed, and – you know the rest.'

'Rose was just in the wrong place.' Alex stared into space. 'It could have been me. Why wasn't it me? Why should Rose be the one to die?'

'These things happen, Alex. I'm not religious, but they say there's a pattern.'

'What pattern? How can there be a pattern that takes Rose away from us? Away from Simon? She'd only just learned to love and she was so happy!'

'I know, I know.' Don held Alex's hand. 'I'm just trying to find something to make sense of it all. But there is no sense.'

A tale told by an idiot, thought Alex, who had heard Arthur quote the line from the 'Scottish play' so many times. She tried to picture her father declaiming, and Jamie listening, but their faces would not come to her. All she could see was Rose's last bewildered, beautiful gaze.

'When will Simon come back?' she asked, as Don rose to go.

'Tomorrow, I expect. That's when Rose's parents arrive.'

'Rose's parents are coming here?'

'Apparently a flight has been arranged for them. They want to see where Rose died. They want to see Rose.'

And me, they'll want to see me. Sweat broke out on Alex's brow. She couldn't face Rose's parents. No, she wouldn't see them.

The next day, she and Simon with a senior nursing officer and the station commander went to meet the plane bringing Mr and Mrs Burnett to Nicosia.

The usual strong sunlight was beating down, as the plane landed and taxied to a halt. There was a short delay as steps were placed in position, then the doors opened and an attendant came out, followed by three figures dressed in sombre clothes.

'Three,' whispered Alex, half to herself.

'I believe Rose's brother has come, too,' Simon said in the expressionless voice he had lately adopted.

'Her brother?'

'I expect you know him, don't you? Tim?'

'Yes, I know him.'

Walking slowly beside Simon, Alex followed the senior people towards Rose's family. It didn't seem strange that the sight of Tim, very pale, wearing a grey jacket and flannels and black tie, meant nothing to her. He wasn't Rose, was he? She could only focus on Rose. The Group Captain was presenting her to Mr and Mrs Burnett. Rose's friend, Alex, who had been with her when—

No, don't say it, don't say it! cried Alex inwardly. Oh, how they'll hate me for being alive when Rose is dead!

But Rose's mother took her hand and said, 'How good of you to come today, my dear, you must have had a terrible time.'

'Terrible,' agreed Mr Burnett, who looked old and ill.

Tim, showing no surprise at seeing her, said her name quietly, then looked at Simon.

Oh, poor Simon! Alex's heart went out to him as he stood on the tarmac, such a spectre of grief, greeting his lover's family, who might one day have been his family. Thank God he and Rose had taken the chance of happiness when it was theirs to take, and Rose had found the love she'd always thought she'd never need.

'Rose told us so much about you,' Mrs Burnett was saying tremulously, as Simon took her hand. 'We were so looking forward to meeting you, weren't we, dear?'

'We were,' Mr Burnett agreed.

'And we'll be able to see you again and talk?' Mrs Burnett looked at Alex. 'And you too, dear, if you wouldn't mind—'

'Of course, we'll talk, Mrs Burnett,' Alex murmured. 'Please ask me anything – anything!'

Oh, but please don't ask me to go back to Kyrenia, she fervently prayed. Don't ask me to do that!

She and Simon were alone, walking towards his car. The Burnetts had been driven away to the Group Captain's house, where they were to be his guests; the senior nurse had returned to duty. Simon was very pale and holding himself as tightly coiled as a spring.

'Got through that,' he murmured, trying to smile. 'Wasn't looking forward to it.'

'Oh, no!'

'They were to have come out in September, you know. For a holiday, Rose had it all planned.'

'I think they were truly glad to meet you, Simon. Rose must have told them how much you meant to her.'

'You think so?' His face lightened a little. 'Well, they did seem to want to see me. And I liked them. We'd probably have got on well.'

They took their seats in the car, but Simon did not immediately drive away.

'Tim's not much like her, is he? Not much like Rose. I was thinking he would be.'

'No,' Alex agreed. 'He's not like Rose.'

'They're taking her home, you know. They're going to have the funeral in Edinburgh. I'm getting leave to go. I want to see everything to do with Rose. Her home and where she went to school, where she worked – everything. Will you show me all that, Alex?'

'I'll be glad to, Simon.'

He gave her a lift back to the nurses' quarters, where she told him she hoped soon to get a flight home. The Group Captain had been very helpful and had said she could sign a statement to be left with the police, in case there was ever a case brought against Rose's killer. Not that it was likely. His fingerprints from the knife were not known, and no one could identify the knife itself. By now, he might well have got off the island altogether.

'He'll never be found,' Simon said broodingly. 'You didn't actually see him, did you?'

'No, he was just a presence in the doorway.'

'Just a presence in the doorway?' Simon laughed harshly. 'And he took Rose's life and ruined mine. By mistake. As though that makes a difference.'

They were both silent for a time, then Simon asked when she thought they might meet the Burnetts again. Alex wouldn't leave without seeing them?

'No, I know they want to talk to me. Ask me about Rose.' Alex swallowed painfully. 'How – she died.'

'We'll tell them she didn't suffer.'

'She didn't, I'm sure of that.'

'It's we who are suffering,' he said in a low voice. 'That's always the way, isn't it? For the ones who are left?'

Chapter Forty-Six

Her father and Jamie came to meet Alex's train at Waverley Station. When she saw them, though she had kept dry-eyed all the way back on the flight, all the long night hours in the hotel in London, she burst into tears.

'Oh, Dad! Jamie!'

'Poor girl,' Arthur said gently. 'Poor wee bairn!'

'It's Rose I'm crying for, no' maself, Dad.'

'Aye, but you've been through the mill, eh? Anybody can see by lookin' at you, you're that thin. Is she no' thin, Jamie?'

'She's no' so bad,' said Jamie, hugging her. 'Come on, I've got the car. And you're lucky I have, seeing as I nearly sold it.'

'Why didn't you, then?'

Jamie put Alex's cases in his minute boot. 'Didn't need the money, after all.'

'He's fancy-free again,' said Arthur, getting into the car. 'Heather's given him back the ring.'

'Oh, Jamie, she hasn't! Oh, I'm so sorry! What happened?'

'Got tired of waiting for me to come up with a house, I suppose. Thinks she can do better and probably can.' Jamie shrugged. 'Come on, I know you never liked her. Let's just say it's a chapter closed and get you home.'

'Och, what a thing to happen!' Edie cried in hushed tones, as Alex took off her jacket and sat down to await the ritual cup of tea. 'That poor girl! Murdered! And her a lawyer's daughter, eh?'

277

As though that made it worse, thought Alex wearily. Her head was spinning, she longed just to close her eyes and sleep at the table, but knew she would not sleep wherever she was, whatever she did. Kyrenia. All she ever saw was Kyrenia, and the blinding light on the water, the little boats bobbing. The shadows of the lace shop, the man in the doorway, and Rose. Rose, on the floor, her great eyes pleading. What's happened? What's happened to me? Am I going to die? And the stain on her dress growing and growing. It was too much to expect, not to see that, wasn't it? Alex thought she would always see it.

'Here's your tea, pet. I'll bet you've never had a decent cup o' tea the whole time you've been away!' Edie was bustling around, setting out plates with food, but Alex said she could eat nothing. Just the tea would be lovely.

At least, she reflected, the Burnetts had not asked her to go with them to Kyrenia. They had gone there themselves, though. Mrs Burnett had told her, when she came to see her at the nurses' quarters. Alex had thought her so elegant, so brave, but the façade had soon cracked when she spoke of seeing the lace shop, of seeing Rose in death.

'She was so beautiful, Alex,' Mrs Burnett sobbed. 'Did you go? Did you see her?'

'No,' Alex whispered. 'I couldn't.'

'We felt we had to see her, to accept what had happened. Just as we had to go to Kyrenia. We had to be there, where she had been.'

'Rose didn't suffer, Mrs Burnett, I promise you, it all happened too quickly.'

'And you and Simon were with her. I'm so glad about that – that she wasn't alone.' Mrs Burnett dabbed at her eyes. 'We were really taken with Simon, you know. Such a fine young man. Rose was happy with him, wasn't she?'

'Very happy. Happier than I'd ever known her.' Alex stopped and flushed. 'Well, more relaxed, I mean. I know she was happy in Edinburgh, too.'

Mrs Burnett looked at her thoughtfully.

'It's all right, my dear. I know that Rose wasn't altogether happy with me. She believed I favoured Tim, but it wasn't true. I just thought he needed me, you see, and Rose didn't, she was always so strong. But maybe I did expect too much of her. I was selfish, I had my bridge—'

'Don't blame yourself,' Alex said quietly. 'Rose did love you, she did want to be close to you, she told me so.'

'She told you?'

'She did.'

Mrs Burnett gave a tragic smile. 'What a comfort you are, Alex! Rose always said you were a wonderful nurse, now I can see why.'

It was Alex's turn to be comforted.

Edie was talking again, as she passed sandwiches to Arthur and Jamie and refilled Alex's cup.

'Tell you who I saw in ma butcher's yesterday – your bookshop friend, Alex. Och, he looked like a lost soul, so he did, buying a wee piece o' steak and a couple o' sausages.'

'Neal?' Alex asked faintly.

'Aye, you've only got one friend with a bookshop, eh?' Edie took a hearty bite from a fish paste sandwich. 'I says good morning and he says good morning, then I says, Mr Drover, there's been a terrible accident in Cyprus, and he went so white, I thought he was going to fall right doon where he was on the sawdust!'

'Edie, you should never have told him like that!' cried Arthur. 'He'd have thought it was Alex!'

'Well, I said as quick as I could it was Alex's friend, we'd had a telegram, and I held him up by the arm till he got his breath, but he was in a state, all right. One o' the lads brought him a chair, but he just took his bit parcel and left.' Edie gave Arthur a truculent stare. 'Don't blame me, Art, I never meant him to get upset!'

Alex got to her feet. 'I'll go round right away. No, honestly, Dad, I'm OK. The fresh air'll do me good, and it's a lovely evening.'

'You're white as a sheet!' cried Edie. 'You're no' fit to be going anywhere!'

But Alex was putting on her jacket and already on her way.

'Come on, Edie, give me some more tea,' said Jamie. 'And let Alex do what she likes. She's been through enough, OK?'

Neal's shop was closed, but he opened his door at once when she knocked, stared at her for a long heart-stopping moment, then swept her into his arms.

'Thank God, thank God, you're safe!' he murmured against her hair. 'I've been in hell ever since your stepmother told me about Rose, thinking what I'd have done, if it had been you. I don't know what I'd have done. I couldn't have borne it!'

'Well, it wasn't me,' she said dully. 'As you see, I'm here, all in one piece.'

Neal let her go and looked into her face. 'My poor girl,' he said softly. 'You're still shocked, aren't you? They shouldn't have let you come home, you're not fit. Come and sit down.'

'I don't want to sit down, I don't want to rest. I can't rest. Let's walk somewhere.'

'All right. Just let me put on my jacket.' He took his keys and locked the door, while she stood trembling on the steps, waiting. Then he took her arm. 'Where would you like to go? It's a lovely evening.'

'Yes. So pale, though.'

'Pale?'

'Yes, all the colours seem muted. After Cyprus.'

He smiled faintly. 'Well, Edinburgh's not the Mediterranean, I suppose. Let's go up to Princes Street Gardens and then have a drink somewhere. You look as though you could do with one.'

'I'm all right, but what about you? I'm so sorry Edie blurted out the news about Rose. I should've sent you a telegram, too.'

'Don't worry about me. Now that I've seen you, I'm fine.'

They walked in silence through the warm evening air, Alex looking at the city as though she were a stranger. She had only been away two weeks, yet it seemed as though all that was here belonged to another age. Certainly, she felt much older. Neal himself noticed the change in her.

'You're different, Alex,' he told her, as they entered the gardens below the Castle, and mixed with the tourists strolling there.

'I know. I feel different.'

'It's the shock. You're vulnerable.'

'Yes, that's true. It's like when my mother died, I feel I'll never be safe from losing someone.'

Neal took her hand. 'It'll take time to get over something like this, a very long time. But you're strong and brave, Alex, you'll make it. And you have someone who loves you, remember that.'

She turned her sad eyes on him. 'I said I'd give you an answer, Neal, when I got back, but it's no' the time to talk about ourselves. You do understand?'

'Of course, I do. All I want is to be here for you and help you. You will let me help you, if I can?'

'Neal, I'm sorry, the only thing that can help me now is work. I'm going back to the Jubilee tomorrow.'

He nodded. 'I won't try to dissuade you. It could be what you need. But don't forget me, will you? Come to me whenever you want. We'll have a meal and talk, there'll be no demands. And anything I can do, I'll do.'

'There is something you can do, Neal.' She smiled a little.

'Something practical. Will you let me make that call to Martie you once offered? I've got the number of the sanatorium, it was on one of her letters. I'd like to tell her myself – about Rose.'

Somehow, sharing her grief with Martie made Alex feel better. They had had the same sort of relationship with Rose, they had known her since the old days in the Colonies, they had been butterfly girls together. Martie had been stunned, of course, but her familiar voice seemed to send strength to Alex in a way that poor Neal's willingness could not do.

'If only I could've been there with you,' said Martie. 'I am there, Alex, in spirit. Believe that, eh? Is the funeral to be in Edinburgh?'

'Yes, when the Cyprus authorities let Rose be brought back. Her parents are out there now, I think they'll be able to organise it.'

'When the funeral is arranged, shall we send flowers together?'

'Yes, I'll order them.' Alex hesitated. 'Are things all right with you, Martie?'

'Fine, thanks.'

'Is the wedding going ahead?'

'Oh, yes. No date yet.'

'You'll let me know?'

'I'll want you there.'

'I don't know if that'll be possible. I can't think of anything but Rose at the moment.'

'After I've taken it in,' Martie said, after a pause, 'I'll be the same.'

When she had put the phone down, Alex turned to Neal and kissed him.

'Thank you, Neal. I'm very grateful to you for that.'

'I'm glad I could do something.' He held her close. 'Oh, Alex, you don't know what it means to me, that you're safe. I keep thinking—'

'Don't, Neal. There's no point.'

'But I'm thinking of Rose's family as well. Her parents, and Tim. Did you see Tim?'

'Not to speak to. I talked mainly with her mother. But there's someone else suffering. Rose had a young man, a pilot, someone she really loved. He was there, with me, when it happened.'

'Poor devil,' whispered Neal. 'Is he coming for the funeral?'

'Yes. You'll be coming too, won't you?'

'Everyone will come,' said Neal.

Chapter Forty-Seven

Everyone came. Neal was right. To Alex's eyes, it seemed that half Edinburgh had attended Rose's funeral service at St Mary's Episcopalian Cathedral, though a good many of the mourners were people who had not been close to her. There were judges and advocates and women who had played bridge with her mother, relatives she hadn't seen for years, and girls from St Clare's who had never been her special friends. But then there were the real mourners. Her family. Her colleagues from the hospitals. Patients such as Neal who appreciated her care. Even Sister Clerk, up from London, who had respected her as a nurse, although they'd had their differences. There was Chris MacInnes, who had been more than a colleague, and Alex's father and Jamie, whose memories of Rose stretched back to the days before the war. There was Alex herself, and there was Simon.

Poor, tall, bronzed Simon, who was staying with Rose's family and had been asked to join them at the front of the cathedral, but had preferred to sit alone at the back. While the choir sang Rose's favourite hymns and a family friend gave the eulogy, he kept his head bent, still holding himself like a coiled spring, as Alex could tell, but afterwards, when the coffin had been borne away, he seemed to sag a little and looked for her in the crowd outside. She would have gone to him, but Chris MacInnes appeared at her side and touched her arm.

'Who is that fellow?' he asked hoarsely, nodding his head towards Simon. 'Was he in Cyprus?'

283

'Yes.' Alex lowered her eyes. 'He's Simon Dawson, he was a friend of Rose's.'

'A friend? More than that, I should think, to come all this way.'

'Dr MacInnes, we can't talk now.'

'We don't need to talk at all. I can guess what you're not telling me.'

Alex looked up, forcing herself to see the misery in Christ's eyes.

'Don't envy Simon,' she said quietly.

'I shall always envy him,' said Chris.

Rain had begun to fall, as the family and close friends stood at Rose's grave in the Dean Cemetery. Alex had wanted sunshine for this last farewell, as Rose had so loved the sun of Cyprus, but maybe it was better this way. The falling rain chimed with the mourners' sorrow, as they watched the funeral director and his assistants arrange the flowers and wreaths and then step respectfully aside. Everyone said their last prayers. The clergyman bowed his head and began to move away, his vestments blowing in the breeze that was unseasonably chill. Mrs Burnett, leaning on her husband's arm, followed, her handkerchief to her eyes, and one by one, the mourners, some putting up umbrellas, made their way down the long mossy path to the gates and the waiting cars. Only Simon, Tim and Alex remained.

'You're coming to the Caledonian?' Tim asked Simon.

Mourners had been invited back to a reception at the hotel. There would be something to eat, and wine, all very tastefully done, thought Alex. It would not be the usual Scottish sending off, or an Irish-type wake.

'I think I won't, if you don't mind,' Simon answered. He ran his hand over his damp hair. 'I think I might just walk for a while.'

'I understand.' Tim put his hand on Simon's shoulder, then he and Alex watched, as Simon, too, took the path out of the cemetery. Tim turned to Alex, and for the first time, she looked at him. He seemed thin in his dark suit, his neck, like a boy's, too narrow for his white shirt. Was he well? she wondered, and hoped he was.

'You'll come back?' he asked softly.

'I can't, Tim, I'm on duty.'

'I believe Neal Drover is waiting for you at the gates.'

'He'll probably just walk with me to the Jubilee.'

'I thought you'd moved away from there?'

'I did for a time, but I'm back now.' Alex put up her own umbrella. Her eyes were on the flowers piled on the mound that was Rose's grave. 'I suppose it will be some time before they can put up a stone?'

'Some months, I believe. But Rose is with the family here, you know. All the Burnetts are buried in this part of the Dean. I'm for cremation myself, but Mother wouldn't hear of it for Rose.'

Alex's eyes had found the spray of pink and cream carnations she had sent on behalf of herself and Martie. She would have liked to look at the card, but was conscious of Tim standing beside her, his grey eyes resting on her.

'I'd better go,' she said at last. 'Though I don't like to, I don't like leaving her alone.'

'No.' Tim cleared his throat. 'She's near the others, though, as I say.'

They both knew Rose was alone.

'Goodbye, Tim,' Alex said quietly. 'It was nice seeing you again.'

'Let's walk together, shall we? I'll hold the umbrella for you.'

'Is there a car waiting for you?'

'I told them I wanted to walk round to the hotel. Felt I needed a breath of air.'

'Shouldn't get wet, though. Look, I'll give you ma umbrella.'

He laughed shortly. 'I'm no longer an invalid, Alex, I can stand a few drops of rain.'

'You're keeping well?'

'Very well, thanks.'

'So is Neal at the moment.'

'Good for him.' Tim suddenly halted. 'He's there, Alex, waiting for you. Look, I just want to thank you for all you did for Rose. It's been a great comfort to us all, to know you were with her. I should have said that before, when we were in Cyprus, don't know why I didn't.' He shook his head. 'Everything that happened there is a blur.'

'I know.' Alex could see Neal standing at the cemetery gates, his dark head bent before the driving rain, his eyes on her and Tim. 'I shall have to go,' she said quickly. 'Goodbye, again, Tim. Are you sure you won't take the umbrella?'

'Quite sure, but I might give you a ring some time, if that's all right?'

'No, I don't think so, Tim. Please don't do that. Please!'

As Neal came towards her, Alex ran to him. He tucked her arm into his and they hurried away together, both beneath the shield of the umbrella, neither looking back. Tim stood still and watched them, while the rain beat down on him and on the flowers covering his sister's grave, on Alex's pink and cream carnations and her carefully written card.

'To Rose, in love and remembrance, from Alex and Martie, the Butterfly Girls.'

Part Four

Chapter Forty-Eight

Martie had been hard hit by the death of Rose. Though never so close to her as to Alex, Rose had been a link with home, with the old days, a link that had now been severed. Then, the suddenness of the event had been so shocking. People died from time to time in the sanatorium, but they were ill, they were expected to die. Rose was young and strong, like Martie. She should never have died, and the fact that she had, was frightening. It might have been Alex, thought Martie. It could still be me. Some lunatic breaks in – pulls a gun – throws a knife – that's it. Lights out.

'Why don't you take a vacation, Martie?' Dr Viner asked sympathetically. 'You look all in.'

'Thanks, but I'm better at work,' she told him. 'No time to think.'

'Well, any time you feel like a break, say the word. Don't want you cracking up before your big day.'

She flushed. 'What big day?'

Dr Viner smiled faintly. 'Come on! Everybody here knows you're biding your time till your wedding.'

'I don't believe it! Who told them?'

'I guess these things get out. Mr Adamson's always here. You and he have been seen around. One nurse tells another. Gets back to me.'

'And we'd been so careful . . .' Martie's look was so chagrined, Dr Viner put his hand on her shoulder.

'Cheer up, it's not the end of the world. It'll all come out one day, won't it? Why the secrecy, anyway?'

'Warren didn't want people to think he was rushing to get wed again too soon.'

'I should say it's nobody's business but your own. Only thing that bothers me is that I'm going to lose a damn' fine nurse!'

'Not just yet,' said Martie.

Warren had been very kind, very comforting, deeply shocked by Martie's news of Rose. Lois had told him about the beautiful young nurse; that she should now be dead, killed by mistake, was almost too tragic to accept. What it was like for his poor Martie, he couldn't imagine.

'Would you like to take a trip home?' he had asked gently. 'I could book you a flight?'

'Oh, no. No thank you, Warren.' As she had told Dr Viner, Martie told Warren, she was better off at work. 'And there's nothing I can do, you see,' she added. 'I didn't really know Rose's family.'

'Well, it's up to you. I couldn't leave the bank myself right now, I've too much on. And then there's Brent's wedding.'

Brent and Julia were to marry in early June, though Lois had not yet been dead a year. The ceremony was to be held at Julia's home in Rhode Island, and would be followed by a long honeymoon in Europe. Martie had not been invited, which suited her very well, but the snub had infuriated Warren.

'I really don't mind,' she told him.

'That's not the point. It's an insult to you. You looked after Brent's mother, you have every right to be invited!'

'You know why they don't want me, Warren. Don't make any trouble, it's no' worth it.'

'I'm just going to speak to him. Ask him what he's playing at. After all, if he doesn't ask you to his own wedding, what the hell's he going to do about ours?'

'We're no' getting wed yet, let's leave that till we come to it.'

Warren took her hand. 'I was thinking we might announce our engagement after Brent comes back from honeymoon. That'd be about the right time.' He hesitated. 'After Lois.'

'Everyone here seems to have guessed about you and me, anyway.'

'The hell they have!' He frowned. 'I know Frank Viner, of course, but I've never given him any hint.'

' "These things get out", he said.'

'At least, this isn't New York. I don't want the news to break there till I'm good and ready.'

Martie knew he was thinking of his mother's reaction, but felt too dispirited, too grieved about Rose, to raise the point at that time. It was strange, but all she wanted, as she had told Dr Viner, was to keep working. Especially as things in their field, as he had described them, were 'hotting up'. The tests for the latest TB drug, isoniazid, in which Mount Forest was now involved, were proving the most hopeful yet.

'All gone to my head!' the director told his staff. 'I tell you, this is it! Sanatoria will be closing down around our ears before we know it, but who cares? If we can get people off Death Row, that's all that matters!'

Behind his back, his staff were still sceptical. And it was true, though there were some amazing successes, there were also failures. There was still work to do.

Brent's wedding went off as planned, and Warren attended, though, in deference to Martie's wishes, he said nothing to his son over her exclusion from the guest-list.

'Did feel like knocking off a nought or two from the check I gave him,' he told her, over a restaurant dinner, 'but maybe you're right, it's better not to make a quarrel over it.'

He had brought the wedding photographs and she spent an interested time studying Julia's dress, which was of heavy brocade and seemed to her to have been based on Princess Elizabeth's, back in 1947.

'Not what I want at all,' she said, with satisfaction. 'Far too grand.'

'Nothing's too grand for you, Martie,' Warren said at once. 'I want you to look stunning on your wedding day.'

'So do I! But I want something that's right for me, as well as something I can afford.'

He looked at her indulgently. 'Darling, you don't have to worry about costs. I'll open an account for you wherever you like. All you have to do is go along and order what you want.'

She hesitated. 'Warren, I'm earning good money. I want to pay for ma dress maself.'

'That's sweet of you, just what I'd have expected you to say, but it's not necessary. Life's going to be very different for you, my dearest, and I'd like for you to start thinking about that.'

'How d'you mean?'

'Well, take your job, for instance.' He smiled a little uncertainly. 'It's fine, it's been a great fill-in for you, but maybe you should be handing in your notice now. If we're going to have a fall wedding, you're not going to have much time. Things need to be organised.'

'Warren, Brent's no' back till September. How are we going to be ready for a fall wedding?'

He put his hand on hers. 'Honey, why hang about? We announce the engagement and then, say six weeks later, we have the wedding. What's wrong with that?'

'I think a winter wedding would be better. I don't want to leave work right now, you see. There are some pretty exciting studies being done with the new drugs. I'm needed.'

His mouth tightened, his eyes were hurt. 'You want to stay on at Mount Forest? Because they're studying new drugs? For God's sake, Martie, this is our wedding we're talking about! The start of our future! I thought you'd be raring to get back to New York, begin making plans!'

'I do want to make plans, Warren. I've got some time due, maybe I could come over for a few days, stay at some hotel? Make a start?'

He brightened. 'That would be fine. You could take a look round the apartment at the same time, see what changes you might want to make.'

'The apartment?'

'Mine,' he said gently. 'You've scarcely ever been there, you know.'

'I have been there,' she answered, remembering her unease. That apartment had been Lois's home. Martie had felt an interloper, looking into another woman's life, a life shared with the man Martie herself was to marry. No wonder she hadn't felt able

292

to look at Lois's things: all her clothes still in the closets, her music on the piano stand, her pen on her writing desk. There had been a portrait too, hanging in the drawing room. It showed Lois and Warren just after their marriage, so young and radiant, Martie had found her eyes brimming with tears. What the hell am I doing here? she had asked herself. It seemed that Warren hadn't wanted to change a thing. So, how could she?

'I think of the apartment as Lois's,' she said, raising her eyes to Warren's.

He had immediately understood. 'I'm sorry.' He touched her hand. 'I've been thoughtless. Should have realised you wouldn't want to live there. We'll find some place else.'

'Warren, you're making me feel bad. I don't want you to give up your home, that wouldn't be fair.'

'No, it makes sense. We're both starting a new life, we need a new house, too. The only thing is, if we have to go house-hunting as well as organising a wedding, we'll need to get busy.' He drank some wine, would have filled Martie's glass, but she put her hand over it. 'Have you thought about getting your parents over, for instance? Maybe your mother could help you with the arrangements?'

'My mother?' Martie laughed. 'Warren, she'd have a heart attack if she had any idea of what we were spending! I don't know that I dare even ask her to come at all. Or, ma dad.'

'You will ask her, though? You'll need somebody from your side, you know.'

'Yes.' Her eyes were thoughtful. 'If we had a church wedding.'

'I thought we'd decided we would.'

'It could just be a civil ceremony. Maybe that would be better. When I've so few folk who know me here.'

'Martie, I want you to have a proper wedding. The sort you'd have if you were marrying somebody your own age. Somebody back home.' He set down his glass. 'Listen, how about that? Why don't we go back to Scotland to be married? You could have your wedding at home. What do you say?'

Home for the wedding. Martie'd never thought of it, perhaps because she couldn't associate Warren with her home. Even now, the image of herself and Warren emerging from the kirk, with her parents looking on and all the girls who would remember her silly skipping games smiling and sneering . . . Rich Man, Poor Man. So, Martie's got her Rich Man, eh? Old enough to be her father, or even older . . . Well, the best o' luck, what folk'll do for money, eh? Of course, Alex wouldn't be sneering like that, but even Alex, Martie knew, would be wondering at her choice, and as for Jamie, she could just picture the expression in his toffee-brown eyes . . .

'I think it'd be easier here,' she said quickly. 'Though it's a nice idea. Thanks for suggesting it.' She glanced at her watch. 'Better be getting back. I'll call you as soon as I can, about the weekend, eh?'

'Can't be too soon for me,' said Warren, summoning the waiter for the check. 'I want to make your reservation.'

Chapter Forty-Nine

Martie had to endure some good-natured ribbing before she left Mount Forest for her little vacation. Everyone knew she was still mourning her friend and most soft-pedalled the jokes, but there were some who couldn't resist references to weekends with Rockefeller, and when Martie said she was NOT having a weekend with Rockefeller, they only giggled and advised her not to do anything they wouldn't do.

'When are you having your shower, Martie?' Alice Penn asked softly, watching Martie pack her case.

'Shower?'

'Bridal shower. You know, over here, girls throw shower parties for weddings, engagements, babies, anything that's going. Then all their friends bring gifts and have coffee and cake and a good old gossip. Guess you don't have that sort of thing back home?'

'Can't afford it,' Martie said shortly. 'It's all we can do to give one present, never mind shower presents. Alice, will you get off ma bed? You're sitting on ma stockings.'

Alice slid off the bed and gave Martie a long cool look.

'You're awful lucky, you know. I mean, they can say what they like about money not bringing happiness, but who'd turn down a guy like yours?'

'I'm no' just marrying for money, Alice!'

'Oh, of course not!' Alice gave a placatory smile. 'That's why you're so lucky.'

*

After Alice had left her, Martie fastened up her case and took a last look in her mirror. It seemed to her that she did not look herself. See those shadows under her eyes! It was all the grieving over Rose, it was waking in the night and thinking about things. Smile, she told herself, try to look happy. Laugh and the world laughs with you, that was what folk said. Martie turned away. Maybe, right now, she didn't want the world's laughter.

The hotel Warren had chosen for her was something from her dreams. A place where you could be pampered and at the same time left alone. Where everything was on the grand scale, from the ballroom, restaurants and public lounges, to bedrooms and 'his and her' bathrooms. Where the very beds would have housed an Edinburgh tenement family and still have space to spare. Well, almost.

'Like it?' asked Warren, watching Martie hang up her few things in the enormous closets.

'Warren, you know it's perfect!'

'Has a view over the park. Thought you'd like that.'

'Oh, I do. I like everything.' Martie, glancing in the dressing-table mirror, thought she was looking better. Who wouldn't look better in a place like this? Well, the patients at Mount Forest, for a start. She knew as well as anyone that all you could buy here was comfort. Health and happiness weren't for sale.

'Why so blue?' Warren asked, gently taking her into his arms.

'Who says I'm blue?'

'You look – I don't know – not my usual Martie.'

'I expect I'm just tired.'

'My experience of you is you're never tired.'

'And that's what you like about me?' She kissed him and drew away.

'That's what attracted me at first.' He caught at her hand. 'Now I love you, anyway.'

'I think, what it is, I'm still shocked over Rose. When someone your own age dies, you feel vulnerable.'

'I know, I know.' He gathered her to him. 'You think death should be for someone who's had more time, and then you realise that's not the way things work. But if you're not going to have for ever, you should try to do just what you want to do.'

'Yes,' said Martie. 'That's exactly right.'

For some time they stood together, locked in a long quiet embrace, before Warren finally sighed and said maybe they should go down to dinner.

'We could have room service?' Martie suggested, a little dryly. 'If you're worried about who's in the restaurant.'

'Darling, we're due to announce our engagement soon. Why should I mind who sees us?'

'You want me to wear ma ring, then?'

He hesitated, only fractionally. 'Of course, wear your ring.'

As it happened, they didn't see anyone Warren knew. Martie couldn't help feeling he was relieved.

Next morning, she was on her own, free to range through New York's grandest stores while Warren was at work, for of course it wouldn't be correct for him to see her wedding dress before the day and Warren was nothing if not correct. Oddly enough, she would have liked him with her, perhaps to stave off memories of the day she and Alex had gone shopping in Logie's with Lois. As it was, that day kept coming back too strongly; she could not seem to concentrate on the dresses the assistants kept bringing to her, felt hot and uncomfortable, though the departments were cool, kept seeing Lois on her silk-covered sofa, ordering this and that, delighting in giving such pleasure with her chequebook, never knowing she had so little time left to give pleasure ever again. Afterwards, they had met Rose, who had looked so well, so beautiful, yet over her too had hung a shadow none of them could see, and now the shadow seemed to have transferred itself to Martie.

'It's no good,' she told the assistants, wiping her brow. 'I just can't seem to make up ma mind. I'll have to come back.'

'Would Madam like to consider couture?' they breathed.

297

'These dresses are beautiful, but all ready to wear, now if Madam would prefer to consider a custom-made design—'

'Yes, that'd be better,' Martie agreed at once. 'Something just for me would be ideal. I'll definitely think about it. But no' today.' She glanced at her watch. 'I have to meet someone for lunch.'

They quite understood, they pressed cards with telephone numbers into her hands, they escorted her to the elevator, but when she got out of the store, Martie threw the cards away, shook back her hair and made for Central Park. She had no lunch engagement, she wasn't meeting Warren until the evening, all she wanted was to be free of wedding dresses, of memories, of everything. She wanted to run, run, run, even in the heat of a New York summer, run until she was too tired to think any more, too tired to make choices, too tired to do whatever a voice at the back of her mind was telling her she should do.

'Hi!' said a voice, as she sat collapsed on a bench. 'You OK? You want I should get you some water?'

She slowly turned her head and met a pair of concerned blue eyes in the freckled face of a young man. Though he was sitting on her bench, she could tell he was tall – his legs in light canvas trousers seemed to stretch out a long way before him on the gravel pathway. He had long thin arms, too, and ginger hair to go with the freckles. Seemed a nice guy, but who knew anything about a stranger on a park bench? Better not get into conversation. She shook her head.

'There's a fountain right there,' he told her. 'With paper cups and all. Won't take me a second.'

What the hell, why not?

'OK, thanks,' she said grudgingly.

He was as quick as his word, and the water he brought was good. What she needed, in fact She told him so, and he grinned.

'Guess you'd been doing too much, looked kinda drained.' He drank from his own paper cup. 'Say, are you on vacation? From England?'

'Scotland,' she corrected coldly.

'I knew it! Recognised your accent straight away! What do you think of New York, then? I'm from Pennsylvania myself. Here for an interview. Got my suit back at the hotel.' He groaned a little. 'Thought I'd kill time, walking, thought I'd feel better. Guess I feel worse.'

'What's the job?' Martie asked, interested in spite of herself.

'Oh, financial services, junior accountant. But my dad's a trucker, thinks I'm going to set the world on fire.' He shook his head and crunched his empty papercup very small. 'Guess I'll have to.'

'Guess you will,' said Martie warmly. 'What time's the interview?'

'Three-thirty. If I last that long.'

She leaped to her feet, all her old energy returning. 'Come on, let's find coffee and something to eat. I'm starving, bet you are, too.'

He unwound his thin length, his eyes dancing. 'Say, is this a pick-up? My mom told me never to speak to strange women on park benches, you know!'

'You just did.' Martie was laughing, amazed at her own actions. She held out her hand. 'Let's introduce ourselves, anyway. I'm Martie Cass, a nurse from Edinburgh, temporarily working in Massachusetts. Who are you?'

'Sam Riley.' He bowed his ginger head. 'Very glad to meet you, Martie. You can pick me up any day you like, whatever my mom says.'

They found a place that reminded her of the little café where Warren had taken her on that wintry day when he had proposed. Warren had chosen it because he wouldn't know anyone there, they because it was cheap. Even so, Sam said he didn't think he could eat anything, his stomach was full of butterflies. Butterflies? Och, another memory, thought Martie, and crisply ordered hamburgers and double french fries for both of them.

'Come on, you've got to keep your strength up,' she told Sam, drinking the coffee, which arrived first. 'I'm a nurse, I know about these things.'

'I bet you give the patients hell,' said Sam, admiringly.

299

'No, I'm very kind, they all adore me.'

'I can believe that, too.' His intelligent eyes found the ring on her left hand, and he leaned forward to touch the handsome stones. 'So, it wasn't a pick-up,' he said softly. 'Might have guessed.'

Martie too looked down at the ring. 'Yes, I'm engaged. In fact, I'm in New York to choose ma wedding dress.'

'So, how come you were in Central Park?'

'Needed a break, I guess.'

'Needed a break? Never thought a girl'd need a break from that!'

Silk, satin, cotton, rags. 'Neither did I,' said Martie, as their orders arrived.

'Want to talk about it?' he asked, pouring ketchup on his French fries and beginning to eat. 'Say, this is good, just what I needed.'

'Why should there be anything to talk about?'

He shrugged. 'I'm getting a kind of feeling there is. But don't worry, I'm not prying. I'd like to help, that's all. You've certainly helped me.'

'I have?'

'Sure. I feel one hundred percent better about the interview already. Just as long as I give myself enough time to get back to change into that damned suit!'

Martie shook her head. 'I'd like to talk, but I can't. It'd no' be right.'

'Disloyal to the guy who gave you that?' Sam looked at her ring again. 'Fair enough. He's pretty rich, though, right? Hell, he'd have to be.'

'Yes, he's rich. Sam, I don't want to say any more.'

'All I want to say is, I hope he makes you happy.'

'I'm no' worried about that.' Martie took a refill for her coffee and sat gazing at Sam, who was still eating. How young he looked! There was not a line on his brow, not a single crinkle by his eyes, everything about him was as bright as a newly minted coin. He had it all before him, just as she had. She too was new and bright, just like him, with no lines, no crow's feet, no grey in her hair. If she were marrying someone like him, they would face life together. On her finger, her beautiful ring glowed.

'You know what,' Sam was saying, slowly, 'I've got to go. Know something else? I don't want to. I feel I've known you all my life. Is that crazy, or is that crazy?'

'It's no' crazy, I feel the same.'

They reached across and held each other's hands.

'Think we'll meet again?' asked Sam.

'No,' said Martie. 'But I'll never forget you.'

'Same goes for me.'

They exchanged long deep glances, then Martie pulled away and said she'd get the check.

'What are you talking about? This is my treat!'

'I asked you.'

'I would have asked you, if I'd had the nerve.'

'Let's split it, then, but I'll leave the tip.'

They came out into the street, both damp with the heat of the day and their own emotion.

'I'd better take a cab,' gasped Sam. 'How about you?'

'I'll walk back to the hotel.'

He fixed her with sad young eyes. 'Couldn't we at least exchange phone numbers?'

'Better not.' She touched his cheek with her fingers. 'Good luck, Sam. I'll look out for you in the Wall Street Journal.'

'And where'll I look for you?'

She was silent, watching the traffic flaring by, thinking of Warren, asking her to marry him.

'I don't know,' she answered simply.

'Good luck, anyway,' said Sam.

She was waiting in the vestibule when Warren came to find her. He hurried towards her, arms outstretched.

'Had a good day, darling? How did it go? You find something?'

She did not meet his eyes. 'Warren, can we talk?'

301

Chapter Fifty

They took the elevator to her suite, standing with other people, not speaking, not meeting each other's eyes. Martie was certain that Warren was already afraid, had already guessed. Yet how could he have done? Were those words 'Can we talk?' enough to make a man in love fear a woman might no longer be in love? She never had been in love with him, she thought, clenching her damp fingers, meeting on her left hand, that great ring. That's what was wrong. It was true what Brent had said, she'd been dazzled. Dazzled by the light of all that Warren had. Somehow, now, the blinding light had died, and she could see again. And didn't want to, if it meant telling Warren. Only, she had no choice.

In her sitting room, he went straight to the hotel drinks tray, poured drinks for them both, rattled in ice from the tiny refrigerator, passed Martie her glass and drank deeply from his own.

'Needed that,' he said, glancing at her, trying to smile. 'Damned hot, eh? You must be exhausted.'

'I do feel weary.'

'Sit down, then. Why are we standing?'

'I think, maybe I'll stand, Warren. Just while we talk.'

'I wish you didn't look so serious.' Warren laughed. 'I'm beginning to feel nervous.'

Martie set down her glass and put her fingers to her lips. 'Oh, God,' she whispered, 'there's no easy way to say this. I don't

302

think I can say it at all. Warren, help me! Please don't make me say it!'

He had gone very pale, but he was quite composed, keeping himself well under control as he poured another drink and sat down on one of the large, soft sofas by the fireplace that was filled with flowers.

'Come and sit by me, Martie. It doesn't help to stand there, looking shipwrecked. Sit by me and tell me what the hell is going on.'

She sat beside him, let him run his hand down her face, look into her eyes.

'You look so sad,' he said gently. 'My poor girl, what's wrong? Tell me what's wrong.'

Martie swallowed and pulled her hand from his. 'Warren, I can't marry you. I only decided today. It wouldn't work out. Brent was right—'

'Brent? What the hell has he got to do with this?'

'Nothing, he just said once – look, don't think about him. I'm the one who's in the wrong. You can blame me all you like. I've made a terrible mistake, taking everything and giving nothing, and now I feel so awful because I'm going to hurt you!'

'Hey, slow down, slow down! I guess I just don't know what you're talking about.' Warren was trying to smile. 'You haven't taken anything from me I didn't want to give, and as for giving me nothing – Martie, you don't know what you've given me. A new life, a new hope, all your love and strength! You haven't the faintest idea what you've done for me.'

'Warren, Warren, don't you understand? I'm saying I can't marry you! I can't give you ma strength and ma love!' Martie's eyes were glistening with tears. 'I don't love you. That's what I have to tell you and why I feel so bad, so terrible – Warren, can't you see?'

He sat back, seeing, and as he saw, his face grew grey and his eyes seemed to sink into their sockets. He was handsome, still, but the spark that had kept him young for his years had died. He looked his age and more.

'This morning, you went out to buy a wedding dress,' he said slowly. 'You were quite happy. Quite yourself. As far as I could see, there wasn't a cloud in the sky. This evening, the heavens have fallen. For God's sake why, Martie? Why should you decide just like that – 'he snapped his fingers '– that you don't love me, don't want me, and everything's over. It doesn't make sense!'

'I didn't decide just like that.' She brushed the tears from her eyes. 'It'd been in ma mind for some time. Only I wouldn't face it.'

'Why face it today, then?' Warren's gaze suddenly sharpened. 'Did something happen today? Something different?'

Martie caught her breath. 'No, nothing,' she said quickly.

It was a lie. Something had happened. She had met Sam Riley. But how could she explain to Warren what that meeting had meant? She hadn't fallen in love at first sight, or anything dramatic like that. All she had seen was Sam's youth and had known that it matched her own. Had known then, what she had been trying not to admit for some time, that she could not marry Warren.

But he was looking at her now with new hope, and her spirits sank, as he clutched at her hands like a drowning man.

'Martie, my love, I've just realised what all this is about. It's just wedding nerves! Lots of girls have them! They don't mind the engagement, they wear the ring, feel wonderful, but then when it comes to facing the real decision, knowing it's so important, the most important thing in their lives, they chicken out, look at the wedding dresses, think that's not for me, get all weepy—'

Martie freed herself from his grasp and leaped to her feet. For a moment she stood looking down at him, despair in her gaze, then she pulled off her engagement ring and laid it in the palm of his hand.

'Oh, Warren, it's no' like that. I wish it was, I wish it was!' She folded his fingers over the ring. 'But I do care for you, I do, honestly! You're the most important thing in ma life, I really admire you, worship you – but I don't love you. No' the way I should love you, to be married. No' the way Lois loved you. And that's what you deserve, Warren. Someone like her. But I'm no' that person. I'm sorry.'

He rose slowly to his feet, still holding the ring. 'Was it the money?' he asked, after a silence, during which Martie silently wept.

She looked at him, wiping her eyes. 'Partly. I'm going to be honest. You were ma Rich Man, the one I always wanted. When I was a kid, that's what I thought would make me happy.'

'Partly?' He shook his head dazedly. 'What else was there?'

'What I felt for you. Feel for you, I mean. Och, it wasn't just the money, Warren, it was you as well. But maybe you'll no' believe me.'

'Oh, I do. If there hadn't been something real between us, I don't believe I could have been so happy.' He moved away to stand looking down at the flowers in the fireplace, flowers he had ordered himself, along with the arrangements of roses, orange blossom and honeysuckle, elsewhere in the room. 'Guess I was at fault as much as you, Martie.'

'No, no, Warren!'

'Yes. You spoke of taking. Wasn't I taking? All your youth – vitality? I'd no right to any of it. Old guy, who'd had far too many bites at the cherry already.'

'You're no' old, Warren! You're in your—'

'Don't say it. In my prime?' He smiled wearily. 'And thirty years older than you. No, I should have kept faithful to my Lois, not gone crazy for a dream. Guess I was crazy, wasn't I?' He shook his head. 'There's a price to pay for craziness. It's going to take me some time to get over you, Martie.'

She closed her eyes, wincing. 'Warren, I'm so sorry—'

'No, listen, will you keep the ring? I'd like you to have it.'

'I couldn't take it.'

'You needn't wear it. Just keep it.'

She burst into bitter tears and he put his arms around her, holding her until the paroxysm passed.

'These things happen,' he said quietly. 'Don't blame yourself. You've been honest and I appreciate it. Give me your right hand.' He slipped the ring on to her third finger. 'There, if you were a

305

Continental, you'd still be engaged. Don't they wear their rings on the right hand?'

'Oh, Warren, I feel so bad, why can't you be horrible to me?'

'Because I'm the one in the wrong. I wanted too much.'

'So did I,' said Martie.

Chapter Fifty-One

Climbing the Archangel Steps again. Sometimes, Alex saw them in her dreams. And the ghosts. Faces, figures. Herself and Martie as children. Jackie, Jamie. Rose, in her St Clare's uniform. 'May I play?' A tall, slim figure in cricket shirt and flannels at the top of the steps. 'Rose, Mother wants you!' Oh, it was sad to wake up! Feel the tears drying on her cheeks. But today, she wasn't dreaming. The steps were real. The October day was fine, with golden sunshine touching the tops of the houses in Cheviot Square ahead. Alex was on her way to tea with Mrs Burnett.

Rose had been dead six months. There had been changes. Simon was in Singapore, feeling better, he reported in his occasional letters, though Alex wondered if that were true. Chris MacInnes had returned to the Jubilee, taking over Dr Senior's post on his retirement. A research group had been set up in Edinburgh hospitals, to monitor the effects of the new TB drugs. Everyone was hopeful, though cautious, particularly as results seemed mixed and new cases kept coming in. Alex and Neal had parted.

He had taken it badly back in the summer, when she had finally found the courage to tell him she couldn't marry him. He'd been so patient with her after Rose's death, so kind and considerate, just letting her take her time. But all along, of course, he'd been expecting good news, and when her answer was the reverse, the glitter of pain had come back to his eyes, and the black dog of depression had descended.

'It's nothing to do with your health,' she'd told him, but he'd said he wished it had been. That would have been easier to accept.

'I do love you, Neal, but no' the way you want.'

'And me everyone's favourite film-star!' He had laughed bitterly.

'Oh, Neal!' Alex caught his hand. 'We can still be friends, can't we? I don't think I could do without your friendship.'

'If you find it hard, consider what it's like for me. I'm doing without hope.'

She'd had to look away from his painful gaze. 'I can't blame you for not wanting to see me again,' she said at last. 'Why should you?'

'Why indeed? I daresay I feel now the way you felt about Tim when you split up.'

'Let's no' bring Tim into it, Neal. He has nothing to do with us.'

'And of course it's not fair to class you with Tim. He changed, you didn't. You never pretended to love me.'

'I said we shouldn't talk about Tim.'

'Strange, though, you only came to your decision after seeing him again.' Neal had taken Alex's wrist in a surprisingly strong grip. 'You still care for him, Alex?'

'No! If you want us to say goodbye, Neal, let's say goodbye. It'll be for the best in the long run.'

'So much for not being able to do without my friendship,' he said caustically, and Alex burst into tears. He put his arm around her.

'It wouldn't work out, Alex. I mean, our trying to keep on seeing each other. Too difficult for you, too painful for me. But if you ever want a good second-hand book—'

She had shed more tears, but the glitter had faded from Neal's eyes and at least they'd parted as friends, even if only on the surface. For some time afterwards, she'd hoped he would contact her, suggest a meal, or a cinema visit. He hadn't. Nor had she been to his bookshop. She still thought of him as someone special, and was glad in a way that if there was no one in his life, there was no one in hers, either. That seemed only fair.

Here was Rose's house again, looking as well cared for as ever. Mrs Burnett no longer had a full-time maid, but her bevy of 'girls', or 'ladies who obliged', kept everything just as she liked it. There had been no slipping of standards since Rose had died, in house or occupants, though Rose's father still looked ill and Mrs Burnett herself had mysteriously aged. You couldn't put your finger on it. She was as beautifully dressed as she had always been, her make-up and hair as immaculate, but she did not look the same. Something had died behind the splendid front she presented to the world, and would not be brought back to life, however hard she kept up her standards, played her bridge, and sought comfort from Alex in the little tea-time calls she asked her to make from time to time.

As she stood looking up at the façade of the house, Alex remembered how fearful she'd been on her first visit in case Tim should be there. She hadn't seen him since the funeral; he'd never telephoned, which was just as well. Though something had stirred for her at that meeting by Rose's grave, she'd resolutely crushed whatever it was, and in the rush of grief she'd been experiencing for Rose, it hadn't been difficult. Luckily, she hadn't met him at his mother's, that first time or since. He had his own flat now, Mrs Burnett had told her, and during the day would be at the office, working hard, sending out bills to clients, no doubt. Wasn't that what lawyers did? Maybe she shouldn't be so cynical, thought Alex, ringing the Burnetts' bell. And came face to face with Tim.

He was wearing a dark business suit, with a white shirt and grey silk tie. He had filled out a little since the funeral, and looked less stressed. When he saw her, his eyes lit up, which filled her with surprise and strange unease.

'Alex! Come on in, we're expecting you.'

She stepped into the flagged hall, where a mahogany table held one of Mrs Burnett's large flower arrangements and a silver tray for cards. Darkened paintings of Edinburgh lined the walls and at the far end rose a twisting stone staircase with a wrought iron balustrade.

'Shouldn't you be at work?' she asked.

'Had to see a client – one of our neighbours – thought I'd cadge a cup of tea from Mother.' He gave a friendly smile. 'You're the bonus. I didn't know you were coming today.'

'Alex!' Rose's mother was rapidly descending the stairs, holding out her hands. 'Oh, it's so good to see you! Tim, Alex is so kind, gives me her time, lets me talk about Rose, looks at my photographs. Go up, my dear, I'll get the tea.'

'I'll get the tea,' Tim said grandly. 'Come on, I can put on a kettle!'

'Nonsense!' Mrs Burnett was already on her way to the basement. 'You take Alex upstairs, Tim. Come down in a few minutes, if you like, to carry the tray.'

They stood together in the drawing room, looking out at the sun gilding the trees in the gardens, a view Rose must have seen so many times, thought Alex. She stooped to stroke Smoky Joe, who had been watching her from his favourite chair by the fire, and felt ridiculously pleased as he began to purr.

'Mother thinks he still misses Rose,' Tim said softly. 'I don't know if it's true. Rose used to say he counted us, the way dogs do.'

'He's very intelligent. I'm sure he does miss her.'

As Alex straightened up, Tim kept his eyes on her.

'I didn't phone, in the end. Thought I shouldn't.'

'There wasn't much point, was there?'

'If you were seeing Neal.' Tim moved a little closer towards her. 'Are you? Seeing Neal?'

'Do you think you have any right to ask me that?'

'No, no right at all. But, are you?'

Alex glanced towards the door. 'Weren't you going down to help your mother?'

'I'm on my way. You're not seeing him, are you? I can tell.'

'Why ask me, then?'

Tim bit his lip. 'I'll get the tray.'

There were tiny scones with butter and honey, a cake with lemon icing, china tea in delicate cups. How hard it must have been for the Burnetts, thought Alex, sipping her tea, to accept something so wrong as violent death when their lives were so right, so wonderfully correct. But then they'd had a little taste of the tricks life could play, hadn't they? When Tim had been found to have a shadow on his lung? Alex looked at him now, eating a scone, cheerfully brushing crumbs from his suit. At least, he was well. Thank God, she amended, he was well.

'How's the Jubilee?' he asked, sensing her gaze. 'Ticking on the same as ever, I suppose?'

'There've been some changes. Dr Senior has retired and Dr MacInnes has taken over. We're all thrilled he's back.'

'Poor Chris,' sighed Mrs Burnett. 'I see his mother, you know. He's still devastated over Rose.'

There was a sad little pause. Alex went on: 'We're also part of a project to test the use of TB drugs in Edinburgh hospitals. That's something new.'

'When you say drugs, that'd be streptomycin?' asked Tim.

'Oh, there are others now. Streptomycin has some bad side-effects and it doesn't work for long on lung TB. There's a new one everybody's very hopeful about. It's called isoniazid.'

'What a mouthful!' cried Mrs Burnett. 'Is it expensive?'

'No, it's much cheaper than anything else they've tried so far, and they've had some wonderful results.' Alex smiled. 'Patients dancing in the wards because they feel so well!'

'My God, picture that at the Jubilee!' Tim exclaimed. 'I can just imagine Sister Clerk's face if I'd tried a few steps! No, seriously, that's wonderful. Is this the breakthrough, then?'

'That's what they want to find out. It's too soon to say. No' everyone's done so well, you see.'

A cloud passed over Tim's face, and Alex guessed he was reflecting on his own good luck. After a moment, he shrugged, and slowly unwound himself from his chair.

'I'd better be getting back, I suppose. Shall I take the tray down?'

'Oh, please, dear.' His mother rose and kissed his cheek. 'So nice to see you, I wish you'd look in more often.'

'You know what it's like, Dad keeps my nose to the grindstone.' Tim glanced at Alex. 'Maybe you could bring the hot-water jug, Alex?'

At the foot of the stairs, he put down his tray. 'Think that was too obvious?' he whispered.

'No, I'm sure your mother never even noticed,' Alex answered honestly. Why would Mrs Burnett think Tim wanted time with her? Such a thought would never cross his mother's mind. Did he want time, though? What was he up to?

'I had to see you alone again somehow.'

Alex set the hot-water jug on the tray. 'Tim, I want to tell you, I don't want to get involved.'

'All I'm asking is that you give me a ring.' He took a business card from his pocket. 'See, I've written my home number on the back of this.'

'You've a phone in your flat?'

'Of course.' His expression was serious, his eyes very steady on her own doubtful face. 'I'm leaving it to you, Alex. Putting the ball in your court. If you want to see me, get in touch. If not – tear up the card.'

'Tim—'

He shook his head. 'Take the card and think about it. Now, I'd better take this down and get back to work.'

As her fingers closed over his card, he picked up the tray and the hot-water jug and ran lightly down the basement stairs. She could hear him whistling, knew he would soon return, and herself ran up the staircase to the drawing room.

'There you are, dear!' called Mrs Burnett. 'Come and sit by the fire. Move that naughty cat and we'll have a nice little talk.'

What did she want? Alex asked herself, hurrying back down the Archangel Steps. The sun had long gone and lights were shining through the blue dusk. This was the time when the streets of the Colonies were filled with men returning from work and children racing to finish their games. 'All in, all in, wherever you are!' sang the young voices over the pungent autumn air, and Alex, as she reached her father's door, felt her eyes pricking with foolish tears. She hadn't always been happy as a child. No, but there had been lovely times. Lovely times when Ma had been alive. If only Ma had been waiting for her now! They'd have talked, Alex would have been able to make up her mind. Decide what she wanted. For she really didn't know.

312

At least, Edie wasn't at home, this was her afternoon for playing whist at the church hall. Arthur, back from work, had been given his orders and was peeling potatoes at the sink. He'd already put a cloth on the table, set out the pickle jar and tomatoes, and two plates of boiled ham.

'Hallo, pet!' he called, when he saw Alex. 'Want a cup o' tea?'

'No thanks, Dad, I'm going to change into ma uniform and get back.' Alex took off her hat and ran her fingers through her damp hair that was curling on her brow. She could still feel the pain of old grief like a stone in her chest. Strange that it should have come back now.

'You all right?' asked her father. 'Look a bit pale.'

'I'm fine.' She hesitated. 'Rose's brother was at Mrs Burnett's today.'

Arthur's brow darkened. 'Him!' he snorted. 'He's no' been upsetting you again, Alex?'

'No, not at all.'

'You should've married Neal. You'd have been safe with him.'

'Maybe I don't want to be safe.'

'You do want to be safe, Alex. You're no' Martie Cass, remember. She's the one for risks, no' you.'

'I'll go and change,' Alex muttered, anxious to get away before Edie came home to put her sharp eyes through Alex's defences. 'Better get the water on for the potatoes, Dad.'

'Aye, or I'll be getting wrong, eh?'

Back in her uniform, with her cloak around her shoulders, Alex felt less vulnerable. As Staff Kelsie, she knew who she was and what she should be doing. But it wasn't true to say she'd never taken risks. Why, look at all those times she'd visited Tim in his chalet! Yes, and look where that had got her! As she kissed her father goodbye and set off back to the Jubilee, Alex's heart sank. Maybe her dad was right and she should have married Neal. No danger there, no fear of being twice burned, as with Tim Burnett. She knew she could never have married Neal.

So, what was she going to do? When in doubt, don't, folk said. All right, she wouldn't. Wouldn't phone. There, decision taken.

What a relief! But as she reached the Jubilee, she was already checking to see if she had Tim's card safe in her bag.

Then all thoughts of Tim were forgotten, as Jill Berry came skidding down the corridor from Butterfly Four and grabbed her by the arm.

'Alex, thank God you're back! Quick, get ready – poor old Sal's collapsed. Another haemorrhage.'

'Oh, God, I knew she was worse when she came in this time!' Alex was already tearing off her cloak, and running with Jill. Seemed no matter how many wonder drugs appeared, there were still times when they had to run like this to save a life.

And they did save a life, that time. It was a miracle, but Sal pulled through and was put to bed in a side ward to lie, paper white, not requiring tea or anything else. Someone made tea for the staff, though, and they stood together, wearily drinking it.

'Well done,' said Chris MacInnes. 'She's made it.'

'Till the next time,' said Jill. 'How often do we say that?'

'Too often, but it might be different in the future. New patients will have a better chance of responding to drug therapy without relapsing. That's the thinking, anyway.'

A cold hand tightened on Alex's heart. If Neal's TB returned again, he would not be a new patient, he might be one who would not respond to treatment. So might Tim.

'Come on, Alex,' Chris said lightly. 'Don't look so sad. We've had good luck tonight.'

She managed a smile, but later, snatching a moment to herself, she looked again at Tim's card. It was too late to ring him then, but she knew that she was going to make the call tomorrow. OK, she was foolish. Taking a risk Why not? Life was made up of risks. And this time round, seeing Tim, she would be better prepared. She would expect nothing.

Chapter Fifty-Two

Tim had a car. When she saw it waiting for them, outside the Jubilee, Alex's eyes widened.

'Tim, is this yours? I didn't know!'

He opened the door for her. 'I expect there are a lot of things you don't know about me. It's only an old Triumph. My father gave it to me for a graduation present.'

'Some people might say you were lucky,' she said coldly, as Tim drove away. 'My brother bought himself a car, but he nearly had to sell it, because of getting married.'

'You mean, he was going to give up his car for his bride?' Tim laughed. 'Greater love hath no man, et cetera, et cetera! I take it he didn't, though? Give up his car?'

'The engagement was broken off.'

'Ah. I'm sorry.'

'These things happen.'

'Yes.'

They were both silent, Tim concentrating on the traffic, Alex thinking the evening had got off to a bad start. They were to have dinner at some little restaurant Tim knew in the Old Town; luckily, nowhere she'd been with Neal, and not expensive. She had expressly told Tim she didn't want to be wined and dined.

'Did I ever meet Jamie?' he asked, reaching George IV Bridge and turning down the High Street.

'You might remember him playing "Kick the Can". Of course, you never played it yourself, did you?'

'I could quite enjoy it now,' he said sharply. 'Sometimes I feel like kicking something. Look, don't take it out on me because you think I'm lucky. I don't feel particularly lucky, anyway.'

'I'm sorry,' Alex said quietly. 'Perhaps I'm no' being fair.'

'You're here, anyway.' He glanced at her quickly. 'That's what matters.'

The Old Town restaurant was more of a café, a bright and cheerful high-ceilinged room, serving peppery beef and smoked fish, apple pie and heavy cheeses, with not a sign of a salad. The clientele was mainly students, and Tim said he'd often eaten there as a student himself. He looked a little out of place now, in a light grey suit and one of his good ties, while Alex, in a new green dress and matching jacket, said she felt a hundred years old.

'Well, you did say you didn't want to go anywhere smart or expensive,' Tim reminded her, as they ordered the beef. 'So here we are. I only aim to please!'

'It's fine, it's exactly what I want. And if you took off your tie, you'd look just right.'

'I shall not be taking off my tie.' Tim leaned forward. 'But why wouldn't you let me take you to a proper restaurant? You can get a decent meal in Edinburgh, if you know where to go, rationing or no rationing.'

'As I said, I don't like too much wining and dining.'

'That's not it. Be honest. You just didn't want me to pay a lot, did you? Didn't want to be beholden to me?' Tim sat back in his chair. 'You think if we just go out for a cheap little dinner, it won't mean so much. And you don't want this evening to mean very much, do you?'

Alex looked down. 'I agreed to come, Tim.'

'Yes, but I get the impression you wish you hadn't. I get the impression you're afraid.'

Her head shot up. 'Are you surprised? You hurt me very much; it took me a long time to get over you. I don't want to go through anything like that again.'

'You won't have to, Alex, I promise! I'm never going to be a fool like that again.' Tim put his hand to his brow. 'When I think, what I did, letting you go—'

316

'Two Beef and Mashed Tatties,' droned the waitress, setting down filled plates in front of them. 'Want anything to drink?'

'Yes, may we have the wine list, please.'

The girl laughed. 'No wine list here, sir! We've no' got a licence.'

'Oh, God, I'd forgotten! Some mineral water, then, or whatever you have.' Tim gave Alex an apologetic smile. 'Just as well you said you weren't keen on wining and dining, Alex! Next time, we'll do better than this.'

She concentrated on her meal, making no reply.

'There is going to be a next time?' he asked quickly.

'I don't know, Tim.'

'Look, I've told you, I was a fool before. A crazy idiot. I still don't know why it happened, and that's the truth.'

'You fell out of love. It's no' so unusual.'

'I don't think I did. I don't think that was it.'

'What was it, then?'

'You don't know how often I've asked myself that question.' Tim looked down at his plate. 'Maybe it was something to do with getting well again. Thinking I'd be getting back to my old life. I don't know. Maybe.'

'And I was your nurse,' Alex said softly. 'I belonged to the Jubilee. I wasn't part of your old life.'

'Alex, don't punish me for what happened before, please!' The anguished appeal in his eyes made her feel suddenly exhilarated. She was on top here! She was in charge! It was a new experience for her with Tim, and she found herself savouring it like the good wine she had not drunk.

'Why don't you eat up your beef?' she asked. 'It's getting cold.'

Coming out after the meal into the chill of the night and getting into Tim's car was another thing to savour. No waiting for the tram! No shivering in the biting wind that was sweeping down the Canongate, blowing poor unfortunate pedestrians before it like so much litter!

'Oh, what a treat, Tim!' Alex snuggled into her seat. 'I think I'll start saving up for a little car maself!'

'You like to be independent, don't you?'

'Yes, I do. I'm no' looking for a man to give me things.'

Tim, as he drove away, smiled, while Alex enjoyed herself, looking out at Edinburgh by night. How beautiful the lights were from the Mound! This was her favourite view of the city, with the Castle on the skyline and the glitter of Princes Street laid out below.

'How's Martie?' Tim asked. 'Now she was looking for a man to give her things, wasn't she?'

'She's found him.'

Alex told him something of the events at the Fidra Bay and what had followed. Tim seemed impressed.

'And this fellow Adamson owns a bank? I'm not surprised Martie's keeping tight hold of him. He'll be a rich man, all right.'

'He's older than her father, Tim.'

'So what? She could still have a happy marriage.'

'Yes, but I get the feeling she's no' all that happy at the moment.'

'You've been in touch with her?'

'I told her about Rose.'

The name hung between them. Neither spoke until the lighted gates of the Jubilee shone through the darkness. Tim drew up some distance away and gave a long deep sigh.

'We should talk about her, Tim,' Alex said quietly.

'I think about her. I don't need to talk.' Tim turned his head. 'She brought us together, you know. It was at her funeral I saw you again. I don't count Cyprus, I was punch-drunk then, didn't know where I was, never mind who I was seeing.'

'We all felt the same.'

'Yes. But back home, when we were saying goodbye to her and I saw you, I felt – this may seem far-fetched – but I felt you part of me again. Maybe I never really stopped feeling that.'

'Oh, come on!' Alex laughed nervously. 'You expect me to believe you?'

His eyes in the shadows were steady on her face. 'I don't expect anything. I'm just hoping.'

'We're different people now, Tim. We can't just pick up where we left off, as though nothing had happened.'

'Why not?'

'Well—' She twisted in her seat. 'What about all the others? And don't say what others! There must have been some girls after me.'

'No one special. No one any more special to me, than Neal Drover was to you.'

'As a matter of fact, Neal is special.'

'As a friend.' Tim drew Alex towards him. 'Not as a lover.'

He kissed her face gently, first her brow, then her lips, and the old magic flowed from him to her, the old rapture filled her as though it had never gone away. In spite of herself, she would not have moved from his arms, but he let her go, as though demonstrating his caution in not trying to take too much too soon.

'Will there be a next time?' he asked breathlessly.

:Tim, I don't know. I don't know if there should be.'

'You do know. You do.' He ground her hand in his. 'Say we can meet again.'

'I don't get a lot of time off, I can't say when it will be.'

'Will you ring me, then? I warn you, if you don't, I'll ring you and make you unpopular on the ward!' When she said nothing, he bent his head and kissed her hand in his. 'Say you'll ring me, Alex. Promise.'

'That's all I'm promising, then.'

They moved as one into a quick, strong embrace, until Tim finally released her and left the car to open her door.

'I'll walk up the drive with you.'

'No need, Tim, it's well lit. And we might meet Matron.'

'You're allowed to be seen with a man, aren't you? Anybody'd think Florence Nightingale was still alive!'

He won the point and escorted her to the door of the nurses' home, where they met no one and all was quiet. With a last serious look, he kissed her cheek and watched her go inside, and she, running up the stairs, caught a glimpse of him from the landing window, walking quickly down the drive.

In her room, she picked up her hand-mirror and looked at herself, looked at her face, haunted by memory, alight with passion.

'Am I still in charge?' she asked herself. 'Am I still on top?'

Why talk as though there were some sort of competition between herself and Tim? Some sort of battle? If there was love, there should be no war, The point was, she couldn't be sure of the love. It had died once. But there, in the mirror, the girl was smiling. Alex laid the glass down, and went smiling to her bed.

In the darkness, Rose's face came into her mind, as it so often did, followed by Martie's. She felt she would have given anything to be able to talk to them, but Martie was so far away and Rose for ever beyond her reach. Neal had let her talk to Martie on his phone, but guilt made her shy away from thinking about Neal, and anyway, talking on the phone was never the same as face to face. What would Martie say, if she knew about Tim? After the way she was organising her own life, she wasn't in a position to be critical, that was for sure. Oh, but I do miss her! thought Alex. And I miss Rose! She couldn't write to Rose, but she could write to Martie. Surely she would reply sometime? Before she was married?

Chapter Fifty-Three

Alex and Tim did meet again. And again and again. There was something very sweet and dangerous about these meetings for Alex, but she couldn't help herself, she had put herself into the position of wanting to see him again. She had promised herself to expect nothing, and she really didn't expect anything, except perhaps trouble, but right through October and into November, whenever she was free, she met him.

Sometimes, they went to the cinema, sometimes the theatre, or concerts. Tim was fond of orchestral music and Alex, who had no knowledge of it, was learning fast, but what she really liked was to go dancing, wearing one of the dresses Mrs Adamson had bought for her, enjoying the admiration in Tim's eyes as she appeared in the cream silk, the apricot chiffon or dazzling emerald green, taking sad pleasure in knowing Lois would have been happy for her. She might have been happy for herself, if she had known what she was doing, or where she was going. What was in Tim's mind? She could have no idea when she wasn't sure what was in her own.

Although they took delight in kissing and caressing in his car neither sought more, which, if Alex let herself think about it, was surprising. Back in those early days in the Jubilee chalet, it had seemed as though they would have given anything to be able to have sex. Now, they never spoke of it, which, considering she didn't know what she wanted from this relationship, was just as well.

Meanwhile Edie was already asking questions, and Arthur was looking glum, and Alex decided it was time for Tim to meet her family and see her home, whether or not there was anything serious between them. When she asked him to collect her from the Colonies before a concert, he immediately said he would be delighted.

At the idea of Tim Burnett's coming into their little living room, Edie was thrown into a panic, and went about brushing and dusting, black-leading the stove, straightening mats, setting out the best cups and saucers and special iced biscuits, even though Alex had told her they wouldn't want anything, they were going straight out.

'Och, you can always do with a cup o' tea!' cried Edie. 'I'd no' want Mr Burnett to think we couldnae rise to that!'

'Edie, you heard Alex, they're going out,' Arthur growled. 'And I don't give a damn what Tim Burnett thinks. I've no time for a fella like that, and neither should our Alex have time either.'

'Dad, you know I've been going out with him,' Alex said quickly. 'I wanted you and Edie to meet him.'

'Why? He's no' your intended, is he?'

'No, but—'

'And I seem to remember he let you down before. You canna trust him, Alex, he's bad for you. When he came after you again, you should've told him where to go.'

'Now don't talk to her like that, Art,' Edie said sharply. 'I think Alex is very lucky Tim Burnett's turned up again.'

'Aye, but when he had the consumption, you sang a different tune, did you no'?'

'He's better now, is that no' right, Alex? Folk do get better, you ken, you canna hold a thing like that against them for ever!'

'He is better,' Alex agreed, crossing her fingers. Pray God, he stayed that way, she thought, and then her heart jumped at the sound of his footstep outside and his knock at the door.

As soon as he came in and shook her hand, Edie again collapsed into nervous agitation, insisting on offering the tea and opening the biscuits, and when Tim said he would quite like a cup of tea, radiantly smiled and looked triumphantly at Arthur.

'There you are, Art! They do want tea, after all!'

Arthur, refusing to be impressed by Tim's charming manners, only shrugged and tapped out his pipe on the stove.

'I'm really happy to meet you at last, Mr Kelsie,' Tim was saying earnestly. 'Alex tells me you're something of an actor.'

'Could've been.' Arthur sat with his arms folded and his expression stony. 'Ma dad was an actor at the Royal Lyceum, I should've followed him on the boards. Things were against me.'

'I'm sorry to hear that, Mr Kelsie.'

'Aye, had to settle for second best.' Arthur's eye ran over Tim's good-looking face, his excellent clothes, his gentleman's hands. 'Shakespeare's ma favourite writer, Mr Burnett. See here, I've got all the plays.'

'Och, Mr Burnett's no' got time to be looking at your books, Art!' cried Edie, but Arthur still put into Tim's hand the Shakespeare volume Neal had given him. 'That was given me by Mr Drover who runs the bookshop,' he said with meaning. 'He wrote in it at the front – see there?'

Tim read the inscription – 'With all good wishes to Alex's father, from Neal' – and, carefully not glancing at Alex, gave the book back to Arthur.

'Very handsome,' he said politely. 'Mr Kelsie, I wish you'd call me Tim.'

Alex, on pins, said they must be going, they had tickets for a concert at the Usher Hall.

'Plenty of time for tea,' said Edie sunnily, and it was not until they'd drunk the tea and eaten her iced biscuits, that they were free to make their farewells.

'Thank you so much, Mrs Kelsie,' Tim said, shaking her hand again. 'So nice to have met you. I look forward to seeing you again, and Mr Kelsie.'

'Oh, yes!' breathed Edie, seeing them to the door, watching them descend the steps. 'Come again, eh? Any time! Art, say goodbye now!'

'What a nice young man!' she exclaimed, when Arthur had banged the door shut. 'My word, Alex'd be lucky if she hooked him, eh?'

'Do you mind no' talking about ma girl as though she were a fisherman?' Arthur asked sharply. 'I'm no' happy about that fella, Edie, and I wish he'd never come back into Alex's life. There'll only be trouble.'

'Och, you see trouble where there's none! If you ask me, he's really in love. Every time he looked at Alex, I thought, aye, he's in love all right!'

'He was in love before,' said Arthur shortly.

Walking towards the Usher Hall, for they had decided not to try to park the car that night, Alex said self-consciously, 'Well done, Tim. You were wonderful in there.'

He bent his cool gaze on her. 'In what way? I enjoyed meeting your father and his wife.'

'His wife, yes, but no' ma mother,' Alex murmured. 'I wish you could've met ma mother, Tim. You'd really have liked her.'

'I told you, I liked your people anyway. Even if your father did make it pretty clear he would have preferred Neal Drover to me.'

'Nonsense,' Alex said awkwardly. 'He only took to Neal because he kept a bookshop.'

Tim shrugged. 'Well, I still like your father, whatever he thinks of me. And your home.'

'Rather different from your home, though.'

'I thought it very comfortable, very cosy.'

Alex laughed. 'You mean, small?'

'Why are you talking like this, Alex? We don't all have to come from the same sort of background.'

'That's no' what Edinburgh folk think. I mean your sort of Edinburgh folk. If you've no' been to the Academy, or St Clare's, they don't want to know.'

'That's not true. My parents, for instance, admire you very much, more than any girl they know.'

'Really? Have you told them you're seeing me?'

'Of course.' As they crossed to make their way up Lothian Road towards the Usher Hall, Tim took Alex's arm. 'You haven't seen Mother lately, or you'd know just what she thought, wouldn't you?'

Alex bit her lip. It was true, she hadn't seen Mrs Burnett recently. In fact, she hadn't called at the house in Cheviot Square since she and Tim had begun seeing each other, and had made an excuse not to go the last time Mrs Burnett had invited her.

'What's wrong?' Tim asked in her ear, as the concert-going crowds surrounded them. 'What did you think my mother would say?'

'I don't know. Maybe something disapproving. And I didn't want her not to approve.'

Tim squeezed Alex's arm. 'You've nothing to worry about. Both my parents think you're the tops.'

A warm feeling flooded Alex's being, which lasted until they were in their seats, waiting for the conductor's entrance and a Rossini overture to begin. Tim's parents believed her the tops? She hugged the thought to her, lost in relief, though why it should have mattered so much what his parents believed, she could not have said. As her own father had remarked, Tim was not her 'intended'. No intentions had been expressed on either side. Even so, she was very glad that Tim had told her she was well thought of by the Burnetts, and that they knew she and Tim were going out together. It was only when the conductor entered, made his bow, and drew his players into the sprightly strains of 'The Thieving Magpie', that Alex's thoughts went to Rose. It's because of Rose Tim's parents like me, she suddenly thought, only because I was a friend to her. Why, they probably don't even see me as a person in ma own right! In their eyes, I'd have nothing to recommend me if I hadn't been with Rose, if they couldn't have seen her in me!

All her euphoria fell away, and glancing at Tim's unconcerned profile, she felt overcome by depression. How would it all end, this new relationship with her old love? She'd promised herself she would expect nothing, but that had been a piece of nonsense from the start. If she didn't want his love, why was she seeing him? Oh, God, what a fool she'd been to get involved again! All the time, at the back of her mind, was that day at Corrie House when he'd told her he had changed. But he said now he regretted that, he said he'd changed back. And that was possible, wasn't it? She'd changed back, herself – if she had ever really stopped loving him, which she was now beginning to doubt.

She stared down at the concert programme on her knee, letting the music flow over her, hearing nothing. What should she do? She knew what she should do. End it. End the whole thing. That very evening. For a little while, she felt better, felt she had been true to herself and could be proud. But when they came out of the concert, Tim asked her back to his flat.

Rain had been falling while they were inside the concert-hall. Now they stood together, watching people stream away towards taxis and tram stops, as the steely rods hissed along the pavements and filled the gutters.

'What a night!' exclaimed Tim. He looked down at Alex, as the rain plastered his fair hair to his head, making it seem dark, making him seem a stranger. 'Listen, why not let's make a run for it to my place? I'm only round the corner, past the Caledonian.'

'You're asking me back to your flat?' asked Alex, lightly. 'Never done that before.'

'Has to be a first time,' he answered, equally lightly.

'Well – I wouldn't mind a coffee, if you're offering.' She gave a shaky laugh. 'We are getting rather wet.'

'Do you remember that time you wanted to lend me your umbrella?' Tim took her arm and hurried her across the road, skipping through the dazzle of car headlights, smiling down at her as they reached safety. 'That was when it all began again, wasn't it? Our renaissance?'

'Renaissance . . . that's a beautiful word, Tim.'

'Yes. Born again. Fits our love, doesn't it?'

Skimming with him along the pavement, Alex thought she was doing the right thing. She couldn't very well end their affair in the street, in the rain, could she? They could talk in his flat, she could explain things. Besides, she wouldn't mind seeing where he lived. Before they said goodbye.

'Here we are,' he said, pausing at the door to a dark, terraced

326

house, mainly converted to offices it seemed, from the names on the bells. Only the top one said simply, Burnett.

'Up the stairs, Alex,' Tim cried, unlocking the main door. 'Come on, I'll race you!'

He won, easily, and Alex, reaching him and breathing hard, was filled with joy at his good health. Oh, she was so happy for him! She did love him, she couldn't deny it. Why didn't she just give in and accept that he might love her, too? As he showed her across the threshold of his flat, all her resolution to end their affair melted away.

Chapter Fifty-Four

Her nerves took over, as she gave him her wet raincoat to hang up. She tried to conceal them, but her hands were trembling as she put back her hair, curling as it always did in the damp, and she did not trust herself to make comment on his flat, though she was impressed.

'Spacious, isn't it?' Tim asked, turning on a gas fire. 'That's because it wasn't converted from rooms for the maids, they'd have slept in the basement. I've had a look at the plans and this room was the old billiard-room.' He stood in front of the fire, smoothing back his own damp hair. 'Interesting, eh?'

'Very,' Alex whispered.

'Sometimes I lie in my bedroom, imagining I can hear the click of ghostly billiard balls, then feet walking round the table and some man calling out the score! Frighten myself to death!' Tim laughed and held out his hands to her. 'But come and get warm, why are you standing over there?'

'I'm admiring things. It's all so modern, isn't it?'

'Too right.' Tim looked with some satisfaction at his long low sofa and square armchairs, light oak bookcases and spindly coffee-table. 'Mother wanted me to take a stack of her ghastly Victorian stuff, but I said no thanks! A client of ours had brought this over from America, then went bankrupt and I took it off his hands. Would've been damn' difficult to get anything like it in the shops.'

'Yes, I'm sure it would.'

As Alex stood shivering by the fire, Tim gently put his arms around her.

'Alex, you're frozen! I'll have to make you coffee before you catch cold!'

'I never catch cold.'

'I'll make you coffee, anyway. Stay there, thaw out.'

'No, I want to help.'

'I warn you, my kitchen's not very tidy. Every so often, my mother sends a cleaning lady round to sort me out.'

As though she would care about his kitchen! Anyway, it was as neat as a pin, and very smart, too, with the sort of fitted cupboards you saw in the American films, and the kind of modern gadgets that would appeal to a man. There was nothing for her to do, only stand and watch Tim make the coffee in a stainless steel percolator, put out brown sugar and home-made shortbread presented by his mother, listen to him humming Rossini, wonder what in God's name, was going to happen next.

'Like black or white?' asked Tim. 'Shall I heat some milk?'

'Oh, black will do.' Yes, yes, black would do . . . She couldn't stand any more of these preliminaries. If they were preliminaries.

They took the coffee through to the sitting room, which was now beautifully warm, and Alex sat in Tim's chair, and Tim sat on the floor.

'Coffee OK?' he asked.

'Lovely.' She sipped it, staring at him over the cup, took a deep breath. 'Tim, tell me truly why you never asked me here before.'

'Couldn't trust myself.'

She laughed, uncertainly. 'Can you now?'

'I don't know.' He set his cup aside. 'Things are different tonight. I took heart, because you invited me to meet your folks.'

'Why should that make a difference?'

He took her cup and placed it with his own, then stood up and pulled her to her feet. 'Made me think, if I asked you to marry me, you'd say yes.'

Alex went scarlet. Her lips parted, but she could say nothing.

He drew her towards him. 'Would I be right, Alex? If I asked you, would you say, yes?'

'Try me,' she said, at last. 'Oh, God, try me, Tim!'

All that they had wanted, back in the chalet days at the Jubilee, came to them that evening. Then, the holding back had been so hard. Now there was no holding back, and they gave themselves up to the sort of pleasure that was new to Alex and Tim, too, though he didn't deny that there had been others for him before her.

'That's men for you,' he whispered, as they lay back in his modern bed, looking at each other, 'you mustn't mind, my darling, they were all meaningless compared with you.'

'You wouldn't have said that to them,' she answered, tracing her finger down the planes of his face.

'No, but I didn't ask any of them to marry me, either.'

'Did I ever say yes?'

'I reckon what happened just now was a yes, wasn't it?'

'Yes, yes, yes!'

They clung together passionately, until, Alex leaped up, in a panic, and though Tim cried, 'You're beautiful, you're so beautiful!' she began hurriedly to dress.

'I've got to go, Tim, I'm sleeping at home tonight and they don't like me to be late.'

'Alex, it's not even midnight!'

'I know, but Dad's old-fashioned, you know how folk are. Oh, God, where are ma shoes—'

'This is ridiculous,' sighed Tim, getting into his clothes. 'The sooner we're married the better.'

'You might be right about that,' said Alex, combing her hair at Tim's mirror. 'If you know what I mean.'

He spun her back into his arms. 'You'll be OK, don't worry about it. Hardly ever happens the first time, does it?'

'Have you no' heard of honeymoon babies?'

'Well, if we're getting married anyway, it won't matter if we're having a non-honeymoon baby, will it?'

Alex gave a tremulous smile. 'I can't believe any of this is happening, Tim. I mean, one minute we're going to a concert, the next we're talking about babies!'

'Don't worry, we'll definitely have the wedding first!' He laughed and kissed her. 'If you've found your shoes, I'll get the coats.'

'You're coming with me?'

'Of course I'm coming with you! I'm driving you home.'

In the car, something came into Alex's mind, she didn't know why, she hadn't thought of it in years.

'Tim, you know my locket? What did you do with it?'

'Your locket?' His eyes were on the road, he was humming Rossini again. He looked very happy.

'Yes, you remember, I gave it back to you.'

'Don't remind me.'

'But what did you do with it?'

'Why, I kept it, of course.'

'Is it in the flat, then?'

'You're thinking you'd like to have it again?'

'Yes, of course I would. It meant a lot to me.'

'I wasn't even sure you'd like it. Seemed an old-fashioned sort of thing to give these days.'

'I'm old-fashioned, then. I loved it.' Alex hesitated, as Tim drew up outside Number One, Mason Street. 'Did you say it was in your flat somewhere?'

He took her hand. 'Actually, I think it's still back in my room at Cheviot Square. In a drawer. I'll get it for you, I promise, but don't forget, I'll be giving you a ring. That'll mean a lot more, won't it?'

'Yes, but I'd still like the locket.'

'All right, I'll find it. I know it's in the house.'

They kissed long and passionately,

'I think of it as a reminder of our first love,' she told him, as they drew apart. 'It's important.'

'I know. For me, too.'

There was no prospect of sleep for her that night. She wished she could have taken a bath, but the stove was out and there was no hot water.

'You're a wee bit late,' Edie commented, filling the hot bottles. 'Go on somewhere after the concert, did you?'

'Er, yes. Just had something to eat.'

'Mr Burnett spends a lot on you, doesn't he?'

'Too much,' muttered Arthur, winding his watch and staring at Alex. 'What's he after?'

'Look, you may as well know—' Alex paused. 'He's asked me to marry him. We're engaged.'

Edie's squeals of joy were cancelled out by Arthur's scowl, but Alex suddenly felt too drained of all emotional strength to try to put the case for Tim as son-in-law, or to answer any of Edie's questions. She was going to bed, she said, she had to be up early in the morning, they could all talk later. Goodnight, goodnight!

Having washed as well as she could in cold water, Alex studied her body that Tim had called beautiful. It didn't look any different, that was the strange thing, and she might even be pregnant. Probably she wasn't, but you never knew. If her father thought she shouldn't take risks, she was certainly taking them now. Putting on her nightdress, diving into bed to clasp the hot-water bottle waiting for her, she faced the truth. The biggest risk of all was taking Tim himself, one she couldn't avoid. But she was committed and wanted to be. It was only as her eyes were closing in sleep, that she again remembered the locket. She wished Tim had taken it with him to his flat, but it didn't matter. He would surely find it.

Chapter Fifty-Five

Everyone, except her father and Jamie who were united in disapproval, said Alex was just so lucky. The luckiest girl in the world! Why, she'd be on Easy Street for the rest of her life, wouldn't she, marrying an Edinburgh lawyer with the sort of money he could make? And though Sister Piers thought that giving up nursing was always a waste, she had to agree that Alex seemed to have done well for herself. Chris MacInnes said he was particularly delighted, Tim being such a fine chap who had made such a wonderful recovery.

'I can assure you, you need have no worries about his health,' he told Alex, which perversely made her worry again. In spite of Tim's ability to run upstairs, there was no guarantee that he might not have a relapse. The TB bacillus was notorious for returning, just when it seemed to have been vanquished. Consider how often Neal Drover had had to return to hospital. And poor young Ginnie Fleck, re-admitted to Butterfly Four, who was not responding to treatment.

'Och, don't take it so hard,' Jill Berry told Alex. 'These things happen, there's nothing we can do.'

'But with all the success we've had with the new drugs, it's so awful that they don't work for her, Jill!'

'Aye, well, they can't help everyone, I suppose. But she might still pull through, you ken. I mean, never say die.'

But Ginnie did die and Alex, seeing the terror in her young face at the end, had needed all her courage to stay with her, though she did stay and held her hand, as she had done before. No amount of comforting from Tim could cheer her, for when she looked at him, she only feared for him. He too had been a patient who had apparently got well.

'I have this nightmare that Tim or Neal Drover will have to come back into the Jubilee,' she told Chris MacInnes when they were on duty one evening, 'and that nothing works for them, just as nothing worked for poor Ginnie. I come out in a cold sweat when I think about it, because all anyone says is, there's nothing we can do.'

'That's not what people said when they worked their guts out on these new cures,' he reminded her quietly. 'And we have a team of doctors here in this city who are going to wipe out TB in Edinburgh before very long, and that's a promise. You know how much is being done, Alex, you're just letting yourself get depressed. Happens to us all.'

'I know, I'm sorry. I can't help thinking about Ginnie and her folks.'

'And you lost your own mother,' he said gently. 'But I truly believe that Tim's going to stay well, and Neal Drover, too. Hang on to that and keep on keeping on, like the rest of us. It's the only way.'

She gave a reluctant smile. 'You're right, of course.'

'Always am! Well, mostly.' Chris rested his hand on Alex's shoulder. 'Why don't you take a quick peep at your ring? I bet that'll cheer you up!'

But Alex's beautiful diamond solitaire ring was safely in her room, she didn't wear it on duty. She might have worn her locket, hidden under her uniform, but Tim hadn't found it. At least, not yet.

'I can't understand it,' he told her, when he took her to Cheviot Square shortly after their engagement was announced. 'I've searched everywhere and Mother has, too. I'm afraid it looks as though one of our cleaning ladies has been a bit light-fingered.'

'Why didn't you take it with you to the flat?' asked Alex, who could not pretend that losing the locket didn't matter.

'I should have done. Darling, I'm sorry, I really am. But it could still turn up.'

Alex said no more, but braced herself for the formal meeting with Tim's parents, for though Tim had said they thought her the 'tops', whether that made her an eligible daughter-in-law was by no means certain. She need not have worried, they welcomed her with kindness and warmth, told her they knew she was a caring and compassionate girl, who would make their son very happy, and that she could count on them to do all that they could to make her happy too. At the back of her mind, Alex knew that if Rose had not died, things might have been different. Their values might not have been shaken, their view of her world compared with their world, might have been enough for them to withhold approval of her. But Rose had died, and nothing for them was ever to be the same again. Even their ideas on the perfect wife for Tim.

'We must have a little dinner with your parents, my dear,' Mrs Burnett said, passing slices of one of her lemon cakes, 'or if they would prefer tea, we could arrange that instead.'

'I think they'd like to come to tea,' Alex replied.

'We'll fix it up, then. I'll write your stepmother a little note.'

Oh, God, thought Alex, wait till Edie gets that!

In the event, the tea-party went off better than anyone could have expected. Arthur wore his good suit and talked to Mr Burnett about books and drama. Edie wore a new twin-set with her best tweed skirt and talked to Mrs Burnett about recipes. When everyone had had the usual delightful tea, Mr Burnett produced sherry, saying the sun was over the yardarm, it was time to have a snifter, and the farewells that followed were very pleasant indeed. Edie, holding Arthur's arm, went home floating on rosy clouds, and even Arthur said the Burnetts were pretty nice folk, considering who they were.

'Aye, and I think Mr Burnett was impressed with you, Art,' Edie told him. 'I mean, I bet you knew as much as him, eh, about thae plays and stuff?'

'Just because a man works with his hands doesnae mean he's got nothing in his head,' Arthur observed, finding his key. 'I reckon I gave a good account of maself.'

335

'You did, Dad, I was proud of you,' said Alex. 'But do you feel any happier about me marrying Tim?'

He sighed heavily. 'If he's what you want, lassie, I'll say no more. Just as long as he treats you right.'

'That's the point,' said Jamie, rising from a chair by the stove. He had let himself in, eager to know how they'd got on with the Burnetts. 'Will that guy make you happy, Alex?'

'Everyone says I'm the luckiest girl in the world.'

'But what do you say?'

Alex unbuttoned her coat and flung it down. 'I just wish you'd leave me alone, Jamie. I didn't go around interrogating you when you got engaged to Heather, did I?'

'Maybe you should've done. Might have saved me a lot of trouble.'

'People have to work things out for themselves, that's what I believe.'

'Quite right,' put in Edie. 'But if you think your sister can do better than Tim Burnett, you need your head examining, Jamie. He's class, he is.'

'There's more to life than a posh accent and money,' Jamie snapped, at which Edie laughed.

'You've got a lot to learn! Here, let me put the kettle on, that sherry's made me thirsty. Och, but it was nice, eh, Art? Were you no' impressed with the house, and the flowers and the china and everything?'

Arthur had taken off his jacket and was putting on his comfortable old cardigan. He shrugged. 'Aye, but thae things are no' important, Edie. Happiness is people.'

The right people, he means, thought Alex, but Edie'll no' see it. Luckily.

'How's Martie doing these days?' Jamie asked her, as Edie busied herself setting out cups and saucers. 'Does she write?'

'No, I haven't heard from her in ages. I expect she's married by now.'

'Come on, she'd have told you!'

'I don't know. I don't know one thing about Martie any more.'

'Out of sight, out of mind, eh?'

'Seems like it. Well, I've got enough to think about without worrying about her.'

'I wish you would think,' Jamie said, in a low voice. 'Just have a long good think about what you're doing.'

Alex did not reply. Jamie did need his head examining, she told herself, if he believed she hadn't thought about what she was doing. She thought about it all the time.

Chapter Fifty-Six

Alex had another worry about Neal Drover and it was not about his health. She hadn't seen him for months, had no idea how he felt about her, yet ever since she'd become engaged to Tim, it had been in her mind to give him the news. It might seem cruel on her part, rubbing things in, but the thought of someone else telling him was too much to face. She would have to go down to the bookshop and tell him herself. So much she owed him, so much was clear. The only problem was she couldn't seem to do it. Every time she set off for the shop, an excuse presented itself and she turned aside. Every time she tried to write a letter instead, the words would not come. Finally, one lunch hour, she made it. Hurried down, keeping her mind blank, so that no excuses could work their way in; reached the shop, tried the door, found it locked. There was a notice she'd been too agitated at first to read.

'Back at two o'clock.'

Damn, damn, damn. The time was then half-past one and she must be back herself at two. She couldn't wait. She would have to write a letter, then, but she knew she could not.

Someone spoke. It was Neal's voice, deep and pleasant. 'Alex? What are you doing here?'

She swung round and saw him, but he was not alone. A young woman was standing beside him, a hand on his arm, and Alex recognised her. She was the sandy-haired girl who had visited Neal when he was in Butterfly Two. A teacher, someone had said. So, why wasn't she teaching?

'I came to see you,' Alex told Neal. 'But I don't want to inter-rupt, I can come some other time.'

'This is Penny Renton, Alex. Penny, may I introduce Alex Kelsie? Alex used to nurse me at the Jubilee.'

Something in the young woman's pale blue eyes flickered, before she smiled and shook Alex's hand. She knows about me, thought Alex. Neal has told her.

'You must have done a good job,' Penny murmured. 'He's very well.'

He did look well, though had put on no weight. Alex thought he seemed calmer, not too troubled at seeing her, anyway, which made things easier for her. She felt ashamed she wasn't more grateful, but she couldn't get used, somehow, to thinking of Neal with another woman.

'Penny and I had just been for a bit of lunch,' he explained. 'Should have gone separately, but we thought, what the hell, why don't we just go together? Got back earlier than we expected, so I may as well open up.'

'I'm helping Neal these days,' Penny said in confiding tones, as Neal took out his keys and opened the shop. 'I've given up teaching – it was so terribly wearing – and Neal's doing better these days, he does need an assistant.'

'I'm sure.' Alex smiled uncertainly. 'It's been very nice, meeting you, but I'd better be getting back to the Jubilee.'

'Staff nurse now,' Neal said over his shoulder. 'Doing well.'

'Really? Oh, that's very good. You look so young.' Penny was beginning to edge into the shop. 'But didn't you want to speak to Neal? I'll just sort out that box of paperbacks—'

'Mind talking on the pavement?' Neal asked Alex, when Penny had tactfully removed herself.

'No. I – Neal, I just came to tell you – I'm going to marry Tim Burnett.' Alex's face had taken on a hard, dry flush, as Neal looked down at her without expression. 'I thought I'd like to tell you maself.'

'Thank you. I appreciate that.'

'You didn't know, did you?'

'I did, as a matter of fact. Your father told me.'

'Dad?'

'Yes, he comes in here often. We have some good talks.'

'I never knew,' Alex said, feeling stupid. 'I needn't have come.'

'No, it's good that you did. I'm glad to know that you thought enough about me to tell me yourself.'

'Will you – wish me well?'

'Of course.' He bent to kiss her cheek. 'I'll always wish you well, Alex. I hope you and Tim will be very happy.'

'You seem happier yourself, Neal.'

'Yes, I'm getting along pretty well. With my assistant.'

'Are you – is Penny—'

'No.' He gave a strained smile. 'Not yet, anyway.'

'Oh, Neal, I do want you to be happy!' Alex cried. 'And I want you to stay well! If you ever have the slightest worry, you will go for a check-up, won't you? It's vital to catch anything new in time, because we have these wonderful drugs now—'

'I do have regular checks, don't worry. Look, give my congratulations to Tim when you see him, will you? Tell him he's a bloody lucky man.'

They held each other's hands in a strong convulsive clasp, then Neal moved to his shop door and Alex turned to run back to work, aware that she was going to be late, aware that she had tears in her eyes. What's got into me? she asked herself. Getting weepy for no reason. It was lucky she'd discovered that she wasn't pregnant, or she might have been worried. As it was, she knew she was feeling the wrench of making a last goodbye to Neal. He was getting over her, and she was happy about it – no, honestly, she was! But there was something bitter-sweet, all the same, about meeting a lover who no longer loved. Even though she had Tim.

There was a letter waiting for her when she arrived back at the nurses' home that evening. It bore American stamps and the sender's name was Cass. Alex could scarcely believe her eyes. Martie? Martie had written at last? And she was still calling herself Cass?

340

Although it was nearly time for supper and she wasn't in the least ready, Alex tore open the letter on the spot. People brushed past her, smiling. Someone said, 'Hi, Alex, are you no' hungry?'

'Coming,' she murmured, not taking her eyes from Martie's huge sprawling hand.

> 'Dear Alex,' Martie had written, 'I feel ashamed, not having written for so long, but you know me! Anyway, here goes. The big news is that Warren and I have parted. (Do I hear your jaw drop?) Yes, well, it had to be. He's the most wonderful man, the kindest, most generous guy you could wish to meet, and I know he'd have given me anything I wanted. Thing is, it just gradually dawned on me, I couldn't take it. I was the luckiest girl in the world, but I didn't want to be. Warren's too nice, he deserves somebody who really loves him. And somebody who'd fit in with his life better than I ever could. He was pretty upset when I told him, but he was so nice, you wouldn't believe! Even made me keep the ring, though I didn't want it. I felt so awful, Alex. That's why I didn't write.
>
> This all happened back in the summer and I've been working on at Mount Forest ever since. But now I've decided to come home. By the time you get this letter, I'll be on my way. Can't wait to see you, and everyone. Please give my love to your folks, All my love, Martie.'

Alex finished reading and dazedly went upstairs to wash her hands. Came down, found a place for supper, still lost in wonder at Martie's news. She couldn't decide which had astonished her more, Martie's splitting up with her Rich Man, or her coming home. It all seemed so strange, so casual. But there was one line of the letter that stood out in her mind, and kept returning. 'I was the luckiest girl in the world, but I didn't want to be.'

Eating sponge pudding and solid custard, Alex pondered on

those words. They sent something into her heart that was so cold and sharp, she laid down her spoon and got up from the table.

'Had enough?' her neighbour asked, with a laugh.

'Yes, for now,' Alex replied.

Chapter Fifty-Seven

'Why all this fuss about Martie Cass coming home?' Tim asked Alex. 'Didn't you think she would?'

He and Alex were having a meal in a dark little restaurant in the West End before going to a cinema. Alex had been telling him – bending his ear, he called it – about Martie's letter.

'I thought she'd marry Warren and stay in America.'

'You're glad she's split up with Warren?'

'Yes, he wasn't right for her. They'd really nothing in common.'

'I feel sorry for him. She probably made him feel his age.' Tim finished off his wine. 'Not the most tactful of girls, your Martie. Never liked me, either.'

'She didn't dislike you, Tim, she just thought we shouldn't have been – you know – risking your health, the way we did.'

His look softened. 'Whatever we did, it was worth it. If Martie finds something against me again, you wouldn't listen to her, would you?'

'I didn't listen to her the first time, did I?'

'That's true.' He covered her hand with his. 'But we've spent too much time on her tonight. Shouldn't we be discussing our own plans? Setting a wedding date, for instance?'

'I suppose we should.' Alex looked from the large diamond on her finger to Tim's face, so well-proportioned, so classically handsome, it seemed perfect to her. To spend her life with the owner of that face had been all she'd ever wanted at one time. She was suddenly aware that the cold sharp pain in her heart seemed not to have gone.

'Do you want a winter wedding, or to wait until spring?' Tim asked.

'Maybe spring would be best.'

'It's a long way off.'

'Well, there's a lot to plan.'

'Were you thinking of St Bernard's? Or the Cathedral?'

'I think, St Bernard's. If you don't mind?'

'No, that's fine. How about the reception?' Tim hesitated. 'Look, I don't want to tread on your toes, or your father's, but my parents have said they'd like to help. I mean, why should it all come on you? Mother said, if we were thinking of the Caledonian, or somewhere like that, they'd be more than happy to share. What do you think?'

'Dad and me would really rather pay for things ourselves.' Alex looked down at her empty glass. 'But I don't mind, if it's what you want—'

'Darling, I only want what you want.'

And I don't know, she thought wildly, what I want!

'Isn't it time to go to the pictures?' she cried.

They saw an adventure film that Alex forgot as soon as the credits came up, but it passed the time and took their minds off themselves, which helped. Just lately, there had been a little constraint between them. Neither had spoken of it. Better not.

When they came out into the early December cold, Tim suggested they go back to his place. Alex said she couldn't.

'I've to be back at the hospital, Tim, I'm sorry. I did tell you I'd agreed to swap and do this one night-shift for Jill Berry.'

Tim studied her for a moment. 'Is it my imagination, or are you getting good at finding excuses not to come to my flat? You haven't been there since that first time, have you? Don't you want to sleep with me again?'

'It isn't that, Tim. It's just – well, we took a risk, didn't we? We got away with it, but I think maybe we should wait now.'

344

'We are engaged, Alex. There's no need for us to wait. And we can take precautions.' Tim took her by the arm. 'Look, let's go back to my place and talk. There's something going on here, and I want to know what it is.'

'I told you, I've no' got the time to come to your flat tonight.'

'OK, we'll go and get the car. I'll drive you to the Jubilee and we'll talk on the way. Come on, hurry!'

They arrived at the hospital with time to spare and Tim parked in the road near the gates. He shut off the engine and turned to Alex, whose eyes were cast down.

'What's wrong?' he asked directly. 'Please just say.'

She looked at him. 'I don't know how to tell you, Tim.'

'Sounds bad. Don't tell me you've fallen out of love with me?' He gave a short laugh. 'That would be ironic, eh? Tit for tat?'

She knew he didn't believe it, as he needn't. It wasn't true.

'I haven't fallen out of love with you. I'll always love you. When you gave me up, I tried to stop. I never really did.'

'Then what the hell is all this about?'

'I don't think we should be getting married. I – made a mistake.'

'Made a mistake?' She could see his eyes shining with disbelief. 'Alex, haven't we just been discussing our wedding reception? Are you telling me you've changed your mind in the last ten minutes?'

'No, I've been thinking about it for some time. In fact, I should never have said yes.' Her voice trembled. 'I should never have said yes in the first place.'

'I don't understand – you've just now said you loved me! What are you playing at?'

'I keep remembering that time you changed!' she cried.

For a long time, Tim was silent, sitting staring straight ahead at the cars moving towards Stockbridge. 'I thought we'd been over all that,' he said, at last. 'It was a long time ago.'

'I know, but it's there, in ma mind. It's always there.'

'Why did you say you'd marry me, then? Because we had sex?'

'No!' Alex wiped tears from her eyes. 'I suppose it was because you'd come back to me. At one time I'd have given ma soul for

345

that. So, I thought I must be happy. We made love and it was wonderful—'

'Go on.'

'And you said there was a renaissance of our love and you wanted to marry me. I thought why not?'

'Why not, is right.'

'No. It was all too late. If you'd never changed up at Fort William, everything we're doing now would've been right. Making love, planning the wedding, everything. I really could've felt I was the luckiest girl in the world, there'd have been no shadow between us.' Alex reached out and took Tim's hand. 'But there is a shadow, Tim. There's a scar.'

'Like my lung, you mean?' He gave another short laugh. 'I did recover, Alex.'

'I didn't,' she said quietly.

'I'm not taking the ring back,' he said bluntly, when they had left the car and reached the door of the nurses' home. 'You're going to change your mind about this, Alex, I know you are. We're so right for each other!'

'We were.'

He looked for a long time into her face. 'Are you sure you've not been influenced by Martie Cass? I mean, she's thrown over a man who loves her, hasn't she?'

'I'm no' even going to answer that.'

'Well, it seems a strange coincidence, that just after she's told you what she's done, you do the same.'

'Haven't you been listening to a word I've said?'

'I can't accept it, Alex. It's just nonsense. I know I let you down, but it's in the past, I thought you'd forgiven me.'

'Tim, I have to go—'

'It's not because of the locket, is it? I know I shouldn't have lost it—'

'It's no' because of the locket. Tim, I must say goodnight.'

He caught her arm. 'You're leaving me? Just walking away? Don't you care at all about my feelings? You blame me for what happened before. Aren't you acting just the same?' His eyes were desperate in the dim light. 'Alex, this isn't some kind of revenge?'

'How can you ask me that?' she whispered. 'Oh, Tim, you don't know me at all, if you think I'd want to hurt you. I'd never do that, never!'

He caressed her hand in his. 'I know, I'm sorry. I take it back. It's just that you have hurt me, whether you wanted to, or not. It's all been such a shock, you see. I thought you were happy.'

Tears were streaming down her face, yet she had no thought for how she would appear on the ward. The only person in the world for her just then was Tim, and she clung to him, kissing his beloved face for the last time.

'We must meet again, Alex. We must talk this thing through.'

'No, it wouldn't help, it wouldn't help! It's been hard enough to tell you now, I couldn't talk again.'

'You say you still love me,' he said blankly. 'What's more important than love?'

She wavered in his arms, trying to find the words that would make it clear why she was tearing them both to pieces.

'I suppose,' she said, at last, 'you might say trust.'

He let her go at that, but did not move. As she went from him, she remembered the time she had gone to an upper window to catch a last glimpse of him, and ran there now, weeping silently. For a long moment, she watched him, until he finally turned and walked slowly down the drive.

Thank God I'm on duty, she thought, making her way to her room to change into her uniform. I needn't try to sleep tonight.

347

Chapter Fifty-Eight

'Och, you've never done it, Alex!' Edie cried, her face quite anguished. 'You've never given up that lovely young man! I'll no' believe it! I canna believe it! Are you crazy, or what?'

'Oh, crazy,' said Alex. 'That's what everyone says, so it must be true.'

'Lassie, you've seen the light!' said her father, hugging her. 'If I'd been a praying man, I'd have prayed for this, and maybe I'll still thank God. He was no' right for you, and now you've seen it. Nobody else could see it for you, you'd to see it for yourself, and you did. There's ma girl!'

'You're two of a kind, you are!' groaned Edie. 'To turn down a fine young man like Tim Burnett – well, it's beyond me, so it is! He's a lawyer's son, he's a lawyer himself, he'll always have money, Alex'd never have had to do a hand's turn. And then there was his parents. Such lovely people! Never a bit o' snobbery! No looking down on us, because we'd no' got what they'd got! When I think o' the way they welcomed us—!'

'Don't,' Alex murmured. 'Don't say any more about his parents.'

'Aye, you'll no' be going there to tea again, will you? You've finished with all that, and for what? No good reason, that I can see. Honestly, Alex, it'll serve you right if you never marry at all, if you end up one o' thae dried-up old spinsters running hospitals—'

'Edie,' said Arthur shortly. 'Shut up.' He drew a few copper coins from his trouser pocket. 'Alex, let you and me go and phone up Jamie from the call box, eh? Tell him the good news?'

'Dad, you're making too much of this. Tim's no' as bad as you make out, or I'd never have cared for him at all.'

'He made you suffer, Alex. Fathers don't forget who hurts their children.'

'He's suffering now, then,' said Edie. 'That young man really cares for you, Alex, I'm telling you!'

'Aye, for how long?' asked Arthur. 'Till he gets tired, eh? Alex, dinna fret. He'll be wanting you now, because you've given him up. That's the way of the world. But if you'd been happy with him, I'd no' have given you six months. Now, let's away and ring up Jamie!'

'Dad, I'd really rather just go round to Mrs Cass and ask if she knows when Martie's coming home. It can't be long now.'

'I can tell you that!' cried Edie. 'I saw Tilda this forenoon and she says she's had a letter. Martie's coming home by liner, she's due into Glasgow tomorrow. Then, would you credit it, she's taking a taxi all the way over here! Tilda's having kittens, as you might guess. She'd niver take a taxi, if she was dying! Aye, but Martie's got money to burn, eh? Must have.'

'Did Mrs Cass say if Martie said anything else?' Alex asked uneasily.

'You mean, about the fella she was engaged to? Tilda just said it was off. I suppose that's why she's coming home.'

'Didn't say who the man was, or anything?'

'No, Martie never told them that. They'd no' but a couple o' letters the whole time she was away. Tilda said to me she sometimes wondered if their girl'd ever learned to read and write!'

'I'm dying to see Martie again, but I don't think I can get off duty until Sunday,' Alex said, no longer listening to Edie. 'I expect she'll be wanting to spend time with her folks first, anyway.'

'Might,' sniffed Edie. 'On the other hand, she might not. If I know Martie Cass, she'll be out on the town before you can say knife.'

Out on the town . . . What does Edie think we nurses get up to? thought Alex. 'If you see Martie before I do, tell her I'll be along on Sunday, will you?' she said aloud. 'And if Jamie comes, tell him when Martie's arriving. He always pretends he's no' interested, but I know he is.'

'Aye, and I'll tell him about you and Tim Burnett and all,' said Arthur. 'He'll be interested in that, all right!'

He came with Alex to the door, adding in a low voice, 'If you've a minute, Alex, why do you no' go round to Mr Drover's bookshop? He'd be glad to see you.'

'Forget the matchmaking, Dad,' Alex told him. 'Neal has another girlfriend now.'

'Och, he's no' interested in that girl who moves the books around and thinks she's helping!' Arthur put his hand on Alex's arm. 'Go and see him, pet! He's a grand fella, he's worth a dozen o' that Tim Burnett, and you'd make him very happy!'

'I don't want to make anyone happy or unhappy ever again,' cried Alex. 'Just leave me alone, Dad, just leave me alone!'

Looking forward to seeing Martie helped a little to ease the pain of Alex's break with Tim. It had come as something of a surprise to her, that she was suffering almost as much as when Tim had broken with her at Corrie House. Sometimes she felt worse, for she had also the anguish of wondering if she'd done the right thing. Supposing she'd been unjust to Tim? Supposing she could have just relaxed, knowing that he would never change again? No, no, she wouldn't accept that. She hadn't been able to relax, she felt she never would have been able to, and what sort of foundation would that have been for marriage? It was true, after all, that after their first split, he hadn't cared enough to keep her locket with him. Yes, but supposing that couldn't be taken any more as a sign of his future feelings? Supposing his renaissance as he called it was truly genuine. All this torture would have been for nothing! So her thoughts went round and round on a wheel of self-doubt and misery, and she longed for Martie's comforting presence, her robust common sense, her probable willingness to think Alex had been right. Apart from all that, there would be the interest of hearing Martie's own experiences. That would surely take Alex's mind off her troubles for a little while! All she had to do was wait for Sunday.

Until then, she had to endure her colleagues' views on her parting from Tim. There were some, she knew, who thought he must have been the one to drop her, who gave her sidelong looks of commiseration, and said things like, 'Och, men!' and 'What a shame, eh?' Others accepted her version, that it had been her decision to end her engagement because it would never have worked out, but commented as Edie had done, that she must be crazy, needed her head examining, must have a screw loose, et cetera. Only Sister Piers seemed genuinely delighted that an excellent nurse had been spared for the profession, while Chris MacInnes confessed himself troubled.

'I know the family, you see,' he told Alex. 'They're good, genuine people. Well, you know what Rose was like, don't you? Tim's the same. You'd have been happy with him, I'm sure of it.'

Seeing tears welling into Alex's eyes, he added hastily, 'But, of course it's not for me to interfere. Marriage is a big step and you're absolutely right to be careful. Oh, look, please don't be upset! Here, take my handkerchief! Oh, God, forget I said anything at all! Who the hell am I, to go putting my foot in it?'

'It's all right,' she said, blowing her nose. 'I know you're a friend of Tim's. Don't want to see him hurt.'

'I hope I'm a friend of yours, too, Alex. I don't want to see either of you hurt.' He hesitated. 'I suppose there's no question, you might reconsider?'

I could easily reconsider, she thought. I could run round to Tim this minute and take him back again. But it wouldn't do, it wouldn't do.

'There's no question,' she told Chris, and he said no more.

Sunday afternoon came at last. Alex had just changed into her own clothes when a probationer brought a message that there was someone to see her in Reception.

'Says she used to work here,' the girl said dubiously. 'Doesn't look like a nurse to me.'

'Is it Martie?' cried Alex. 'Is it Martie Cass?'

'That's the name. Shall I tell her you'll be down?'

'I'll tell her maself! I'm coming down this minute!'

In what seemed less than a minute, Alex was out of the nurses' home and into Reception, hands outstretched to the young woman rising from a chair. 'Martie!' For a moment, she did a double take. This wasn't Martie. Oh, how embarrassing, she'd made a mistake. Then the young woman said, 'Hello, Alex!' And it was Martie's voice.

Of course it was Martie. Just a very slender version, wearing a beautiful American coat, with her honey-coloured hair cut stylishly and a general air of seeming different. Being away has changed her, thought Alex, but she's still there, she's still Martie.

She made to throw her arms around her old friend, but Martie put up her hand.

'No hugging or kissing,' she said, in her familiar voice that had just the faintest hint of an American accent. 'Off limits right now, Alex, but I guess we could shake hands.'

Aware that the receptionist, Joanna Tay, was staring at them curiously, Alex shook Martie's hand.

'Whatever are you talking about?' she whispered. 'Hugging and kissing off limits?'

'Come on, can't you guess?' Martie was smiling in a strange, fixed way that sent arrows through Alex's heart. 'It's happened to me. What we all dread. I'm coming back to the Jubilee as a patient, Alex. I've contracted TB.'

Alex, moving like a robot, fetched her coat, and went walking with Martie in the grounds.

'Might as well see the cabbages again!' said Martie. 'If I'm lucky, I'll be out here weeding, eh? And it's no colder outside than it is in Mum's house!' She laughed. 'Nothing changes, Alex. Except me. But you look just the same, only more so. Prettier than ever.'

'And you're very thin,' Alex said huskily. 'Oh, Martie, I don't know what to say! I can't believe it, I just can't believe it!'

'Snap. I couldn't believe it either when Dr Viner made the diagnosis.' Martie took a paper tissue from her bag and wiped her lips. 'That wasn't long ago, either, so I'm still coming to terms with it. Frank wanted me to stay at Mount Forest, of course, but I just told him I was coming home, coming to the Jubilee. I didn't know for sure I'd get a bed, but I'm ex-staff so I was hopeful. I wrote to ma doctor and saw him yesterday. Seemingly, I've hit lucky, they're fitting me in.'

'Thank God for that,' said Alex, shivering in the wind. 'Look, could we go somewhere and talk? Have a cup of tea, or something?'

'Guess there won't be anywhere open on a Sunday.'

'There's the visitors' canteen here.'

'The visitors' canteen!' echoed Martie. 'Perfect! Let's go.'

Chapter Fifty-Nine

While Martie, unbuttoning her handsome coat, sent that fixed stare she seemed to have adopted round the other customers in the visitors' canteen, Alex, sipping tea, studied her. Now, at close quarters, she could see that Martie's slenderness was gauntness, and that the honey-coloured hair, though so elegantly cut, was dry and dull. There was no flush on her cheekbones, but Alex took no comfort in that, for Martie had never had cheekbones before, not that you could see. They helped to give her that look of difference Alex had first noticed. And of course Martie was different, wasn't she? She was ill.

Oblivious of the rattle of cups and the hum of voices around them, Alex leaned forward.

'Why didn't you tell me about it?' she asked in a low voice. 'Why didn't you write?'

Martie studied her coffee in the paper cup she had requested. 'I haven't known for very long. Like I said, I came straight home, soon as I got the news.'

'Tell me now, then.'

'It was the worst day of my life, Alex.'

'When they gave you the news?'

'When Frank Viner asked me to take a sputum test.'

As Alex waited, looking stunned, Martie thought back to the beginnings of the nightmare. She had not been well since the summer, had begun to feel very tired, which was not like her at all.

It had been easy to explain it. She'd quoted to herself the shock of hearing about Rose, the strain of breaking with Warren, but she'd known all the time that such things wouldn't have affected her physically, wouldn't have made her feel tired. Heavens, she'd never known what tiredness was! Warren always said that it was her vitality that had first attracted him to her. As for being ill, she'd never been ill, never had a cold. Suddenly, she began to get one cold after another, and by the fall, had developed a small cough. No one had noticed and she'd never taken any notice of it herself. Even Frank Viner, who'd begun asking her out to dinner, never noticed, and he had the sharpest eye of any doctor she knew. But folk never really looked at people they saw every day. It was only when Frank had once glimpsed her in the distance, that just for a moment he'd seen her objectively. And had feared.

'Martie, you've grown thin!' She remembered how he'd run to her and taken her hands, holding her away from him, scrutinising her with narrowing eyes. 'My God, have you been dieting?'

'No, of course not. I never diet!'

'But you have lost weight? You know that, don't you?'

'Sure.' She laughed. 'I've had to take in a few waistbands.'

'You've had some colds, I seem to remember. Any cough?'

'No. Well, just a bit.'

'And sputum?'

'Hardly any.'

'But some?'

She'd begun to fear too. 'From time to time. No' much.'

'Why didn't you come to me?' he had asked gently. 'You know the score, Martie. It's the easiest thing in the world for a nurse or doctor to contract TB. You have to be on the watch the whole time.'

'Look, I didn't have anything to tell you! I'm no' ill!'

'Maybe not, but any member of staff here has a duty to report symptoms. You have a cough, you have a little sputum, that's enough to warrant tests, Martie.'

Her face was ashen. 'I honestly never thought anything of it, Frank. I'm never ill, you see. When have you ever known me to be ill? Didn't I first come here when everybody'd got 'flu and I never got it!'

'I want you to report for a sputum test first thing in the morning, Martie, and I want you off duty now. Go to bed and lie down.'

'Frank, I've no chest pain! I've never brought up blood! I'm OK, I must be!'

She'd pulled her hands from his, but he'd taken them again, lending her strength.

'It's just a precaution, one we have to take. But try not to worry.'

'Try not to worry!'

'Listen, if the test's positive, it's not going to be the end of the world. You know what can be done with chemotherapy now. You're young and strong, you'll be well in no time. I'll look after you myself.'

Martie had said nothing. She was already making plans.

When the result of the sputum test came though and was positive for TB, Frank Viner himself had broken the news to her.

'We'll do another, to be sure, Martie. And take X-rays, and a blood count—'

'I know the drill,' she'd said drearily.

He'd tilted her face, made her look at him. 'Martie, as I told you before, this isn't the end of the world. You are going to get well. I'll get you well, but you have to help. You have to look this bug in the face and say you're going to beat it. You can do that, probably better than anyone else I know. So, promise me you'll work with me on this. I can't do anything without you.'

'It's very kind of you, Frank, to want to help me. Don't think I don't appreciate it. But I'm no' going to be here. I'm going home.'

'No, Martie, you're not. It would be most unwise. Don't even think of it.'

'I'm no' too bad, I'm in the very early stages. I can travel. I can go by ship where I'll get fresh air. I'll be very careful no' to mix with folk, eat in ma cabin, all that sort of thing. But I'm going back to Scotland, Frank, and you're no' going to stop me.'

He stared at her with sudden helplessness. 'For God's sake, why? Why go home when you're in the very place for a cure here?'

'I want to go to the Jubilee, Frank. It's where I trained, and I know they're doing great things for TB in Edinburgh. I've read there's a team of doctors there that's going to lead the world.'

356

'You think they can do more than I can?' he'd asked shortly.

'I don't say that. I just feel I must be at home. In the Jubilee.'

He'd given a great sigh. 'You put me in a terrible position, you know. If I start treatment, it may not be what the Edinburgh doctors want to continue. We're all just feeling our way with these new therapies. What the hell am I going to be able to do for you, if you insist on leaving me?'

'The sea voyage is only a few days, then I'll be home, then I'll be all right.'

'I wish things could have been different,' he said softly. 'They might have been, you know, if you'd stayed.'

'I don't think so, Frank.'

'You're remembering my ex-wives? I did say there'd be no more marriages, but a guy can change his mind.' He smiled faintly. 'Or, is there someone waiting at home for you?'

'There's no one waiting at home.'

'How about Warren? Are you going to tell him about this?'

'No! And please don't you tell him, Frank. I don't want him to know. He'd – well, he'd probably want to charter a plane, or pay for ma passage, or something, and it'd be embarrassing.'

'May I pay for your passage? I want you to have as much comfort as possible, not to mention privacy.'

'I can manage, Frank, thanks all the same. With the kind of salary you pay me, I could probably afford to go on the Royal Yacht!'

Frank had laughed. 'There's my Martie! Oh, God, get well!' He'd kissed her briefly on the cheek, and when she'd pulled away in alarm, told her, 'Don't worry, I'm immune.'

'I used to say that once,' she'd said, hanging on to tears.

Over and over again on the voyage home when she'd kept apart from the other passengers, barrier-nursing herself, as she put it, she'd gone over all that Frank had said, trying to come to terms with what had happened to her, and failing. That she, who had always been so strong, should suddenly be like one of the patients she'd nursed and felt sorry for, was too much, too hard to take. She'd carried an image of herself all her life, and it wasn't of one who had to lie in bed, being stuck with needles, coughing up rubbish, facing death. Why me? she kept asking herself, and knew that countless others had asked that question and found no answers. The last thing she wanted was to go over her problems with Alex, or anyone, but there was poor Alex sitting expectantly, waiting for her to tell her tale, so that she could comfort her. Oh, Lord, I'd better let her do it, thought Martie, and began. And of course as soon as she'd finished, Alex did take a deep breath and tried to find words to console her.

'Your Dr Frank was right,' she said, with immense confidence that Martie was sure she did not feel. 'You will get better. You're young and fit, you've never had TB before, you'll respond to treatment straight away. Honestly, Martie, I'm no' just saying this – you're going to be OK.'

'What's the success rate?'

'Well, I haven't facts and figures, and every case is different, but you know we've got this team of doctors working in the hospitals? They're getting some amazing results. Chris MacInnes says in a year or so, they'll be controlling TB right through the city, and it'll be on its way out.'

'I'll believe that when I see it. If I see it.' Martie gave Alex a suddenly sweet, grateful smile. 'Och, it's good to be home,' she said quietly. 'It's good to be back with you. But here I've been talking all this time about maself. What's been happening with you? Are you engaged? Married? Courting?'

Alex looked her bravely in the eye. 'I was engaged. To Tim Burnett. As a matter of fact, I've just broken it off.'

'Tim Burnett? How the hell did he come back into your life?'

'At Rose's funeral.'

'Oh.'

'He really seemed to care for me, Martie.'

'Did he?' grunted Martie. 'Och, he could always turn on the charm to get what he wanted.'

'This time he wanted marriage. I had a beautiful ring.'

Martie smiled sadly. 'So did I.'

'And I got on well with his parents, he met ma Dad and Cousin Edie, it all seemed to be working out.'

'Well, thank God it didn't! What made you change your mind?'

Alex stirred the remains of cold tea in her cup. 'I don't know what brought it to a head. It was just – I couldn't seem to forget he'd given me up. I felt – afraid.'

'I should think you did. You'd have been crazy to trust that guy again.'

'You think I did the right thing, then?'

'I know you did. And if you're wondering, I did the right thing, too, when I gave up Warren. Though I had different reasons from you.'

'He'd have taken such wonderful care of you, Martie.'

Martie shook her head. 'Well, I'm just glad he doesn't have to. He spent all his life taking care of Lois, he deserves a break.' She glanced at the clock over the canteen counter. 'Think I'll be getting back now. Can I call a taxi? You know I take taxis everywhere? Drives Mum crazy!'

'How've your folks taken your news?' Alex asked diffidently.

'Och, they've no' said much. Probably think it's judgement on me, racketing around the world!'

'No, they don't, they don't! They care too much about you!'

'News to me,' said Martie, rising. 'But I'm going to get a bigger fire going tonight, if I have to dig the coal out maself!'

Back at the Colonies, Martie paid off the taxi, brushing away Alex's offer, and said she'd see Alex later.

'Right now, I need to rest,' she said glumly. 'Imagine me, resting!'

'When shall I see you again?'

'Call in any time you like. But I'm hoping I won't have to wait too long for the bed at the Jubilee. You'll see plenty of me then. Are you still making folk rest all day?'

'Oh, no. Not with the chemotherapy they're using now. Some people even have treatment as out-patients.'

'What, no hospital bed-rest? Sister Clerk would be crying her eyes out!' Martie laughed, then began to cough. Coughed and coughed, while Alex held her, and gave her paper tissues. When the paroxysm was over, Alex took Martie's arm and walked with her to her door.

'I'll see you soon,' Martie said hoarsely, and Alex, not trusting herself to speak, nodded and ran up the steps home.

Her heart sank when she saw Jamie sitting at the table, with Edie pouring tea, as usual, and her father passing sandwiches.

'We didnae wait,' said Edie. 'Are you no' late back?'

'I've been seeing Martie.'

'And how's Miss US of A?' asked Jamie cheerfully.

'I'm just going to wash,' Alex replied.

She took several moments to calm herself, then splashed water on her face and scrubbed her hands. When she returned, those at the table stopped talking until she had taken her place. Jamie looked at her thoughtfully.

'Anything wrong, Alex?'

'Yes, there is as a matter of fact.'

'No' with Martie?' cried Edie. 'Why, I saw her go off in a taxi yesterday, looking that smart, and Tilda's no' said anything.'

Alex looked straight at Jamie. 'Martie's coming into the Jubilee as a patient. She's contracted TB.'

Into the silence, the kettle began to whistle, and Edie, her hand to her mouth, ran to turn it off, while Arthur sat like stone and Jamie stared down at the sandwich on his plate, his freckles standing out against sudden pallor.

'It's all right, Dad,' Alex said, at last. 'She's no' as bad as Ma.'

'When can I see her?' asked Jamie.

Chapter Sixty

To Alex's relief, a bed was found for Martie in Butterfly Four, her own ward, which meant she herself would be able to nurse her. Sister Piers, however, decreed that she must make her usual introduction, whether the patient was Alex's friend or not, whether she was ex-Jubilee trained or not.

'Quite right, Sister,' Martie agreed. 'I know what you have to do.'

'Well, Martie – you'll no' mind if I call you that? – things have changed a bit since you were here, and for a start we don't insist on absolute rest the way we used to do.' Sister Piers gave a loud laugh. 'Unless you were going under the knife, it was all we had in the old days, eh? But rest is still important, especially for your first few days when you have to have your assessments, so we'll no' want you running around, using up your energy, eh? Is that understood?'

'Yes, Sister, don't worry, I'm going to be your best patient, you'll see.'

'Aye, well I hope so! I'll tell you frankly, Martie, the worst patients I've ever known have been doctors and nurses, so surprise me, eh? Now, you'll know all about the sputum bags and what to do with them, so I'll leave you to have a word with your friend, who's been dodging around behind yon screen. Staff Kelsie, come on over – but no' staying too long, mind!'

Alex, smiling, came to Martie's bedside. 'I've no' brought the grapes, yet, I'll bring them tomorrow. How are you feeling?'

'No' so good. I think maybe I was a fool to come back, Alex.'

'Don't say that, Martie!'

'Aye, I thought I'd be able to put up a fight when I got here, but now I can't bear to think how I used to be and how I've changed.'

'Listen, no one's comparing you with how you used to be.'

'Well, I am!' cried Martie, and great tears suddenly coursed down her cheek. 'Oh, hell, I'm sorry, Alex. Don't you stay. I'll feel better when I get used to things.'

'Jamie's coming to see you as soon as he can,' Alex told her, reluctantly moving away. 'Though I said he should leave it a day or two, until you'd had your tests.'

'He came to see me at Mum's,' Martie said indifferently. 'I'm sure I don't know why he wants to visit an invalid.'

'You're no' an invalid, Martie!'

'I'm no' a butterfly girl, either. Remember how they used to call us that?' Martie coughed and turned away her head. 'I think I'll rest now.'

Alex, deeply depressed, returned to her duties.

It was some time before Martie's tests could be completed and her condition assessed, but as soon as she thought there was anything he could tell her, Alex began stalking Chris MacInnes. Finally, she cornered him in his office.

'OK, OK, I know what you want!' he cried, with a good-natured grin. 'But give me a chance, Alex. I do have other patients apart from Martie, remember.'

'I know, but I'm just as selfish as all the usual friends and relations. Please, tell me the prognosis!'

'It's good.' Chris took a file from his desk. 'Martie's given us her doctor's notes and findings from America and they pretty well coincide with ours. Sputum test is positive, X-rays show some soft shadows, white blood count is low. It appears she has a primary lesion in the upper part of her right lung, but no cavities.' Chris looked up at Alex. 'A mild case, you see.'

'A bit like Tim's?'

'Not quite as mild as his. Thanks to Rose, he came to us pretty early on. Martie hung about a bit.'

'Couldn't believe she was ill.' Alex looked expectantly at Chris. 'So, what's she going to have?'

'What we're trying with all new patients now, on the advice of the Professor's team. We'll treat with a combination of three drugs – PAS, streptomycin and the latest one, isoniazid – and keep things going for several months to make sure there's no relapse. Chris came round his desk. 'I know Martie's your oldest friend, Alex, and you're very worried, but she's young and strong and she's contracted TB at the right time, just when we're seeing a real breakthrough. I'd put my money on her making a complete and speedy recovery.'

'Thank God!' Alex gave a sigh. 'And you, Chris.'

'Don't thank me, thank the folk who've made this breakthrough possible.'

'Well, thank you for talking to me.' Alex moved to the door. 'Now, I'd better get back to work. Just one thing – will Martie be able to take her treatment as an out-patient?'

'We'll see how she goes. It'll help that she's a nurse herself and can be trusted to know what to do.'

Alex, on wings, flew back to Martie's bedside.

'Martie, Martie, have they told you? Your prognosis is good, you're going to get well in no time! Now, did I no' say that very thing!'

Martie, sitting up in bed, with a magazine on her knees, did not smile. 'Aye, seems I'm no' too bad.'

'But aren't you pleased, Martie? Aren't you relieved? The new drugs'll cure your lesion and you won't even have to stay in hospital! Come on, cheer up, don't look so glum!'

'It sounds so easy, eh? The new drugs'll cure your lesion . . . One of those drugs is streptomycin, and you know what that can cause, don't you? Deafness, amongst other things. And we were always told it never worked long for lung TB, so why include it at all?'

'Because it works very well in combination. The team working in Edinburgh have discovered that if new patients get the three drugs together, they've a very good chance of complete recovery. As for the side-effects – no' everybody has them, and you'll be monitored the whole time.'

Martie's expression did not lighten.

'Look, you're going to have to try to be more positive,' Alex said with sudden sharpness. 'The doctors can't win this battle by themselves, you know.'

'I just feel so low,' Martie whispered. 'I just feel it's no' worth living in a world that can kick you in the teeth like this. I can't cope.'

'Martie, Martie, don't give in! Remember, you were always the strong one!'

'I realise now I was never strong.' Martie fixed her strange bright gaze on Alex's face. 'Remember how I went to pieces after Lois died? You and Rose were the strong ones. You could face the bad times. I'm for fair weather. That's why I wanted a rich man, eh? To keep the rain out?'

'You turned the rich man down, Martie, you were strong there!'

But Martie only shook her head, and Alex, deeply troubled, had to leave her.

'How's she doing?' Jill Berry asked in a low voice, as she and Alex gazed down the ward at Martie in her bed.

'She's very depressed. Thinking of everything that can go wrong.'

'Aye, there's nurses for you. We know too much.' Jill sighed sympathetically. 'Poor old Martie. But somebody cares about her, eh? Did you see her flowers?'

Alex glanced at the chrysanthemums and carnations grouped with other patients' flowers at one end of the ward.

'We sent the chrysanths, I think ma brother gave the carnations'

'I'm no' talking about them. I mean the whopping big arrangement that came today. Alex, it looks like half Logie's flower shop! And came from America – they must've phoned in the order!'

'America?' Alex's heart sank. Surely only Warren Adamson would have sent flowers from America? 'Did you see who sent them?'

'Aye.' Jill gave a contrite smile. 'I peeped at the card. Said "We love you, Martie, get well soon!" And it was signed Frank Viner and the staff of Mount Forest. That's the sanatorium where she used to work.'

'Ah,' said Alex. She'd forgotten Dr Viner.

'We've had to put them in Reception, far too many for here. Have a look next time you go through. Where we'll fit in the Christmas tree, I can't think!'

'Was Martie no' thrilled when they arrived?'

'Never took the slightest notice. Och, she's no' the Martie we used to know, Alex.' Jill began to move on, then stopped. 'Hey, did you say your Jamie had sent her carnations? Is he interested, then?'

Alex shrugged. 'Who knows?'

Jamie, after visiting that evening, seemed as depressed as Martie. He told Alex he might give up the visiting for a while. Martie was in a world of her own and would not leave it for him.

'Do you want her to?' asked Alex. 'I've never been sure what your feelings were for Martie.'

'She was always looking for someone different from me.'

'I'm no' so sure she is now. You know she's given up Mr Adamson?'

'She ever say why?'

'Said she didn't love him.'

'How about the guy who sent those flowers in the hall?'

'That was just the doctor and the staff of the sanatorium where she worked.'

'The doctor signed it Frank. I saw the card.'

'There's nothing between them, Jamie.'

'His flowers certainly put ma carnations in the shade.'

'I've an idea Martie would prefer your carnations, if she was herself. Look, she starts treatment tomorrow. You're right to leave the visiting for a while. Just at the moment, she's ill and depressed. You'll see a big change soon.'

'Aye. Hope so.'

Alex, watching her brother walk slowly down the corridor to the exit door, could not help reflecting how badly things were going for those she knew. There was Martie ill, and Jamie saddened. Warren Adamson, broken-hearted. Herself and Tim, devastated. Rose, of course, gone from them all, leaving Chris MacInnes and probably Simon Dawson still grieving. Only Neal Drover seemed to have overcome his adversity. She had been astonished and a little chagrined to see his engagement to Penny in the paper a week or so before, but was glad, of course, that he was happy and that he had stayed well. There had been a time when she'd worried he might relapse; Tim, too. But she wouldn't let herself think of Tim. The one person she'd never expected to see in a Jubilee bed was Martie. Her treatment started tomorrow, pray God it worked!

'Staff Kelsie, give me a hand with this bed, will you?' came Sister Piers's voice.

'Coming, Sister.'

'And try to look a wee bit more cheerful, eh, for the sake of the patients? You look as though you've lost half a crown and found a sixpence!'

'Sorry, Sister.'

'And remember, it's no' you having intramuscular strepto injections tomorrow!'

As though that makes me feel any better, thought Alex.

Chapter Sixty-One

There were two weeks to go until Christmas. A tree had been put up in Reception, vying with Martie's amazing flowers. No doubt, nearer the time, a few decorations would be allowed and the usual token gifts exchanged. Alex's heart twisted, as she remembered Tim's locket and chain, but she had become adept at putting him out of her mind and in any case had other things to think about. Martie had begun her treatment and was doing well!

'It's like a miracle,' Martie told Chris, when he stopped at her bedside on his morning round. 'I feel so much better, already! I can't believe it!'

Chris glanced at his accompanying young doctors and smiled. 'We often get this immediate improvement. You'll note that Martie's slight fever has cleared, her cough is easier and her sputum count is down. When we come to take X-rays, we'll probably find similar good news.' He picked up Martie's wrist and felt her pulse. 'Any side-effects at all? Apart from feeling a bit sore. I know the streptomycin injections aren't pleasant.'

'No, I feel fine.'

Alex, standing to the side of the doctors, could see that Martie's eyes were already looking different, already losing the fixedness that had been so disturbing, and that she was even smiling. When had she last smiled in the Jubilee?

'No dizziness, ringing in the ears, anything of that sort?' asked Chris.

'Nothing at all, thank God! I don't mind telling you, I was really worried about deafness.'

'That's rare, Martie, and usually found in older patients.'

'Aye, but I've read cases of young folk being affected, too.'

'Not you,' Chris said cheerfully. 'I'm very pleased with your progress. We'll see you tomorrow, but if you have any problems, you'll tell us straight away, OK?'

'OK,' Martie answered sunnily.

The little white-coated group moved on down the ward, and Alex, who was supposed to accompany them, quickly pressed Martie's hand and gave a radiant smile.

'Didn't I tell you?' she whispered.

Martie pushed back her hair and grinned. 'Thing is, I'm starving, Alex! What would I no' give for a couple of American doughnuts!'

There were some wonderfully happy days after that, when Alex walked on air, and Chris smiled at her every time he saw her, saying her relief for her friend was like a tonic to him. Jamie visited regularly, listening closely while Martie talked and laughed and was told to settle down by Sister Piers, but said she felt far too well to settle down, felt more like flying.

'Guess I'm a butterfly girl again!' she cried. 'Now I understand why those patients danced in the wards when they first got their treatment. If I don't get round to flying, maybe I'll start dancing too!'

'Count me in!' said Jamie, who stood up and bowed. 'May I have the pleasure, Miss Cass?'

'Charmed, I'm sure, Mr Kelsie!'

Martie's parents usually came in the evenings after work, bringing some marked-down item from Sid's shop, and sitting uneasily in the ward, not looking at the other patients.

'For all the world as though they might catch TB by looking!' Martie told Alex. 'And your Edie's the same when she comes with your dad, but I shouldn't complain, it's good of them to visit me, when I know they're terrified of illness.'

368

Alex said nothing of Martie's own terror that had so patently been conquered.

One morning, however, Martie woke feeling unwell. Her eyes felt heavy and strained, the lids swollen, and her mouth was sore. When she dragged herself up to a sitting position, the woman in the next bed, Norah Harrison, a middle-aged, long-term patient, gave a little shriek.

'Och, hen, you should see your face! Have you got the measles?'

Martie, her heart racing, fumbled for her compact mirror in the bedside locker drawer, took one look at herself, and groaned. She was covered in a dark red blistering rash that meant only one thing. Reaction.

'Nurse!' she called weakly. 'Nurse!'

'Nurse!' echoed Norah. 'Nurse, come quick, eh? Help this poor lassie!'

'Yes, it's reaction,' Chris said glumly, when Alex had run to fetch him. 'Oh, Martie, what can I say? You were doing so well!'

They had drawn the curtains round her bed and were looking down at her, Chris, Sister Piers and Alex, all, it seemed to Martie, wavering indistinct figures, no longer showing the false cheerfulness she had often had to show herself, though any minute now they would begin to tell her that this was nothing, just a temporary set-back—

'No need to worry, Martie,' Chris said, bringing out the optimism as she had predicted. 'This is just a temporary set-back. You've developed a rash and fever, so obviously one of the drugs is not agreeing with you.'

'Which one?' she asked painfully. 'Strepto?'

'Probably, but I think what we'll have to do is stop all three drugs, let this condition improve, then try some tests and gradually get you back on medication.'

Martie closed her eyes. 'That's going to take for ever,' she whispered.

'Not necessarily.' Chris managed a smile. 'We'll give you

something to make you feel more comfortable and I think for the time being put you in a side ward. You probably won't feel like any visitors for a while.'

'While I look like this, I don't want to see anyone at all.'

When Alex and Jill had moved Martie into a side ward, Alex stayed with her for a moment, trying to find something to say that would bring comfort, but Martie kept her swollen eyelids tightly shut.

'The symptoms won't last long, now that we've stopped the medication,' Alex told her. 'You'll soon feel easier.'

'Och, give it a rest, Alex,' Martie finally responded. 'If I don't get medication, I don't get better, do I?'

'You will be getting the drugs, as soon as they can sort out the right ones. Please, Martie, try to be positive, try to fight, it's the only way!'

'Just tell Jamie I don't want to see him today. He'll understand.'

But that afternoon, another visitor arrived for her, who said he had come so far, he must be allowed in.

'All right,' Jill said doubtfully. 'But I'll have to see Sister about it. Miss Cass is feeling very poorly.'

Sister Crosby had come on duty. She too looked doubtful, but finally said in view of the circumstances the visitor might be allowed a few minutes. If he were not willing to accept that ruling, he would not be allowed in to see Miss Cass at all.

'Oh, I'll accept it, Sister. Just take me to her. Please!'

'A visitor to see you, Martie,' Jill whispered, showing the visitor into the side ward. 'He's promised no' to stay long.'

'Is it Jamie?' asked Martie, struggling to look up. 'I did say no' to come today, Jamie.'

'It's no' Jamie, Martie. It's a Mr Adamson .'

The room seemed to swing and several Warrens danced before her eyes. Then the swinging stopped and there was only one Warren, looking as immaculate as ever, but with such dismay and horror in his eyes as he took her hands, she could only turn her head away.

'Oh, my God, Martie, what's happened to you?' he whispered. 'When they told me you'd got TB, I couldn't believe it, but now I see you—'

'Who told you, Warren? Was it Dr Viner? I asked him to keep it to himself.'

'It wasn't Frank Viner, it was one of your colleagues, Alice Penn, and I'm very glad she did tell me. What on earth made you try to keep this secret from me, Martie? Who can help you better than I can?'

'You've had enough of illness. I didn't want you involved.'

'Well, I am involved, and as soon as I got that girl's call, I booked myself a flight and came straight over. Frank Viner did tell me the name of this hospital when I asked him, so I knew where to come. And here I am.' Warren's voice faltered. 'Finding you need me even more than I thought. What in God's name have they been doing to you, Martie?'

'It's just a reaction to the treatment. Nobody's fault.'

'I dare say, but this is no place for you to be, my poor girl!' Warren looked swiftly round the little side ward, which couldn't have been more bare. 'Why, I've seen better holes than this when I was in the military! Tomorrow morning, I promise you, I book you into the Fidra Bay.'

'They don't take TB patients there, Warren,' Martie said wearily. 'And I'm staying here.'

'I'll take advice, find out the best sanatorium, have you moved immediately. In the meantime, I have a basket of fruit for you, and some flowers. We'll cheer you up, get you the best doctors going—'

'I already have the best doctors. In Edinburgh, they're leading the field. Please, Warren, it's wonderful of you to come, I really appreciate it—' Martie's voice died away for a moment, then hoarsely returned. 'But you must just leave me alone.'

'My darling, I'm going to look after you,' he said softly. 'There'll be no strings, I won't ask anything of you. All I'll do is give you the best. All that you need. You won't be struggling on your own any more, you'll be able to lean on me until you're well. That's all I want. To see you better.'

She was silent, letting his words wrap her round in a beautiful

371

vision of comfort and peace and well-being. When he took her hands and kissed them, she didn't stop him, only lay without moving, like a child being lulled to sleep.

'Listen, Alex, guess who's here?' cried Jill, finding Alex in the sluice. 'That American guy Martie was engaged to! I'm sure it's him – name of Adamson?'

'Warren? I don't believe it!'

'Aye, it's true. He's in seeing her now.' Jill glanced at her watch. 'Which reminds me, Sister Crosby said he wasn't to stay more than a few minutes. I'd better kick him out.'

'I'll go,' said Alex, washing her hands.

The door to the side ward was shut and she gave a gentle little knock before opening it.

'Mr Adamson—' she began, then stopped.

Warren was sitting by Martie's bed, holding her hand, looking intently into her poor, mottled face, but her eyes were closed. She was peacefully asleep.

Alex caught him when he came out of the side ward, and at the sight of his exhausted face, felt compunction that she could not welcome him. He, however, greeted her with affection, managing a smile, kissing her cheek.

'Alex, my dear, it's good to see you!'

'Warren.' She shook his hand. 'I can't believe you're here.'

'Had to come. Martie needs me.' He wiped his brow with a silk handkerchief. 'Can you imagine how I felt, when that nurse from Mount Forest told me the news? Beautiful, strong Martie, struck down with TB! I made a reservation to come over right there on the spot, and am I glad I did! Now that I've seen her, Alex, I intend to fix her up with 'somewhere good' before it's too late!'

'Too late? What are you talking about? Martie's in no danger, she's just suffering from a drug reaction, it happens all the time.' Alex's large eyes were diamond bright. 'And what do you mean "somewhere good"? This place is good, the best. You won't find better doctors anywhere in the world than there are here in Edinburgh at the Jubilee!'

He smiled indulgently. 'Alex, I know the medics are first-rate. It's the surroundings I want to change. My God, there isn't even a carpet on the floor!'

'It's a hospital,' Alex told him, as patiently as she could. 'And it's where Martie trained. She's at home here, she won't want to go anywhere else. Anyway, Dr MacInnes wouldn't give permission. He's in charge of her case, he's going to get her well.'

'I'll see him in the morning. Right now, I need to catch up on some sleep. If you need me, I'll be at the North British Hotel.' Warren gave a tired smile. 'Had to book the honeymoon suite, can you believe? They're full up for Christmas.'

'Warren, I'm sorry I've had to argue with you.' Alex spoke awkwardly, as she escorted him to the door. 'It's no' that I don't appreciate you coming all this way to see Martie.'

'That's all right, I quite understand.' He put on the overcoat he had been carrying on his arm. 'Mind if I ask, though – who's Jamie?'

Well, I told him, she thought, walking fast back to Butterfly Four. I told him Jamie was my brother, young and good-looking, and in love with Martie. And I just hope that that registers. He's ruined everything, arriving like this.

Chris MacInnes was approaching her, his look rueful.

'Alex, I'm so sorry! This set-back for Martie, it's hell for her, but pretty bad for you, too.'

'For all of us, Chris. But these things happen, they're nobody's fault.'

'Try not to worry. We'll get her treatment sorted out and get her back on course as soon as possible. Did I hear her ex-fiancé from America had arrived?'

'He's just left for his hotel.'

At the tone in her voice, Chris gave her a long, intelligent look. 'And you wish he'd leave altogether?'

'Chris, he wants to move Martie to a private sanatorium! He thinks she should be somewhere with carpets on the floor!'

A look of thunder darkened Chris's brow. 'Move Martie to a

private sanatorium? Over my dead body! Nobody takes my patients away from me, Alex!'

'No, Chris.'

'Besides, Martie would refuse to go.'

'Maybe.'

'What do you mean, maybe? Martie'd never leave the Jubilee!'

'I don't know, Chris, I expect you're right.'

But as she left him to return to the ward, Alex was remembering something Martie had said. 'I realise now I was never strong.' Perhaps they would see now just how strong Martie really was.

Chapter Sixty-Two

Jamie was outraged when he heard that Warren Adamson had reappeared.

'Oh, well, that's it, then,' he said curtly, when Alex telephoned him at the office where he worked. 'If the US Cavalry's arrived, Martie won't need me. I'm told no' to visit, but he's allowed? And she's supposed to have given that guy up?'

'She has given him up, Jamie. It was his idea to come, no' hers. And the only reason she doesn't want you to visit is because she's worried about what she looks like. She has this terrible rash, you see—'

'As though I'd care about a rash! No, I've had enough, Alex. I always thought I'd be a fool to get mixed up with Martie Cass, and it looks like I've been proved right. I'm keeping out of her way in future.'

'Jamie, please! Martie does need you, this is just the time you have to let her see you care!'

'Well, maybe I don't. Sorry, Alex, I've got to go. Can't spend time on the phone in work time. Company policy. 'bye.'

So much for Jamie, thought Alex, leaving the public call box in the hospital vestibule. Well, thank God, she was going off duty. Sudddenly, she'd had enough of fighting Martie's battles, of worrying over Warren's arrival, Jamie's truculence. What of her own life? She still felt a hole in her chest when she thought of Tim, which was why she did not allow herself to think of him, and if he was thinking of her, he certainly had given no sign, for she had not set eyes on him since that night when they had parted. As for his parents, thoughts of them brought pangs of guilt. They had been so kind, particularly Tim's mother, and it was nothing to do with them that she had broken with their son. If she could find the courage, maybe she would send a Christmas card, with a little note. But what she would say in the little note, heaven only knew.

For some moments, she stood still, thinking what she might do. Look in and say goodnight to Martie? No, she'd probably still be sleeping, better to leave her. Go up to her room and lie down?

She was tired enough, she ached in every bone, but she longed suddenly to be with people. Or, even one person. Longed just to be going somewhere for a drink or a meal, some place where she could relax, forget the Jubilee for a little while. But she couldn't think of anyone to go with, and the dismal thought came to her that in the whole of that city, thronging with men and women, she was alone.

'Hi, Alex! Going off duty?' asked Chris MacInnes.

She swung round, flushing, because she'd never thought of him. Why should she? He was Rose's. He would always be Rose's.

'Yes, and very glad. It's been quite a day.'

Still in his white coat, he stood smiling at her, a little self-consciously. 'I'm taking a few hours off myself. I was wondering, would you care to—'

'Alex! Dr MacInnes!'

Their eyes that had been meeting moved in surprise to the man that had joined them. It was Neal Drover, looking well in a long overcoat and red woollen scarf, and carrying a large paper bag and a bunch of flowers.

'I've only just heard!' he cried. 'Alex, why didn't you tell me about Martie?'

'I – well, I was going to, but it all happened so quickly—'

'Dr MacInnes, how is she? Actually, I was coming in to see you, anyway. Alex, will you hold these flowers a minute?' Neal set down his carrier bag and took out two bottles of wine which he put into Chris's hands. 'For you and the staff, with all my thanks. By way of being a Christmas present, though nothing much. But how is Martie?'

Chris was shaking his head over the wine labels. 'There was no need to do anything like this, Neal, you're far too extravagant! As for Martie—' Chris glanced quickly at Alex. 'She's not so good today, actually. Had a reaction to the therapy, so we're going to have to sort things out.'

'May I see her?'

'I think maybe not tonight, if you don't mind. She's got a bit of a rash.'

'That's OK, I understand. Alex, could you give her those flowers?'

'Of course. I'll find a vase now.'

'And then maybe we could have a drink? I've got a little Christmas present for you, too.'

Alex's eyes flew to Chris, who shrugged and grinned.

'I'll say goodnight. Thanks for the wine, Neal. We really appreciate it. And you're looking very well, you know. You're a credit to us!'

'Wasn't breaking anything up just there, was I?' Neal asked, as he and Alex went down the drive, walking easily arm in arm.

'No, of course not. Chris is still carrying a torch for Rose, everyone knows that.'

'I don't know. As soon as I'd asked you, I thought I'd put my foot in it. He had a certain look on his face—'

'Forget it. There's nothing between us.'

'Just good friends, eh? Tell me, what happened to you and Tim?'

'I suppose Dad told you we'd split up, did he?'

'Why didn't you?'

'Why didn't you tell me about your engagement?'

'I meant to. But you didn't send me congratulations, either.'

'I meant to.'

They went into the bar of a small Stockbridge hotel which had once been a favourite of theirs, sat down near a roaring open fire, and ordered gin and tonics.

'How come we're having a drink together?' asked Alex. 'Won't Penny mind?'

'She's out with her parents at some lecture tonight, I skived off, but I'll tell her. We've vowed to have no secrets from each other.'

Their drinks arrived and Alex smiled as she squeezed a twist of lemon. 'I'm glad you decided she was the one for you,' she said, after a pause. 'I hope you'll be very happy.'

'She's not exactly the one for me.' Neal held out a still thin hand towards the fire. 'Sometimes, you can't expect that. But I do love her, in my way, and she's sure she loves me. I think we can make a go of things.' He fixed Alex with his fine dark eyes. 'But after all I used to say about Tim, I'm sorry you broke up with him. You seemed to be so happy.'

'I made the decision. I don't regret it.'

'You must have felt a certain satisfaction?'

'No, I didn't! There was never anything of revenge about it!'

'I'm sorry.' Neal snapped a small cracker in half. 'Tell me about Martie.'

She told him, watching his shoulders droop, his good humour fade.

'Oh, God, that brings it back,' he muttered. 'It hits you for six, you think, why me, why me? You try to pull yourself together, but you wonder if you're on the long long road to nowhere. Even today, with all the medication, it must be a hell of a blow to take.'

'Yes, and Martie hasn't taken it too well. We all thought of her as so strong—'

'The very type not to be able to accept what's happened. And until you accept, you don't get well.'

Alex covered his hand lying on the table. 'I'm so glad you're well, Neal. I used to have nightmares that you'd have to come back to the Jubilee and the drugs wouldn't work.'

'Did you?' His look on her was tender. 'I'm touched. But look, I haven't given you your present.' He began to delve into his paper carrier again, as Alex said she felt bad, she had nothing for him.

'Come on, this is just something I had on my shelves. I thought, like father, like daughter – maybe you'd appreciate the Shakespeare sonnets. If you really don't want them, give them to your dad.'

He put a small package wrapped in Christmas paper into her hands.

'Why, Neal, that's so kind! Can I open it now?'

'Why not? It's nearly Christmas.'

She tore off the paper and took out a slender, leather-bound volume.

'It's lovely, it's really lovely! But you haven't written in it!'

'I thought I shouldn't, in case you gave it to your dad.'

'I shan't be giving it to him. I'm going to keep it.'

'All right.' He took a pen and after a moment's thought wrote, 'To Alex, daughter of a Shakespeare man, with all good wishes, from her favourite bookseller.' 'There, how's that?'

'Perfect!'

'You'll note I didn't put, "with love".'

'No, you're a married man now.'

'Well, almost. Will you come to my wedding?'

'I wouldn't miss it for anything.'

He glanced around the bar, saw that no one was watching, and swiftly kissed her cheek. 'Thank you, Alex, for all you've been to me. We probably won't be meeting again on our own, but I wanted to see you this last time, tell you how much you did for me, when I needed it.'

'Neal, I didn't do anything. You're making me feel terrible.'

'Let's have a quick sandwich,' he said cheerfully, 'and then I'll walk you back to the Jubilee.'

They made a last goodbye at the gates, saying no more, for they'd said all that was to be said, then she ran up the drive and he walked back to his shop, wondering if Penny had returned yet from her lecture.

Back in the nurses' home, Alex thought she might as well have an early night, found a bathroom that was free, ran the usual tepid bath and shuddered back to her room in her dressing-gown. The wind was howling down the chimney like a wild thing, and as she climbed into bed with a hot-water bottle, Alex wondered, as everyone wondered, if the old house would survive another winter. Probably it would soon be pulled down and some new building erected, always supposing the authorities wanted to keep the Jubilee going. Maybe it was true, what folk had been suggesting, that hospitals and sanatoria for TB would one day be unnecessary. Certainly looked that way, as in-patients turned into out-patients and bed-rest became a thing of the past. But Alex, picking up her Shakespeare sonnets, thought of Martie. It seemed to her that they still had a long way to go before they could say they'd seen the last of TB.

She turned over the pages of Neal's present. The edition was a good one, beautifully bound and printed, something to treasure. And she really would read the poems, she promised herself. Whenever she had a bit of time. Like now.

'Let me not to the marriage of true minds
Admit impediments,' she read. 'Love is not love
That alteration finds . . .'

Famous words. And false. She'd never believed them. Why, when you found out the person you loved had altered, wasn't that the very time you stopped loving? She closed the book and switched off her light, staring into the darkness. But you haven't stopped loving, a voice whispered in her mind. Yet you found alteration.

This time, I was afraid of alteration, she answered. And I was right to be afraid.

It was a long time before sleep came to her. In the morning, she realised that Christmas was almost upon them yet again, and she still hadn't written that card to Mr and Mrs Burnett. Without giving herself time to think too much, she picked out one of her more elegant cards, sent good wishes, signed her name and put the card in the post box before breakfast. OK, she hadn't managed a note, but it was the thought that counted and she was certainly thinking about them.

'Anything for me?' she asked one of the junior nurses, who was putting letters into pigeon-holes.

'Sorry, Alex. Not this morning.'

Alex went on to breakfast. She hadn't really expected anything.

Chapter Sixty-Three

It looked like being a dismal Christmas.

'Awful sad, eh?' commented Edie, on Christmas Eve. 'When you think of the poor Queen! First Christmas without her husband.'

'You mean the Queen Mother?' asked Jamie, who had called in for a mince-pie after work. 'The Duke of Edinburgh's alive and kicking, last I heard.'

'Och, I can niver remember these new names! Yes, I do mean the Queen Mother, and what I say is it's very sad for her and all of us this year.' Edie gave a meaning glance at Alex, who was waiting to go. 'Take that poor Mr and Mrs Burnett, for instance, without their daughter!'

'And poor Mr and Mrs Cass, with Martie ill,' Alex said quickly.

'But that was a lovely card Mrs Burnett sent you, Alex,' Edie steam-rollered on. 'Very forgiving of her, I say.'

'I'm afraid I have to leave now.' Alex fastened her cape. 'There's a little do for the nurses at six tonight – just a drink with the doctors. I don't want to be late.'

'That nice Dr Chris going to be there?' asked Jamie. He glanced cheekily at Edie. 'I've heard rumours he's sweet on Alex. How'd he suit, Edie?'

'A doctor?' she asked, with interest. 'Alex, you never said!'

'Jamie's teasing,' Alex replied calmly. 'Dr MacInnes was very attached to Rose. He hasn't got over her death yet.'

'These things pass in time, Alex.'

'Sometimes,' said Arthur, from behind his paper.

'Look, you've got all your presents, haven't you?' Alex kissed first her father, then Edie. 'I'm sorry I'm on duty tomorrow, but I'll see you Boxing Day. Jamie, are you coming over to the Jubilee?'

'Why should I?'

'Don't you want to see Martie? I told you she was feeling rather better.'

'And meet that American guy? No thanks.'

Alex tightened her mouth. 'You're pretty hard, aren't you? Never relent.'

'If I thought Martie wanted to see me, I'd be there like a shot.'

'Och, get yourself along there, Jamie!' said Arthur. 'It's Christmas!'

'All right, all right! Anything for a quiet life!' Jamie went to get his coat.

The Jubilee was strangely quiet. A ghost hospital, Jamie called it, but of course there were still patients and staff about. What was different from previous years was that more patients had been allowed home for the holiday, trusted to take their medication away from the hospital. If things had gone well for Martie, she too might have been allowed home; as it was, Alex and Jamie found her in her room, listening while her parents talked.

She was out of bed, dressed in a blue twin-set and tweed skirt. Her rash was fading, her eyes only slightly swollen, she was certainly looking better. Almost the old Martie, in fact, except that the vigour and vitality that had characterised all the old Martie's movements were absent. She still seemed very weak.

'Evening,' Jamie said to Tilda and Sid as they rose from their chairs. 'Hello, Martie.'

'Jamie!' Her eyes lit up. 'My, it's nice to see you! Where've you been?'

'You did say I wasn't to visit.'

'That was only the first day, when ma rash was bad. I thought you'd come in after that.'

383

'He's been held up at work,' Alex said smoothly. 'But he's been asking after you. Don't go, Mrs Cass – Mr Cass – I'm no' staying, there's plenty of room.'

'Och, we'd best away,' said Tilda. 'We just looked in with Martie's presents.'

'Thanks, Mum. I'll no' open them till you come tomorrow.'

'You're looking that well, pet,' said Sid, bending to kiss Martie's cheek, but she moved her head away.

'Better not,' she said with a smile. 'Goodnight, then. See you tomorrow. Happy Christmas!'

'She's that brave,' Tilda whispered to Alex. 'Niver a word of complaint.'

'No' exactly true,' said Martie, attempting a grin, as her parents left her. 'I complain night and day.'

'Och, we've both known worse.' Alex held Martie's wrist with a cool hand. 'You know, you really are much better. They'll be able to start the tests soon.' She glanced at Jamie. 'To see which drug is causing the problem.'

'I do feel better,' Martie said slowly. 'I think even the bit of treatment I had did some good.'

'You'll probably recover on just the two medications, without the strepto. People do.' Alex glanced at her watch. 'I've got to go now, but I'll see you later, shall I, Jamie?'

'What you mean is, am I going to stay? Yes, I am.'

As Alex slid away, Martie and Jamie looked at each other.

'What happened to your friend?' asked Jamie, clearing his throat.

'He's at his hotel.'

'Having dinner, I suppose?'

'I guess so.'

'It wasn't true, you know, what Alex said. I wasn't held up with work. I didn't come to see you because I thought you wouldn't want me to. When you'd got Mr Adamson.'

'Warren? Come on!' Martie's eyes flashed in the old way. 'You knew we'd split up, didn't you?'

'Martie, he flew across the Atlantic to see you.'

'Because I'm ill. He wanted to help.'

'He still cares for you, then.'

384

'Yes, he does. And I'm very fond of him. But no' enough to marry him.'

'Alex said he wanted to move you out of here, set you up in some private hospital, look after you.'

'Sure, but I told him I was staying right here. I crossed the Atlantic too, you know, to come to the Jubilee. The doctors here are the best, and I'm no' joking.'

Jamie moved uneasily in his chair. 'If you'd no' fallen ill, would you ever have come home?' he asked in a low voice.

Martie put out her hand. 'Do you mind holding ma hand, Jamie?'

He took and held it. 'You know the answer to that. But would you, Martie? Would you have come home?'

'Oh, yes. If I'd thought you'd be waiting.'

'I think I've been waiting a long time.'

'You were engaged to a girl called Heather, if I remember rightly.'

'You were engaged to a guy named Warren, if I remember rightly.'

They burst into laughter, and for a moment it seemed as though Martie would cough again, and their eyes met in apprehension. But the moment passed. She did not cough, and Jamie let out a long sigh.

'Can I no' kiss you, Martie?'

'No. Strictly forbidden.'.

'So, it's back to waiting, is it?'

He was joking, but she pulled her hand away. 'Oh, Jamie, do you want to? I wouldn't blame you, if it was too much, honestly, I wouldn't. In fact, that's what I thought was wrong, when you didn't come. I thought you couldn't face things—'

He took her hand back. 'Never say anything like that to me again, Martie. I don't give a damn about your illness. I'd promise to look after you, but I know you're going to get better, anyway. Aren't you?'

'Yes.' Her voice was firm, positive, quite the old Martie's voice. 'I believe I am.'

*

Over in the doctors' office, the staff was, as Jill said, living it up on tea, coffee, mince-pies, crisps and one glass of sherry each.

'Got to keep a cool head, eh?' Jill asked one of the junior doctors, who had already suggested they might have danced, if they'd had any music, or maybe they could dance anyway? 'With two glasses of sherry, who knows? I might have done a tango!'

'Not with Sister Piers watching!' he said with a grin, and Jill agreed.

'She'd need three!'

'Enjoying yourself, Alex?' Chris MacInnes asked, offering her another mince-pie.

'Yes, thanks, but I'll pass on those. I think if I have any more I'll have mincemeat coming out of ma ears!'

'How was Neal, when you saw him the other night?'

'In very good form. You know he's engaged?'

Chris's eyes flickered. 'No, I didn't. Well, well, another good man gone.'

He laughed and moved on, and Alex thought, he's wondering why Neal should be offering me a drink and giving me a Christmas present. But he's no' really interested. Sweet on me? I don't think so. He felt like a bit of company the other night, and so did I. That's all that was. Still, a drink with Chris might have been nice.

The little party broke up. Everyone had to get back to duty. Alex, anxious to see how Jamie and Martie were faring, was hurrying towards the side ward when she saw Warren standing in the corridor, shaking raindrops from his overcoat.

'Alex! Hello there! Merry Christmas!'

'How's the North British?' she asked politely. 'Very festive?'

'I'll say! They certainly know how to put on a party! Listen, is it OK for me to look in on Martie right now?'

She hesitated. 'Warren, could I have a word?'

His gaze sharpened. 'She's not worse? Why, she was looking so much better—'

'Martie's all right. Or, will be.' Alex drew Warren to one side. 'The thing is, my brother's with her.'

'So?' Warren's look was suddenly wintry.

'So, they're in love. I don't think it would be a good idea if you were to go to her at the moment.'

He bit his lip. 'All I want to do is help her, Alex. I came thousands of miles to do just that. And she needs me, you know she does.'

'No, Warren, she doesn't.' Alex put her hand on his arm, her gaze very gentle. 'I'm so sorry.'

'But there's so much I could do for her! I wouldn't have asked anything of her, you know, I wasn't trying to get her back, or anything like that. But she made me very happy once and now she's sick, I just want to take care of her.'

'She really appreciates all you've done, Warren, and she will want to see you again, but I wouldn't try to see her tonight.'

'I guess you're right,' he said dully. 'Guess I was a fool to come.'

'You heard she was ill, you were shocked. It was understandable.'

'So what do I do now? Go home as soon as I can get a flight, I guess.' He sighed. 'Heaven knows what my son will say. I didn't tell him where I was going.'

'Why don't you come in tomorrow?' Alex asked softly. 'We try to make Christmas Day happy for people. Martie will want to see you.'

He shook his head. 'As a matter of fact, I have an invitation for Christmas lunch at Fidra Bay.'

'Fidra Bay!' Alex stared. 'With the Raynors?'

'Yes. I called them when I arrived. Thought I'd like to go back, see where Lois spent those last weeks. They asked me over and I said I'd come if I could.' He shrugged. 'Might be best if I went. I have my hire-car.'

'You will see Martie again, though? Oh, look, she wouldn't want you just to go. You mean a lot to her, you know.'

'I'll say goodbye.' He took Alex's hand. 'Thanks for being so understanding, Alex. You're a fine person. Anyone tell you that? I hope there'll be happiness for you one day.'

'I'm happy here, Warren.'

'That's good, that's very good.' Warren put on his overcoat. 'You'll tell Martie I came?'

'Of course.'

She watched him go, walking slowly towards the end of the corridor, his shoulders hunched, his fine head a little low.

'Remember me to the Raynors!' she called, and he looked back.

'Sure, I'll do that. Goodbye, Alex.'

'Goodbye, Warren.'

Fidra Bay. She hadn't thought of it in an age. Remembered Hugh Raynor now and those talks on the shore – Mrs Raynor, blowing up, then apologising – poor Lois – Warren – Martie, crying because she thought she couldn't go to the States. All seemed so long ago. She herself had been getting over Tim, and was still getting over Tim. On she hurried to Martie's room.

They were both laughing over something, Martie and Jamie, Martie looking prettier than she'd looked since her return from America, Jamie looking different. How different, wondered Alex? Happier, that was all. She realised with a pang that it was a long time since Jamie had been happy.

'Sorry to break things up,' she told him, 'but it's time to go. Visiting's over.'

'Come on, Alex! It's Christmas Eve!'

'Sorry. Martie has to rest now. You can come tomorrow.'

'I'll bring your present,' he told Martie. 'Don't you go opening your mum's before tomorrow!'

She smiled delightedly. 'Wonder what she's found for me? Woollen undies, I bet you, or tea towels for ma bottom drawer. But I shouldn't make fun. They mean well, you know, Mum and Dad, and they do care about me. Only thing is, I've no' very much for them. Jill got me chocolates for everybody. Had to borrow the sweet points from Dad.'

'From Logie's, I suppose?' asked Alex, as another memory pierced her heart.

'Where else? Only the best for me!' Martie lay back, looking suddenly weary, and at a sign from Alex, Jamie kissed her hand and said he'd better go.

'That'll have to do for now,' he whispered, folding her hand over the kiss. 'I'll see you tomorrow.'

'Right, let's get you settled for the night,' said Alex briskly, as Jamie sidled slowly away. 'Want me to help you to the bathroom?'

'No, I can manage, thanks.'

'I'll do your bed, then.'

On her return, Martie sank into a chair, watching Alex remake the bed with all the efficiency that had once been her own.

'Alex, I'm sorry,' she said quietly.

'What on earth for?' asked Alex, hanging up Martie's dressing-gown.

'For being such a pest. Honestly, I'm ashamed of maself! When I think of how I used to tell patients to pull themselves together, and when it came to me, I just fell apart!'

'You'd every reason to do that. Anyway, you're on the right track now.'

'Thanks to Jamie. He's made all the difference, Alex. I feel I have a goal now, and I'm going for it.'

'OK, you can get back in bed now.' When Martie was back in her beautifully neat bed, Alex looked down at her. 'I think I should tell you, Warren was here.'

'Oh, no! Oh, God! Alex, I feel so bad about him. I just wish there was something I could do.'

'You didn't ask him to come over, he knows that.'

'Goes deeper, doesn't it? I shouldn't have got involved with him in the first place.'

'Took two for that, Martie. Look, don't upset yourself. I had a word with him, I told him about Jamie, and he understands.'

'He does?'

'Yes, and he's going home.'

'I still feel bad. Is he coming in tomorrow?'

'No, he's going to the Fidra Bay. The Raynors have invited him.'

'The Fidra Bay . . . that's where it all began.'

'Well, it's ended now. Warren will come in to say goodbye and that'll be that.'

'No' really. You never really close relationships down completely, do you? There's always a part of you remembers, eh?'

'But you move on,' said Alex. 'Goodnight, Martie.'

It was with some relief that she shut the door to the side ward, before Martie thought to ask her how well she'd closed down relationships in her own life.

Chapter Sixty-Four

Before he left for America, Warren presented the Jubilee with two television sets, one for the staff, one for the patients.

'That's very handsome of you, Mr Adamson,' Chris told him. 'I'm not quite sure when the staff'll have time to watch, but the sets are most welcome. We're very grateful.'

'I'm grateful to you, too, for all the care you're taking of young Martie, and I'm sorry if I upset you, wanting to take her elsewhere. Believe me, I was only thinking of comfort, not medical care. I know you guys are the best.'

'Kind of you to say so. We'll think of you when we switch on the box.'

'Be sure not to miss the Coronation!' cried Warren. 'That'll be some show, with your Queen and the Abbey and all the works.' He shook Chris's hand. 'Well – guess I'll say goodbye, have to be getting along to the ward, see Martie.'

Her rash had cleared and she had returned to Butterfly Four, but she was up and dressed and said they could talk for a moment in the hospital library. There probably wouldn't be anyone there at that time of the morning.

'Ah, Martie,' Warren groaned, when they were alone. 'I shouldn't be putting you through another goodbye. You thought you'd finished with all that, didn't you?'

'I'm very grateful to you for coming here,' she said earnestly. 'I'll never forget what you've done for me, I'll never lose touch, I promise.'

'I like Jamie, you know. I know he doesn't like me, and that's understandable, but I think he's a fine young fellow and is going to do well.'

'He's never going to be a rich man,' Martie said, with a smile. 'But we'll get by.'

'If he should ever want a job in the States—'

'He'd never leave Scotland,' she said firmly. 'But thanks all the same.'

'Is there anything else I can do for you? Apart from send a wedding present?'

She shook her head. 'And we'll have to wait for the wedding present. Till I'm better.'

'When are they going to get you back on medication?'

'Very soon. They're pretty certain it was the streptomycin that caused the reaction, so they'll test for that last. If I'm OK with the other two drugs, I'll go back on to them and see how I get on.' Martie took Warren's hand. 'I feel quite confident now that I am going to get better, and that's half the battle.'

'Got to put some weight on,' he murmured, caressing the thin hand in his, then kissed her cheek.

'You're no' supposed to kiss me, Warren!'

'What the hell – if I couldn't take a little risk like that, I'd be a pretty poor sort of guy. Will you come to the door to say goodbye to me? I have my car there, need to check it in, then take a taxi to Turnhouse.'

'I'm sorry you missed Christmas with your family, Warren.'

'That's OK, I'll have New Year's. Probably with my mother.' He grinned. 'She's still the same, Martie.'

'I'll bet she is!'

They embraced quickly, disregarding the covert gaze of Joanna Tay on Reception and the interested stares of one or two patients passing by.

'Take care!' cried Warren.

'And you!' Martie returned.

The glass entrance door slammed and he was gone. She followed, standing on the step to wave, as he turned the hire-car round, gave a last smile and drove away.

392

'Come on, Martie,' said Alex, appearing at the doorway. 'Let's get you back to the ward. They want to start your tests.'

'I wish I didn't feel so bad about Warren, Alex.'

'Just concentrate on getting well now. You need all the energy you can get.'

But Alex was no longer really worried about Martie, who was so different now in her attitude to her illness. The doctors would sort out the best drugs for her, she would take them, she would co-operate in every way, and she would get well. It would take months, because the treatment had to be continued long after the patient felt better so as to avoid the risk of relapse, but in the end, Martie would be Martie again, her old strong vital self. She would marry Jamie, maybe stay on at work for a while, have a family, return to work, end up Sister, at least.

Heavens, thought Alex, leaving Martie in the care of young Dr Robbie, I've worked out her whole life history! Maybe some of it wouldn't happen. Most of it would. Maybe I should look into the future for myself, she thought. But that was different. She couldn't picture anything for herself.

The dead days between Christmas and New Year passed, and New Year's Eve arrived, the best time of the year for Scots, at least, Scots who liked partying. Hogmanay! The very word conjured up something very different from the English New Year. Something special, something magical. With plenty of drink, said the cynics. But most people set out for a good time, and most didn't want to work.

'I don't mind doing New Year,' Alex had volunteered. 'I'm no' doing anything in particular.'

'Well, you should be, fine girl like you,' said Sister Piers. 'But you worked Christmas, so you needn't work Hogmanay as well.' She added in a whisper, 'Dr MacInnes is taking it off this year, you know.'

'That right?' Alex shrugged. 'OK, I won't say no. Thanks, Sister.'

Yet not partying on New Year's Eve if you were free, made you feel worse than if you were working. At least, then, you had an excuse not to be going anywhere.

393

'Goodnight,' she called to Joanna, as she passed through Reception. 'Happy New Year!'

'Going somewhere nice?' asked Joanna.

'Just home. I'll see the New Year in with the neighbours, I expect. Jamie'll be coming, after he's seen Martie.'

'Lovely!' Joanna was being very polite. 'I'm away dancing, soon as I've finished here. Ma boyfriend's collecting me.'

'Lovely,' echoed Alex, turning away.

'Hey, I nearly forgot, there's a parcel for you. Package, anyway.'

'For me?' Alex took the neatly wrapped parcel with typed label and studied it from all angles. 'Did someone leave it? There's no postmark.'

'Aye, it was hand-delivered. Didn't see the fellow, though. Just found it on the desk.'

'Might have been a woman, then.'

'Might have been. Why don't you open it, see what it is?'

'It's just chocolates, I think.' Alex put the package into her bag. 'Nothing exciting, I'm sure.'

'From an unknown admirer?' Joanna asked with a giggle.

'Probably a patient. They sometimes send us sweeties.'

All the way home, Alex thought about the package in her bag. As soon as she got in, she went up to her room to open it. How cold her room was that night! No heating, of course. Her hands were shaking, as she tore off the wrapping with her nail scissors. Inside – she'd been right – was a box of chocolates. It had a scarlet ribbon and a picture of the Scott Monument. It was Logie's Talisman Selection.

Logie's Talisman Selection. Alex sat on her bed, holding the box, looking at the picture, as voices echoed in her head.

'Present from a patient, we all got them . . . My word, he must have some money . . . And sweet points too . . . Wait a minute, pet, if I'm no' mistaken, that box has been opened already. . . '

She should open the box, she should look. She couldn't look.

There was a letter, and after a moment, she opened that.

'My dearest Alex,' she read, 'Can we meet? I'll be on the steps tomorrow at two. All my love, Tim.'

Then she opened the box. Inside, on the top layer, wrapped in tissue just as before, was her locket.

'Alex, are you coming down?' came Edie's voice. 'Tilda and Sid are here!'

'Just getting ready, Edie.'

There was Christmas cake set out, a bottle of port and glasses, sandwiches and the usual mince-pies. Neighbours were arriving, Edie was flushed and excited, pushing at her tumbling hair, Arthur trying to be sociable, looking lost.

'We'll wait for Jamie, eh?' asked Edie. 'He'll no' be long, coming from the hospital. How was Martie today, Tilda?'

'No' so bad. They were saying she might come home, when they get her treatment sorted out.'

'Aye, we're going to make things comfortable for her,' put in Sid. 'Spend a bit on the house, eh? I mean, what's money for?'

Into the stunned silence that followed this remark, Jamie arrived, calling greetings. Happy Jamie, thought Alex. His happiness was like an aura, gilding him, setting him aside from ordinary people. She had had that once.

'Who'll we get to first-foot?' asked Edie, beginning to hand the sandwiches, as Arthur opened the port. 'Jamie, you're no' dark enough. It'll have to be you, Sid.'

'If you'd kept up with Neal, we could have had him,' Arthur said to Alex, in a low voice. 'Tall, dark and handsome, just the fella, eh?'

'He'll be doing his own first-footing, Dad.'

'No' going out anywhere tonight, Alex?' asked Sid, coming up with a glass of port in his hand. 'Thought you'd be sure to be out at some do on Hogmanay.'

'I might be going out tomorrow,' said Alex.

'Aye, well they say what you do on New Year's Day is what you do the rest o' the year. So watch your step, Alex!'

'Art, put the wireless on!' cried Edie. 'Let's get the chimes – it's nearly midnight!'

Happy New Year, Happy New Year. They circled, kissing, as the tolling of Big Ben heralded 1953.

'Happy New Year, Jamie!' Alex whispered, kissing his freckled cheek. 'I know it'll be a good one for you. Martie's going to be all right.'

'I wish it could be good for you, Alex. There should be somebody somewhere to make you happy.'

A band on the wireless was playing 'Auld Lang Syne', and they all joined in, linking arms and singing loudly.

'Should auld acquaintance be forgot, And never brought to mind? Should auld acquaintance be forgot, And auld lang syne?'

Old acquaintance . . . Alex had an old acquaintance. He would be waiting for her tomorrow on the Archangel Steps, where she had first seen him, in the days of long ago.

'We'll tak a cup o' kindness yet,' she sang, with the rest, 'for auld lang syne.'

And kept her mind a blank.

Chapter Sixty-Five

He was there, standing at the top of the Archangel Steps, looking down. He wore a black overcoat and grey scarf, but no hat, and his fair hair blown by the wind was a little long, as though he hadn't thought about getting it cut for some time. When he saw her, he came running down the steps, his hands outstretched, but she was carrying flowers and could not take his hands.

'You came.' His grey eyes were alight. 'I didn't think you would.' He stopped, said awkwardly, 'Remember when I said something like that to you once before?'

'I remember.' Her voice was stiff, a stranger's voice. 'How did you know I wasn't on duty?'

'I rang the Jubilee.'

She looked down at the flowers. 'You found the locket, then?'

'No.'

'No?'

'I never found it. I bought another.' He gave a faint smile. 'You see, I'm being honest. It's just the same, but I had to order it and they couldn't get it for Christmas. So, I gave it to you for New Year. I thought it would be appropriate, a new locket for a New Year. A fresh start.'

'Who says there's to be a fresh start?'

'I'm asking for one, Alex.'

She began to walk up the steps and he walked with her.

'Thank you for the locket – and the chocolates.' Her eyes went to him, and away. 'But nothing's changed.'

'You didn't think it was childish? Sending the chocolates, the same kind as before?'

'I guessed why you did.'

'To try to put the clock back. You think we can't?'

They had reached the square, they were in sight of his parents' home. Both halted, exchanging long sorrowful looks.

'I stopped loving you,' Tim said quietly. 'And then my love came back. Don't you believe that could happen?'

She looked away, long, long into the past. Once she had loved Tim, and that love had died. Oh, but it wasn't the same! A childish infatuation couldn't be compared with an adult's love. Yet her feeling had been real enough at the time. And it had returned. Stronger than ever.

'When love returns, it can be deeper than it was before,' Tim went on, watching her, echoing what was in her mind. 'That's what I've found, Alex. You say nothing's changed, but I have. I'm not the same man who hurt you. My love isn't the same, either. That's what I'm asking you to believe.'

'I'm afraid, Tim.'

Afraid for herself, afraid for him. Maybe all lovers were afraid of the future. She felt her resolution turning upside down, struggled to hold it, let it go.

'There's no need for fear,' Tim was saying gently. 'I love and trust you, Alex. Won't you trust me?'

The bitter smell of the chrysanthemums in her arms rose between them, as she looked up into his face. There were those who called him arrogant, but she saw no sign of arrogance then. He was as vulnerable as all who love, dependent on her, as she had been dependent on him. Was still dependent, would always be dependent, which was why she would give him her trust, as he gave his to her.

'Where are you taking the flowers?' he whispered.

'To the Dean. To Rose's grave.'

'May I come with you?'

'If you want to.'

'Let's take the car, it's parked just here.'

*

The cold and damp air hung in vapours over the Dean Cemetery. Moisture clung to the walls of green stones, where the names of the dead slid into obscurity, and ran in rivulets down the obelisks of the wealthy. On the paths, they had to take care, for fallen leaves were slippery and moss was growing through the gravel.

'What can we put the flowers in?' asked Tim, with sombre expression.

'There are some jars near the tap,' Alex replied.

She filled a jar, as Tim took the flowers, and they made their way carefully towards Rose's grave. Other mourners too were walking the paths; more than usual, perhaps, because it was New Year. Alex and Tim stood in silence, looking at the etched letters on the still new-looking stone marking Rose's place.

'It's a lovely stone,' Alex commented.

'Yes, we were pleased with it.' Tim watched, as Alex placed her white chrysanthemums in their jar on the grave, next to a large wreath of holly and ivy. 'We came at Christmas. That's our wreath.'

'I couldn't come at Christmas, I was on duty. And Martie, of course, was ill.'

'Martie? Is she back?'

'Didn't you know? She came back some weeks ago.' Alex held Tim's arm. 'Tim, she's contracted TB.'

The colour left his face, leaving it pinched and worn.

'I didn't know. How bad is she?'

'It's mild, only a shadow—'

'Only a shadow!'

'But she was very depressed at first.'

'Do you blame her?' He shuddered. 'So, how's she going to be?'

'They think she'll make a good recovery, the treatment's so different, you see, from when you were ill. And, Tim, she's given up Warren. She and Jamie are going to be married as soon as she's better.'

Tim's face cleared, as his colour began to return. 'Martie and Jamie? That's terrific.' His gaze returned to his sister's stone. 'Poor Rose. So many things happening that she knows nothing about. Life goes on, they say, without the dead.'

'I know, it has to, but it hurts, doesn't it?'

'It hurts.'

A crunching footstep on the gravel made them turn their heads.

'Why, it's Chris!' Tim exclaimed, as the doctor approached, carrying a sheaf of lilies and another of the cemetery's jars.

'Hello!' Chris, with obvious effort, moved into cheerful mood. 'I didn't expect to find you two here.'

'You mean, not together?' asked Tim.

'Are you together?'

'Yes. I think we could say that, couldn't we, Alex?'

She hesitated. 'Yes, we're together, Chris.'

'Things have worked out, then?' He shook Tim's hand and kissed Alex on the cheek. 'I can't tell you how glad I am to hear it. But what's Sister Piers going to say if you desert us, Alex?'

'I'm no' deserting. I'd like to work on for a while.'

'I wish you would. This is a great time to be in our field, you know.'

'I know.'

'Working with the Professor and the team, seeing the changes happening before our eyes. I'm not joking, I wouldn't swap my job for any money.'

'You really think you've cracked it?' Tim asked warily. 'Killed TB for good?'

Chris shook his head. 'I wouldn't say that. It's the strongest bug in the world, it'll come back time and time again, like a boxer that's out for the count and still gets up. But, we've never been so hopeful, put it that way.'

'I used to feel I was on the edge of the abyss,' Tim said, holding Alex's hand. 'It was like being in the war, others dying, you were sure you'd be next. All came down to luck.' He raised his eyes to Chris. 'Seems that might not be true any longer.'

'I hope not.'

'There's not a lot one can say – except thanks.'

'Don't thank me. I use other people's work.'

'I am thanking you, Chris. And Alex. And everyone.'

400

'Be happy,' said Chris, with an embarrassed grin. 'Both of you.'

They left him, putting his lilies on Rose's grave, and were silent as they made their way back to the car, their thoughts with Rose and the men who had loved her. In their seats, their eyes met.

'So you plan to stay on as a butterfly girl?' asked Tim softly.

'No one calls us that nowadays.'

'But you still are.'

'Yes. I want to be. Just now, I'm needed.'

Alex looked back at the gates to the cemetery.

'I'm the only one of the three of us who can work, Tim. Martie will come back, I'm sure, but she's going to need time. Rose'll never know what wonderful things are happening. There's only me. You do understand?'

'Of course. I want you to do what you want to do. But, I was thinking, maybe we'd like a family some day.'

'Oh, yes, I want children, Tim! But I'll come back. When they're at school.'

They stared at each other, imagining themselves as married people, with school-age children, a house, responsibilities.

'You do trust me,' Tim whispered.

They kissed, solemnly and passionately, uncaring of passers-by, but on that chill afternoon, no one saw them.

'Have you got the locket with you?' asked Tim, sitting back.

'Yes, I put it in ma bag.'

'And what about your ring?'

'That's there, too.'

'Will you put them on?'

They made a little ceremony of it, Tim fastening on the chain and locket, slipping the ring on her finger.

'I thought we might call in on Mother and Dad,' said Tim. 'They'd be very pleased to see you. Give us a cup of tea.'

'Oh, I don't think I could, Tim! I'd feel so embarrassed!'

'Got to face them sometime. Same as I'll have to face your father and Jamie. Not to mention Martie.'

'If I call on your parents, will you come down to see Dad and Edie?' Alex smiled. 'Get another cup of tea?'

'It's a deal.'

They drove away, tremulous in happiness, afraid, yet strangely confident, while at Rose's grave, Chris steadied his jar of lilies and did a little weeding. In the Jubilee, Martie and Jamie held hands, watching Warren's new television, and the butterfly wards were quiet.

More heartwarming sagas by
Anne Douglas available from Piatkus:

CATHERINE'S LAND

Madge Ritchie moves her three young daughters into
Catherine's Land when the death of her husband leaves
them in reduced circumstances. By 1920 Madge can't
imagine life without her noisy neighbours; though two of
her girls, ambitious Abby and artistic Rachel, both dream
of making their escape. Only Jennie, the middle child most
like her gentle mother, is happy in the hurly-burly
atmosphere of the tenements.

But when Jim Gilbride and his sons Malcolm and Rory
move onto the Ritchies' stair the lives of both families are
to change dramatically – and bonds of love and hatred,
jealousy and forgiveness are forged that will bind them all,
in their hearts, to Catherine's Land forever.

978-0-7499-3036-3

AS THE YEARS GO BY

Forced by the post-war boom to leave their shabby
Edinburgh tenement for a new bungalow on the outskirts
of the city, Madge Gilbride is comforted by the fact that
at least she has her family near her. And when her
grandsons, Will and Hamish, fall in love with local girls
she is delighted.

But life is not plain sailing – especially for Will. In love
with the fiery Kate Rossie, he discovers she wants both a
husband and a political career. Conventional Will makes a
choice he will regret for years – a sensible marriage of
convenience to the suitable Sara.

As she watches her grand-children with their own families'
joys and troubles, Madge can't help but remember her old
tenement home and hope that the new generation of
Gilbrides never forget their roots . . .

978-0-7499-3125-4

BRIDGE OF HOPE

Josie Morrow and Lina Braid are best friends. But although Josie has an understanding with Angus, Lina's brother, her mother has far more grandiose plans than for her to marry a local boy. She sees civil engineer Duncan Guthrie, a lodger in their Queensferry boarding house, as a much better catch. However, it is Lina who Duncan falls for, forcing her to break her promise to her childhood sweetheart in order to marry him.

Josie believes she could never hurt Angus in that way . . . until she meets Firth of Forth bridge worker Matt MacLeod. But there are more barriers to her relationship with Matt than the fact that she is already spoken for. Matt is an atheist and unacceptable to her staunch Presbyterian father. Josie is torn between her family and her love for Matt. Does she have the courage to follow her heart and accept the consequences?

978-0-7499-3232-9

GINGER STREET

The Millar family live next door to the Riettis on Ginger
Street, a row of Victorian tenements on Edinburgh's south
side but their circumstances couldn't be more different.
Ruth Millar would like to stay on at school but her
father's salary as a grocer's assistant is barely enough to
put food on the table, let alone such luxuries as an
education. By contrast the Riettis own the local corner
shop and a little cafe at the end of Ginger Street.

Ruth's father dreams of one day owning his own business.
Meanwhile Ruth secretly dreams of Nicco Rietti. But not
only is Nicco older, he is Italian and Catholic, three things
which make him out of bounds for Ruth, especially with
the threat of war on the horizon . . .

978-0-7499-3383-8

A HIGHLAND ENGAGEMENT

After their parents die, Leslie Mackenzie and her two siblings are taken in by their Auntie Peg. Leslie knows that given the poverty and unemployment in and around Leith, she is lucky to have a roof over her head – albeit her aunt's tenement – and a job to go to. So she can hardly believe her luck when she manages to escape the poverty of Leith and earns a position at the Hotel Grand Forest in the highlands of Scotland.

However, it couldn't be more different from the Edinburgh hotel Leslie is used to working in. The luxury spa hotel is in the highlands of Scotland, in the small village of Glenmar, and caters to the whims of its rich, high society guests. But whilst in many ways it is her dream job, strict rules govern the behaviour of all Grand Forest's employees and staff are forbidden from mixing with guests. But then Leslie meets Christopher Meredith and falls in love . . .

978-0-7499-3501-6

THE ROAD TO THE SANDS

The war has brought devastating changes to the people of Portobello, a seaside district of Edinburgh. But as VE day nears, Tess Gillespie and her mother are feeling hopeful. Tess is looking forward to being able to walk on her beloved beaches for the first time since war was declared. More importantly, her father and sister will soon be back home and they can all be a family once again.

However, the war has changed Don Gillespie and he is no longer content to settle back in to his former life. The future will bring both betrayal and heartbreak for all the Gillespie women. And it will take all their courage and resolution to rebuild their lives and find new happiness.

978-0-7499-3729-4